D1468756

EQUILIBRIUM

By

Elizabeth Lydia Bodner

Author of

UNCOMPROMISING: FAMILY STYLE

EBW Associates
Kennebunk, Maine

ISBN: 09657162-2-8

Library of Congress Card Catalog No. 2004115001

This book is a work of fiction.
Certain real locations, products and public figures are mentioned
but all other characters and event and dialogue
described in the book are from the author's imagination

Manufactured in the United States of America

EBW Associates
68 Port Road
Kennebunk, ME 04043

DEDICATION

This book is dedicated to all of our families in equilibrium.

My dearest love, Jim Cumiskey

For our children who have taken the journey with us.

Bridget
Susan
Andrew
Thomas
John

Original pastel art cover design by
Tina Ambrose

And loving contributions of family members, Joseph M. Bodner, Theresa Bodner Surgeon, and Catherine A. Bodner

TABLE OF CONTENTS

Prologue

The Great Depression unflagging from 1929 and into 1936 ravished the veritable core of American life to the physical and moral hopelessness of every man, woman, and child, not withstanding the cities and towns in which they lived across the landscape of America. Every assertive expectation, dream, and promise was crushed as so many burgeoning buds chopped at their roots. Lives were interrupted with no future in sight. In many cases, ordinary people had no comprehension of what had happened to discontinue life, as they had known it in the "prosperous twenties."

Incessant worry about physical survival, food, shelter, and warmth permeated families. Hunger was rampant; fifty men could be found fighting over a barrel of garbage set outside the door of a restaurant. Long lines of tiresome, haggard men and women waited for dry bread or thin soup. How did the nation get into such a deplorable state? Many blamed President Hoover for standing by and doing nothing when, historically, the economic system of the United States had been spiraling out of control for over two hundred years.

Adam Smith wrote *The Wealth Of Nations* in 1776, the same year the United States declared its independence. Amidst this fresh new fertile economic soil, the country had been cultivated for economic freedom. Smith stated that labor, and not land or money, is the real source of a country's wealth, favoring free trade and free market, and unrestricted by government controls or private monopolies. His theory of classical economics taught that individuals know what is best for them, and under influence of profit motive, they will turn out products society most desires. In this manner self-interest would be harnessed to the common good. Ideal in theory and what might have been a perfect practice turned into chaos as businesses grew larger and government intervention increased, forcing financial destruction.

The trusted classical economics worked well for many years, since farmers could at least feed their families when money became scarce. However, by the 1930s, as cities became less rural with fewer farming practices, urban industry began to control large populations, which were exposed to the market economy. Loosing jobs and wages disadvantaged people whose lives became dependent upon the company where they worked. The enormous economic crisis had gripped the nation, with ten billion people out of work by 1932, as factories closed and banks failed. Twenty thousand people committed suicide in 1931 alone.

Through the desperate ensuing years, a large portion of the middle class of the country turned into a blanketed humanitarian disciple bringing social justice to the poor and downtrodden. The thirties became a time when people reached out to each other more than ever before in American history. Endearing relationships resulted from this interdependence and shared sacrifice.

Family life became a day-to-day struggle of scrimping and saving for years and often never getting what one wanted. People walked five miles to save a five-cent carfare, skipping meals and wearing clothing to shreds and shoes until huge holes appeared in the soles. A means of solitary endurance evolved which omitted rampant materialism, as Americans had known it to be in the past decade.

"We were poor but we didn't know it, but so was everyone," one survivor said. Money had little to do with the quality of anyone's life, no one bought things they didn't really need, and they "made do." Essentially, people united against this external enemy that completely changed life, as they had known it in past decades.

Trust was an unfaltering virtue; poor strangers showed up regularly at people's homes and were given work and food. Houses didn't have locks, and keys were left in the ignition of cars. Natural dangers not people were what scared children.

Despite these hard times, in the heavily industrialized city of Pittsburgh, Pennsylvania, acrid smoke spewed hourly from nearby mills sacrificing the landscape with mounds of soot crunching under worker's feet as they walked along side tall wire fences. Labeled the "Steel Capital of the World", it's citizens struggled to breathe within the confines of the smoggy choking air, which remained hazy throughout the day, as many wore masks to cover their nose and mouth during outings.

Officers of United States Steel announced in 1934 the astounding gross earnings of 35,218,359 dollars. The prosperous company turned out more than 53 million ton of iron ore, coal, coke, limestone, pig iron, ingots, and finished steel items, with more than a quarter of a million tons of by-products from ammonia to cement. The corporation owned mills, coal and iron mines stretching from Canada to Brazil, a fleet of ships, and miles of railroad tracks to move its cargo.

Twenty miles southeast of Pittsburgh lay the manufacturing borough of Eastburg, where the George Westinghouse, Andrew Carnegie, and Edgar Thompson plants lay, and thousands of workers remained unemployed. Common laborers who were able to work continued to be grim and hopeless in 1933, as no fulltime worker was on their moneyed rolls. Regardless of steel profits, the average steelworker in Braddock at the Carnegie Mill earned $369 a year in order to support an average family of six.

Safety conditions in plants were far worse than the wages, with occupational diseases, including carbon monoxide poisoning, and hot mill cramps (exposure to temperatures up to 220 degrees F) at the furnace mouth. Pneumonia took hundreds of lives every year. Every week a man could expect his clothes to catch on fire, and if he did not burn to death, he had to replace his clothes with his meager earnings. One safety manager admitted a lot of equipment was out of date, had no safety devices, and was liable to break down, causing an accident at any time. He said the company had no plans to scrap the equipment therefore 22,845 humans in 1931 were disabled in accidents, 242 were killed, and 21,410 were laid up temporarily.

John L. Lewis as head of the *Committee for Industrial Organizations* stepped forward as steel spokesman. FDR would hear him loud and clear, and so did the rest of the nation. By the end of this bloody decade, American workers once scattered and beaten by industrial bullies, ignored or opposed by politicians, would assume rightful places as first-class citizens.

EQUILIBRIUM

PART ONE

Equilibrium

1. Resolve Among The Ruins

The growing, lively city of Eastburg where Lizzie and Zach Albred had founded their successful Albred Hotel at the prosperous turn of the century exhibited signs of neglect. Paint peeled freely from dirty white wooden houses with broken windows, doors falling off their hinges, and shingles lying on the ground. Failed business establishments boarded up along the street displayed the rubbish of their wares, much of which had been picked apart months and years ago by desperate hands of need. The steeped trash piles with remnants of meager possessions littered sidewalks, indicating a hasty tenant evacuation for a better job, or promise of better living conditions elsewhere.

The once new two-story brick and wood frame homes, built with skillful hands of Italian and Czech brick-layers and carpenters soon after their arrival in America at the turn of the century, looked shoddy and forlorn, as if their occupants were entombed within, never to emerge again into the discouraging social stream of life.

Many of these residents, who had been eager to find their American dream, had worked and lived through good economic times, and progressing through almost two generations to become group leaders in the city, now found themselves dead-ended to help their children fulfill their own promises as well.

Eastburg's employer and benefactor, Westinghouse Electric Company, which had employed most of the people, had all but shut off the lights and closed its doors on the faithful local workers who now spent much of their working time in the hotel restaurant eating, drinking, and remonstrating. The townspeople's favorite gathering place had prevailed, despite multitudes of patron's daily consumption of food and drink on hotel credit, totaling up an extensive deficit to the steady depletion of the hotel's finances.

The convivial, old, brick building had become a port in the storm, accommodating as many as 500 borders under its withering roof. Profits were non-existent, but unlike the stock market, good will, hospitality and charity were immeasurably abundant.

For the last thirty years the name of Albred remained synonymous with magnanimity, since Lizzie and Zach had assisted many people through much of these troubled times. Food lines at the back of the hotel were a regular sight, as Dell, their daughter-in-law, and one or two of the hired girls passed out stale bread and left-over stew, soup, or any other scraps from the day before's menu. Some days, large steaming kettles of plentiful eastern European peasant food consisting of dumplings or noodles and cabbage, haluska, were brought out and ladled into individual bowls, cups or whatever other vessel was brought by hungry families crowding around to fill their containers.

Usually one or two of the people in line needed medical attention or were desperate for a place to live, that was when their son, Johnny came out to get their name, so that he could get in touch with the local doctor or social worker to help them.

Now with the passing away of the famous local Albreds, the down trodden would depend on their sons, Johnny, his wife Dell, his brother, Philip and their self-centered sister, Agatha who struggled to maintain business as usual. Notwithstanding the family's economic obstacles, were unyielding attitudes in their path from the outset.

An immigrant of Bratislava, Czechoslovakia, the industrious Lizzie brought many inherent gifts to America in the mid-nineteen hundreds among these were strong moral conviction, sprightly enthusiasm, fortitude and business acumen and a good sense of security to introduce excellent cooking skills of Eastern Europe to her new homeland. Concurrently, she worked long hard hours to achieve professional success with other business leaders in the local area.

With the opening of her hotel at the beginning of the twentieth century, Germans, Hungarians, Irish, Slovaks, and French boarders honored the hotel. The immigrants who knew the common languages congregated daily, keeping touch with their countrymen. News from the villages from across the sea had traveled fast via letters and gossip regarding their loved ones they had left in order to find the "golden streets of America".

The camaraderie, under the soulful watch of Lizzie and her quiet, easy going husband Zach, became the daily drawing card for hotel guests to gather in the friendly communal surroundings.

As the years went on, the regular boarders made conjectures regarding the uncompromising Albred family, each one taking their part in the management of the business under Lizzie's professional acumen. Many of the customers held secret conjectures about the presence of their roguish son.

"If only Lizzie could command her mischievous son Philip and spoiled daughter, Agatha, as well as she lays the law down in her restaurant, there would be no problems with her family." The Albred's oldest son, Johnny, escaped criticism with his nickname "the professor" of the hotel, as his words of wisdom and counsel helped many back to the salvation of the Catholic Church.

His only mistake, according to Lizzie, was to meet the love of his life, Dell Gesner, the summer before while working at Dell's father's, Pops Chrysler's garage. He would leave the seminary after only six month's at St. Vincent's College in Latrobe, to marry Dell in defiance of the wishes of his headstrong mother.

Despite her ambition for Johnny, Lizzie became an anchor for his growing family, cherishing her three grandsons implicitly lavishing love on each one of them abundantly, a virtue she never displayed toward her own children. She and her soft-spoken husband, Zach, who prevailed as the mainstay in her life, believed his wife to be a queen. He spent his married life as her subject, working to keep her kingdom smoothly run, supporting her mien.

On Easter of this year of 1932, they both succumbed to pneumonia. The doctor, whom Lizzie would deny was in attendance, diagnosed her and then her devoted Zach, as having advanced stages of influenza, leading to the critical pulmonary pneumonia. Doctor Newhouse would not have been there through Lizzie's protests, had Johnny not called him as a last recourse, since Lizzie did not respect the "moods" of the medical profession.

The devoted couple was buried the summer of that year side by side in St. Joseph's Cemetery in East McKeesport, leaving Johnny and Phil as proprietors of the Albred Hotel.

A heavy downpour of rain this November election evening hastened chilled drenched customers clamoring through the squeaky wooden louvered doors to take "regular" barstools and tables, all the while hurling political insults at Republican incumbents. And with almost 100% Democrats in the Eastburg area, most were safe in voicing sharp opinions openly.

Dark oak wainscoted walls covered the huge room, composed of more than thirty white porcelain-topped tables, complete with bent wood rounded chairs. Every table had a fresh white cloth covering the porcelain top, protecting it from scratches. Dark brown wood floors had been polished to a shining finish.

This historical evening, excited voters were present after the polls closed to listen to radio station KDKA's broadcast for the outcome of the 1932 presidential election. Tonight the drinks would be half off anticipating a Roosevelt victory. And although the risks of drinking in business establishments were tenuous, the promised ratification of amendment twenty-one to the constitution, kept the bar open for public consumption.

"Hoover's presidency is buried up there in St. Joseph's Cemetery," yelled one stringy wet haired, high-spirited customer, throwing off his soppy jacket onto a chair.

"Trow da bums out – dint dey do 'nough damage in de government!" Shouted Phil, dark sheep of the family, from the kitchen. Rumors had it that Phil still kept close company with many criminals, some even as far away as Chicago and New York. Even in his thirties, at first glance Phil Albred looked like one of Al Capone's boys, and of this he was extremely proud. Always dressed in a pinstriped suit and dark tie, his dark straight hair remained laquered down on both sides of his head in an unwavering straight middle part. Brown sharp eagle eyes took in all of the insider's activity with one scan across the room and exits, and a double check on those who might be questionable.

4

"Yeah, almost as much trouble as you've caused, Phil," shouted a lowly irate Republican, eager for a chance to be heard in the hot political group, seating himself in a back safe corner table beside his wife.

"Look who's talkin'," retorted Phil.

"You voted for Hoover twice, I seen ya. We was aways in trouble wid your boy."

Charlie Greenbacher, a regular outspoken hotel patron, sloppily spit his slimy chew onto the floor, missing the shinny brass spittoon nearby, and broke out in song. The emotional patriotic momentum grew, as *happy Days are here again, the clouds above are clear again.*" The Democratic National campaign song broke throughout the smoke filled acrid bar filling the patrons with hope for Franklin D. Roosevelt's promised New Deal for the struggling nation.

"We will sing a song of cheer again…"

Johnny Albred stood tall at five feet, ten inches, behind the long, broad, dark oak bar this evening, pulling draughts, his left and right hands adroitly moving Iron City and Duquesne Beer handles simultaneously, while his clear tenor voice rose above the spirited throng. The wall sized gilt edged mirror behind him reflected the back of his crisp white apron wrapped high around his midriff, and stiff white shirt sleeves rolled up to his elbows exposing red garters between the folds.

Sparse sandy hair on a high thinking forehead crowned his head revealing more rosy scalp than he preferred, but then he would reiterate, *"Grass did not sprout on a busy path"*. This was just one of the reasons for Johnny's "professor" moniker by most of the locals.

Advice, information, philosophies of the great thinkers, art, literature, or whatever subject was introduced, flowed from the educated archives of the cardinal bartender. On these long dark Depression days, Johnny was the reason most people came in, because they always left feeling better about their predicament, knowing that everything changes and nothing lasted forever, no matter how terrible.

"Ah, it won't last too much longer, FDR will get in and change everything for the better. Sure it's been tough, but all in all, maybe some of us have become better people. And just maybe we've become closer to God. This guy will be a president for the forgotten man. And that's us, the people in this town."

On this night as on so many others, his old friend Alfred Goss was perched on a bar stool close by, where they could have their usual dialogue to pass the night away. Johnny had met Al in St. Vincent's Prep School when he was just fourteen. They were two of a kind, both destined for the priesthood at one time, and both were steered away by the physical loves of their lives. As the years went by, they learned to be better husbands and fathers than parish priests. At least Johnny had triumphed in his choice of wife and family.

Alfred managed to hold on to his position through bad times as foreman with the Westinghouse Electric Shipping Department, primarily because he could do different jobs, and had extensive seniority. A tall dark hared man with an olive complexion and mild demeanor who listened more than he spoke, therefore, he and Johnny always understood each other.

"You know, Al," Johnny said, after the customers had settled down to their shots and beers.

"It isn't like I enjoy this job being out here everyday taking punches, its just that Mom left us this hotel and we're going to have to make a go of it. This was Mom's dream, she worked, or rather slaved, twenty-four hours a day here, cooking, cleaning, balancing the books, worrying over the finances." Al always acknowledged Johnny's proclamations with an "Hmm," which Johnny knew to be total agreement from his quiet friend.

Once in a while Al would stay too late and have one shot too many. This happened rarely, but when it did, he would reveal his innermost thoughts for Johnny's ears only. A secret they both shared was the passion that Al held for Johnny's sister, Agatha. It was more than common knowledge that Agatha was more beauty than brains, as her long wavy auburn hair and blue starlit eyes could charm even the coldest customers, these being mostly men.

Al revealed his true feelings for her one evening after he had consumed more shots than beers at his place by the bar. Agatha had strutted over to him in all her splendor, wearing one of her slinky chemises, which revealed hidden curves beneath. And though more form fitting dress styles had come into vogue, Agatha had not kept up with the trend, having had her clothes allowance cut back by her brothers, about which she complained daily.

"Look at these old fashioned rags," she'd say.

"I should be wearing the new dresses showing my waistline. And if I were to buy the new styles, I'd look like Mae West did in her last movie."

"Yeah," Phil broke in curtly. And I'm Wallace Berry."

"Stop it, Phil. Johnny, make him stop makin' fun of me," Agatha would cry out, her beautiful face all puckered up in a frown.

This afternoon Agatha lingered longer than usual by Al's side, arranging the steaming heaped plate of sauerbraten for his lunch with great care. But try as he might, he could not concentrate on the tangy beef brine, the mountains of mashed potatoes or the layers of sauerkraut. His senses were dizzy with the nearness of Agatha, caught up in her plump hips and buxom bosom undulating beneath the thin dark georgette dress. *What a woman*, his brain kept flashing. He wanted desperately to feel her warm skin for just an instant. Hastily he reached out his hand and slowly ran his fingers lightly up her smooth side.

"Ouch," she cried out into the crowd of hungry lunchtime eaters.

"Keep your hands to yourself, mister," she retaliated. All eyes were on him.

"I didn't do anything," he said, raising both hands in the air and looking red-faced straight at Johnny.

"Go and start the potato soup, Aggie. Where's your apron? What the heck is wrong with you, Al?"

Al had felt ashamed to face his friend the next evening. Everyone knew that Al and his wife, Bedelia, weren't happily married. They had seven kids, every new one cuter than the last one, but that was the one that forced poor tired and worn out Bedelia to abstain from sharing her bed with Al. Birth control was a taboo in the church - no couple could get absolution if they were preventing conception from occurring. Unfortunately, abstinence or ultimately secret adultery were the only obvious choices.

Nevertheless, after Al's expressive behavior with Agatha, Johnny kept an eye on him, and on Agatha, who was engaged to be married to a redheaded Austrian, Joe Lasky, who worked in the pattern shop at Westinghouse. Aggie had no idea just how she affected these love-starved men. Johnny watched her closely to see that she did not wear provocative clothing, just as his mother had in the past. She had no idea how a man's mind worked -- a good bit of the time on their conquests with women, in fact it was a downright obsession with some of them. Johnny tried to talk to her like a caring brother.

"Hey look, Aggie, there are a lot of married men being tempted by you and your body. Wear one of those big aprons and flatten yourself out, will ya?"Agatha stared at her brother with big blue eyes, retorting in the softest appealing voice.

"No, this is the body that God gave me, and I'm not ashamed to wear it proudly. If you men are thinking something else about it, then you have to just keep your hands to yourselves. What's the commotion about anyway?" Agatha replied smugly.

Oh, God. She really doesn't know about the facts of life, Johnny thought. *Nope, I can't picture Ma telling her anything. The poor thing. Nobody has ever told her about the physiological exploits of men, or women for that matter. Here she is going to be married and should know something about what she may encounter on her wedding night. Maybe I'll ask Dell to talk to her.*

Suddenly havoc reigned in the back of the room, a struggling sound as if a force were being held back, and then a man's cry came forth.

"Let me in, damn you. I need a doctor for my wife," the distressed man shouted despairingly, as he forced against the constraints of Phil Albred's grip with his last drop of strength.

"Yeah, youse guys'll say anything to get in ta de joint dese days. Ya hobo."

"What about you, ya damn crook, everyone knows yer ma bailed ya outa jail, and if it weren't for yer money, you'd a been in the big house years ago. So there." An agreed calm came over the room, as they stared back at Phil, waiting for the fistfight to begin, as the wrath of Phil got the best of him, as he pulled the poor man upright by his shirt collar.

"Hey, Phil, let him go. What the hell's wrong with you, beaten up on a man when he's down," Johnny yelled at his brother.

"I was jus doin' my job." Phil would always look down snobbishly on society's victims, assuming that he was well above this caliber of men.

"Johnny, you're too soft on dese guys, its bad for business havin' the likes of 'em aroun' here," Phil replied, reluctantly letting go of his suspect.

"Hi, Eddie." Johnny knew this poor bent down man in rags, holding his crumpled dirty hat in his hands. He and his family of three had lived behind the hotel in an old railroad boxcar in an alleyway for the last year, barely surviving the tough times. Dell had often taken boxes of sandwiches and baskets of food to them, and sometime tonics and herbal remedies when they were sick. They had no other family or benefactors.

"Johnny, the baby is dying. Me and Mary can't hear him breathing." He whispered in a hoarse frightened voice across the bar, his red eyes bulged out in distress. A sleeve of his worn and tattered tweed jacket brushed across the bar wiping a puddle of spilt beer. Patched filthy pantlegs nearly covered his worn down shoes, water-soaked cardboard flapped out of the sides of their soles as he walked.

Now only the muffled voice of KDKA's broadcaster announcing the nightly news could be heard, as the room became silent with only the sound of clinking glasses being washed back behind the bar, as they stared with pity at the intruder in their midst. Many murmured words in a compassionate tone among themselves with respect to some of the people they knew who were worse off than this man who represented the "man on the street."

9

"Eddie, I'll get Dell, maybe she can call Dr. Newhouse or come and see Mary. Go back to your family. They need you," Johnny told this poor disconsolate creature tenderly, moving with speed toward the back archway.

"C'mon, Phil, watch the bar while I get Dell upstairs."

"Okay, but I got a date, tonight," said his brother, eyeing the wretched little tattered man, who would spoil his plans for the evening. Johnny's face became bright red with anger and frustration as he watched his brother and so called business partner walk off muttering under his breath. *What kind of a world did he come from?* Johnny thought. Did he even acknowledge that times were bad? Mom had allowed him to go unscathed through life - at her own expense.

Johnny ignored Phil's indifference as he ran back into the dark and dusty wooden hallway toward the steps. Taking two at a time, realizing a little life was lingering without hope, Johnny glanced remotely at the walls and woodwork, which his mother had dusted and cleaned, so that they shone to a gloss, and now showed outward signs of deterioration at every turn. Cracks in the plaster ran horizontally on almost every wall, chunks of the white powdered mortar mixed with dust in every corner of the hotel. And even though they tried to keep the debri swept up, he worried that his children would pick up the pieces of plaster and put it in their mouths while playing.

Johnny could almost see his mother passing in the hall, her strong arms full of laundry, and her head wrapped in a white babushka. His eyes teared up at the thought. He could hear her telling him, in her strong authoritative voice.

Johnny, watch over your brother. Sometimes he gets into trouble, and Agatha, she's not as smart as you, she needs your help.

The strong pungent fragrance of her Eastern European culinary masterpieces no longer permeated the air circulating through Eastburg, but most strongly evident, Lizzie's strong resounding principles no longer held reign within the family business milieu.

The loss of Lizzie's presence and command begot anarchy of the worst kind among her offspring, pitting brother against brother as altercations broke out between the two men during the daily operation of the hotel. Johnny became more and more exasperated about his brother's irresponsible behavior. Just yesterday he was moved to rage.

"Dammit, Phil, you left the beef brisket to spoil in the sink in the kitchen. It stunk to high heavens. Why the hell did you let Molly take the afternoon off yesterday? That meat should have been cooked and stored properly. What on earth is wrong with you? You are costing us money."

"You, you're wits wrong wid me, college boy. I can't do anythin' right around here. Molly was sick wit that time o' the month or something. Ma would've let her go too," Phil replied.

"No, you're wrong, she wouldn't have, she wouldn't have let her best friend go - not Mom, no one was ever excused from work."

Johnny couldn't believe that he and Phil came from the same mother. Where was he when she preached about perishables, principles, or anything else as far as that was concerned.

"Listen, little brother, don't go making any decisions about letting the help take an afternoon off without talking it over with me, do you hear me?" The veins on the side of Johnny's face stuck out as he watched his brother and so called business partner walk off muttering under his breath.

"Tap, Tap." Johnny knocked on the door of their tiny apartment. The door was always locked so that none of the boys would try to open it and walk out into the main corridor of the hotel. But this time it was open, and he stepped inside.

"Dell?" he inquired, walking around to the kitchen.

"Daddy, Daddy." Three tiny boys ran from the other part of the room into his arms as he entered and kissed Dell, his loving wife of almost five years. As Johnny held the two older boys, one in each arm, they put their soft warm head up next to their father's. Johnny loved his family more than life itself, and would sacrifice throughout his entire life for their well-being, come what may.

"Brother! It feels good to get away from that lousy bar, and remind myself why I'm trying to make this business go in the first place. It gets harder every day, Dell." His wife greeted him in her warm gentle way. Never having been a gregarious person, she would nevertheless reach out to people with amenable bearing.

"Johnny, I know, your mother always shielded your sister and brother, even when they were in the worst of trouble. Like the time that Phil was stealing cars, he should have done his jail time, but instead Lizzie paid the police off, and bought them a new car from Pop's garage. He just did it to see if he could get away with it, it isn't like he couldn't afford to get a new one. I'm sorry; I shouldn't be saying these things, but they're true. May her soul rest in peace." Dell's bright gray eyes conveyed all the hurt that his family had brought to her, which broke Johnny's heart.

"Daddy, daddy, Aunt Aggie has chocolate covered peanuts and won't give us any," spoke up Tommy, his oldest son, who seemed to be aware of everything going on, and usually spilling his troubles out for his father's ears.

"She went into the bathroom with them and never came out - we waited for a long time outside the door because she said she'd give us some." Hmm, Johnny thought that sounds like his self-centered sister Agatha.

Tommy was the favorite precocious child of the hotel regulars, who often teased him to get back talk so that they could laugh at his retorts. Singing the popular tune of the day, "Brother, Can You Spare A Dime," he stood in front of the diners while they ate in the restaurant, before his mother could find him and disapprove of his shenanigans. He was pleased when they gave him a penny, and sometime he'd dress up in a coat or big hat they had left hanging in the cloakroom. Tommy didn't know why, but this would make his mommy mad.

Ben was a stocky little boy, built more like Johnny and born just a year later. He liked to wander outside into the tiny yard by the alleyway between the buildings. Dell would sometime sit on the porch holding Joel, while Ben sat digging worms to put into a mud pot he had nearby.

A third son, a fair haired, delicate boy, Joel Michael made his quiet entry into the world on a blustery windy March evening, just a year and a half ago. His easy birth, after Dell's difficult labor while having Ben, helped restore her faith in less painful deliveries. Joel was an easygoing boy who soon became a favorite of his mother's.

Just learning to walk, Joel followed his brothers around playing in empty hotel rooms, and sliding down the old wooden banister, while pestering the patrons of the hotel much to the repulsion of Dell, who wanted more than anything for them to have a home of their own. Consequently she tried to keep them locked up in their three hotel rooms, not nearly big enough for a family of five.

"Hi honey," Johnny kissed his wife endearingly, holding her close to his heart. His poor hard working wife, who had spent all of their married life heretofore laboring at the hotel. She seemed to be thinner than he had ever seen her before. Holding her out from him, he looked into the clear gray eyes that showed signs of crying.

"What's wrong, Sweetheart? You look as if you've been sad about something." His compassionate voice would always summon a flow of heartbroken words from the deep recesses of her insides, since she had so much on her mind these days. Dell's teary red eyes looked up at her husband.

"Oh, I was just thinking about last year when your mother died and when she called me to her bedside to ask for my forgiveness while she was dying, with the last breath of air that was in her body."

She could still see the diminutive body lying there under the flowered pedina in the big dark mahogany bed. Lizzie seemed to be a small fraction of former herself. A pure white, thin plait hanging down on her frail shoulder, most of the loose hairs framed her round haggard face. At just five feet, Lizzie's stature came from within, her very own level of attainment started with thinking productively. Dell had known her mother-in-law, Lizzie, since she came there as an eighteen year old. Lizzie had never spared her even while pregnant with her sons, from any hard work; she had to do the daily grind at the hotel. Changing all the bed sheets, dusting, washing the dark clapboard with strong soaps to make sure there were no lice or bedbugs in the wood.

On what would be Lizzie's last day on earth, she had just brought dinner on a tray with her favorite, stuffed cabbage to her mother-in-law, when she spoke with a weak voice.

"I haven't always done the right thing with you, my dear." She took her hand within her large rough hands, taking all of her strength.

"Please try to understand the hardships there for me, you've been a good woman for our John, and mother to those sweet sweet boys, and the new little poiska". And with that she smiled, falling off into sleep.

"Yes, I know, she wanted your forgiveness for the way you were treated around here - I'm glad she talked with you." The truth was that Johnny felt guilty for not defending Dell against the unkindness of his mother, but she was stalwart against everyone, especially him, and he was very much afraid to speak up to his mother.

"Johnny, I know Lizzie picked on me, but I still miss her around here, and my dear friend Zach, that sweet man. In a way it was good the way they passed away, each one not knowing the other had died, exactly one day apart. They would have been heartbroken, especially Zach, to know that his anchor, Lizzie, was no longer around.

"I remember Zach sitting by Lizzie's bedside holding her hand the day before he got sick too, saying, Lizzie, I'm going to bring you up some moonshine from the cellar - remember how we always said it's really sunshine because it makes us happy when we shine."

Johnny and Dell laughed.

"Zach could always make Lizzie laugh, even in her darkest moments," said Dell.

"No, Johnny, There doesn't actually seem to be a reason for us to be here anymore, with those two gone. Your brother and sister are not to be trusted; I have to continually hide our money in a different mattress in the hotel, hoping that Phil does not find it."

Holding each other, and deep in thoughtfulness, Johnny suddenly remembered remorsefully, why he had come bursting in there.

"Dell, the Stewart baby is deathly ill again. Can you go back there, or call the doctor? Eddie came into the bar all red eyed, poor guy, tell Doc to come fast."

"Johnny, I'll try to call, I feel as bad as you do, but what am I going to do with the boys? The baby was ill last month, I don't think he'll get well until they move into a warm apartment, that old box car they're living in is so cold and damp. I'll call Dr. Newhouse immediately. At least when Lizzie and Zach were here one of them would watch the kids, I can't leave Aggie or Phil here, I don't trust them," Dell said, sorry that she could not run out to help Eddie's poor sad little family.

"Okay, thats all we can do, Sweetheart. Oh, and Tommy, don't worry I'll bring you a big bag of some kind of candy home, it'll be a surprise, okay?" Tommy looked up into his dad's kind eyes, and knew he would bring back something wonderful and sweet to eat. But it was Ben who answered his father's promise.

"Daddy, you always help us when we're in trouble." Johnny bent down and put his arm around his little dark haired boy, holding him close. They were all his treasures, and what made life worth living.

Johnny walked back to the office he had once shared with his mother. The walls in the hallway looked dirty and dingy and in desperate need of a good coat of white paint, just one of many improvements needed. If only he could find some extra cash in the account books. Brass handles and railing, once polished daily and even hourly where he could see a reflection, now were smudged and even looked pitted in some places.

What happened to the professional staff they once had? It couldn't have been Lizzie's constant badgering and hassling that got things done around there, or could it? Was that what was needed for upkeep in the establishment? Well, he didn't think he had it in him to harass the people who worked for them all day long to get their job done right. I must have taken after my dad after all, he mused. The easy going, Zach, loved growing flowers most of all. He smiled noticing five tiny fingerprints made by one of his boys. It was a sad place for a child to grow up, Dell is right about that. Maybe we can at least rent a home until we can build one, he thought, wanting to remember to get the wanted ads from the newspaper.

Sitting down next to the big oak roll top desk where he and his mother had spent so much time going over accounts, Johnny opened the giant ledger book to all the negative numbers in the deficit column. The finances looked grim, more deficits than profits by a long shot. How much longer could they hold on here? At least they owned the building, thanks to Lizzie paying off the mortgage five years ago. For the first time in his life, Johnny wondered if it would be a good time to sell the hotel.

At two a.m. the next morning, Johnny and Phil had just turned the last table and chair upside-down so that Nellie the scrubwoman could clean the filthy floors turned into worse than a refuse heap by the overexhuberant election rebel rousers. Election returns still reverberated from the radio high above the bar, until finally an over-stimulated, but concise announcer spoke out the final count and sent the following historic message.

"Folks, we have a new President of the United States. Franklin Delano Roosevelt has won an overwhelming victory over Herbert Hoover; he has carried 42 out of 48 states, with 472 electoral votes. Hoover on the other hand had 59 electoral votes. The New Deal triumphs."

Johnny prayed a silent thanksgiving for this Godsend.

Finally crawling into bed beside Dell, who was sleeping peacefully, Johnny was dead tired from the important political day's events. He could hear her smooth even breathing as he drew near to kiss her goodnight. Pulling himself gently up next to her warm, lithe body, he fell into a deep fast sleep.

Deep in a slumber state, his sense of smell registered something strong and pungent cooking on the huge iron stove in the hotel kitchen. Suddenly the powerful odor penetrated his nostrils until his brain finally distinguished it as smoke. Jumping out of bed disoriented, and holding on to a nearby chair for balance, coughing and choking, he held onto the walls and furniture. Something was burning, maybe a pot left on the burner? A cigarette ashtray?

Panicked at the thought of an all-consuming fire coming to trap them upstairs in this old hotel, his first impulse was to run to get the boys.

"Dell, Dell," he cried. He could feel his heart pounding in his chest, as he grabbed his robe from the coathanger.

"Johnny, what is it?" she cried, her face a look of fright, as she too doubled over coughing harshly with strong response from the smell.

"There's a fire somewhere in the hotel, come on, honey, we've got to get out, oh God, where is it? Call the fire department, Dell, grab whatever valuables you think we have and run out fast, I'll get the boys."

"I'll go with you, Johnny," Dell replied, pulling her housecoat around her, wanting desperately to know that they were all right as well.

"Please, honey, I'll have them out in a second, go straight outside." He thought of the sixty people living there, some of them older now.

"We must warn the boarders. They've got to be evacuated fast. Maybe they're already up and out." He found himself talking in spurts, as if the whirling gases suddenly seized him, becoming stronger by the minute.

"Jesus, Mary and Joseph, please help us," he prayed. He could hear high-pitched sirens coming closer and closer blasting into the night, as he stumbled to the boy's bedroom. He could hear the rumble of people running downstairs, carrying their few treasures out into the night.

"What's wrong, Daddy?" Tommy muttered, rubbing the sleep from his eyes.

"Boys, we have to move fast and get out, there's a fire. We must all work together here. Please listen to daddy. Put your slippers on quick and take your blanket from your bed and put it around your head and shoulders." He tried not to scare them, just to alert them of the oncoming danger. Johnny wrapped Joel soundly and picked him up, holding him tight.

"Now follow me wherever I go, boys." Tommy and Benedict, both tall boys for four and three, walked swiftly behind their dad, their blankets dragging through the hall. They could all hear the fire crackling downstairs, their eyes stinging with tears, as the thick choking deadly smoke rolled up the steps.

Avoiding the open hallway, Johnny led them to a side entrance with a firescape, only to see great tongues of fire blazing out of the side of the door. With the next draft they would be encircled in flames.

"Oh dear God, please help us to find a way out of here. Mom and Dad, if you're up there, please ask God," he implored in anguish. Now full of terror, Johnny thought of one more exit. He hoped in his heart that capable firemen were helping all of the boarders and his sister and brother find a way out of this inferno. Just then some boards fell out of the ceiling right behind them, embers flew everywhere almost hitting them.

"Daddy, are we all going to burn up in the fire?" Tommy screamed in terror, while Ben's eyes reflected his brother's words completely. Then little Joel began to cry, struggling in his father's arms making him difficult to carry.

"I want Mommy. I want my Mommy," he chanted, his tiny fists rubbing his sore eyes

" I know honey, I know Joel, it'll be alright. I hope your mommy is way outside of the building by now waiting for us." Now they ran to the back of the second floor, where his mom had kept a special supply of linens. She used to sit in here handling all of the beautiful crocheted Hungarian dresser scarves, bedspreads and handiwork from Europe, he thought. It was all right there were no flames around there. He pushed at the old door that hadn't been opened for years, which wouldn't budge, it must have been painted shut at one point in time.

Johnny grabbed the end of the old sewing machine, butting the end up against the door. He knew it opened onto an iron staircase, because he used to play on it as a child while his mother sometime did her handiwork.

"Okay, boys, let's get this door open, I know you're all little but every ounce counts. One, two, three." Everyone including little Joel pushed with as strong a force as their young lithe bodies could thrust. After two hard shoves, the door flew open, releasing the fresh autumn night air, and revealing the others down on the ground, a distance away watching the building burn. Two firemen made their way up the iron staircase, quickly reaching for the children.

Dell met Johnny and the boys, her face full of loving relief, as they made their fast exit away from the steps. She ran to them holding them all as far as her arms could reach around her little family.

"Oh, thank God, Johnny, it seemed like you left so long ago and I know it was just minutes. My life would have been over if anything happened to any of you." When they spied Agatha standing alone sobbing, they walked over to her and put their arms around her as well.

"Don't worry Aggie, you can come with us." Johnny said in a moment of benevolence.

"It's alright Johnny, Joe and I are gonna be married in a couple of weeks, until then I'll stay with my friend Gladys." Agatha said, her beautiful face restoring itself after her despair.

They all huddled together in the chilling November night watching a rain of fiery red embers falling like snow from the fourth floor of the hotel. Then the entire building became engulfed in a pillar of fire that reached high into the dark sky. Raging and roaring, the flames pushed through room after room, propelling the storm of red-hot cinders on to new unburnt sections of the hotel, until the entire structure was covered. Iron and bricks came down as if thrown from a blast furnace, as the unsound wooden frame revealed itself.

Turtle Creek and Braddock fire engines roared to the scene, sirens blaring, as firemen battled the wild blaze. They heard happily, that all sixty people were able to get out of the building safely. That in itself was a blessing. Another condition that firemen were grateful for was that there was no wind that night to carry the sparks to nearby buildings, the capable firefighters wet down the roofs of each as well.

The newer added banquet room where Lizzie held large dinners for the area's aristocratic businessmen like George Westinghouse and, Andrew Carnegie, was one of the last to burn. The family could see remnants of green brocade drapes dancing as the power of the firehoses shot through the windows. The works of art that Lizzie had selected personally, designated to be a refined cultural room became ashes in no time at all to the observers.

Johnny stared into the ruins, mesmerized by the devastation of the Albred hotel, the building and way of life that controlled his life, his mother and father's dream, where they laid roots down in America. He knew they never left it ever, not even to take a vacation. It would be the end of this part of his life, and Dell's, as they knew it, but with God's help, they would begin a new, knowing it would be a long hard climb back to prosperity.

2. A New Neighborhood

Electric Avenue was the direct route for the trackline of the 87 Ardmore. The red and white streetcar trundled through the little residential section of Eastburg every half hour going west. Clickety clacking over the tracks, stopping to pick up a few passengers on their way to Forrest Hills or Wilkinsburg, the speedy transit then traveled on to its Pittsburgh destination.

Whereas, most local people walked the short route to the commercial center of Eastburg, unless of course they had shopping to do and heavy burlap bags to carry. As people boarded the lighted streetcar, compressioned folding doors made a long shhh sound that could be heard all around as they opened and closed behind passengers.

After depositing a worn metal carcheck into the glass receptacle by the door, riders grasped the looped straps hanging from the ceiling as they quickly made their bumpy way to a vacant seat, if there was none, they continued holding on to the strap or seat in their precarious standing positions, since the electric car sometimes jostled passengers quite vigorously while it traveled on the single track.

This manner of transportation carried Westinghouse workers to and from their job shifts at all hours of the day, was in fact, where the streetcar motor had been developed. The Company of Westinghouse Electric undertook production before the turn of the century, when inventor Nikola Tesla, an immigrant from Austria-Hungary, sold his patent to George Westinghouse. Tesla introduced it at a time when advocates of alternating current were seeking this type of motor with coils arranged so that when alternating current energized them, the resulting magnetic field rotated at a predetermined speed. Consequently, this style of transportation ran safely and swiftly throughout the city for almost fifty years. And although Germany invented the first electric railway, this unique design began a new trend in public transportation.

At 1449 Electric Avenue sat the dark insulbrick two-family, three-story house with its big up-hill yard taking up the entire large corner. To the left of the house, the narrow bricked road inclined steeply upward through Chalfant Borough. The road was bordered on the right by a rocky enclave of cliffs, and on the left side by homes that were reached by a descending stairway, as they were tucked into the side of the downward hill. Most of the older people had trouble navigating the precipitous route to and from their hillside homes, and most, not having automobiles, had to negotiate the terrain at least twice a day, to and from home mornings and evenings.

Craftsmen were skilled at building around the mountainous geographic composition of the Pittsburgh area, where stone ledges held up most large family homes. At the turn of the century, carpenters and bricklayers came to the city in great numbers to find work at Westinghouse and steel mills in the surrounding area, usually staying in construction because of the desperate need for housing. Some companies, such as the Westinghouse Air Brake Company in Wilmerding and Edgar Thompson Steel Mill in Braddock, constructed their own brick row houses for employees.

The handiwork of these early settlers, who were sometime commissioned to build more stately executive mansions in more affluent areas of Pittsburgh, demonstrated magnificent skill. Ornate wooden Victorian homes were elaborately decorated with ironwork gates and fixtures, along with brick and stone structures boasting fanciful masonry. Many of these homes that had stood the test of time lined the western part of town on Electric Avenue.

And though these structures had seen better days, having just gone through the Great Depression, they were still inhabited by later generations of the same families whose father or grandfather built them, more or less manifesting the solid character of the people living within.

The day before the early morning disastrous fire, which demolished the long withstanding Albred Hotel, Dell had come to see the home and new neighborhood where they might move. She had promised herself to bring Johnny here to see her new discovery the very next day, never dreaming that they would make haste to move sooner than expected.

They had taken whatever belongings they were able to rescue to stay with Dell's uncle Frank and Aunt Susie who lived nearby on Cable Avenue for a couple of nights. Immediately the next morning, Johnny went back to examine the remaining ashes and debris and to claim whatever goods were unharmed and help investigators try to discover what initiated the blaze. He had also hoped that Phil would be there to explain where he had been the night before. Johnny knew that his brother would definitely show up to collect his share of the fire insurance money.

For some time Dell had been secretly planning to move out of the hotel, especially after the death of her mother and father-in-law the year before, since the atmosphere had deteriorated from bad to worse after Lizzie's strong moral code was no longer enforced. But most of all because the standards of incoming hotel guests were now of a lower quality of character just to make money. Drunk and unscrupulous tenants roamed the halls, often hollering to each other loud and rudely using profanity, many vulgar words she had never heard before. The once highly regarded hotel was becoming little more than a rough college fraternity house, but even that institution kept its tenants in tow.

Dell worried constantly about her family under these living conditions, and was concerned that her children would hear or encounter these brash individuals. She had complained about this to Johnny, who made excuses one after the other, often ending with rationalizing why he had to continue the business objectives through devotion to his mother and father.

"I know, honey, I'm thinking about turning it over to a broker who'll sell it." His brown eyes flashed with concern toward her, trying to sift through her worried look, and tenderly enfolding her in his arms. But Dell knew deep inside that his mother's domination to keep this business going was deeply imbedded in the soul of John Aloyisius Albred, and there it would remain until the day he finally left the stronghold of this structure. Consequently, complacency would be his until something radical happened to change the tide.

Johnny's brother Phil, who was supposed to look out for the possible illicit behavior of incoming boarders, was himself an example of unethical character, who would steal their last penny in order to gamble or buy drinks for his crooked friends. Criminals and their dealings enamored him. The exploits of Al Capone had always thrilled him in the past, no matter how dastardly. A double feature made up of gangster movies, like *Little Caesar*, starring Edward G. Robinson, and *Public Enemy* had just come to the Rivoli Theater. Phil loved to imitate James Cagney with his rough gangstyle voice.

"Hey baby, whadaya doin' tonight, wanta pull a heist?" he'd say crudely in Cagney style to Dell in passing, winking slyly, with a dark curly haired ringlet falling over his eye. Always impeccably dressed in a white shirt, tie and dark pin striped suit, Phil tried but never looked the part of a gangster. His baby face got in the way.

"Oh, Phil, act your age, you don't even sound like the movie star," Dell admonished him, trying to sound a bit like his mother, and thinking that Lizzie probably would have never said anything to her "baby" even if she were present, about his worshipping crime figures and their living habits. Lizzie's neglect to discipline him, like letting him get away with petty thievery at the cash register, probably started him out on the crooked road he chose.

"Phil, will you please speak to the Kellys on the fourth floor?" Dell directed, starring into his shifty, dark shiney eyes and trying to break into his fantasies. "They've left their garbage outside their door, smelling up the hall," Dell said, forthright, keeping her message firm.

"Okay, sista, gimme de hard line, I don care.... Say, did ya hear 'bout Pretty Boy Floyd gettin'away wid three huntret dollas in cash de other day?" He smiled, devilishly arching his eyebrows, reminiscing about the evil deeds of one of his heroes.

"Yes, well the good Lord is going to punish him too, one of these days, Phil, he will only get away with it for so long." Dell preached. Phil knew she was a religious woman, and cringed at the thought of God and the church, looking once again like a mischievous innocent boy. Maybe his mother, who never missed mass in the morning, did have some effect on him, Dell mused. But Phil went on with his quips, trying to convince his sister-in-law of the partial goodness of the criminal mind.

"Hey, Dell, whata 'bout dat rascal Capone, he's really a good guy underneath, ya know? He offered a reward up to ten tousand for de chump dat kidnapped de Lindbergh baby."

"Well, then, why is he in Alcatraz now, for not paying his income tax? Come on Phil, be reasonable. I read the papers," Dell said, all the time thinking about the difference in him and Johnny, and how their mother treated each so differently. And though she never had time due to her busy schedule at the hotel to discipline Phil and Agatha, she devoted the other part of her life to trying to force Johnny to be a priest.

Dell shuddered when she thought of living in the same building with Phil. She tried to be charitable toward him, since the teachings of her Catholic faith advocated humility which meant restrain from judging another, not for us to live the lives of others, but to try to understand the infinite forces at work in another's life. Johnny had taught her these and other precepts of the Benedictine way of life from his education from Brothers at St. Vincent's in Latrobe.

The boys' aunt Agatha, seemed to be a little more honest by nature than her brother, Phil, though she had become even more lazy and self-indulgent than ever before without her mother to watch over her. Dell told a few of the townspeople that she wanted to move her family somewhere else, even though she worried about whether Johnny would move or not when given the actual choice.

An opportunity had arisen the week before when Dell walked up the street with the children to Kreck's Meat Market to buy some links of special sausage that were on sale for 22 cents a pound. Money was still very tight, and when she saw an advertised bargain she usually would investigate. Peering into the butcher's refrigerator display to look at the other prices, she noticed that steak was 29 cents a pound this week and bacon was 22 cents, while pork chops were 20 cents a pound.

"Mr. Kreck, prices are so high - it's hard to feed a family these days. I did want to get some bacon, but I'll just have to take six pork chops, plus the sausage. And then that'll be all." She knew that Mr. Kreck's prices were fair, for he supplied all of the meat at the hotel and kept special cuts for her to pick from. He then looked into Dell's eyes to mention quietly, so that other customers would not hear, about a friend of his who had a house available to rent.

"Mrs. Albred, you should see this big house, your family will have plenty of room to run around in, two whole floors. Just go up and see it. You know it's not easy to find a place these days. Go straight up Electric Avenue, you'll see Mr. and Mrs. Farkash's store on the left," he said in his kindly shopkeeper voice, as his immaculately clean white clothes reflected his shinny red cheeks - chilled from going in and out of the huge meat locker. Gently moving Tommy, who curiously stretched to peek into the cold storage unit out of the way, he addressed her again.

The sheepish look on her innocent face revealed a rising pink tinge from her neck up to her cheeks, telling him that it was a personal decision and that it was she who wanted her little family to strike out on their own. However, Jack Kreck was a wise old man who knew both the Gessner and Albred families, and the people who Lizzie rode hurd over in the past. And presently the town's people knew Johnny was tied to the Albred hotel physically and emotionally by Lizzie and Zach and lately to their spirit that haunted its dark halls.

Ignoring her apprehension, Mr. Kreck continued.

"Mrs. Albred, didn't you make a remark that you were looking for a new place to live the last time you were in here?" he said, while wiping his cold red hands on his apron, then ripping a large piece of white paper to wrap the meat up in. Dell looked over at Tommy and Ben drawing tracks in the sawdust-filled floor with their little worn out shoes. She gazed at them, while wondering if she should take the big step of even just looking, without Johnny's consideration.

"Tell Mrs. Farkash that I'm recommending you, and that you're Lizzie's daughter-in-law. She knew Lizzie, you know; yes her brother Frank stayed at your mother-in-law's hotel for a whole month back in 1907 when he arrived from Russia. And then she helped him to find a job too. She was a fine woman. May her soul rest in peace." He spoke with assurance, keeping silent about Lizzie's formidable side. With restored confidence, Dell spoke back surprising him.

"Yes, I know Mr. Kreck, thank you, I think I will walk up today." Her stomach quivered, she had never made any decisions of this importance without Johnny's permission, but this time it had to be done for her family's sake. Besides, she would be "just looking." Johnny could still work at the hotel - they would just be living somewhere else.

Her father, Pop, had told her in a letter to go ahead and try to make plans to move. *You have to get the boys out of that smelly hotel, with all of the drinking and smoking around there, its unhealthy for them growing up, he*'d written in his last letter. *They've got to have a yard to play in, they're growing fast. Please start looking for a nice home to rent, until home mortgages become available again - the economy is beginning to get better.* He had also included a one hundred dollar bill for a down payment, which was a fortune to behold in these days at the end of the Depression.

Dell had not shown the check to Johnny. She was afraid he might get resentful and be angry at Pop, for trying to interfere in their lives. Her father always saw Johnny as a complacent man; one who did not take initiatives toward success outside the hotel business his mother had left him. Dell knew her father thought a college-educated man like Johnny should wield his professionalism out in the world, especially since other jobs were becoming available.

Pop Gessner had sold his Chrysler garage before the Depression began for a good profit, moving his family to Cleveland where he bought a small tool-making company. Dell had been broken hearted when she found out her family was leaving - her only immediate family. She dearly missed her sister Mary, and her lovely mother, Theresa, but they weren't too far away, and she and the boys could take the train to see them. That is, at least until the new baby came.

Dell had not told Johnny that she was expecting again. She was somewhat unhappy about it this time, especially since they were still living in their small quarters. She knew he would be happy as usual when she told him they would have more children, but Dell had hoped not to have any more children born in there, and hoped with all her heart that they would have their own place before the new baby was due, which would be around the middle of April. Joel would be two in March, so she had some time to get ready, and please God, let this be the right place for them to live.

"Tommy, hold Benny's hand while we cross this street. Don't rush out like that, a car may be coming. Now Benny, hold Tommy's hand." She tried to be patient her sons, but aggravating morning pains still persisted after all this time. It was a little unusual for her, since she carried all of the boys without any problem at all and while working hard every day in the hotel. In fact she maintained a very low weight gain for almost five months of pregnancy. She hoped for a girl this time. In fact she was praying a special novena to Saint Theresa The Little Flower, her favorite Saint, which Dell thought would also be a beautiful name for the baby, also after her own mother.

Her mother would not be here to help with the new baby this time. Theresa had made her many new oversized clothes to wear when she was pregnant with Tommy and Ben. In fact the dress she was wearing now was one that her mother had made five years ago, and now it would have to do for her next pregnancy. She wished that there were special clothes made for expecting mothers. Most women just wore larger sized clothes - sometime even their husband's shirts.

Walking down Electric Avenue, she and the boys stopped to look into the large five and ten cent windowpane. The store was usually deserted with just a few articles for sale, but today there were many new articles. Dell was stopped short by their beautiful display of clothes and furniture. A nice suit for Johnny priced at $10, an eight-piece dining room set for $49, that might be something they would need in their new house.

Gazing into the array of fashions there, she spotted a lovely pin checked dress for just $1.95. *What a beautiful dress. Its been a long while since I had something new to wear.* It had been a long time since she and Johnny had gone anywhere special. *They used to go to a Marx Brother's movie as soon as they came to town.* She looked down at the oversized baggy shift she wore, hanging down below her knees. She felt enormous, though she was less than one hundred pounds. *Oh when will I ever wear*

28

normal clothes again? I've been wearing these same big dresses almost since the time I was married. It would be nice just to have one year when I could dress up in a nice outfit, she dreamed. *But then, where would I wear such a fancy thing with a family to take care of?*

Then she reprimanded herself, *I can't believe I'm standing here thinking about myself when I have a family to think about, how selfish I am. This money is going for something much more special, our very first home, away by ourselves. No hotel, clients, huge cooking pots, or Agatha and Phil around.* Dell's smoky gray eyes twinkled with her secret as she thought about the private life they would lead in their own private house. She would put the money down on the house, regardless of how much work it took to fix up - it would do until they could get a real house of their own, whenever that would be.

Dell thought about Lizzie. Making a decision like these would never have been a problem for her. She grew up being independent, making her own rules. It must have been a disposition she grew up with in Europe. Almost six years of living with her in the hotel must make some kind of difference in Dell's life. That was it. She would do what Lizzie would do in this situation. Please God; give me the strength Lizzie had.

The neighborhood seemed nice. They walked through a block where there were many nationality clubs. The Swiss Club, Czechoslovak Club, run by her Uncle Andy and where her family danced the czardas when she was a little girl. She remembered how her mother had laughed out loud at the sight of her husband, Pop, twirling Aunt Pauline, her sister around the room. Aunt Pauline and Uncle Steve lived up on Bessemer Terrace with their children, in another part of town.

Upon the hillside was a grade school where Tommy could start school. He was a bright boy and she knew that he would do well. They might even have a kindergarten, now that the Depression was ending; she heard that schools were starting classes for even younger children maybe Benny could go too. Oh he would like that. Dell's enthusiasm turned into determination with each new step she took.

She was beginning to be enthused about their new independence, finally. She would try to talk business with Mrs.

Farkash without the boys finding out, since they might tell their father, especially Tommy who was the mouthpiece of the group and liked to report everything to his father.

Finally, they came to the little grocery store. Once inside she saw a short stout woman with her wiry gray hair pulled back in a knob standing behind the counter. Her old gray sweater was darned in many spots, some of which needed to be darned over again. *Another sign of the horrible Depression,* Dell thought.

"Mrs. Farkash?" Dell inquired politely.

"My name is Mrs. Albred, Johnny's wife, from the hotel." Dell smiled, thinking to herself that this was one of the first new people she'd met outside the hotel in a long time.

"Hello, Mrs. Albred," replied Mrs. Farkash. She knew from the serious look on Dell's face that she had come to see about the house for rent, since she had never seen her in the neighborhood or in the store before.

"Mr. Kreck said that you have a nice home for rent somewhere in this area, a place for a large family to live." Dell thought of her as a generous woman, who had instantly handed the boys a lollipop and they were now sitting out on the front stoop of the store all together, which she was pleased about.

"Oh, Mrs. Albred, with the bad times, the building is in disrepair, the paint and the wallpaper is peeling." Mrs. Farkash looked with pity at the sad looking little mother of three boys, standing there so forlorn. Her dark brown hair was short and straight and tousled from the youngest boy's arm reaching around her head to look at his brothers.

Mrs. Farkash knew from her line of gossip how hard this young woman had worked at the hotel ever since marrying the Albred's son, Johnny, who left the priesthood to marry her. How could she help not knowing, it was the talk of Eastburg a few years ago or so. And though she was grateful for the help that Lizzie gave to her brother Frank, she knew her to be a slave driver for people who worked at the hotel. She made up her mind to help Dell as much as she could.

"The house is just across the street, do you want to look at it now?" she said to Dell, who glanced back at her with the clearest honest eyes that she had ever seen, stunning her vision for a moment.

30

"What will the rent be?" she asked demurely, looking once again straight into her eyes.

"Forty dollars a month. But it has to be painted and there are a few repairs that need to be done immediately if you are going to move in," Mrs. Farkash warned.

"Oh, Mrs. Farkash, we can paint and fix it up nice," Dell said, enthusiastically, going to take Tommy and Ben's hand in hers, while lifting Joel into her arms once again. *Oh no, she thought,* smelling a powerful odor coming from his diaper.

"I'll bring my husband to see it, when can we move in?" Dell hurried to bring their deal to a close since she could not conduct business with the awful smell prevalent.

"But don't you want to see it first? It's just the second and third floors with a private entrance of course. The first floor is already rented to another family." Mrs. Farkash went on, wondering what was happening for Dell to want to leave in a hurry. Then she began to smell the ominous diaper as well, as she turned quickly to see to another customer's needs.

Dell handed her the envelope from Pop with the money for deposit.

"I'll bring my husband up to see it. Thank you Mrs. Farkash," she said as she ran out the door.

Homes were scarce, as Mr. Krek said, and Johnny would just have to realize that this was a treasure to behold at the tail end of the Depression when every family would be looking for a better place to live. She was proud of herself for acting quickly.

Dell walked swiftly along the sidewalk back down to the hotel, with Joel turned to his side in her arms. If only she knew where the streetcar would stop so that they could all get on. Who was this approaching them, oh no, she thought not Phil. *What is he doing in this neck of the woods?* She wondered in disgust.

Her brother-in-law's usual natty self appeared before her, and if she didn't know that he was on the devil's side, Dell would think that he was the world's finest dresser. Sporting a navy and white pin striped double-breasted serge suit, with a white shirt and tie, Phil strolled arrogantly up the sidewalk. Even through the most troubled times of the Depression, Phil had always managed to be dressed well, making him the enemy of many who continued to struggle. Where did he get the clothes? What group was he connected with?

Dell knew from the phone calls and letters he received at the hotel that he might still have ties with Chicago and Al Capone's boys.

"Hi, sugar." He spoke in his cavalier tone.

"Now what would you be doin' in dis part of town?" he questioned. Dell was not to be distracted from her mission, which was to get Joel changed as soon as possible.

"I've come up to visit my dressmaker to have my winter coat shortened," she yelled back, running to catch up with the boys who were yards ahead. Thank God for their racing ahead, she thought. Usually she'd be hollering at Tommy and Ben to wait up. But she could have asked the same question of Phil: who did he know there, except maybe the "numbers" people? He probably collected their bets regularly, strong arming the poor merchants, she thought.

"Hey, wait a minute, Dell, can ya spare a coupla bucks." She could hear his voice in the distance. Silently she thanked Heaven she had met him on the way back after handing over the money to Mrs. Farkash, otherwise he may have guessed that she had it on her.

Agatha was lost without her panoply of fine clothes. Sitting on the side of the bed in her neighbor's home, she reflected on what had happened to bring her to this beleaguered point in her life. Her mother and father had died, and now all of their loving memories had been destroyed in the fire along with her beautiful cherished wardrobe. She caught her reflection in the small inadequate mirror across the room.

Where was she? Her past had been burned into ashes. Thank God she had survived. She gently touched her long auburn ringlets, which encircled a peaches and cream complexion. Smiling at her lovely image, Agatha breathed a sigh of relief.

"Ahhh, at least I'm safe and still attractive." She spoke out loud, walking haughtily across the room. She turned around and posed in various ways, pleased with her countenance.

"Now if only I had my ensemble of outfits, I would feel so much better about being alone. And my Princess Eugenie Hat that I just paid five dollars for at Sachs Fashionable Womans Store was also burned in the fire. It was still in the tissue." She had loved the story the clerk had told about some royal lady in Europe who loved to wear hats. It looked so perfect on her well-shaped head. She had always looked good in hats of any style.

She sobbed, shedding real tears, as if her clothes were her last friends on earth. Oh, why hadn't she grabbed that hat at least? But when Mr. Greenaway had called "Fire!" down the hall, she had gotten swept in with the rest of the boarders running to safety.

It was true that Agatha loved her clothes more than any of her family. Throughout her lonely existence in rooms full of people at the hotel, she became friends with these material objects. Her wardrobe was known to be one of the most stylish in the area. Fine evening dresses brought in from haute couture in New York City. Complete outfits, including hats, coats, shoes, and other accessories, were designed for her during the twenties by current designers. She loved her collection, even though months went by without her attendance at local charity balls when she would exhibit her splendorous wardrobe. Many of her outfits were now looking very dated due to the effects of the Depression and decline of business in the hotel, and she had not replenished some of the older "flapper style" dresses.

The "twenties" were the haymaking days of the hotel, when her mother had sometimes allowed her to go to New York City by train on weekends where her cousin Johanna lived. Her mother never knew that Agatha would spend hundreds of dollars on a single outfit. Every month Lizzie would call her into the office after the invoices arrived.

"Agatha, five hundred dollars for a single dress? And did you have to get the expensive shoes, hat, and purse too?" Lizzie would frown at the paper in her hands, putting more blame on the store than on her daughter's imprudence.

"Mother, you know I have to look good for the Policeman's Ball, Officer Popovic may be there and you know how he has eyes for me." Agatha told her mother in her best little girl pleading voice - which she knew her mother would respond to, rather than have a confrontation with her daughter. And since Lizzie knew she had not given her daughter the attention she needed since she spent so much time working at the hotel, she obediently paid her bills. Lizzie sincerely hoped that Agatha would meet a nice young man.

Agatha put on the same navy low-waisted sailor style dress she had worn for the last two days. The borrowed outfit looked drab and ugly on her, almost as bad as some of the rags that her sister-in-law Dell wore. But then she had to wear them, since Dell was always pregnant - but then who knew, she was such a string bean, and was never known for her fashion and style.

She slid her hands gracefully down along her ample sides wondering if she had a waistline to reveal under her full dress. She knew that fashions were becoming transformed, as dresses reached a mid-calf point or lower. Photographs showed small pert hats, dark nail polish that matched with lipstick. Color was once again abounding with decorated apparel and accessories. Physical shapes of models had changed as well; no longer the flat-breasted long-waisted female with perpendicular lines unnaturally accented; now the waist was permitted by style to be where mother nature had intended it to be, no longer flattening the figure.

"Aggie, I have a tray here, would you like some tea and toast for breakfast?" Asked a kindly voice outside the door where she was staying.

"Ugh!" She mumbled quietly to herself. *I hate it when people call me Aggie.* But instead she responded cautiously, not to hurt the feelings of her friend who had taken her in during the emergency. She had learned how to pretend to be nice to people, since all her life was spent waiting and greeting the public in the hotel business. Even on a bad day she would try to smile, and sometime it would take root and she would not feel as discouraged working there.

"Yes, thank you, Gladys, that's very nice of you."

She never dreamed she'd be staying here in this dump. She held the bed linens in her hand. *Look at this torn bedspread, its darned all over, not like my beautiful chenille cover. And this old mahogany furniture, why it looks like George Washington slept here. How much longer do I have to put up with these squalid conditions?*

But then her wedding to Joe was just a month away. Maybe he would give her some money to buy some respectable clothes. She knew that Dell would let her borrow the wedding dress that she wore when she and Johnny got married. Dell could be a kind sister-in-law when she wanted to be. Anyway, her mother bought the dress six years ago - so it was hers anyway - even though Dell wore it for her wedding.

She remembered how baggy and ugly it looked on Dell. She had no figure at all - just skinny, straight up and down. She couldn't see what her brother Johnny saw in this skinny minny. But he must have seen plenty, because she was always pregnant. They already had three little boys. Maybe she would ask Dell about some of the intimacies she was about to face in married life. She was scared to death.

Joe would be a good provider; she knew he had a good job at Westinghouse as a patternmaker or something. She hated it when he tried to give her wet kisses - oh how horrible.

She wondered how many other awful things she would have to do with him on their wedding night. In all of her nineteen years she had had nothing to do with men physically - her mother had made sure of this. To let a man touch your body in any way meant that pregnancy would soon follow. She thought her mother would do something horrible to her if she allowed this to happen, whatever it was.

But Joe had been different from other men from the day she met him. His red hair and fiery personality had won over all of her family, including Johnny, who was now the head of the family after her mother and father's death.

Joe Lasky was a tall fair guy who was full of fun, telling stories that made them all laugh, including herself. Their attraction to each other was almost immediate; he seemed to focus on her with his uplifting charm and happy disposition, even when the rest of the world was weeping because of the Depression. They really began to go together after their trip to Kennywood Park at the Westinghouse Company annual picnic.

Agatha couldn't wait to ride the Jack Rabbit roller coaster with the double dip. She screamed so loud that Joe had to put his arm around her to protect her from the near death experience. Then they had to run with excitement to the comparable Racer with two separate tracks racing against each other. Phil and Mugsy were in the other one that ultimately won on its track. Of course he flaunted their winnings all day as they passed each other on the picnic grounds, even when they ran into them again in Noah's ark.

Noah's Ark was a brand new feature of the park, just built this year. It was a huge Ark built high so that it could be viewed from all over the park. It had moving sidewalks, teetering barrels and rollers embedded in the floors. The enormous structure continued to rock as people entered.

Last of all they rode in the Old Mill, which could have been called the "tunnel of love," The dimly lighted boat ride through narrow canals showed a scenic tour into the life of several cheery skeletons. This was the romantic occasion when Joe held Agatha's hand and asked her to marry him.

*"Let us concentrate upon one thing. Save the people
and the nation and, if we have to change our minds
twice a day to accomplish that end, we should do it"*

Franklin D. Roosevelt to
Commerce Secretary Dan Roper

3. The Special Baby

Johnny and Dell sat back in their chairs with the rest of the nation to listen to the first of President Roosevelt's fireside chats on the radio, the evening of March 12, 1933. His informal talks would begin a series where he would make known to the people exactly what the government would do to strengthen their depressed social situation and how they would be directly affected.

During the first 100 days of the new administration, Roosevelt's leadership had stirred the country out of its apathy. In just three months time the government gave 500 million for cash, food, and shelter to the destitute. The New Deal was described as a use of government authority as an organized form of self-help for all classes and groups and sections of our country. Conservatives, the wealthy, and many businessmen bitterly attacked the policy, but most people stood behind it.

In a 99-day session, The Democratic congress had passed a history-making number of bills. It approved any measure the president urged coming directly from the White House. One created the Federal Emergency Relief Administration, which paid out three billion for relief or wages on public works.

Johnny and Dell were relieved when Phil was called to work with the Civil Conservation Corps, which would be working in the state of Oregon. This program would employ almost three million young men to plant and restore forests, build roads, and construct flood control. He would receive thirty dollars a month and room and board. His group was leaving on a train the next week, westward bound for Portland. And though he was apprehensive about going so far away from home, he seemed as if he was excited about the opportunity. They felt it would be a good way for him to stay in tow before he found a new way to make a living after the hotel burned to the ground, which had left them all to find a new way of life. He showed up at their doorstep looking entirely different from his old self, and dressed in the new uniform he would wear.

"Look at deese rags, did ya ever see the likes of "'em before. Now dis is ugly duds." He yanked his khaki sleeves, poking fun at his new appearance.

"Not on my worst day in hell would I wear 'em. Wally Berry never even wore deese when he went to da Big House. Hey maybe I'm gonna break prison like he did." Phil joked, with his underworld humor. But despite their doubts, Johnny and Dell had to laugh at him. It would be a change from his old ruinous pattern at the hotel at least for the time being, and before he got into more mischief. He would trade his flashy clothes for khaki ones. He wore his uniform with dignity, a big change for him, since he narrowly escaped jail several times for boot legging, gambling with the numbers racket, repainting cars for racketeers, and many other illegal businesses. And people in town always said, "If it wasn't for his mother Lizzie always bailing him out of jail, he would have ended up in the big-house years ago".

"So now he's working for the government. Ha." Johnny grinned at the thought of his troublesome brother actually doing something legal, and actually having to follow the laws of the United States.

"Well we'll see how this turns out, maybe they'll make an honest man of him, but I doubt it. And somehow I can't picture him in some forest cutting down trees. But who knows, stranger things have happened, maybe he'll meet up with good company around the campfire out there."

Now Johnny wondered about his sister, Agatha. She had just married Joe Lasky. He hoped she had made a good marriage, but serious doubt clouded his thoughts. They hadn't been in touch with her for a few weeks; maybe he would stop over to their new apartment soon. For some reason, he thought the newlyweds should be left alone for now.

Now, as he examined the *Pittsburgh Sun-Telegraph*, Johnny read details about the merits of the new National Recovery Administration, which would put industry on its feet by shortening hours, raising wages, and stopping cutthroat competition. This bill concerned him, since he had just accepted a new position with Westinghouse as an inspector for their products. And since this would be the first time other than his job stints at Pop Gessner's Chrysler garage, where he worked on his summer's home from college, that he would work outside of their family venture. His friend Al Goss had come up at Thanksgiving to describe the position available, telling him to go immediately to the employment office and fill out an employment application. Johnny had gotten the quality assurance spot that day after a quick interview and an annual salary of $1558, primarily because of his family owning the hotel; he knew everyone and their families in the plant subsequent to the day George Westinghouse built it, and he was welcomed with open arms. His friends in management knew that being a member of the ambitious Albred family, he would bring pride to the thirty-year-old company, which now had over 10,000 employees under their Eastburg plant roof.

Dell had carried steaming thick gray restaurant cups of coffee into the living room after dinner, which Johnny recognized instantly as the few pottery pieces salvaged from ashes of the fire. This was their moment of solitude before they put the boys to bed for the evening. Johnny smiled and winked at Dell, who bloomed as so many lovely flowers in her eighth month of pregnancy. She would have their fourth child next month in April sometime. They both hoped it would be a girl. He loved her with the same exuberance that he felt the wonderful day they had met at her father Pop's garage. She and the boys were everything to him, and he had made up his mind to work as long as he could walk, for their happiness and livelihood.

The old rickety threadbare mohair side chairs were the only bit of furniture their sparse living room contained. They had been left by the last tenants and stood for another forgotten time, when many living rooms were luxurious enough to comprise different types of occasional furniture. The hotel had been such a place, with two or three rooms filled with many distinct ornate styles of Victorian furniture.

Three of the more priceless pieces were a Philadelphian Chippendale chair, a small table, which sat in the main hall off the large dining room, and an oak carved American chest and cupboard procured by Lizzie during the prosperous years. Over one hundred years old, these had probably fed the flames as so much fodder. Then there was imported Bohemian glass and porcelain exploded into a million pieces in the rubble.

A brand new Philco radio purchased with the money from the fire insurance proceeds sat in the corner of Johnny and Dell's new living room. They were pleased with the new console, which now provided many hours of entertainment for the family. Tommy and Ben would crowd around the speaker for hours listening to the adventure stories of the cowboy Tom Mix and his horse, Tony. Dell loved to tiptoe in without them seeing her, to watch their eyes light up, as vivid imaginations actualized the activities of their heroes, their little heads up close to the speaker unit. Ventriloquist Edgar Bergen and Charlie McCarthy were also favorites.

Johnny had taken the two older boys to one of their movies recently at the Rivoli Theatre, a few blocks down from where they lived. In the afternoons after Johnny came home from work, they would turn on the afternoon "soap operas." Stella Dellas or Just Plain Bill, a serial that narrated the adventures of a hometown newspaper reporter, were broadcasted. They would have tea before dinner was cooked. Johnny wouldn't admit his interest in the moving drama, however, and Dell would tease him.

"Shall we turn on the radio, John? Let's listen to our program." Then he would get comfortable next to the speaker. They would laugh together at the exploits of the imaginary radio characters going through their escapades. This was a good way for Johnny to escape from his humdrum work-a-day doldrums.

The five-room apartment was not yet adequately furnished, lacking the material accouterments to give it comfortable surroundings. But the rooms were large enough for their growing family on the second floor with two extra bedrooms for the boys up in the third floor attic. A private entrance led from a big back porch and yard where they could play and Dell could hang her wash on Mondays.

Struggling up two sets of steps with an overloaded wash basket filled with wet clothes from the side door in the basement, Dell was careful not to disturb the nice family living on the first floor at street level. Jumping up to secure the washline to a pole, she stretched it out as far as it would reach to the next post. Pinning each piece in orderly fashion was strenuous for the soon to be mother of four.

Upon entering through the back door, a big warm kitchen, which always smelled of freshly baked bread, greeted guests. Two colorful rag rugs, which Dell had crocheted herself this past winter, adorned the old worn linoleum floor. Cutting uniform strips from old clothing; she wove these into a colorful herringbone pattern with a thick wooden needle. These would suffice as a good washable floor covering for her active boys who usually bounded in with muddy knickers and wet knee socks.

She and Johnny had managed to buy a secondhand Tappan range from a former boarder of the hotel, Jacob Johannsen, who had recently transferred to another steel mill job in Cleveland. He had sold it to them for twenty dollars, which proved to be a good bargain. The only problem that Dell could see was defective side storage doors on each side which sprung open swiftly, giving her a start as baking pans flew out onto the floor with a crash. This infuriated her to the extent that she sometime swore, a rarity, especially when it happened in the middle of her baking and cooking process. Johnny would laugh when this happened, watching her all disheveled with her big apron askew as she bent over to restore the trays.

"Aw, that's nice Dell, a good Catholic woman like you." And then they both broke up at the ridiculousness of the situation, since they were both always able to laugh at themselves and situations. A commonality between them lay in their easeful way with each other. They were able to chuckle at everyday foibles, not taking life seriously together. Their love was effervescent and was surrounded by their deep faith in God and in each other.

Beside the range stood a brand new Westinghouse refrigerator bought with an employee's fifteen percent discount. Dell and Johnny continued to hold on to the old icebox from another era, sitting symbolically in the back corner of the porch, and used only during the winter.

Johnny sipped the dark brew, feeling the warm soothing steam gently move up his face. He was blessed, as was his whole family, by the series of events which led them here to a home in an opposite part of town, a nice residential section of Eastburg. He reflected for an instant on how these events, in just three months, had changed the course of their lives. The neighbors were good people as well, and many Johnny knew by name from the hotel restaurant. He would miss those good old days, holding court behind the big oak bar, keeping the camaraderie of the patrons constant. Living as a nearby resident instead of in Eastburg's prime business district would require some getting used to, he thought.

"Bro-o-om." Tommy ran his toy car over the old worn Turkish rug given to them by their kindly landlady, Mrs. Farkash, the day they moved into the house. Benny, a boy who liked to tackle more intricate tasks, was building a tall building with different sized colored blocks, while tiny Joel watched his brother with devoted anticipation.

FDR's resonant voice came over loud and clear over KDKA, but try as he might to concentrate, Johnny's mind drifted back to the frightful fire that burned the evening after his election, leaving his family destitute for a night.

They had stood holding each other, with the frightened children clutching at their robes, for what seemed like an eternity in the dark night, while flames swallowed up all of their life possessions into cinders. He had cried desperately, searching his mind for answers, his face blackened with soot and dirt from helping the firefighters get the rest of the boarders out alive.

"What will we do, honey? Where will we stay? Which one of our relatives will take the five of us into their home? We might stay with Uncle Andy for a while, but will he take all of us since his home is so small?" Suddenly he became acutely aware that he had never faced a problem of this magnitude before in his life. His whole family literally out on the street.

And being perfectly honest with himself, he experienced a cold realization that his mother had always been in the forefront solving everyday problems before they began to be troublesome for the rest of the family.

His whole life had been one of a favored existence. The Albreds had wallowed in luxuries during the twenties. Johnny had driven the most expensive Chrysler available. Money was never an object to worry about. He never knew what it would be like to struggle for your last nickel or penny in an embittered economy.

He had been "Joe College", football star, wearing the latest dapper clothes that Brooks Brothers had to offer on campus. And even though the money was there to be used frivolously, one of the best gifts handed down to him was his faith, which could never be bought in any store. This he called upon daily to get him through life's difficulties. Johnny believed in prayer, and learned how to truly love through his devotion to God, the church and the sacraments at an early age. Showing early promise for the priesthood, his mother became instrumental in entering her son into St. Vincent's College prep school in Latrobe at the young age of fourteen.

The Albreds comfortable life ended abruptly during the last few years of the Depression. Many businesses were lost fast at the beginning of the downslide The family had been lucky after Lizzie and Zach's death to coast through most of this terrible time, made possible because of his mother's parsimonious financial system. Her method simply meant that she never trusted banks, hiding all her money beneath the heavy wool mattress in her room.

At any rate, he believed they could never rebuild the hotel into what it once had been when his mother had all forty rooms filled to capacity furthermore, he did not know if he had his mother's strength to work from morning to night, ignoring his family as she did.

He was drawn back abruptly into the present as he heard Dell's gentle voice.

"A penny for your thoughts, John". He glanced over at his dear wife, the woman who surprised him by finding the nice place they were now living in. He would never underestimate her ever again, never dreaming that she would go ahead and carry out a plan like this for the family. If only he hadn't been so preoccupied with the business, and had given his family the attention they needed. He also wondered if they would ever find out the mystery of why and how the fire started. Could it have been foul play? And how much of a role did Phil play in coordinating this form of larceny?

"Huh? Oh, Dell, I'm just going over everything that has happened to us, and how we came to move here, in my mind again. I guess I'll never be able to erase all the horror from my mind".

"I know". Dell nodded compassionately, her dark bobbed hair falling down around her thin face. "It was an experience we won't forget for a long long time."

"The boys still have nightmares about the fire. Did you hear Tommy hollering last night? He was coughing too, as if smoke is still in his lungs."

"Do you miss our life at the hotel at all, Dell?" Johnny reminisced. Dell couldn't even begin to tell him how much happier she was living here - just the five of them. *Thank God we're out of there, I worked like a dog in that place. She* thought. Outwardly she showed compassion to her lonesome husband.

" I miss Lizzie and Zach, and some of the nice people who came and went there. But Johnny, you know yourself that Phil and Agatha were too much to control. Just like big kids who'll never grow up. One of the best things is that we are now away from them." Secretly, Dell told herself that it was a catastrophe that she was somewhat grateful for deep in her heart, though she would never forget the night scene either.

She had never seen him raging like this almost into delirium. His once strong and controlled voice weakened with cries of anguish. He was her husband and lover, who always seemed to have the answer to everything. But then, suddenly, his usual strong resolve had been burned along with all of their other worldly goods. She had stood with the boys crying silently.

Caught up in the disastrous moment, Dell had almost forgotten that their most important problem, of immediate housing was solved, because of her spontaneous actions before that evening's circumstances. She looked over at her tortured husband and began to relate the news of what she had done the day before. She had been holding back for just the right moment to tell him, and destiny had intercepted swiftly by burning down the hotel, the only home they'd ever known. Fixing her clear gray yes on his, Dell held tight onto his arm, hoping that he would not be startled by what she was about to say.

"Johnny, the boys and I found just the place for us yesterday. Mr. Krek suggested that we look at it. We walked up the street to see the house and we liked it. We can probably move in right away." Johnny looked at her incredulously. His stare was of one of suspicion, and frightened her, shaking her previous confidence.

"What do you mean you found a house, Dell, how could you have? Where did you get the money?" His questions came fast and furious, making her confused as to what her answer should be. *Should she tell him the truth and compromise Johnny's relationship with Pop - or tell a tiny white lie for the sake of family unity?* Ultimately she had chosen to tell him that she had been saving for years to get a home of their own, and had put away just enough for a deposit on this rental. And whatever route they had taken to get there, providence had put them on a single road to change their life for the better. And she would see to that.

The Faraday family lived directly next door to the right of them, occupying the entire house, unlike some other families who had either the upstairs or the downstairs. Mr. and Mrs. Faraday had two daughters, Dolores and Mildred, who would sometime watch Ben and Joel, when Dell had to go down the street to shop or go to the bank or post office. Just two sidewalks divided the houses, so that they could see right into their house as they went about their day-to-day living. One evening as Johnny observed their neighbors for an instant through their kitchen side window, he noted that they were having dinner. He thought it was odd that they all ate from a large pot in the middle of the table. All he could do was think that it was another quirky habit developed during the Depression when food was scarce.

Residing on the first floor, beneath them, was the Zbyosky family who had come over from Czechoslovakia. Mr. Zbyosky was a butcher for Farkashes store across the street. Most of their children were grown. Because of their Bohemian heritage and years serving the immigrants at the hotel, Dell and Johnny would frequently have conversations in Czechoslovakian with them as they passed on the street or met in the hallway to the basement. Their second language would be with them always, especially when sharing secrets in front of the children. This tactic would frustrate the Albred children, who never learned to speak the language of their heritage throughout their life.

As six-year-old Tommy grew and began to think about getting ready to go to school, he wanted to make friends with the nearby boys his age. Dell worried about his crossing, as the front street was dangerous with streetcars coming and going fast close by their house.

"Mommy, I want to go up to see Walter today, he has new soldiers he got for Christmas, can I, please?" Dell was moved by her little boy, his blue eyes twinkling with prospect. Tommy was a small, thin, boy, not at all built like his stocky father. He favored her side of the family, with his tousled dark hair, a few strands always fell down in front of his forehead. Tommy always seemed to have a plan in mind, and this was the one he wanted to carry out today.

Dell still carried guilt pangs from when he was a baby and she had to lock him up in the room upstairs of the hotel. And while serving restaurant guests, she would steel away after her customers' first course to listen for his cries at the bottom of the steps. Sometime she would run up the steps panicked that he had fallen from his crib or smothered under his blanket, or even that one of the boarders would open the wrong door and let him out. She breathed in a sigh of relief. Oh, what a release to know those days were over.

Dell loved being a mother. She felt that she had so much to give her children - most of it nurturing. Watching them growing up was a good reward for all the time she put into everyday work around the house. She believed that children brought out the best in a mother, and maybe some of the worst, but she enjoyed her time with them, and was happy to be having another baby. And just at that moment, the baby within her jumped almost with joy. She smiled at the unborn child. Next month would be delivery, if she had counted correctly.

She stooped laboriously to give Tommy a kiss and a hug; he would always be the big brother. His lips were still sticky from the raspberry jelly that was on his breakfast toast this morning. But then she also wondered how he knew about his friend.

"How do you know he has these toys? You've never been up there to his house."

"Remember, mom, when we saw him and his mommy in the store yesterday, we talked."

"Oh yeah, I do." Dell had to laugh. This little guy was meeting more people than she had in the almost five months that they had lived there. Well just about everyone who lived around there would meet at Farkashes during the course of the day. This was a close store, where they'd need to buy a loaf of bread, laundry powder, or jumbo lunchmeat and usually got some good choice gossip on the side. Dell kept quiet while some neighbor talked about another. She had enough to do with her three boys; besides, it wasn't charitable for a good Catholic to talk against another's good name.

The little neighborhood store was a little too expensive for her budget, when the Giant Eagle supermarket was down the street for the larger orders of food, especially since coffee was now .26 cents a pound and eggs were .29 cents for a dozen. She could bring home two burlap shopping bags of food for ten dollars to feed her family for a week.

"Tommy, we'll have to talk this over with your father tonight," she said to her son. "I promise that your father will ask Mrs. Kovic tomorrow if you can play with Walter. You're just too small right now to go up there alone." She hoped she was not being too protective with him, but not knowing all the people around here made her hesitant. Johnny seemed to know many by name, but then he had always been much more outgoing than she. Tommy took after his father in that way. She had to broach the fact that Tommy was very socially inclined. He made friends easily and would probably have many friends in his life.

By contrast, his younger brother Ben, a quiet and somewhat thoughtful boy, seemed to sit for hours with worms and bugs of every variety in the backyard, with most of these personally collected by him to inspect for various points of view.

Now and then he would put ants and flies into the spider webs, adorning the stonewall in the back yard. He could be happy just playing in one place, or with Joel. He would entertain his little brother by setting up bridges of large blocks, and letting him pull them down. With this the little tow headed Joely would fall down with giggles. Of course Joely would follow his brothers everywhere, his diaper sometimes drooping behind.

Johnny was strict with the boys, much more so than she - he especially wanted them to have good companions. A principle rule that he pointed out was that if they were present while another was acting out wrongly, they were just as responsible if they did not correct the harm done. Dell thought it was a tough rule for them to follow, but would not question their father about it, since he was the head of their family.

The steep hill up to North Avenue to the left of the house seemed to comprise of a different group of people. One thing she noticed about the entire area was the freedom with which everyone went about their business. It was a different way of life here. This section seemed to hold more freedom to go about the neighborhood, and yet she didn't know the people that well yet.

Dell thought this attitude probably had to do with the aftermath of the Depression - many people had formed a bond of helping each other through this terrible time. She knew many of these people. But contrary to this, there were the others who remained suspicious, and still hoarded food and scrimped to the last penny depriving their family of needed necessities.

After a dark and dismal winter, spring had come to Eastburg. The sumac trees sprouted pointy leaves to form long willowy branches. The hardy variety was one of the only trees growing profusely through soot layered hilltops and cliffs of Eastburg and the surrounding area. Dust and ferrous crystals descended upon the area regularly, blending in with soil during plant growth.

This area, as opposed to that of the Albred Hotel, was at least sheltered from nearby Edgar Thompson in Braddock, which regularly spewed a steady drizzle of soot. Dell remembered Pop saying not to complain about the dirt, because it means that everyone is working again and prosperity is booming in the area.

48

The sun shone brightly on soot crystals embedded in the sidewalk, sparkling like jewels, as the little group ascended. Dell, Ben, and Joely walked tediously up the steep graded hill, with Tommy running far ahead eager to get to his friend's home. Dell felt hot and sweaty in her dark wide dress, as if she were pulling three times her weight with her protruding stomach.

The evening before, as Dell questioned her husband about Tommy's motives, Johnny had mocked her abject concern for a suspicious group of people on North Avenue, saying,"Honey, the Kovics are good people. Mrs. Kovic will probably welcome you with open arms today. You've got to start trusting people, there are many good people around here." Johnny had arranged with the Kovics to leave Tommy there until Johnny came home from work at 3:30 p.m., then he would walk up to bring him home.

Johnny was right. Mrs. Kovic was a kindly gregarious heavyset woman very close to Dell in age. Her tight blond curls bounced around her chubby face as she stretched her arms out to help Dell down her back steps.

"Mrs. Albred, oh my goodness, you poor lady, walking all that way," she sympathized.

"When are you due? C'mon in, would you like some tea? My sister is to deliver next week." The two women commiserated over a cup of tea that Mrs. Kovic had poured for them. A sweet smell of cinnamon had filled the cozy room. Dell broke off a tiny piece of the freshly baked roll. She looked around at the colorful little kitchen with bright shades of red and blue plaid curtains and a tablecloth to match. She had never seen such an attractive little kitchen and vowed to do a similar scheme in her own place. She decided to ask where she bought them. She hoped she wasn't going to be too forward, but she liked this woman and began to feel at ease.

"Mrs. Kovic, where did you get the nice curtains and matching tablecloth?" Dell said interestedly. Her new friend smiled with delight that Dell had noticed her handiwork.

"Oh, I made them, I was fortunate enough to find some inexpensive material at *Murphy's Five And Ten Cent Store*. Then I used my mother's old sewing machine, and I just put a seam in them," she replied cheerily.

Dell was not sure what to say next, and looked down at her lap shyly. Soon she became embarrassed about her behavior and knew she could not keep up this idle conversation any longer. She felt funny to be this familiar with someone she hardly knew. Suddenly, jumping up, she started for the door, leaving her new neighbor bewildered.

"We have to be going." She collected Benny and Joel, leaving Tommy to play with his new friend. She would ask herself over and over why she couldn't just relax in another person's presence. Why did she feel so nervous under these conditions? She had seen her mother do it time after time. But then Theresa had been a Hungarian immigrant adjusting to entirely new conditions everyday. No, she was intimidated by being around people generally. She hoped that someday she would overcome this feeling. Or would she?

In late afternoon, while Joel was taking his nap, Dell was dampening her clothes to be ironed the next day. She spread each shirt, pillowcase, apron and hankey out individually on the kitchen table for a shake of spray from her pop bottle, dampening them all evenly. Then she rolled each piece up carefully, laying them back in her clothesbasket. Just then, Johnny came in through the back door. He came over to kiss her as he always did, but she saw him looking behind her, his dark brown eyebrows knit together in a frown.

"Did Tommy come in, Dell?" he asked.

"Mrs. Kovic said that he wanted to come home a little earlier, and she walked him down the hill, and that he went through the backyard." Dell felt a chill come up her spine.

"No, John, I haven't seen him." Her voice quivered with panic.

"Now, don't worry, I'll go out in the yard to see if he is lurking out there. Maybe one of his friends stopped by." He knew that Tommy was not out there, because he had looked all around before coming into the house. He put his arm around his wife's shoulders. In the meantime Dell ran out to the back porch calling frantically.

"Tommy, Tommy." Her voice rang out, urgently. Johnny ran down the back steps two at a time, priding himself on his agility of the athlete that he had once been - though he now blamed his incessant smoking habit for the bad cough he had developed. It was a miserable habit he could not now stop easily, but what the heck, it got him through moments like this, when his kids made him nervous.

Looking everywhere for his young son, he peered into every nook and craney that he might have squeezed into. He was just about to come back in and call the police, when someone called to him from next door. It was Mrs. Faraday leaning over the fence to answer their call. She spoke calmly.

"Mr. Albred, your Tommy is in our basement watching my husband work. He must have wandered down there. You can come over and get him." *Thank you dear Jesus*, Johnny thought, taking a moment to thank God for his neighbor's help.

"Oh, Mrs. Faraday, thank you, he is a roamer, that boy. I don't know what we're going to do with him."

"You know what they say, Mr. Albred. He's going to be traveling away all his life, it's in his blood," she prophesied, smiling.

After telling Dell, who smiled and shook her head in disbelief, Johnny ran down to the street level basement to find his son, who sat next to Mr. Faraday, watching him repair a heel on a pair of women's shoes.

A deep rawhide and shoe polish aroma penetrated his nostrils as he entered the dimly lit room, reminding him of his last pair of new shoes probably bought years ago before the Depression. He used to love to put on a new pair of Florsheims.

"Hey Daddy, look at the shoes Mr. Faraday has made around here," Tommy cried, standing close to his neighbor's shoulder with renewed interest.

Johnny wanted to grab his son by the scruff of his neck and teach him a lesson. But soon he too became absorbed by the craft of Mike Faraday, who had all the tools of his trade. Set up around the room was a big sewing machine, leather cutters of every size, spools of brown and black heavy thread, different sized iron shoes, and other equipment set at various stations. Along one whitewashed wall was a supply of shoes of many sizes, styles, and colors, with a long wood bench and a large mirror for trying them on. *Was this a business?* John asked himself. *If so, who were his customers? The neighbors must all bring their worn out shoes to him.*

"Hi, Mike," Johnny said, his voice filled with relief." Looks like you have company here. Is he bothering you?"

Mike Faraday did not look up but stayed with his task at hand. He was known as Big Mike, who commanded Gate 15 into the Transporting Division of the Eastburg plant. Recognized for his tall, broad stance and sharp, to the point, one-word answers at work, he kept everyone confused except the insightful person, who might hear these transmitted with volume and elocution. If perchance one did not catch his answer properly, it was never repeated. Now Mike replied to Johnny's question with a profound response.

"Nope." He uttered, nose to the grindstone continuing to cut hard leather soles out of leather with an enormous pair of shears, his dark hair falling down around his face.

As Johnny looked back into the room again, he caught him looking at his shoes. Who would have thought that Big Mike would fix shoes on his time off?

Johnny couldn't wait to tell Dell about Mr. Faraday's "boot-leg" shoes next door. He had to laugh to himself, as he and Tommy walked up the steps to their house. He came to the conclusion that his neighbor had found a way to have a quiet repose to himself, since it was common knowledge that Mrs. Faraday ruled the roost. *The poor guy probably just wants some time to himself,* he mused.

The little family sat around the table saying grace with the boys' little hands folded over the yellow printed oil tablecloth.

"Bless us O Lord, and these Thy gifts which we are about to receive from Thy bounty through Christ our Lord, Amen." And even though the little ones did not know all of the words, they bowed their heads and prayed with their mom and dad. Then Johnny began his discourse, looking directly at Tommy, who sat timidly, waiting for his bawling out.

"From now on, you will let your mother or me know where you are going, young man." He looked directly into his eyes.

"Do you understand?" Johnny stressed. There was no need to punish his young son this first time, he thought. Tommy stared at his father then spoke.

"We learned in church that Jesus disappeared without telling his parents where he was going once." His blue eyes wide, trying very hard to make the best of a bad situation. His parents fought back a giggle, but Johnny did not relent to his son's charm, and said nicely. "Jesus was the son of God, Tommy. His meeting the doctors in the temple was all part of a divine plan that God had to help the world welcome people back who had done wrong deeds in their life. Although in a way, you're right, Mary and Joseph were also very upset at his disappearance, until later when he said, don't you know that I must be about my Father's business. Then they understood that he had many deeds that he would perform in God's name."

Tommy seemed to be satisfied with his father's explanation. Ben now spoke up.

"Dad, did Jesus have a bicycle? His father was a carpenter - did he make him a wagon to play with in the old days?"

"Probably, why do you ask that, son?"

"Because that's what I want, a bike," Ben said, looking his dad square in the eye.

"You know it's against my principles to have something like a bike around where you can fall and hurt yourself," Johnny said.

"Does it mean you don't trust us?" Ben said. Johnny knew he could never win an argument with his son Ben, who was always one up on him.

Fraught with severe cramps in the middle of that night, Dell was convinced that the baby was on its way, since she felt her water trickling beneath her. In her misery, she realized who was missing in her hour of need. Lizzie's ubiquitous presence would be a terrible loss for her right now, since she was vigilant until the babies were born, and did everything but deliver the baby. She not only made her feel stronger, just by being there. She would also delegate work to all those present, sometimes even the doctor. When the hard birth of Benedict took place, it was she who had helped him into the world, when one of his tiny shoulders had appeared; Lizzie then gently nudged the rest of his body out of the opening. Oh, how Dell wished she were here at this time, and she began to pray to her mother-in-law to guide her during this terrible ordeal.

Dell thought about Mary's letter that she had received today, about her marriage to a local Cleveland boy. They had gone to the Justice of the Peace in nearby Solon, Ohio. Pop and mom were happy because he was Hungarian, which made him a fellow countryman. She was glad for Mary, but the oncoming baby interrupted her, with another excruciating pain. This time she felt it even deeper. Dell clutched the folds of her flannel nightgown; hearing the threads give way, ripping a hole in the seam. Now Johnny was lying there on his side looking at her with deep concern, intrinsically ready for this moment.

"It's going to be okay, Dell," He said, patting the side of her head. It hurt him to see his wife already weakened with labor pains. She felt sorry for him, but she was involved in a process that only women who had gone through it could understand. Dell knew that all deliveries were risky and had seriously thought about going to nearby Columbia Hospital in Wilkinsburg to have this baby. But she simply could not imagine exposing herself to a medical team in a cold, strange operating room. Her friends had warned her about some of the infections, which could take place during home birthings like puerperal fever, an infection of the placenta site. A friend of hers from Westinghouse had contracted this disease, which went right into her blood stream, and killed her.

"I'll call Dr. Newhouse, I'm sure he's expecting our call." And even though he'd witnessed three other births at the hotel, he asked himself in this tense moment. *Now what did my mother do at the very beginning of the boys' births?*" He closed the bedroom door to keep the room warm. Then pulling the blinds down, and stacking towels around the bed, he prepared for the period ahead. He hoped with all his heart that Dell would not be in labor too long.

The pains became sharper and faster, and Dell held her body tautly, hoping that each one would be the last, but her common sense told her it was a few hours too early. She must have slept for a moment, but was awoken by the children in the kitchen as they ate breakfast. She could hear their spoons hitting their bowls as they ate. The steam of water cooking added to the beads of perspiration already building up on her forehead. Johnny must have made them Mother's Oats for them to eat so heartily. They loved it with brown sugar on top.

"But where is mom?" Tommy, the most curious, said. She could just picture his inquisitive face leering up at his dad, insisting upon an answer.

"Mommy is not feeling good today, Tommy." Now that the boys were getting bigger and more inquisitive, Johnny did not want the children to see the harshness of labor and trials of bringing forth a baby. But he could not stop the curiousness of his oldest son, as he peeked through a crack in the door. Dell could hear him breathing quietly there. She could see his little dark head level with the bed, probably worried for her safety.

"Hi, Mom, is our new baby coming?" he whispered sweetly.

"Yes, honey, she muttered above the quilt, between spasms, trying to smile at her little boy. He did not smile back at her, but had a look of deep concern. This made her feel horrible with guilt. She could not reason why.

"Take care of your brothers, it will all be over soon." Then there was a knock on the door that told her the doctor was there. Barging into her bedroom, he immediately measured the opening of the cervix.

"It looks like you're about 8 centimeters dilated, Mrs. Albred. It won't be long now" She wondered at his projection. Dr. Newhouse had never been a man of many words, and certainly not a gentle, compassionate person, but he was a notable doctor in town, and had many years of experience behind him. Again she wished that Lizzie was here to look over his shoulder, which used to aggravate him, but at least Dell could watch her face for any imminent danger during the delivery.

The next contraction was the most powerful that she had felt thus far - now she screamed and Johnny was there in a flash to witness her look of agony. She was glad that he had taken the boys over to the Faradays as they had planned.

"Dr. Newhouse had now donned his long sterile white robe, cap and rubber gloves, so that she felt that the final stage was here.

"Now push a little more, my dear." He grumbled through his facemask. Why was he calling her dear? She mused, in her misery, he's the same age as me.

"Your baby is almost here," he continued.

"And it's a girl," He said, cleaning and wiping the blood from the baby. Dell looked at Johnny for affirmation, but he was not smiling back at her. His look was one of deep concern and consternation. Holding the new infant in the crook of his arm, he was stunned by something overwhelmingly unexpected that he could not control.

"Johnny, is she okay?" Dell insisted, a fresh fear grabbing hold of her senses.

A mixture of joy and deep hurt seemed to overtake him while holding his new daughter, as he looked over dumbfounded as the doctor clamped and cut the umbilical chord, then delivered the placenta.

Johnny then wrapped the baby in a clean towel, and placed her in Dell's arms as he had done three times before with their sons. But the feeling was completely different today, as they contemplated their new baby's appearance with tears rolling down their eyes. Little Theresa appeared to have two vertical splits on each side of her upper lip. Dr. Newhouse then approached the side of the bed. Still very clinical and without emotion, he explained her medical condition.

"Your baby has a double hair lip, this is why her nose has spread into a flatted position. She may also have a gap inside her mouth called a cleft palate, which usually accompanies the birth defect." He stated technically, not skipping a beat, and throwing off his hospital clothes into a pile next to the bloody instruments on the floor beside his black leather bag.

"The problem at this stage is that you'll have to work on a way to feed her because she'll have trouble sucking, unlike your other babies. Try to make the nipple hole bigger – see if that works." And though Johnny and Dell stared concentratedly at him for help, advice and anything else he could add to alleviate their predicament, he had one foot already over the threshold of the door, yelling one more thing in transit.

"Oh, yes, you must take her to Children's Hospital as soon as you are able. She will have many operations throughout her life as she grows, to correct this deformity." His harsh diagnosis met their ears as incongruous to the delicacy of caring for another of their loving children. And as soon as the doctor had slammed the backdoor behind him, they held each other with baby Theresa between them, sobbing openly.

"Oh, John, we have our baby girl and she needs us to help make her right," Dell whispered in disbelief, exhausted with the ordeal of the morning. Little Theresa did not make a sound, but seemed to innately know of the tough road ahead of her.

"Operations on a tiny infant?" Johnny said disappointedly. He had no words to console Dell, but ultimately they vowed together to do the one thing that they were capable of outside of medical science, and that was to love her and endow her with a strong spirit, against her adversities in society. As with anything else unusual, people would tend to stare

Dell and Johnny would question themselves the rest of their lives about what could have gone wrong during the conception and pregnancy for their daughter to be born this way.

4. A Formidable Family

Lying back against the satin chaise cushion, she luxuriated in the plush fabric, breathing in deeply the pungent scent of lavender emanating from a glass jar on the table next to her. Now raising milk white arms, Agatha opened her silky hands with pink painted fingertips, and gracefully spread out her soft printed pongee negligee, resembling a glorious butterfly about to soar gently up into the room alighting on all of her subjects. A magazine featuring her favorite movie and society stars slid from her lap as she became transfixed into their enchanted world.

Fantasizing her role through Cafe Society, a new fashionable elite group that frolicked frequently in and out of all of the posh supper clubs of New York, Agatha would hob-nob with the likes of Brenda Frazier, trendsetter and heir of millions. Culminating a close friendship of "years together", the twosome would then taxi over to the luxurious suite of Barbara Hutton, queen of the Woolworth five and dime fortune worth forty-five million.

A gathering in the Waldorf Astoria, where the brightest and first class societal echelon would come together. Hors d'oeuvres and canapés of every variety would be crowned with Russian caviar and placed carefully around a vast circular table covered with a white linen tablecloth. The guests would dine on imported sweetmeats and cheeses from Europe, savoring their rarity.

In the center of the cheerful throng, Agatha imagined a magnificent pink fountain of Champagne cascading through lovely pink alabaster angelic fingers, drizzling on to all of those devil-may-care guests daring to delight in its milieu.

At that moment, another illusion caught her daydream, as a Latin rhythm pulsated in the background, floating over radio waves. Gently lifting herself into dainty pink satin slippers, each toe tipped with a furry pink pom pom, Agatha then popped a bon bon into her mouth, and in a timely fashion swung out the diaphanous material around her ample body. Moving into tempo with the syncopating beat of the music, she simulated Ginger Rogers in *Flying Down To Rio*, the movie she'd just viewed at the Rivoli Theatre, paralleling Fred Astaire's quick limber steps. Self-assured that she looked even lovelier than Ginger in her clinging white satin gown, Agatha glided around the room. Gazing rapturously at her image in a mirror across the room. She in fact could have been a star of this magnitude, she sighed in reverie, reflecting on long wavy auburn tresses hanging loosely down her back.

All at once, starlight blue eyes fell down over her mid-section; she caught a shocking side glimpse of her body. Agatha brought back to mind the physical condition that had taken over her beautiful body, as she began to seethe with loathing. Oh why had she ever let him touch her? Still feeling his lustful hands all over her naked flesh brought regurgitation and disgust. The memories of her wedding night revolted her into reality. No, she had not been the least bit prepared for the way his hot and sweaty body had rushed at her.

Was this what they called love? Two bodies clinging together, undulating relentlessly? She could not believe that women did these things with men. How could her mother and father and all the virtuous people she had known in her life partake of this horrible activity that men seemed to have a natural desire toward. Were they taught these urges at an early age? It seemed so unfair to girls and women that all the time they were growing up, boys and men were thinking of doing this terrible act, when they were innocently thinking of just being kissed sweetly. It was hard to believe that God wanted babies to start this way.

Agatha had adored the romance in the beginning - the gentle kissing and hugging, not knowing that it would turn into this miserable wrestling match. Well, she now had her own bedroom, and would stay there forever, shut away from the possibility of another brutal physical attack.

Men are filthy, she found herself saying out loud. Her beautiful body was now tainted, used, in disrepair. *My mother always told me not to let men touch me, and furthermore It's a mortal sin. And now because of my offense, my belly is growing bigger every day. How ugly.* Agatha squeezed up her lovely face. Ugh, and to think that now a baby was growing inside of her - it made her more nauseous than usual. Whatever would she do with a baby? Dress him up like Jackie Cooper, who played in the *Our Gang* movies, with a big red bow under his blouse collar? She had always thought Cooper was ridiculous in this role. Maybe she'd have a girl - that might be a little easier, as she would train her to stay strictly from boys at an early age.

Agatha knew only one person that she could talk to about her little "indiscretion". She would have to share her secret situation with Dell, which also disturbed her, to find out what to do next in her predicament. Dell, the perfect little mother, who pranced around the burgh with her precious little boys following her around like a mother hen with three chicks. She knew she would never be that kind of woman, and especially that kind of mother. She would try to put it out of her mind, for now. Oh, if only she were single living in the hotel again.

For now she would force herself to block out this unpleasant reality invading her life, this was a tactic that she was especially good at. Of course it was true that she didn't have an extensive evening wardrobe or accessories. Desperately needing a new beaded cocktail bag, she could never be seen in her old red felt cloche hat, having been out of style for ages. Running both hands down along her now burgeoning frame, she tried to forget her condition for a moment.

She had to give it to Mae West, who made hourglass figures popular again, a shape wanted by every skinny woman this side of the Allegheny River. It was reported that she made $480,833 a year. With this much money, Miss West was always boss in her movies, especially in *She Done Him Wrong*. Mae cut a dashing figure in her floor length black crepe gown, cerise scarf and sable wrap glittering diamonds from heads to toe. And though she didn't entirely approve of the way she lured men to her side, Agatha loved her high style.

There was a time when she used to spend lots of money on clothes. She used to shop from morning until night in Braddock, where most of the finer stores were located. Her mother would give her two hundred dollars to outfit herself from head to toe. She knew her mother expected some money back, since Lizzie never spent a penny on herself, not even knowing the price of a pair of shoes.

She could still hear her yelling when she came home from a shopping expedition, wisps of white hair flying out of her babushka as she pointed her finger endlessly, reprimanding her daughter for being so extravagant. Lizzie's bright hazel eyes reddened with rage, probably taking her hard day of work out on her, Agatha thought, always fearful that the patrons in the restaurant would hear her.

"Agatha, what do you think, that money grows on trees? We work hard here, and you fritter it away in three hours. What will happen to you? I'm so disappointed in you."

"Mother," she would plead.

"This is one of the only pleasures I have. You won't let me work in the office or do any of the important jobs around here. It's always peel the potatoes, polish your precious silver. Johnny and Phil get to do all of the good things here. They meet all the interesting people out front and count the money and order supplies" She was on the verge of tears, and knew she had softened her mother's tone.

"Nonsense, we all work hard," Lizzie would retort harshly. But then she would turn around and hug her only daughter, conscience stricken that she never spent enough time with her, due to being absorbed in managing the hotel. Then her mother would whisper again the promised message.

"You're a beautiful woman, you'll marry a handsome man some day, we'll have a big wedding like we had for Johnny and Dell. Agatha, you'll carry white roses. What a lovely bride you'll make." But then she would be quickly summoned away by one of the parlor maids or the chef, leaving Agatha standing there in the empty space of the hotel entrance hall.

Now, a year later, she began to sob uncontrollably, reaching for a white crocheted edged handkerchief in her pocket. If only her mother could have seen the horrible chapel that she was married in, she would have rolled over in her grave. Nothing about her "Special Day" even compared to the high mass at church and hotel reception that Johnny and Dell had. Maybe if that awful accident hadn't happened, they could at least have had a dinner in the hotel. She knew Johnny would do that for her and Joe.

All she had was that meager fire insurance money to buy a plain old long, white dress with a short veil. That was all she could afford. She had heard somewhere that long ago in Roman times, a bride wore a full-length veil so that she could be buried in it someday. Now she wouldn't even have that necessity around to wear for own her funeral some day.

"Oh!" Her tears turned to anger once again.

"No wonder I'm so miserably married." Johnny had been given everything, and Phil took everything he could. She was the orphan. Her mother who was able to make everything happen, knowing no boundaries, was no longer around to help her only daughter.

At least Joe had some money, but not enough to live comfortably. At least not according to her standards. She looked around at the bare surroundings. She had never lived in anything as dismal as this flat they rented in Turtle Creek, the town next to Eastburg.

The floors were dark bare wood without carpeting of any kind. A small table and two oak chairs were all the furniture that existed in the small dining room, kitchen combination, where the small window looked out onto another gated division of the huge Westinghouse Plant. Agatha's godmother had given them an oak bedroom set that had been hers when she first came from Czechoslovakia. This suite was in good condition and contained a beautiful dressing table with a blue tapestry stool where Agatha sat frequently brushing her lovely hair with the oyster white onyx brush and comb that had also been a wedding gift.

Perhaps her most proud possession was the beautiful chaise lounge that Joe had given her for a wedding gift. This was her island of refuge. Suddenly, her heart skipped a beat. Hearing a step on the threshold, she turned with a start. This would be the end of her solitude this evening. He would torment her about things she didn't want to talk about - like cleaning and especially cooking.

"Aggie, where are you?" Said her husband of six months.

"How about supper?" he said wearily, exhausted from his hard work day at the Westinghouse. *Listen to him raving about his infernal stomach,* she thought, angrily. That redheaded Austrian she had married sure made demands on her.

"Gimme a kiss, Princess." He walked over boldly to her corner of the room, planting a kiss on her cheek, which she reluctantly held out for him. Then he did the unthinkable, and positioned himself next to her, daring to sit down on the corner of her beautiful chaise with his dirty workclothes. The only haven left for her around this crummy place. *Why did he have to invade this one perfect spot,* she thought bitterly. Joe smiled at her, with two big dimples sunk deeply into his cheeks. He isn't that bad looking, she mused. Then as she half-smiled back, he took liberty to come closer and practically sit on her. Then speaking softly, he inquired once again for the twentieth time since they had been living together.

"Aggie, didn't your mother teach you anything about cooking? You must have learned something, because Lizzie was the best cook in Eastburg. I used to salivate all day at work, thinking about all the wonderful pork and sauerkraut she would have on the Saturday night menu."

"Oh, here you go again – asking that one," she retorted angrily, her forehead knotted up in an aggravated frown. Finally she put both fingers in her ears so that his message would not get through.

"For the last time, Joe, did you marry me to be your cook and maid? Because if you did, you got the wrong tomato. I didn't cook at the hotel 'cause everybody else did. My mother and Dell always had a big pot of stew or stuffed cabbage or something else on the stove to eat. Maybe you wanted to marry my mother instead. Did you? Huh? Well, its too late she's six feet under." At this she sniffled, dabbing at her eyes with her lace handkerchief, knowing he would feel sorry for her, which he did.

"Ahh sugar, my little Aggie." He put his strong working man's arm around her, which she pretended was Clark Gable's.

"I'll round us up a little grub," he placated.

"You make me so happy, Joe," she lied. And for the time being he seemed content. Agatha tried to pretend that he was Clark Gable, since he had played a rancher in his last movie, *The Painted Desert.* She could feel the bulge of his muscle next to her shoulder. But then he spoke out, immediately destroying the image she had cast.

"Don't worry about it now, my little chickadee," Oh, no, Agatha's dream was shattered, he was really W.C.Fields and she was Mae West being lured into a phony romance once again.

Agatha had no idea what kind of work Joe did every day at the plant, or if he worked himself to the bone doing it. There was a part of her that envied his right to go out and do something important every day, whatever it was. Men were allowed to do anything they wanted to do, professionally or otherwise. They owned the world, while women were their slaves. There was no place for women in the men's business world.

Her mind rambled on to the few women she knew had come into the hotel while she was growing up there. They were educated and worked in the Westinghouse library. She remembered that Ruthie Higginbotham and Evelyn Corchak were their names. Ruthie had gone to school at the Pitt University's Cathedral of Learning in Oakland. She wondered what had ever become of her desire to succeed and what she had achieved in her career. Agatha would hear her argue intelligently with the silly comments the men would make at the hotel bar.

"A woman in the president's cabinet? You're talking foolishness girl. It's bad enough you women got the vote." Big Bill Johnston would laugh out loud at the thought of it all.

"We are first class citizens too, mister, all we need is to get voted into the state legislature and we're home free from that post," Wiley little Ruthie would proclaim.

Agatha knew that Ruthie was smart from the big words she used. From her viewpoint men and women were on extreme unequal grounds as far as our social system went. She was living proof of how little ground women had traveled since they got the vote in 1920, Amendment 19 to the Constitution. Ruthie had gumption. That was the quality that Lizzie had and could never teach her daughter in a lifetime. In fact it wasn't anything that you were taught, you were just born with it.

Her mother had come to this country from Europe not knowing a single soul and without a penny in her pocket, but she knew what she could do well, and that was work hard as a good cook and hotel owner. No one would speak disrespectfully to her. No one. Agatha once witnessed a customer telling Lizzie to mind her own business, and quick as a wink she turned around and grabbed him by the scruff of his neck, shuffling him out the front door and turning him into a tiny mouse right before all of their eyes. He never spoke up to her again, though he did come back. He knew his place after that. She could never underestimate the power that her mother exhibited. She was not a big woman, and yet she had a force that could not be reckoned with. She proved that strength came from deep within.

Agatha knew she would never tell Joe about the baby coming for a long time; she would keep her body covered with big full clothes around him. Even though it would make him so happy, now why would she want to do that? For her to admit this to him would be to turn over any freedom she had as a woman. She was trapped forever and there was no going back to her carefree days. If only she could think of a way not to have the baby, but it would be going against all of the commandments of the church. And what would her mother have said. They all said abortion was a sin, she didn't have a choice.

Later that evening after dining on eggs and toast once again, they were washing the dishes together, a chore that Agatha didn't mind doing if Joe dispensed with the garbage first. He was wiping while she carefully submerged her rubber-gloved hands into the murky water. Picking up a new wedding gift cup to dry, Joe spoke up with some news.

"Guess who I saw today when we were out in the shop yard eating our lunch?" he said nonchalantly.

"Now how would I know? President Roosevelt was coming through," she replied haughtily, looking down worriedly at her delicate hands getting chafed even with the gloves on in the hot dirty dishwater.

"Your brother Johnny, that's who. Boy, that guy works hard."

"He has to work hard, he's got a brood to feed, mister. Dell just had another one, and I think she's a girl, I've been trying to avoid my perfect sister-in-law." Agatha said, feeling a tinge of guilt that she hadn't been up to see the new baby.

"Well, that's just it Aggie, Johnny wants us to come up for supper on Sunday and see the new little kid. That might be fun, huh?" He talked fast and excitedly now, not knowing whether

Agatha wanted to see them or not, and also never knowing which mood she might be in at the moment. She could be unpredictable about most things, especially concerning her family. And Joe definitely knew she could take or leave Dell, who he thought was a special upright person. Johnny was okay most of the time to him, but he always disapproved of everything his sister Agatha did. But then they had a strange upbringing around that hotel - so did everyone who lived there.

"Oh yeah wise guy, I know, I know, you just want to get a good home cooked meal in your belly, and you know Dell will probably cook something good."

"No, no, that's not true at all." He strongly disagreed, but thought more positively about it as the night wore on as they sat in the living room reading. Agatha had her pile of *Vanity Fair, Bazaar*, and *Photoplay* to leaf through, since she was not adept at book reading. However, spending the evening doing this would once again aggravate Agatha, who glanced over at Joe, who was intensely interested in a thick novel by the famous contemporary writer Studs Lonigan. He praised his written portrayal of real life scenes about struggling farmers in the Midwest during the Depression. This made him think that the manufacturing people in Pittsburgh were better off in many ways, particularly that most of the big companies would keep a skeleton crew on, not letting the employees go hungry through the bad times.

Agatha sulked at his profound knowledge of books, and to think she could barely read and write, having quit school in third grade after a bad bout with scarlet fever. In fact she wouldn't be a bit surprised if Joe wasn't deliberately spiting her by flaunting his reading ability. He also bragged about finishing *Tobacco Road* in just a week. He'd told her about that one with the southern sharecroppers and their struggles. Why on earth would he want to get these books about the depressing times they were living in and were struggling to forget?

The next Sunday, Agatha and Joe got into their brand new Pontiac Chief, which he had bought from a hard-pressed friend, who had to sell it to pay for his wife's hospital operation, at a bargain price of five hundred dollars. Agatha had donned a brand new red straw picture hat with elbow length gloves that she had to buy at the five and ten, to wear for the Easter Parade and church on Sunday. It was a pity she did not have a nice new suit to wear, but her old navy sharkskin would have to do for this spring.

As they pulled in beside the street level basement of the two family home, which stood high on a slope, Tommy and Ben rushed out at them from the sidewalk where they had been waiting for their aunt and uncle to arrive. Agatha cautiously stepped out over the running board and onto the street. They waved and greeted them simultaneously in their tiny voices.

"Hello, Aunt Agatha and Uncle Joe. Will you take us for a ride?"

"Oh, hi boys," Agatha whispered, uncaringly brushing some lint from her outfit.

"Now step back, you'll get Aunt Agatha dirty," she said, without as much as a hug or kiss or any other kind greeting. In the meantime, Joe had wasted no time scrambling over to her side of the car, not to assist her with getting out but to hoist Ben high onto his shoulders, and with Tommy holding happily onto Uncle Joe's pant leg, walked off leaving her in their dust.

"Hmm, isn't he a good uncle". She contemplated snidely. "So he loves little boys, well, maybe we'll have a little something to keep him occupied in the future, that way he won't have these little urchins crawling all over him," she sneered.

Dell came to the door with her usual carefree smile. Notwithstanding, that Agatha saw that underneath it all she wore the victimized housewife look, and had fallen into the abominable pit of relentless motherhood. A flowered apron revealing splotches of cooking stains, probably samples of the food they would be having for supper. This covered an old dotted Swiss dress that Dell used to wear on special occasions at the hotel. And as Agatha recalled, it was unattractive then when it was new, now it was downright ugly. Agatha looked away disgustedly. What her handsome brother had ever seen in this matchstick was beyond her. Dell greeted her sister-in-law kindly.

But more momentous, the heady aroma coming from the kitchen nearly overwhelmed her sense of propriety, as she thought that nothing about Dell's appearance could detract from her wonderful ability to cook like her dear mother. And if she had to admit it, Dell was the daughter-in-law who took after her own mother, Lizzie.

"Hello, Agatha, I'm so glad you two could come." We're having your favorite breaded pork chops and stewed cabbage with homemade bread and rolls." Agatha did not want to show her excitement at finally eating something worthwhile, which would be admitting she was a lousy cook. Dell picked little Joel up, who was tugging at her apron, giving him a big affectionate kiss and hug.

"Ugh," Agatha murmured under her breath, glancing disdainfully toward the dirty little boy so attached to his mother. Then she remembered the new baby girl.

"Hey, Dell, where's little Theresa, we really came to see her." Agatha said slyly. Dell hesitated slightly, wondering how Agatha would react to their new baby's birth defect. She had recently been hurt at some of the comments said at the store, and from some of the neighbors who were ignorant about the physical nature of Terry's deformity.

The baby had been very healthy in every other way, having almost doubled her birth weight. Dell had especially concentrated on keeping Terry healthy, since she would face her first big operation to close the gap in the lip. The doctor had said that this surgery would improve her ability to feed easier, however she had to weigh ten pounds before they would schedule surgery. The cleft palate procedure could be done at two years old, with more operations to come with facial growth at five or six years old.

Dell had prayed fervently to St. Theresa The Little Flower for the health and well being of their baby daughter. This beautiful saint had been canonized in 1925. A Carmelite nun, she had suffered with tuberculosis during her lifetime. She was known for piety, simplicity, and patience, just a few of the virtues she extolled during her sickness. All throughout her life, she was credited with many miracles. And since May was the month of the Blessed Mother, Queen of the May, in their bedroom corner stood a tiny altar surrounded with the fresh flowers of the season. Here they would say the rosary every evening with the boys present. The sweet fragrance of lilacs, lilies of the valley, and violets poured forth as they prayed. She and Johnny knew that their faith would help them through this ordeal.

Dell began to feel squeamish, trying not to expose her daughter to her critical sister-in-law who was one of the most pompous, ignorant persons she knew. She'd seen her embarrass almost anyone on the spot with her wicked tongue, including herself on many occasions. *Oh, where was Johnny when she needed him the most? He would know how to handle his sister when she starting slinging arrows around.*

Dell knew that the men and boys had gone to sit in the living room, probably talking about the new car that Joe had bought, or maybe her husband was discussing the hearsay that Phil was now in trouble with the federal government for running away from his job in Oregon. It wasn't as though she personally was frightened of his sister, but now it was not just herself at the hotel anymore, it was their precious newborn daughter who was susceptible.

"Shhh, she's sleeping now, let's wait a little while to go into the bedroom, " Dell heard herself replying to the tense situation. She had tried diligently to protect Terry from all offensiveness of strangers, or where anyone would harm her, and she certainly felt that her Aunt Agatha could possibly be one of those threats. Nonetheless, Johnny had recently spoken out about her keen protectiveness toward all of the children. Consequently, she worried about her apprehension.

"Dell, we can't hide our family because the world dictates that everyone has to look a certain way. Eventually she'll have those skin grafts and with plastic surgery and with a little more time, she'll be a nice looking girl. Now, though, we have to act as if nothing is wrong. She has to run and play with her brothers and the rest of her friends. You and I are going to work hard to help her be a strong person inside, and to grow up be a good human being. And we'll set the example for the boys to do the same. We're a family, dammit, and we'll face all of our problems squarely together." Dell tried fervently to follow his advice, taking Terry out for her afternoon walks braving some of the disapproving comments of the local people.

The next day another incident happened with Tommy involved. Dell saw him come in the door from school out of the corner of her eye, as she was feeding Joel some baby food after his afternoon nap.

"Oh, what happened to your eye, honey?" she questioned her son, moving toward the refrigerator for ice and pulling the kitchen drawer out for a tea towel, with her heart beating rapidly with dread for reprisals not met with the other boy involved. Placing the cold application on his eye and giving him a kiss and a compassionate hug, she placed his usual after school snack of milk and cookies in front of him at the table. Knowing inside that her oldest son seemed to be the least tolerant of all the boys gave her an insight into his lunging out at another, but John had tried to raise them in a reasonable way, solving problems with words instead of fists.

"Harry Rippen called my new sister a pug nose," he answered resentfully, his black hair hanging down in his face like a regular ruffian, maybe a kid out of the *Our Gang* comics in the movies, with his shirt collar hanging almost torn off and his knee socks pushed way down below his knickers somewhere around his ankles.

"I told him to quit pickin' on her, but he kept going. He said she looked like she ran into a Mack Truck. Then Billy and 'Fish` laughed at her, sayin' yeah, yeah. And I let him have it right between the eyes, just like John L. Sullivan, that fighter daddy talks about." Dell shuttered, listening to his story, and though she didn't agree with the action he took, she knew her son had acted on the circumstance.

Essentially, Tommy was an affectionate boy, who loved and paid daily attention to his new sister, kissing her good-bye every morning before he went to school, while Ben kept his outward feelings to himself, watching his older brother. Dell knew what was coming next, as she sat there almost teary eyed feeling proud of his devotion to his family.

"Don't tell Daddy, Mommy, okay?" he said worriedly, fearing the wrath of his father.

"Now, you know he'll see you with your shiner. How can he miss that?" she mused, still angry that Johnny had shown such open admiration for fighters beating each other up in the ring. Her husband amazed her further by later condoning the way Tommy had handled the problem.

"Dell, I've got a secret to tell you." Agatha used her phony singsong voice to bring her sister-in-law back into the present once again, forcing Dell to smile. Apparently Agatha was back by her side after going to the bathroom where she had removed her hat and gloves for supper. It was uncharacteristic for her to talk so kindly and sweet; consequently Dell was suspicious of her actions once again, especially since she found out that Agatha hadn't even told her own husband that she was in a family way.

All during the sumptuous supper feast that Dell had prepared the conversation centered on where they had spent last spring. The hotel had still been in existence, even though Lizzie and Zach had passed away the previous year. The immortalizing of her mother seemed to goad Agatha into an angry, jealous mood, as she lashed out at them. She had many grievances.

"Well, my mother ruined my life, I could have been an actress," she exclaimed hurtfully, as everyone stared at her sad expression. Dell felt sorry for this poor misguided woman, who was pampered and given everything from birth and yet was given none of the true essential love and guidance to live her life happily. All in all, maybe she is right, she thought, knowing that Lizzie's tough European ways did not cover raising a child the proper way.

Joe stared at the children eating, sometime with both hands, as they loaded their spoon with mashed potatoes and cooked cabbage. The innocence of their gestures filled him with a kind of purity, and he felt uncomfortable at his wife's straightforwardness, wishing that she would show more gratefulness and kindness to Johnny and especially Dell. How dare she bring personal problems to the table here? He loved her, but she was a selfish woman. He tried hard to intercede with a change of subject.

"I hear they opened what is called a drive-in movie theatre in Camden, New Jersey. Now what do you think of that, Tommy?" His nephew smiled, enjoying the attention, getting ready to answer his uncle. But Johnny broke in, inflamed by his sister's remark against their deceased mother. His brown eyes burned with condemnation, as he came to his deceased mother's defense. Agatha straightened up in her chair, ready to challenge her brother's every word, but inside she wondered why he was so defiant and couldn't just merely talk about it with them.

"Ahhh, you were the girl who had everything money could buy. Mother handed out cash to you like peanuts to a monkey, and now you're saying you wanted to be a movie star. Well, you can't purchase that in a fancy department store, it has to be studied and planned for, and a goal has to be set. The path needs strict discipline and patience. This is something you were never taught in your life, which is too bad, since Mother had all the qualifications and background, working like a dog day and night pursuing her dream. You were there, didn't you witness the hard work she put into that damned hotel business?" The room grew still, as heads looked down, with just the sound of forks and spoons hitting their plates filling the room. A momentary whimper from Joel in his highchair almost broke the silence.

Orchestrating her domain of pots on the stove, filling serving dishes with more stuffed cabbage and potatoes, Dell looked up sporadically with rapture at her husband. It seemed he had become the head of the family overnight, and she thought the best one he could educate would be his sister. Though she still felt just a little sorry for her, sitting there as a pathetic little painted bird ready to have her picture taken.

"Besides", Johnny continued with his dissertation." you barely finished the third grade, so how in Heaven's name can you be an actress. This is no longer the time of silent film. You would have been good in those, all you'd have to do is stand around and pose, like Norma Shearer. These women today have to learn their lines, this means that you would have to be a very good reader, pick those movie script lines up fast. You know what I mean." He sat back in his chair with a glib feeling, as though he'd made his point with his sister.

"You think you know everything, College Boy." Johnny winced at the old nickname both she and Phil had given him. Now Agatha was poised for battle, sitting erectly in her chair. Strands of long, hair lay strewn around her face from when she had removed her large hat just before dinner. Dell and Joe watched her theatrical acumen, both thinking that her dream of being on the silver screen may have been a reality if she had been led down the right road to success. She continued vehemently, telling her side of the story.

"As it turns out, Mother catered to you boys much more than me - she actually 'paid' me to stay out of the way, that way she wouldn't have to spend what little time she had on me. It was rumored around the hotel that "she worked like a man", well naturally, that was where her heart was and after all, you men carry all the command, right? You have the final word on everything. If I had been born a boy, I would never have been ignored." Johnny listened carefully trying to interpret what she thought was a sorrowful life, which he'd always thought was easy. He remembered watching her wear all of the beautiful clothes she bought, never knowing that inside she needed something far more important.

He began remotely to see a mother-daughter connection between them. Having studied principles of behaviorism in college, he recognized the symptom of what was called "matrophobia", the fear of becoming one's mother. He could see how the hard-working Lizzie's appearance and the way she conducted business could repel the self-projected Agatha. He remembered the textbook example of how women struggle with the feelings of identification with mother and husband as well, having their divided feelings about each individually. Agatha would always have to rely on her hallow appeal of looks and cunning to get ahead in life.

She and Joe ended up leaving almost abruptly, but not until they had finished the apple pie 'a la mode. And just so they had a supply of the delicious homemade food, Agatha prompted Dell to fill a pie dish full of left over food and put it into a paper bag to bring home.

As they were going down the walk, Ben curiously questioned his uncle.

"Uncle Joe, who goes to the new drive-in movie?" Joe smiled at the inquisitive boy.

"I don't know, someone came up with the idea, son. It probably won't get off the ground. There's this big gigantic screen in the middle of a huge parking lot, and everyone puts a radio in their car for the sound."

"I think it's a good idea," Ben answered thoughtfully.

"I want to go there, to New Jersey," said Tommy, echoing his brother's excitement. Their uncle laughed uproariously, nudging his wife to join him in listening to the kids. But she walked along, still reeling sullen-faced from the altercation with her brother. She didn't even get to see the new baby.

"New Jersey is a long way from here, Tom, but someday you can go to all of those places in your automobile or on the train." The two boys gazed at him wide-eyed as he spoke, contemplating all of the things that might be out there to see. As they watched their guests disappear down the streetcar line, Johnny threw a football up in the air.

"Hey, guys, lets go out and play some ball," he suggested.

"Yeah!" They both yelled together. Johnny laughed as they all ran up to the vacant lot behind the house. I've got a couple of good little quarter backs here he thought as he stretched his right arm high to throw a pass out.

"Okay, Tommy, run out far for a pass, Ben you try to intercept," he yelled.

Dell's right he thought, his sister was incorrigible. His mother was mostly responsible, but she was a product of the hedonistic society growing up. Their family would be different, he vowed. There was unity and strength of character in a strong family, and he and Dell would strive for it, with the help of God.

5. Daunted Courage

"What de hey? It ain't like da farmers wern't ready fer a good deal when we sold dem da fencin' an all dat wood an nails an stuff wholesale out dare in Oregon. Me and Butch Corrigan are businessmen, not boy scouts like de Feds want. Naturly I liked wearin' dose khaki duds from de Gov, but a guys gotta make a livin'. Aw who knows who's watchin' ya out dere." Phil stood there scratching his dark straight shiney hair trying to explain the latest predicament he had gotten involved with and probably the most serious to date.

With a bewildered look on his face, as if he was the innocent party just standing by, his brother sat at the kitchen table sipping strong black coffee that had been made earlier this morning. Johnny watched with utter disbelief that Phil could be so amoral and practically a common criminal stealing and selling government goods, while he was supposed to be helping to build roads, walls and bridges with the Civil Conservation Corp. And what on earth had happened to the resolve to help his country, albeit a weak one, to join in the first place.

"When the hell are you ever going to grow up?" Johnny spoke angrily. His only retaliation against his brother's disdainful actions was to become his parent and reprimand him squarely.

"You are lucky they didn't throw the book at you, especially with your checkered past. Who was the judge anyway?" he interrogated, hoping that none of the children were within earshot of their conversation. Then hearing them playing upstairs, he felt relieved.

It had been a quiet Saturday afternoon when he turned on the Notre Dame vs. Army game, while engaged in reading an article in the *Sun Telegraph* about the new leader Adolph Hitler, who had gained control in Germany. All of the newspapers were full of the formation of the Nazi party, and Johnny was curious about how this Austrian had taken over the people in that strong country - or so it seemed after the First World War. This new organization was gaining control of their national courts, industries, newspapers and schools - what would such dominance mean for the future of the rest of world?

Dell had gone out shopping with the baby to look for a new highchair, since the old one had gone through three boys, when someone started rapping loudly, practically breaking down the back door. Johnny greeted his brother with mixed emotions. He hugged him indifferently, surprised that his brother was in town again after a letter he had received about a month ago from a magistrate. He secretly wished that Phil had been thrown in the brig doing about ten years, after his latest escapade.

Phil never ceased to amaze Johnny as he created yet another story of his fraudulent innocence. This guy could fall in a pasture of cow crap and come out smelling like roses, Johnny thought disgustedly. He was dressed in his usual neatly pressed dark pin stripped suit, white shirt and tie, but when he spoke - he exudes the lowest form of life, Johnny thought. And always in the back of his mind was that Phil had had some involvement in the hotel fire. Though investigators never turned up with a clue as to the actual cause, someday, somewhere, the answer to this crime would emerge, and the guilty person would be brought to justice.

He listened as Phil went on with his implausible testimony.

"Judge Flanigan is Butch's cousin once removed - he's from the Burg - used to dance the czardas at the Slovak Club. You remember him, Johnny, a red-faced chubby guy. He wore dem herringbone jackets and butcher caps to cover his skinhead. The chump went west to find his fortune." Phil tried jovially to reminisce about another moment in time, but Johnny knew his cunning ways, and would have none of it, knitting his bushy eyebrows together in a deep frown of consternation.

"So what happened at the hearing? Did you have counsel?" he asked.

"Naw, Flanigan trew de case out - not enough evidence he says." Johnny was astounded at this news; even the government wasn't safe from vandals like his no-good brother. No one could handle his kid brother, who had been a problem from the day he came out of his mother's womb. How can he ever get turned around now at this stage, he wondered. But as he

76

continued to listen to his brother's jabbering, he thought there might be a tiny glimmer of hope on the horizon.

"Den I met dis dame in Montana. She's a beaute Johnny, honest, an her ole man put de cash up fer de bail, can ya beat dat? Dere real down home folks; dey let us sleep out in de barn for a couple a days. I love 'er." Johnny didn't want to speculate what Phil's idea of what love meant, but he began to think that if Phil found someone he really cared for, that he might change his wicked ways. Could he actually believe that his brother would care for someone outside of himself? Johnny believed in prayer and love as a strong force between humans. After all wasn't that what religion was all about? Why they went to church every Sunday. And though his brother tested him time after time, Johnny thought that just maybe a miracle might occur in Phil's life. Consequently, he took the interrogation to another level.

"So what are you going to do about it?" Johnny queried.

"About what, da dame or da misdeed?" Phil answered.

"Both, you can't bring any innocent woman into a life of crime and transgressions. You have to get a job, mister, and walk the straight and narrow for a few years. Can you do that?" Johnny stared hard into his brother's eyes, which also meant that he would throw in the towel as well, if Phil didn't turn his life around, though he wasn't sure he understood, and whether he had a conscience or not in any of these exploits.

"Where's your woman friend now?" he said, wondering about the truth of his statement.

"She's out on da porch, D'ya wanta meet 'er?" Johnny couldn't believe the audacity of his brother, leaving the poor forlorn young woman out there on a cold winter day. It must have been twenty degrees out there. Especially if she wasn't even from around here, and wasn't prepared for the cold weather, although he guessed that it probably got cold up in the northwest, where he'd never visited. Oh, he didn't know what to believe anymore when it came to Phil.

In the meantime, his brother tenderly ushered a tall gangly young woman into the kitchen, standing with a colorful Indian blanket around her shoulders. Johnny wondered if she had a coat, and started to feel sorry for this woman emotionally mixed up with his wayward brother.

"Mugsy, this here's my brother Johnny," Phil said shyly, even a little humbly. A characteristic Johnny never recognized in his brother before. Good start, he thought.

"My given name is Margaret," she asserted, which Johnny was glad for, since her life would include God knew what if she paired up with the likes of this guy.

"Yeah, but I call 'er Mugsy, don't it fit? Look at that mug, aint it purdy?" His brother kidded her, so that she giggled in a romantic sort of way as their eyes locked in an embrace. That was when Johnny guessed that they must be lovers.

"Oh, Bredie," she responded back embarrassedly. Johnny winced at the pathetic nicknames they had for each other, but put his aversions away, hoping all the while for the new life they might make together. Who knows where this relationship might go -- maybe he could bring her out of the dregs of the Wild West, and she could help him be a decent person going through life.

Just then the door opened, and Dell entered with baby Terry in her arms. She greeted Phil with her usual apprehension and mistrust. The sight of him always put her in a state of anxiety. As usual he smelled like liquor. This would give him the courage to stop by to see his brother. But then, as usual, she tried hard to act like a good Catholic woman, and not judge him too harshly. Her brother-in-law had done so many horrible things to her family, like stealing money they had saved for six months, to go on a week's vacation to Conneault Lake. It was tough explaining this to the kids, who had their hearts set on going.

His girlfriend Margaret seemed nice and began to make conversation with her, while the two brothers continued their own brand of discussion. It seemed that Phil was trying his utmost to convince Johnny of his innocence.

"Oh, she looks like - who's that new kid star out there." She began to motion to little Terry, who began to smile and giggle at the new outsider.

"Aw, you know, we saw it together, Bredie".

"Shirley Temple. She was in *Stand Up and Cheer*. At the Rivoli,"   Dell put in.

"Hey, dat kid is makin' 300 big ones a year, dat ain't cow manure. Younse should teach 'er to sing and dance, den we'd all be rich as thieves." Her brother-in-law *had* to put in his two cents, Dell thought. Leave it to him to think of the money angle. *That'll be the day,* she thought, but went along with the subject at hand, ignoring his comment.

"Everyone says that about her, it's all of her ringlets and curls. They look like little corkscrews," Dell bragged about her baby's beautiful hair. She demonstrated by gently pulling a few tight curls out, which sprung tightly back into place into her dark shinny hair. Terry alighted in the attention of the two women. Dell was glad that Margaret had not mentioned her little girl's lip - which turned up into a puckered smile.

Now that Terry was starting to say some words, like Mama, Da Da, and her brother's names, Dell was taking her to speech therapy every weekend at Children's Hospital in Oakland. Terry loved going on the streetcar on the way to the hospital. At the end of the year, she would have plastic surgery again. There would be tiny skin grafts taken from her upper leg to replace more skin inside her cleft palate, so that she could talk normally. Terry would have a full firm roof built in her mouth, and an intact lip and upper gum against which her tongue could shape sounds, therefore the therapy would be timely with her operation. Eventually they might have a small denture made to help the rest of her teeth fit together and improve appearance further.

Their little girl amazed Johnny and Dell time and time again with the pleasing way she went in and out of the hospital for yet another surgery.

"It's as if she knows that she has to go through this to help herself, John, She's such a brave little girl." Dell said. Her eyes spilled over to have to leave her little girl in the hospital again. Johnny put his arm around his wife compassionately, on the verge of tears himself.

Every bit was going to hospitals and doctors these days, which would probably go on for the rest of their daughter's life. And though there was talk in the company of medical insurance becoming a necessity there, no one had adapted it as yet for company use. Johnny was thankful for all of the overtime pay he'd begun to make at the Westinghouse. They had just moved him over into the new radar division, installing radar sights into heavy machinery. They were only testing this equipment at this time.

Now at the end of the 1930's, he hoped that war was not imminent, however, this new radar would be most probably used for war. This was why he viewed the world situation with great suspicion.

Dell made another pot of fresh coffee, and everyone gathered in the kitchen, including the boys who had came down to be thrown up into the air by their Uncle Phil, who by their standards, was always fun to have around, and not the ogre that Tommy saw in his parents eyes any time his name was mentioned around there.

"Hey, who's dat big guy over der?" he'd razz Tommy. Then he'd do his prizefighter boxer dance, throwing jabs at Ben, who would run up to spar with his uncle pretending to stagger and fall over and be out for the punch. Tommy would count.

"One, two, three, he's out, and the new champion of the world is… Big Benny, the toughest guy in the burgh." Then Uncle Phil lifted his arm high in the air. The boys laughed heartily, including little Joel, who thought his uncle was a real rough and swell guy. Dell and Johnny also joined in, watching the boys cuttin' up with their dubious uncle. Dell was taken aback at Phil's romping around in his perfect attire, his white shirtsleeves rolled up just for the occasion. Now this was truly something different - there was a change in him, she thought.

Dell dished out some apple pie she made the day before and they all sat around the table enjoying her good "home cookin". At least that's what Phil called it, who vividly remembered Lizzie's own good and plentiful meals, as his eyes grew sad and reddened.

"You have a wonderful family, Johnny and Dell," Margaret said. She had finally unwrapped herself from the Indian blanket and was sitting straight as a rod in a shabby brown dress. Not at all the type that Phil had brought by the hotel in the past. He used to sail by the place in the Chrysler convertible with a girl named Maizie, who wore a tight cloche over her bleached blond curls, her face painted like Theda Barra or some film star. The two of them never stopped for more than ten minutes. Lizzie would be perturbed at Phil's slipshod gangster ways, even though he looked like a million bucks, always in a suit; they never saw him in work clothes of any kind. He and Maizie were Eastburg's Bonnie and Clyde, the couple who were shooting up banks in the Midwest.

Margaret looked like a maidservant sitting next to Phil, who was as impeccable as ever. Dell sometimes wondered how he kept his clothes so well pressed, and if he was still getting kickbacks from some of the local gangsters.

"Mugsy and me are gettin' hitched," he said, breaking the silence, while taking a heaping forkful of pie and giving it a push into his mouth with his manicured thumbnail. This prompted Dell to look down at her own war torn hands, which were anything but polished from working hard all day.

"Are you Catholic, Margaret?" Johnny inquired, trying to take their romantic plans to another level. Johnny had been brought up to believe that the sacrament of matrimony was essential for a couple to start off a life right together. Looking over at Dell for her reaction to his statement with mixed emotions, he felt glad for an effort to instill responsibility into the situation as the head of the family.

"No, we never went to church," she answered quietly, feeling that he might be disappointed by her answer. Johnny was encouraged that this might be easier than he thought.

"Maybe you would like to think about converting to Catholicism before you marry." Margaret was surprised by this notion, since Phil had never shown any belief in anything but big cars and money and whatever way he could get them. She didn't know how to answer Johnny and looked to Phil for help, to which he responded with a swift way out of the dilemma.

"Ah, we just tought we'd go to a JP in town." Knowing his brother was still a priest at heart, and would not let the subject rest, he started to shuffle his new Fluorsheims under his chair, getting ready to stand up for a quick exit. Johnny continued to say all the things Phil did not want to hear, and hadn't dealt with for a while.

"Mom would be surprised at you thinking about getting married outside of the church and without your faith," Johnny taunted him relentlessly.

"But then you're breaking every other law, why not the laws of God and our religion." With Johnny's last statement, it seemed that Phil had had enough preaching for one day.

"C'mon, Mugs, let's skedaddle, we ain't welcome no more." And as fast as he had blown in uninvited, he grabbed his Mugsy's arm and away they flew out the door, mumbling slurs against his brother while he quickly bundled his girlfriend once again in her Indian blanket.

"Mr. College priest, aint good 'nough fer de common people like us.... maybe we don't believe in yer kind of God." His face was horrible with anger.

"Yeah, wait'll you're down on your luck and in a sick bed, you'll be the first one on your knees." Johnny finished the argument. Dell felt a little sad. She knew the reunion was too good to last long, as they all stared at the vacated kitchen chairs, Ben finally breaking the silence.

"What happened to Uncle Phil and his new girlfriend? Did they go to get hitched?" This child's understanding of the serious situation broke them all up into the much needed relief of laughter. Dell wondered if they even knew what getting hitched meant.

"What time is it, Mom? Is *Hopalong Cassidy* on yet?" Tommy inquired, wanting to get out of this complicated adult world, now confused that God only liked some people because they went to church or were Catholic. He was also puzzled at how his dad could get so angry at their funny Uncle Phil and poor Mugsy, who seemed to like him a lot, which he was glad about.

Johnny sat alone staring at the artist's interpretation of *The Last Supper* hanging on the wall above the kitchen table. He didn't know why he had to harp on moral and religious problems all the time; it always got him into trouble, especially with his family. But wasn't he just doing what he was trained to do, trying to shepherd the flock? Why did he keep looking for ways to bring his brother back into the religious fold, when he never did acknowledge belief in anything spiritual in his life? Probably because Johnny knew how positive faith in God could make life.

It was so hard facing life's constant perils alone, but to have a divine companion helped so much. Well, he now knew it was a useless situation and realized that being a good example would be best for his brother to experience first hand. Maybe this would be enough, but he doubted it. Even Christ went out of his way to bring the lamb that strayed back into the fold, as the Good Shepherd.

On a warm spring day in May, a bouncing baby boy was born to Agatha and Joe. Joe was ecstatic, having his very own son in his arms. The robust boy had a full head of auburn curls and the bluest eyes the two of them had ever seen. Holding him, feeding him, and pushing him down Penn Avenue in a baby carriage did not embarrass him at all, parading his new offspring in front of his single buddies hanging out in front of all the local bars.

Saloons mostly out numbered commercial stores in Turtle Creek and Eastburg, and it was customary for most workers to head right through the swinging doors as soon as the whistle blew for quitting time at Westinghouse. Consequently, drinking problems ran rampant among the men, making proprietorship among bar owners very lucrative in deed.

Joe prided himself on not yet being addicted to liquor. He would take a drink with the rest of the guys every now and then after work, but never habitually. Nonetheless, life with Agatha was getting more and more difficult, and could probably drive anyone to drink, and drink heavy. But no, he wouldn't let it happen, not with this fine boy around that he had fathered.

They named him Charley, Agatha's father's middle name. She was pleased with herself, but glad that the ordeal was over, vowing it would never happen again. What a horrible and appalling experience, and something a real woman shouldn't have to go through. Ugh, the blood. She shuttered to think of the torment her poor harmless body had tolerated. Now she would avoid Joe like the plague. At least she had a good excuse with the baby - and she would soon think of something for the future. But positively no more kids for her. Oh, the messy terrible diapers she tried not to have to rinse out, at least when Joe was around to perform the terrible deed. Most of the time she would pile them up for him to wash out in the toilet.

Protesting vehemently against the nursing process, Agatha ultimately claimed soreness in her breasts, which would disavow all forms of that depressing activity. Moreover, having that little thing on her all day was insufferable, giving her nervous system anguish beyond compare. Enough was enough; she had done it all when he was born. Whoever said that a woman had to drain her entire body to keep a baby happy? It was probably a man who delivered that speech just to have a son exactly like himself.

"One, two, three, four, five…." Dell numbered the small parade of boys going upstairs to play after school. As usual there was Harry Rippen, Andy Renlus, Joey Hart, and at the tail end of the chain gang were Ben and Joely. They resembled the little dirty waifs in *Our Gang.* She had to laugh to herself. Andy even wore an old cap hanging on the side of his head like one of those characters; she couldn't remember which one, maybe it was Sparky.

"Hey, you kids take off your shoes at the bottom of the steps," she hollered. Dell took Terry out of the bathwater, wrapping her in a big warm towel, as her beautiful hair fell down around her ears into a mass of wet ringlets. She just knew those boys would be bouncing around on the beds upstairs, after she'd just changed the bedclothes that morning. It seemed that when their friends came to play, anything went – including pillow fights. Once she even saw tents hanging from a makeshift rope all the way out into the hallway, resembling an Arabian marketplace created from the clean comforters lining their bedrooms.

Dell didn't often shout at her sons, but she had just labored over eight loads of clothes with the ringer on the blink again. Johnny would have to do his best to fix it, even though he was not mechanical in any sense of the word. He usually knew someone who could eventually do it – but that would delay the process longer. Therefore, she would have to scrub some of the dirtiest work pants by hand, after boiling them in a huge tub on the tiny gas stove in the basement. It was a never-ending battle every washday, especially, in the wintertime when the clothes

84

were hung all around the huge coal furnace in the basement of their building. It took days for them to dry, and then it was time for the whole cycle to start again.

Holding out her red raw hands for inspection, she rubbed some balm over them feeling sorry for herself, always thinking that this was still better than life at the hotel, when she didn't even have the time to look down at her hands or sit down without Lizzie nudging her along to work.

Now hearing the kids trouncing up the steps, Dell caught up with Joely, who toddled slowly behind the rest, happiest when he could tag along with his brothers.

"Honey, wait there for a minute," she said to Ben and Joely.

"What are all those lumps in your pockets?" she asked, stooping to make an inspection.

In the meantime Harry ran back with his prominent limp, his hand-me-down knickers falling down around his ankles with the weight. The limp was due to an accident stumbling from a moving streetcar, when his leg was caught in the door as the conductor began moving the car. His mother, Irma had always grieved that she had been a negligent mother in not turning back to tend to his quick exit. The tall six-year-old looked up at her with a sincere look shining through stringy brown curls hanging down his forehead. His angelic look caught her eyes, and she felt sorry for him.

"Oh its okay Mrs. Albred, we're building an airplane launching pad upstairs, we've got to pile these up until they're high enough, then we're gonna put wood on top of that."

"Yeah, Mom, we're going to make a giant run-way for our planes to whoosh over it into the sky." Tommy, always the motivator for the group, piped up to demonstrate the wind effect. She was glad they were all getting along and having fun, but when she saw that their pockets were full to brimming with dirt and grit, she hollered out.

"Yeah, it sounds good, but all of you get outside now. Take your planes outside too. It's a nice day, what are you doing in here anyway? And don't go up in the woods." She finished her orders by the screen door, as Joely lowered himself one level at a time down the steps, trying valiantly to keep up with the rest.

She watched him safely down, thinking he was in good charge of the situation. They can wonder all over the yard, she thought, but the woods are a little too far up the hill.

She knew from the deep mud on their shoes that Tommy and Ben would go up there now and then. Johnny went as well, saying that it seemed harmless, but near their so-called "hideout" were some mines that he heard might cave in at any time. There were tales around all of eastern Pennsylvania that many unexplored coalmine shafts were dangerous if tampered with, even stories of children being trapped in them for hours at a time. The coal beds could be 2 to 8 feet thick, just deep enough for one of the little boys to fall into a crevice there. The apertures were hard to recognize unless someone started to dig for water or some other natural resource, usually discovering a vein of coal.

Dell worried about these dangers, but immediately thought of the nice things that had happened since they had lived there. Their family had met many of the neighbors, mostly through the boys, especially the Faradays next door, and the Zbyoskis who lived in the apartment downstairs on street level. They always spoke when passing and offered help watching Terry if Dell needed to leave for any reason. And many of the mothers knew Tommy and Ben from coming into their homes or yards to play.

She now felt safe enough to let them roam around the neighborhood without too much fear that anything would happen to them, unlike down in the city, where they could encounter drunks, women and men of ill repute, and immorality in every respect, not to mention their own Uncle Phil. This was an open area where multiple families lived and cared about their children.

Essentially, they were all striving to come out of the terrible Depression years where they had been under siege together, which prompted people helping people, just to get by on a daily basis. Being poor these days meant sharing, like keeping an extra cot or mattress available for someone, even a stranger on the street who needed a place to stay for a couple of days. Dell knew that none of them kept their doors locked for this reason, and over all it was the family-oriented familiarity and interdependence that seemed to keep them honest. As time went by, the neighbors came to know and watch over each other.

Terry was sitting quietly in her high chair as Dell turned back around. She marveled at the good baby she was from morning until night. And now she was sitting up and making noises, which sounded better as the speech therapist, worked with her baby vowel sounds two times a month. She still had scar tissue from the last operation, but at least her mouth was working properly by this time with the roof built up by plastic surgery and she was able to eat solid food.

She and Johnny thanked God that she was responding to all of the treatment from Children's Hospital. She peeped out once again at the boys all huddled around their newly constructed landing strip up in the yard, with a few of them drawing a large circle in the sooty-like dirt on another level part for a game of marbles, which she thought must have been at the bottom of the other debri they had tried to haul in to mess up the upstairs.

She saw Ben stooping to shoot his best lucky green marble; she hoped he wouldn't loose it to some of the other sharpshooters. He probably left the plane flying idea because he probably would not take his beloved planes out. Having just started putting his own version of model airplanes together, however crudely, he would sit for hours cutting and shaping the soft balsa wood model airplane. Sanding the rough spots from the body and the wings required some deftness in a little boy, sometime she or Johnny would help him, but mostly he wanted to tackle them himself.

Ben put the parts together according to the picture on the box, carefully gluing the tissue paper on the parts, and sprinkling it with water to shrink and fit tightly, then setting them to dry securely. No one was allowed near his treasures. He would remind his mother adamantly before going to school in the morning.

"Mom, don't let Joel upstairs, and please don't run the sweeper when you clean." He pleaded in a business-like voice. Dell had cautiously run the hose of the Hoover near his project, but the powerful motor had swiftly sucked one of the tiny propellers into the bag, which they later retrieved by fingering through the dust and dirt laid out on newspapers for inspection.

So Ben was satisfied this time, but she promised herself it wouldn't happen again. With four kids, she tried to let them all have something of their own, which was not easy. Also, she was sad that there was not enough time to spend individual time with each; it was hard to get to know their likes and dislikes, since all four children were quite different.

Tommy and Ben, though they were close in age, seemed to gravitate toward diverse interests, she could already tell this about their personalities. Tommy, growing tall and thin, with olive skin and thick black shiney hair, was more outgoing. He would entice his friends to come over, and they'd sit out on the porch picking on each other and giggling. Tommy seemed to make them all feel individually important, while he listened to their crazy sounding stories. There seemed to be a devoted exchange of friendship there. This was contrary to Ben, who sometimes spent time with Tommy's pals as well but liked being alone more. He loved to work with wood, make things like the planes, or sat for long periods of time over a collection of bugs he'd caught.

The clock told her it was four thirty; she switched on the little radio over the chifforobe just in time to hear the opening music of one of her favorite daytime drama's *Stella Dallas*. Dell put on her other clean housedress; this one had come through a day and a half of cleaning, with splashes of food adorning the front. She tied a clean apron on and went in to start supper. Today she would scavenge the refrigerator and make a vegetable stew with all of the leftovers, and some rice pudding, which they all loved. And even though they didn't eat that much at this age, she had to scrape by to buy milk and all of the staples required to make daily meals.

She was glad that she had watched Lizzie cook so much from scratch in the restaurant. Even with all of the insults she threw out, her mother-in-law had been the true mentor in her life. Dell now realized this more in her day-to-day life, especially when she reached in the oven for the four crusty loaves of bread she baked weekly. Lizzie would have been proud, she said to herself, but would never give her daughter-in-law a compliment in a million years.

She pulled up her sagging stockings filled with runners every direction and said to herself that she would not change these to suit Johnny. No, Johnny wouldn't notice them, and it wouldn't matter if he did. She was comfortable that he loved her for just being herself. She had never worn makeup either. Oh, once in a while, maybe to church on Sunday, she would dab a little bit of Pond's face powder on her shiney cheeks.

And although she had seen a woman going up the hill to Chalfant yesterday wearing pants like a man, she had told herself she could never exhibit her rear end this way. Nonetheless, she thought them practical, especially while raising small children. She knew her sister Mary wore them to work every day to General Electric in Cleveland, but Mary was a stylish dresser, not drab and plain like Dell had always been. No, she felt better in dresses for the time being. Her sister was more of an outgoing and outspoken person than she had been in her life. And now her whole life revolved around Johnny and the kids.

She thought of her mother and dad in Cleveland now. She missed them so much. She was surprised when they moved without even telling her, but then she knew that Pop must have had to report for work immediately at the tool shop there, after he sold his business. Many miles separated them. Dell would take the two older boys on the train to see their grandparents one of these days. But then how could she ever leave Terry and Joel alone here, even with Dolores next door?

"*Prress, Sun Tele paper*" Newspaper boys were shouting from two street corners, as Johnny walked downstreet with Tommy and Ben that Saturday evening. All of their shoes were polished and lined up in the kitchen for church in the morning, and Dell had baked a cake for company on Sunday. It wasn't as though they were expecting company, but she was always prepared in this way. And who knows, maybe Phil and his new girlfriend, Mugsy or rather, Margaret would show up again.

He looked around closely at the shabby Eastburg business district. This was not the same city where he grew up, when the Hotel was right down the street, and businesses were prospering in the twenties. Storefronts were boarded up with defacements written across the front and a few more were gutted out. But two or three were rebounding from the Depression, like where the newsboys were stationed in front of *Murphys five and ten store*, which had Halloween window decoration on display. And a new bakery beside it. Catty corner where the other kid stood was a new Drug Store called *Brown's.*

Johnny handed the boy a dime and received his paper in return, glancing at the headlines. *Italy Marches into Ethiopia.* Oh brother, the world is in turmoil, he thought. People were shocked when *Japan* invaded *Manchuria,* but with all of the power hungry dictators running those countries, they could strike anywhere at any time. *Hitler in charge in Germany. Mussolini in Italy and Hirohito in Japan.* He didn't trust any of them.

Johnny prayed that Roosevelt would keep the U.S. out of war, but the *League of Nations* had broken down, consequently, other countries were threatened as well. The people had great faith in this President, but he only had so much control against keeping the US out of world war.

He'd also heard that Congress passed some new acts that would keep the country from trading with or giving financial credit to any nation involved in a war. He did not believe that any of these tactics would stop these aggressor nations. Interrupting his thoughts, and tugging on his arm was Tommy.

"Alright, boys, I still have twenty cents here, enough for three ice cream cones."

"Let's go to Isaly's like you promised. I want chocolate with sprinkles on it." He said excitedly. Looking down at him, Johnny noticed that he looked inordinately sloppy today in baggy kneed argyle socks, and bigger than usual tweed knickers. He wasn't sure whether they were hand-me-downs from their neighbor, or else Dell had bought a large size from *Penney's* for school, so they'd fit him while he grew.

Oh course Ben would wear them next – and then Joely, the three of them would eventually wear the clothes out, so Johnny chose to ignore his feelings on this one, some kids still had no clothing of their own. They were wearing patched up and torn clothes, whatever they could put together, what was the matter with him? He was a snob, that's what he was, coming from his rich background at their money making business, always having the best while growing up.

"Ooh, that sounds good, what kind do you want Ben?" Johnny said, reaching in his pocket for change, as they crossed over the streetcar tracks to the Dairy store. He knew that his younger son would not come up with a quick answer, since he was always more reticent than his brother. But that was okay; Ben usually thought things over carefully first. Johnny loved spending time with them on the weekends.

When they reached the other side of the sidewalk they turned to stare, as a beautiful new 1934 De Soto Airflow went by. Johnny laughed and waved at the driver, his old friend George Pushcar from the Westinghouse. Leave it to George to be driving a gaudy car like that, but then he was single.

"Nice, huh." Johnny looked over at them. He hadn't been able to afford a car for the last few years because of the Depression, and now being a family man; he had other living expenses, notwithstanding Terry's recent operations. They were talking at work about an insurance plan for the workers, but nothing had come of it as yet. It had to come out of his wages.

He hoped to get a Plymouth in a few years. That was a nice family car. Then he could take the boys fishing, something he loved to do for leisure. Car manufacturers were really pushing the sales of automobiles. Buying one would cost him at least three months' wages. He read somewhere that even in the depths of the Depression, there were still over a million cars sold. People probably went without food to have a damn car, Johnny surmised, since cars were beginning to gain in popularity.

Oh boy, when he thought of how he used to drive and sell those beautiful Chrysler Maxwell's for Dell's dad. And to think how they would get in it just to ride around the block to the store, it seemed ludicrous now that such a thing could have happened before the crash. Yeah, many luxuries were around when they still had the hotel.

But what was most perplexing was the Benedictine's religious philosophy that had manifested itself within his heart, when he was in the seminary at St. Vincent's, with their austere life style and piety, but most of all the example of the Brothers who taught them every day. This was all so contradictory to the materialism taking over the world. He secretly believed that God was punishing all those who had strayed away from their religious beliefs. They had broken the first commandment, in that they had many other Gods like big automobiles being worshipped everyday

But this was the 1930's, not the roaring twenties, and I think I can wait it out, he told himself. Tommy broke into his thoughts.

"Jackie Rostivich's dad has a Pierce Arrow. Jackie rides in it all the time. He says, we're all gonna ride to the ball game someday. Their family went out to Rainbow Gardens to the swimming pool. They're lucky."

"I'll bet Uncle Phil will take us swimming in his Ford V-8," Ben said. Yeah, Johnny thought, and maybe we'll all get in a boat and go to China too.

"Don't worry, we're gonna get a car of our own pretty soon, kids, but they cost a lot of money. Your mom and I are saving in the bank for a good one." This satisfied them for a while, as they dreamed about the places they could go in an automobile. He thought of his ner'do well brother, who drove a repainted stolen car from God knows where. Johnny also hoped he wasn't too hard on him the last time they were together. After all, he was his kid brother and sure needed help morally.

"Hey, boys, let's stop in here for a while." He motioned them into one of the better class speakeasies in the burg. *Tables for Ladies,* it said on the window of Harry's Bar and Grill.

"Hi, Harry, I'll have my regular, and oh yeah, give the boys a couple of bottles of pop and potato chips." Harry Davenport had tended bar part-time for the Albred Hotel and knew them all well. He was a tall, cheerful bald-headed guy with a big apron and kind dark eyes. It was said that Harry was financially fixed.

"Hey, look at these big guys. I remember the day you were born." He smiled down at the youngsters.

"How's your ma doin? Don't see much of her anymore. I don't think she'd ever come in here." Johnny downed his shot and a beer, worrying slightly that Dell would be peeved with him on their return. He promised not to stop at any bars, especially with the boys. But dammit, a man had to have a drink once in a while.

Late October sun streamed through the dreary little three-room apartment of Phil and his Mugsy up in Bessemer Terrace. Coffee perked over the pot's side, spilling onto the two-burner hot plate, streaming down through the cracks in the linoleum on the floor, while they lay side-by-side three feet away reading the new comic strip, Li'l Abner.

"Hey Mammy Okum, go turn 'at thing off, would ya!" Phil yelled, patting her on the back, and kissing her sweet innocent face.

"Go do it yourself, you big Palooka," she said. This sent them into a fit of giggles, as they rolled in each other's arms across the outspread funny papers.

"Oh, I'll git it before this ole dogpatch becomes a bigger piece 'o crap." And he jumped up leaving her breathless at his feet. What could she say? She adored the big dope. Mugsy watched as her lover walked into the tiny kitchen in his maroon silk smoking pajamas and jacket, resembling John Barrymore, with his black shiney hair slicked down next to the part. Oh, wasn't she the lucky one. But then she thought of the gun she'd spotted in the corner of his suitcase last night before he'd unpacked.

"What's that for?" she'd said sheepishly.

"Hey, a guy's gotta protect himself, honey – don' worry, you're safe wit me." Then he hugged her fast and hard to get her mind off the subject. Then she'd remembered her daddy's rifle in Montana. He had it around to chase coyotes away from the sheep ranch, but Mugsy didn't think there were any four-legged critters around here to bother them, therefore it must have been meant for the human kind of pest. She'd have to keep her eye on it – she knew of many accidents happening when a temper flared in the wrong direction, and that was when love could turn to hate mighty fast.

EQUILIBRIUM

PART Two

"In individuals, insanity is rare; but in groups, parties, nations and epochs, it is the rule."

Friedrich Nietzsche
German philosopher
(1844 – 1900)

6. Six and One Half Dozen

She knew her mommy was sad about something these days. She wasn't her usual pleasant self, like when they would go down street and buy something nice for lunch. She loved the ladylock's pastry from Stallings, and could hardly wait to come home and lick the white oozing cream out of the deep sweet powdered center. But this was only after she ate her fried jumbo sandwich with vegetable soup, Libby's favorite. Mommy would usually say, I'll bet I know what you would like for lunch? In her usual cheery voice. And then they would shout it out together happily. But now Libby could see that her eyes were sad, like when the priest talked at Sunday Mass. She thought he must have been saying something serious to make her mother feel this way. She was down in the dumps, as her big brother Joely said.

"I hope they're not going to have another baby. We have enough kids already, and Mom is tired out," she'd overheard her brother Tommy say out on the back porch when he and Ben were sneaking a cigarette one night. Libby had wondered too; she didn't want any little babies around, and probably her mother didn't either. That's why she was sad, she thought.

Libby would start school in the fall at St. Coleman's. This was where Joely and Terry went every morning, when she watched them get on the streetcar with the other kids. There she would learn how to spell her long name, Elizabeth Lydia Albred. She was named after her Grandmother Lizzie, and also Daddy wanted her to be called Elizabeth. He said it was because she was a beautiful patron saint. Her dad knew all about the saints and the good spiritual lives they led, and how we all should pray to them because they were close to God in Heaven.

Terry said that she might let her come along with Mary Ellen and Rita on the streetcar to school. They were her sister's best friends who lived a few houses down from them. But most likely she would stay with Joely; he didn't mind her tagging along like Terry did. It wasn't always easy being the youngest kid in the family. Tommy and Ben were big boys in high school, sometimes they would throw her up in the air, or put her on their shoulders, but usually they were out doing things with their friends. Ben would always try to make her laugh, because it seemed that most of the time she wore a frown, probably because she was working hard to understand everything and it showed on the outside. At least this was what her mom said.

This afternoon after Libby had come in from making her mud pies in the yard, Mommy had called her in so she could wash up her hands and face with a soapy rag, then she put a nice dress on, because she would sit out on the front cement steps to watch for her daddy when he came home from work. This was a very important time of day; sometimes Ben or Tommy would show up as well. And if she got tired of sitting there, she would take two pieces of flat yellow stones and rub them together, to make a fine powder. This was an important job and it took a long while to make enough powder. Later she could sprinkle it on the dried mud pies.

Once Ben sat down and asked her why she was doing this. She ran to get her old strainer that Mommy no longer used in the kitchen, and showed him how the tiny rocks were sifted from the powder. Mud pies were not easy to make the right way. If there was too much water in them they would never dry nicely. Once her friend Sonny Faraday told her not to put too much water in the mix. He sat on the other side of the fence, and they compared their pies after they dried, but hers took way too long to get hard. Finally, when they were dried it was a beautiful sight and she felt so good. After that Ben always asked how the mud pies were coming along.

Libby's favorite thing to do was to watch Mommy iron clothes. She was happy on Tuesday's when she brought the huge straw basket filled with neatly rolled up clothes of different colors inside. Then the big ironing board would spring into an upright position, ready for the hot iron to start pressing. Daddy's work shirts were laid out first on the smooth board and she arranged the big sleeves to press over shoulder and collar seams next. Pssss went the iron on the damp material, steam arising in every direction.

Sitting comfortably on a nearby bed Libby watched Mommy finish everyone's blouses and dresses, then the embroidered pillowcases and dresser scarves with which she took extra care.

While Mommy was putting Daddy's hankies away in his chifforobe drawer, Libby looked out the window to see if any people were climbing up the big hill of Chalfant Boro, the steep road next to their house. Libby thought it would be pretty tough to walk up there, and wondered what kinds of people were up at the tippy top of one of the highest places around.

Hardly any cars drove up there either. Mostly kids like Joely's friend Kovic came down to Farkashes to get pop and lunch meat, but the older people were too weak to walk back up after they had come down to the store, and they would have to call someone to help them get back up to their homes. Libby was not allowed to try it, not even once.

Her family was lucky because their house was down on level ground and all they had to do was cross the street to go to Farkashes store with all of the colorful covered counters full of all kinds of candy. Mrs. Farkash would always give her a sucker, but Libby liked to buy Dixie Cups best. Whenever Mommy would give her ten cents, which was not often, she would buy these first. They were filled with ice cream, but best of all; they had movie star pictures inside their lids, which she would give to Joel because he collected them.

Libby loved all of her brothers because they were fun and she loved to laugh at their hi-jinx, especially Joel. Her sister, Terry, did interesting things. She loved to go with her when she went to visit people in the neighborhood. Not just people who lived close to them, but much farther down the street. Libby would beg to go with her when she heard her planning her day. Terry always had ideas about what she would do in the future. Mommy didn't always agree with what she wanted to do, but sometimes Terry knew how to make them come true, especially if she persuaded Daddy to go along with her, and sometimes he gave her money to spend on candy along the way.

"Okay, I'll take you. Stop crying. But don't tell Mom where we went, or I won't take you ever again," Terry would warn her, giving her a hard push along with it, but it was always worth it no matter how she was treated along the way. Libby learned not to ask too many questions, but just to stop, look and listen. The same thing she did when she came to a street corner.

"Let's wear something nice today, when we go for a walk," Terry said. Libby could tell that she was still putting together an exciting plan; by the slow way she talked. Her sister always knew what was going on around their neighborhood.

"I know, we'll both wear our new striped playsuits that Mommy bought for us last week, they're in style. Or is yours in the wash as usual?" Libby knew it was in the wash waiting to be laundered, but if she didn't find it Terry might change her mind about taking her along. So she didn't waste a moment running to the clothes hamper and dragging out the wrinkled garment. She flattened it out the best she could and put it on, even though the seat of the shorts was muddy from sitting in the yard making a new batch of mud pies. She quickly put a sweater on over it, even though it was a hot summer day, just so it would pass her sister's rigid inspection.

"Oh, you look like a slop as usual, you little mud puppy." Terry gave her the cruel critical eye of disdain. Then much to Libby's surprise, she softened her scorn.

"But that's okay, you're just a little kid, you can get away with it I guess." Libby held her breath. She was lucky this time. She knew that Terry was a kid too, but she would be going into the fifth grade and was a tall girl. Everyone had said so.

They walked together down a long city block, almost to the Booster's parking lot, until they came to Petrosky's Bar and Grill. Then Terry stopped to look up at the apartment upstairs where a light was shinning in the window.

"They're home for a change," she said, excited at the prospect of finding her target.

"Who is it?" Libby inquired, wondering how her sister had all this information.

"They own the junk store in Braddock – they're rich." Terry went in to the vestibule and knocked hard on the door. Libby crouched as far back as she could next to the door. Soon a little old man in a dirty undershirt and an unshaven face appeared through an opening in the door.

"Who is it…. oh, it's you, Theresa. Whatdaya want today?" he grumbled not unkindly.

"Hi, Mr. Solomon, do you have those books you were going to give me?" She answered in the sweetest assuming tone. Libby did not know that Terry owned so pleasant a voice, and stared inquisitively at her sister. This was not her manner at home. Wearing an old torn and dirty undershirt, the man stumbled half way down the steps as if he were going to forcefully chase them away. Then he opened his mouth half full of gold teeth to speak, but hesitated, setting his mouth in an ugly gape. Libby stepped back, thinking he was going to grab them, but instead he smiled flashing his fancy dentistry, speaking surprisingly softly.

"Honey, we're cleaning out the warehouse. When they bring them over I'll call you." Knowing her mother would not approve of what she was doing, Terry answered fast.

"Oh, that's okay, I'll stop by next week, sir. Goodbye." She continued with her appealing tone. *Sir?* Libby remained captivated by Terry's newfound language, but was swiftly wheeled around through the door, as her sister yanked her to the sidewalk outside.

"He was scary," Libby said cautiously.

"Aw, you're afraid of everything, ya baby, even the witch in Snow White."

"That's because you always pretend you're her and jump out at me," Libby confessed.

"Yeah, sure, someday you'll realize that these are the good people in the world." Libby wanted to ask how do you know, but refrained, knowing that Terry often knew many worldly things that she never even thought about. Like where babies came from. She somehow knew that her sister was in on the secret about if and where they would get a new baby. Libby would ask her mother about this problem as soon as she could and was bothered by the fact that her mom hadn't discussed it with her at all.

As they walked slowly, Terry talked about her next hopeful worthwhile stop. Softly they crept back past their house on the other side of the street lest someone in their family was lurking about. Tommy might have been sitting on the porch swing with his girlfriend Dolores, or Joely could have been waiting to have his haircut in a chair in the barbershop next to Farkashes. But none seemed to be around as the two girls made their way up Electric Avenue.

The Gardiners lived under the train trestle in a big white frame house. There were huge trailer trucks parked all around their house because they owned a big trucking company.

"Those girls are older and have beautiful gowns and clothes. Maybe they're ready to throw away something; we might be just in time to get some really good loot. They never wear the same thing twice," Terry said excitedly. "Remember those silver shoes I brought home? They were Jeannie's. She wore them at a grand ball in Edgewood. Now you know they were special." Libby knew the shoes that Terry wore everytime they played "house". She could never touch those or any of her sister's things or it would be the end for her.

The doorbell sounded out pleasant-sounding chimes, and soon a beautiful older girl with long brown curls and wearing a silk Chinese kimono greeted them warmly. She seemed to know Terry well.

"Hi, Terry, are you looking for used goods again, you little beggar girl? And this must be little Libby with the blond pigtails. Hi, honey," She said, pulling one of them. Terry laughed, but Libby was a little embarrassed and wished they were coming there for any other reason than trying to get some old clothes. No wonder their mom got mad at Terry, going around asking for things from people she hardly knew. It wasn't as if their family needed help.

"It just so happens we have some nice things to give you. I'm not sure if you can wear them or not. It just so happens that my Aunt Louise has just returned from China where she was living with her husband stationed with the army in Shanghi. Come on up to the bedroom." As they ascended the thickly carpeted stairway, Terry whispered to Libby assuredly.

"See, I told you, now aren't you glad we came up here?" Libby smiled pensively, wondering what was upstairs that was so good. But as they stepped into the plush bedroom with pale blue damask drapes and matching chaise, an astounding sight greeted their eyes. Large white furniture holding tall delicate glass lamps illuminated the huge room, spotlighting the multicolored pile of Chinese silks spread from one end of the big bed to the other.

Libby stared all around the beautiful room. Two enormous walk in cupboards were stuffed with shoes and dresses. She had never seen so many clothes, except maybe at *The Famous Department Store* in Braddock, and those were hung separately in different departments.

Jeannie began to explain in an intelligent manner how her relations had acquired such an enormous cache of clothes, while the two sisters stared at the young woman who seemed to know so much about where these lovely outfits came from.

"These are legendary prints inspired from the realm of Chinese legend. They represent 25 separate designs. The patterns carry names such as Lotus Maiden, Temples in Moonlight, China Forever. Familiar subjects like jade teapots, fish patterns, Confucious, or others with equal cultural significance. The colors are oriental; peiping green, lotus pink, pagoda red and bamboo. They're used for daytime and evening gowns, for housecoats, beach wear, parasols, bags, turbans and other apparel that the Chinese women use."

Libby thought of what she knew that was Chinese. Chinese checkers that she and Joel played, the Chinese laundry down the street in town that she'd heard people say did the best job starching white shirts. China dishes and cups, and then there was the Chinese chicken man – where her mother bought chickens sometime. Then Terry broke into Jeannie's dissertation, seemingly very interested.

"Were they all shipped over here on a boat?" She wanted to take some of them home, even though their mother would not like it.

"My aunt and uncle purchased these when they lived there. They lived in Shanghai for over five years. These were sold to benefit the Chinese relief fund that Madame Chiang Kaishek held for her people's benefit. Have you ever heard of this famous woman?" she asked the two girls, who seemed to be fascinated by what she was saying. When they both shook their heads, Jeannie went on trying to give them a little bit more information about what they were going to take with them.

"She went to school in the United States, where she helped her husband communicate with President Roosevelt. This helped both of our countries stay friends so that we can trade goods."

"How many can we take?" Terry said greedily, tired of the geography lesson, her bright blue eyes lighting up. Libby could see that her sister was getting fidgety to get some clothes and leave there. She could tell when she started to talk fast, but was interrupted when they heard the sound of their voices being called by Joel down the street through the open window. He sounded mad.

"Oh-oh, they're looking for us," Libby said, staring at her sister. Then she realized they might have been away for a long while, maybe Mommy was worried. But Terry didn't seem to care as she busily rummaged through the clothes lying on the bed.

"Don't worry about him," she said, a wee bit concerned, so that she did look up to Jeannie, then yelled back at her brother out the window that they'd be right home.

That evening everything went well at first, as Mom served chop suey for dinner. Libby thought this was some kind of coincidence, since they never had a choice for dinner. And as they sat eating with new long ivory chopsticks poking out of their braids, the food seemed appropriate for the day's events. Libby wore a lustrous red dress with tiny yellow birds sewn near the shoulder with matching piping, trimming the pagoda on the shiney satin bodice. The size nearly fit her. Jeannie had told her that little girls her age in China had smaller bodies than she did at almost six years old.

A beautiful shiney black two-piece pajama set with red stitched lanterns adorning the sides made Terry look very grownup, especially with her brown wavy ringlets hanging down from her dark thick hair pulled up into the new "up-sweep" that fashionable ladies were wearing now. Tommy and Ben smiled as they sat together across the table spooning rice into their mouths, as if they already knew what was coming to their sisters. But Libby didn't care; she had a wonderful feeling about the adventure they shared today.

In many ways she felt as if they had visited another country, if only by just being told about it by Jeannie, who seemed to describe China as if she had been there, and they knew she had not. Most of all Libby was glad to have been with her older sister, who was happy finding treasures beyond compare.

Nonetheless, Johnny, who was never taken in with showy frills, presented his oldest daughter with a few strong words during supper, an opportunity for him to teach them a lesson in some way or another, and the ideal time to pin them down to attention. His bushy eyebrows were knit together as he spoke soundly to Terry.

"Mrs. Stein told your mother that you were asking for clothes and things at her door today. Theresa, what must these neighbors think about us, letting you go around like this begging for things all the time? Don't you have enough to keep you busy here at home? And poor Joel here looked high and low for you two. Not to mention dragging your little sister around the streets like a vagabond. What is wrong with you?" Libby was disappointed that he had to make his last remark, because it might mean she could not go with her sister anymore.

Terry stared at him, her deep blue eyes focusing intently on her father. Libby could tell she was embarrassed to have this kind of attention brought to her, especially in front of their brothers. But she sat at attention ready to confront him with willful words of protest, carefully trying to place her words so that her father would not be more upset.

"Well, Joel didn't look up the street."

"Yes, I did," her brother put in at his end of the table, defending himself against the blame of his sister, staving off his father's anger toward him. Usually he sat at the supper table quietly and ate everything without comment because his dad would reprimand him on bad table manners if he drew attention to himself.

"Well, we were just a few doors up having a conversation with Jeannie, who told us a lot about the geography of China, right Lib?" Libby shook her head positively. Terry had come up with a good answer because their father liked them learning new things.

At age ten, Theresa had already captured a form of confidence that would overcome those opposing sides to her

102

opinion – even if they did belong to parental authority. Through her early growing years she had acquired strength from the social adversities brought on by the noticeable appearance of her restructured nose and lip, changing through puberty.

Developing an attitude toward on-sight rejection by her peers sometimes led to her eliminating some friends altogether. However, this disposition sometimes materialized into a deep hurt and self-pity bordering on hating herself as well. It was during times like this that Dell had to step in to restore her daughter's self-assurance.

Through experience, Terry now knew that she could win people over with her outgoing personality and keen sense of humor. This took work toward winning some friends her age, but became a worthwhile skill for her at a young age. She loved being with people, and had many friends because of a special effort she made toward getting to know them and their families later. In addition, she loved to laugh, always having a joke or two ready to pop on anyone within range, usually her brothers.

Now, though, their father continued on with his "supper sermon", which was what Tommy and Ben called it.

"I am just thinking of your safety and our family's reputation. Whatever you kids do when you're out there in our neighborhood reflects on all of us – on our good name." In future years, Terry would question her father's own similar motives when he frequented the local bars. But this thought did not occur to her in these early years before the war, when innocence prevailed among children, even those who would soon leave their family circle for foreign shores.

Dell's mind had wondered across the table to her son Tommy who was probably eating one of his last meals at their dinner table, and whose serious expression followed his father intently, though she doubted whether he was listening. He seemed thinner than ever. She had never been successful at helping him gain weight, simply because he never stopped moving long enough.

Her heart was hurting for him, whom she probably loved more than all the rest, especially since they had been through so much together at the hotel. It seemed like yesterday that he had wandered away from there with his little red wagon. She and

Johnny had been in a state of panic, when the next day someone called from Linhart, a town over two miles away to say that he was safe and they had recognized him from when they'd eaten there one day. Dell would never forget the flow of relief that followed the ordeal.

Tommy threw open the back door the next day. Beef stew simmered on the stove for supper and he could hear the familiar music introducing his mother's radio program, Stella Dellas. His father would be changing his work clothes just about now. Harry and Andy and another curly red-haired boy named McGettigan had come along as Tommy's booster section, trailing mindlessly behind him into the room with apprehension. They seemed to always be wondering how their chum would fare in an audience with his father.

There had always been tension between them, since Johnny had seen his oldest son as a restless boy, who could never seem to focus on any interest in particular. The latest incidence involved Tommy taking off with his girlfriend Pauline's family automobile, unlicensed. They had gone for a ride. No one had been hurt, but the cost of replacing headlights and the large chrome fender of the 1934 Chrysler Airflow was exorbitant and had ruined its appearance forever.

The Albreds had watched from their windows as Mr. Sokolowski had shined up his coveted car every weekend over the years. And now the embarrassment that Dell and Johnny felt every time they encountered their neighbor was insurmountable. This bad feeling between the two families probably mounted up to more than the damage to their monthly budget, since they had no insurance to rely upon.

The following week Tommy had gone downstreet to sign up for the Navy, except he was under age at sixteen, and parental permission was needed for processing. Enlistment permission papers had to be signed by his father. He'd been reading about the United States Navy for a while and had often thought it would be an exciting adventure to be out on the seven seas in any capacity. Besides, all he was doing was getting into trouble around there. He'd always had a job. When he was just turning fifteen he lied about his age and got a cookie picking position at

National Biscuit Company in East Liberty. For a short while he brought home mutilated cookies for the gang to eat. They loved every crumb, which was most of the consistency, but those little urchins would devour anything that didn't grab them first.

It was while working for *Shackelford's Flower Shop* that he made the decision to go into the service, since right next door was a central office of the USN. The job of cleaning up flower stems and leaves was easy but boring and going nowhere, just like school, and all he liked about that was the football team. And heck, all the guys were talking about going into the service for their country to help the good old U S of A out in case that louse Hitler decided to bomb their shores. And whether they'd have the guts to sign up – well it was their business.

"Sign here, Dad." Tommy stepped right up to his dad in businesslike fashion, and while nodding back, a long dark curl hanging down the middle of his head, sent a wink back to his buddies who stood in the background wearing it seemed a larger version of the same dingy clothes they had on when they were tiny boys.

Dell noticed this with a lump in her throat, which would not contain itself, as she stood with her arms crossed over the huge pregnant bulge showing beneath her red and white-checkered apron. It was quite obvious to at least most of the family that she would deliver soon, though she never talked about it, or made plans in any way. It was just understood that Aunt Mary would come and take over the household as in past births. But now with Tommy leaving, her heart was breaking into little pieces.

She wondered why it had to come to this. It seemed that Johnny had no patience with their oldest son, who had such zeal to get out there into the world to take part in what was the hardest part of life. As if to justify her reasoning, she brought to mind many of their neighbor's sons who were going into the service. War correspondent Gabriel Heater had just announced that war had started in Europe because of the aggression which England and France had already declared of Germany. Dell prayed that her son would not be involved, and that the United States would not get into a full-scale world war.

Johnny read the release form with his eyes filled. Why on earth would his son rush out and do this? But then, he knew. At first he was reluctant to put his signature on it, but looking hard into Tommy's blue eyes, he tried to convey how this move would influence his young life forever.

The rest of his children, except Ben, who had probably gone upstairs to immerse himself in his model airplane hobby, looked bewilderedly on from doorways, as father and son confronted each other with a break in their relationship. *What would the aftermath bring?* Johnny wondered. *Tommy getting wounded, perhaps handicapped for life out there in harm's way? Would he be signing the epitaph for his own son to be killed somewhere in action?*

As a youth, Johnny had been under his mother's jurisdiction when she sent him to prep school at St. Vincent's, nevertheless, he was not regimented into going off to some foreign land to learn a hard lesson without friends or family anywhere in sight.

"Do you know what you're letting yourself in for?" he asked his son, who stood waiting impatiently for the deed to be done, so he could run off with his pals nearby. In the end Johnny had signed the form, knowing full well that Tommy was too anxious to stay at home. He had to be on the move in some way. It was in his nature to explore everything, no matter which way he chose.

Of all of the family, Terry was the most forthcoming in querying her older brother every day. Where would he be going? Why was he leaving them, and was it safe in that city or country?

"What will you do in the Great Lakes?" Terry said, as if she had any indication of where the Naval Base was located.

"Will you learn how to sail and save other sailors if the Germans sink your boat? Can't you just go up to Lake Erie and learn to how to run a ship, why do you have to go to the Navy for that?" She wanted to get the picture perfectly clear before Tommy disappeared. Tommy had been her champion, defending her against the wickedness of kids her age who insisted on insulting his sister under any circumstance. Her oldest brother would fight anyone on her behalf, never letting anyone say a bad word to his sister about anything. Consequently, he felt like he was letting some of the family down now, especially Terry.

Tommy put his arm around his little sister, his prominent Adam's apple visibly moving in his long slim neck. They sat together and talked about his plans for the future.

"I'm going to fight for peace in our country, kid, you've heard of this guy Hitler, who's trying to destroy countries one by one over there, until they all bow down to him. Well someone's got to stop him, and that's what I'm goin' to be trained to do. Protect the oceans around our nation. No one in this family can go but me right now." He believed himself, and so did those other members within ear range, like Joel and Libby who walked around looking morose that he would just go off, daring to leave the others in his wake.

It was tough for Joel, who loved the security of home life, to believe that his big brother would put himself into some stranger's hands to leave the peaceful house that Mom and Dad had given them. But he also knew that his Dad had run out of ideas about how to keep Tommy in tow, so maybe this just might work, his twelve-year-old mind told him. He thought about an incident that happened just last week when Tommy and Ben were shinnying up the porch pole and rain pipe to get in through their bedroom window long past curfew.

Joel had been in bed for some time, and thought it was a dream when he heard his father creeping around in the adjoining bedroom. Uh-oh, he thought, Dad's found out about their "after hours entry plan". Soon he heard struggling at the window, and Tommy's voice.

"Hey." He had yelled apparently when he saw his father in the room waiting in pursuit to grab the first boy who came in the opening.

"What do you think you're getting away with, Tom." his father said calmly, now that he knew he'd scared the daylights out of him.

"You are to be in this house at nine, especially on a school night, and that's final. This will never happen again. Do you understand?" Then he turned around and left his son, afraid he might say or do something in anger that he would regret. Then Tommy muttered agreement knowing this was the last word, and as his father went down the steps, he mumbled something else under his breath about having the meanest father on earth and how he would never understand his life. This was all Joel could hear. In the meantime, Ben had disappeared into the night, as soon as he got an inkling of his father having caught on to the "entry plan".

Ben laughed at his older brother having the guts to enlist in the war. He had his own plan about where he'd go after graduation next year, and it didn't involve any such risks at the moment. He scoffed at his older brother's daring.

"Ha, just wait till those torpedoes land on your boat. You're gonna shit your pants, kid. I'm never goin' willingly – they'll have to drag me off to the draft," he ranted.

"You wanta be a big hero, huh? You're gonna be watchin' guys die beside you. Better get ready," Tommy laughed at his kid brother.

"Ha, you've been watching too many WWI movies, bud," Tommy said.

Even so, deep inside Ben was anxious about his brother rushing into the fray. He never talked about his plans. Right now anyway he was pretty disgusted about being one of the smallest guys in the junior class. Why even his best friend Tom Tierney towered over him. Well he might be shorter, but he had broader shoulders than his brother.

Joel had his own conflict going on with his father. As a seventh grader he could not see the blackboard clearly. This would raise the wrath of Sister Mary Eustis, a sister of Mercy, who was doing a worthwhile task of pummeling education into the minds of young Catholic boys and girls. Through no fault of his own, Joel had encountered the measles, which had started in his eyes, weakening his sight. This fact was learned only after he had to repeat the seventh grade. He would never forget the look on his mother's face when she read his report card that he would be detained in the seventh grade.

Johnny was livid realizing that his son had failed and decided to close up the ranks on discipline. This stress caused Joel numerous problems, namely stuttering and bed-wetting. One evening as his mother was hearing his prayers before bed, Joel could not seem to get the words out correctly.

"H H H Hail Mmmmmary…" Hearing his son upstairs, Johnny threw his newspaper down and charged upstairs two at a time.

"I'll help him say his prayers," he shouted angrily, trading places with Dell at the bedside. Joel knew it was do or die, as he continued his prayers correctly. But the next morning he hid the sheets under the bed – which his mother found to carry down to the wash load later. She was always on his side, but would not openly defend him against his father's discipline.

Friends and relatives showed up the day before Tommy would take the streetcar in front of their house after he received his orders to go to Great Lakes Naval Base in Illinois.

"Hey, Tom, what battleship are ya goin' out on? I knew a coupla guys who shipped out on dat freighter out o' Norfolk, dey never came back." Looking natty in a broad breasted, wide shouldered zoot suit, Phil told his nephew everything he knew about the Navy, while his Mugsy walked slowly behind obediently. Dell and Johnny looked at each other knowingly, since word had it in his shop in the Westinghouse that Phil was drinking heavily and would often go on out of town junkets of his own trying to find a new business venture. And though he had a steady day job at the plant, it seemed he would search all life long looking for a successful establishment of his own, legitimate or not. The latest of these had been a potato chip factory.

His wife, Margaret, looked the worse for wear in a big dark and gloomy long dress, which Dell identified as an old made-over maternity outfit for their baby, which had been still-born after eight months of pregnancy. Dell knew that Margaret was even now in mourning after five years, and knew her menacing brother-in-law had been the cause with his brutality toward his poor wife, the battering ram for all his failures.

"Yeah, I was in de Merchan' Marines for a while, 'til Mom caught me, and brought me home. Huh, Johnny?" Phil motioned toward Johnny, who stared disgustedly at his brother, not knowing whether to agree with him or smack him across the head, as only a brother should do. All Johnny knew was that Phil tried everything once, having no limits where he went – he was secretly glad to know that his mother had stopped him in his lousy tracks.

Tommy and Ben had to laugh at their crazy uncle dressed in the odd looking suit, which one or two of their friends had, but said they wouldn't be caught dead wearing it in public.

"Hey Uncle Phil, you look like your ship just came in. You're lookin' like a real hepcat." Tommy kidded starting in on the jive talk of the day, knowing that his uncle followed jazz and Benny Goodman's swing.

"You hit on the numbers or somethin'?" Tommy kept razzin' him, knowing his family and his girlfriend Pauline beside him, enjoyed the banter between uncle and nephew. Phil tried to act cool like a younger guy as well and came back.

"Nah, I aint hip to de jive sonny boy, if that's what yer sayin', if I hit I'd be outa here faster den you could wink an eye," he retorted.

"Jimmy Brennan hit dough, last week. He boxed 797 and won both ways. So how 'bout dat. Aw I don' know when my sub boat's comin' in." Then all of a sudden he got a depressing look on his face, like he lost his best friend, an "its never gonna get better look". The boys could never figure out which planet their uncle Phil was coming from.

Just then two little boys ran up the sidewalk to the back porch.

"Hi Tommy, hi Ben, hi everybody." Their cousin Charley was ready to play and have fun. A cheerful friendly little boy with curly auburn hair, blue eyes and a keen sense of humor, he chuckled at most anything. Resembling his mother in looks, it was his father's solid outgoing personality he'd inherited. He and Terry usually hit it off well and would go off and play for hours up in the hills above the house, mostly swinging on the wild grapevines close to the woods.

Joey, Agatha and Joe's younger boy, was near to Libby's age, but she felt that he was a little too quiet for her liking and usually ignored the little fragile blond boy. Also Aunt Agatha would follow them around watching them constantly like she didn't trust her being with Joey.

The older Joe would always wonder if the boy was indeed his son, since he hadn't remembered them sleeping together since Charley was born, due to all of her "maladies". Unless it was that Sunday afternoon that he'd caught her unaware?

Now Agatha and Joe seemed to be having an argument as they came around the corner of the house, looking upset with each other. Dell thought she looked attractive as usual, wearing her long auburn hair in the new fashionable pageboy style. She also wore brand new open-toed shoes, the latest rage, and a short blue rayon dress above her chubby knee. It was hard to believe she could look this way with two little kids around all day.

But then what did Dell know about what women were wearing. She barely had time to take her Saturday night bath, wash her hair and put it up in curlers for church on Sunday. And now with another baby coming any day, who knew when she'd get her shape back. Agatha, who seldom thought about what she was going to say, confirmed her thoughts by the first ugly words out of her mouth, in greeting her sister in law.

"Boy, you sure are big Dell. You'll probably never be skinny again after having all these kids, ya know? You and Johnny'll have to get separate beds," she said, continuously eyeing her up and down. But Dell would have none of it, and spoke back sharply, glad that the kids were not within earshot.

"Agatha, please keep your comments to yourself. This is none of your business. You don't watch my kids, you have enough looking after your own."

"What's that supposed to mean?" Agatha snapped, spying a lemon meringue pie with thick homemade crust on the table, her favorite. *Hmm, I better be careful*, she thought. *Otherwise I won't get any of these good eats.* And if there was one thing she loved about Dell, it was her cooking, which tasted better than her Mother Lizzie's now. For this reason only, she quickly changed the subject to her advantage.

" Poor Tommy, leaving home so young," she cried. Dell looked into her eyes to see if she was sincere, and thought maybe she might be, but did not risk pouring her feelings out to this cruel woman. Besides, she was not feeling good at all this day.

The next day their oldest son and brother left on the eighty-seven Ardmore streetcar for Penn Station in Pittsburgh. As they all watched from the front porch, Tommy and a few other neighborhood boys walked to a seat with a small bundle of clothes, some toiletries and a new black prayer book that Johnny had bought him. Dell had also wrapped a jumbo sandwich in waxed paper and put an apple in a lunch bag, but doubted whether her excited boy would even stop to eat it.

The family observed silence all day until that evening, when Johnny had to borrow a neighbor's car to take Dell to Columbia hospital in Wilkinsburg, where their sixth child was born. She was a delicate little dark haired baby girl, and they counted their blessings once again.

*"We will not defend ourselves to the uttermost, but will make
certain this form of treachery shall never endanger us again"*
Franklin D. Roosevelt

7. War Worries

Soon before the New Year of 1940, Germany had total control of Central Europe. On another front, Japan rained it's military power on China. Through all of this world havoc America stayed within its own border. The United States Government pledged to be neutral with 67.4% of Americans opposed to taking sides with any country.

Dell nursed six-month-old Katrina, while she and Johnny listened to the President's State Of The Union speech. Speaking for the mobilization of America, he now alluded to foreign affairs, asking Congress for 1.8 billion to finance peacetime military buildup, the largest in the history of the U.S. At the outset, the nation was not ready for such organization, far removed from the exhilaration and reverberating preparedness, which marked the start of the First World War in 1917. The country remained complacent due to an independent attitude of the administration.

Seaman Third Class, Tommy Albred had come home on a short leave at Christmas, as one of the first servicemen to leave a lasting impression on the neighborhood and his girlfriend Pauline with his dark slim-fitting uniform and his even more eager readiness to defend his country no matter what. Now all of the Albred's respected his outreach into the dangers of the world, including Johnny who greeted his oldest son with a new form of respectful affection. Even Mr. Sokoloski, whose car would never run or look right again, looked differently upon this young man, who seemed to now be on the right track.

Dell's priorities, besides keeping baby Kat healthy, were watching intently for the daily arrival of the mailman carrying a precious letter from her son. Tommy's letters were filled with interesting tales of his life on a big battleship, taking on a life of its own as it circumvented the waters of the Atlantic coast. His beautiful handwriting spread out over sometime three-page letters was impeccable, as he described Ports of importance and interest for all the members of the family, mentioning them by name. When Dell wasn't reading the letter aloud, all of the family took turns examining the interesting document for information that would concern them.

Hey Ben, a giant Air Craft Carrier passed us yesterday about the size of two city blocks – there were Army planes being transported somewhere – probably to Britain. All the guys came up on deck to watch this big flattop pass by. I think you ought to join the Airforce and fly real planes. Then you can leave the toys behind. Ben just laughed at his brother's remark, but was glad that he mentioned him, the poor sap, out there slaving for his country.

Oh and by the way, Terry, I got a big bolt of some material for you from one of my buddy's at the PX, I thought it looked like your colors.

"Oh boy". Terry yelled, trying to contain herself. She couldn't wait to make something on the old treadle Singer Sewing Machine given to them by her Grandmother Gessner, who had passed away a few years ago. Dell was pleased that her daughter would take up the craft that had been the delight in her mother's life, and thought that she was doing pretty good at sewing on her little scraps of material. It wasn't easy keeping the treadle going and moving your cloth back and forth at the same time. Alternatively, Dell was glad that Terry had an interest that would keep her home and not walking around bothering the neighbors.

Dell read to Libby her paragraph from her brother, as she stared with interest.

An' how are you doin' in school, Libber? Mom says you can almost read now? Behave and take care of that little Kitty Kat you have around there now. Libby wasn't happy that his greeting referred to this new little kid who'd come to live with them. Somehow they'd just sprung this baby on her out of the blue. All of a sudden Mommy was gone with a quick good-bye and Aunt Mary was here to stay with all of them, just like that. She didn't have anything against Aunt Mary, who was a kind and good lady, but she would just keep talking the whole time she was here about this nice little sister she was going to have and won't it be nice to have her around and all that. Libby didn't

114

think it was so good, and would climb up high into her favorite apple tree or stay with her head down low into her mud pies all the time now. It would feel good to bury herself among them and become one of the big lumps of goop. Who cared about her anyway, they were all lookin' at this little limp piece of baby in there cryin' all the time.

The day before Uncle Paul took Aunt Mary back home to Ohio, she heard her Mom and Aunt Mary talking and laughing in the living room. But then Aunt Mary sounded kind of sad. Libby had never seen her crying before and felt sorry hearing her speak so softly.

"Dell, I don't know how to say this, but I've been thinking about it for a long time. Paul and I aren't having any luck at all with a baby and look we're already married five years. How would you feel about us taking Kat and raising her as our own?" Libby peeped in to see her pretty white-haired Aunt almost in tears; she thought this was a wonderful plan. Why didn't her Mom and Dad think of this one? They could share some of their kids.

Her mother looked thoughtfully at her sister, thinking hard for the right answer. Libby wished so much that she would say *go ahead, take her, she's all yours.*

The two Gessner women were very different when it came to having children. Dell had fallen in love with Johnny at eighteen, soon after attending Stenographer night school at Turtle Creek High School, having Tommy soon after. Whereas her sister Mary had a good career going as a tester at General Electric's Light Bulb Division in Nela Park, near Cleveland. Dell was well into motherhood at age thirty-eight and could see her sister's dilemma. Mary was thirty-six years old and wanted to be a mother. Dell felt sorry for her sister, but she and Johnny loved their family, all of them. Consequently, she tried to encourage her sister.

"Oh Mary, I would never give up any of these kids, they're all precious to us. You'll have your baby – you have to pray hard to the Blessed Virgin. Only she knows how much you want to become a mother. I have a special novena that you can take, but you have to say the prayer every day." Libby was sad and then glad when she heard her Mother say these words about how much they were all loved, and thinking a lot about saying goodbye to that new kid who might be on her way to Ohio.

As it happened, Joel had taken Libby to school on her first day, since Dell was even now recuperating from the birth of Kat. Joel and Libby stood with the parents in the back of the room, and then Joel had to leave to go up his own class, so Libby had to maneuver on her own. She was lucky to have the one of the "good nuns", Sister Mary David. The rest of the kids seemed to be afraid of many of them, and she heard worse stories from her sisters and brothers, knowing this lady was okay. At least she never yelled, she just talked a lot about the fires of hell and the suffering souls in purgatory. These scared Libby and kept her from sleeping and wondering when God would destroy the world by fire, as sister had told them.

She was glad that Terry slept in the same daybed. This made things better, but Libby had to be sure to stay on her side of the small bed. The girls didn't have their own bedroom as the boys did in the attic; they slept in a little alcove next to the living room. Dell and Johnny's bedroom, which also contained Kat's crib, was next door. Terry had warned Libby as far back as Libby could remember, drawing a separation with her forefinger.

"Now here is the line down the middle". She made an indentation down the sheet. "You cannot cross it, or the big bad wolf will get you, see?" Terry jumped quickly into Libby's face, who screamed at her sister's shocking spontaneity, laughing at her sister's sudden antics.

Dell was not happy with their living arrangements now in the least. They were starting to bulge out of the seams of the once roomy two-family second story home. And what really upset her is that the neighbors they liked so well, the Zbyoskis, were moving into a home of their own. Dell took heed that the property was being resold to other people who might immediately raise the rent.

Dell deliberated on where they could buy a nice house with maybe a piece of land attached where they would plant a big garden and have a few chickens to help quell the large food bill for the seven of them, now that Tommy was gone, though her oldest son never ate much.

116

She and Johnny were saving lots of money now, due to his long hours of over time at the Westinghouse. One of her primary goals was to get him out of Eastburg and far away from his regular bar visits and hard drinking friends. She thought he was a wonderful man when he did not drink, the same good guy that she fell in love with that day in Pop's garage. But as soon as she heard him whistling coming up the walk, she knew they would have a squabble of some kind. *I hate that damn liquor.* She thought.

And well, she hated cigarettes too, but they didn't change his character like liquor. Nevertheless they stunk bad, and worst of all she thought that Tommy and Ben were starting to sneak cigarettes with their friends – but so far they hadn't tried it around her. She new that Johnny was a bad example in this respect, since he had always been a chain smoker.

Today while Dell was cleaning she felt tears forming in her eyes hearing Bing Crosby, her favorite singer, crooning the old song "My Buddy" on the radio. *Nights are long since you've been away, I think about you all through the day, My Buddy, My Buddy, your Buddy misses you.* This song had come out when Tommy was a little boy, and would always remind her of the little affectionate boy who would always put his arms around her tenderly, caring about her feelings with all that she had to do at the hotel.

She missed him terribly but was reminded that they had five other children to worry about. Ben was the secretive one, not really telling anyone much about school or his friends, and seemed to be doing well in school according to his report card. And nowadays that Joel could see the blackboard with his new glasses, he was doing better in school, though they were usually taped and stuck together with airplane glue from being thrown around into all of the wrong places.

She sincerely wished that Johnny would take it easy on him. It seemed like he picked on him too much, and Joely was a vulnerable boy who seemed to go to all lengths to please them. He was also the one who helped with the two little ones, watching over Libby, and was always around to run over to Farkashes and doing other errands.

Terry was growing up into a strong young lady with her family's encouragement. They would constantly prod her with the fact that she was just as good as anyone else, and not to forget it. Johnny had recently found more studies about cleft palates being common among birth defects, affecting approximately one infant in every 700 born in the United States.

It was a fact that the cause started with a developmental abnormality in early pregnancy beginning at slightly different times and for various reasons. So that the chances that other children in the same family would also be affected by the problem differed with the two separate conditions. Therefore, the odds that the next children would have this similar trait had been somewhat remote.

Therefore Johnny and Dell felt greatly relieved when Libby and Katerina were born. Katerina was named after an elderly aunt who lived in Saxony, Germany. A delicate dark haired baby; she ate reasonably well and was gaining weight normally. And though Libby started out as a baby with eczema, possibly from a food allergy, Dell changed Libby's formula and kept her skin cool, as much as she could in the hot months after her birth in August.

However, she would persistently scratch her tiny arms until they bled, and now at six years old, she was a tough little robust tomboy always active outdoors, even in the winter without a sign of allergies except very dry skin.

Dell would never forget that fog-like day, thick with contaminated air spewing out from the mills all around them, especially during the ride to Columbia Hospital to have her fifth child. The air had already been impure, but now in addition, gritty residue blew off the grinding Westinghouse machinery going on night and day. Depending on which way the wind was blowing, sulphur smelling like rotten eggs blew through their valley. Some people bought gas masks just so they could breath, but most got used to the imperfect air around them.

One of the chief contributors was the Edgar Thompson works in Braddock, less than five miles away. Operating a number of blast furnaces, they integrated iron, steel into coal, and spewed out tons of smoke filled clouds by the minute.

Then there was Homestead, Duquesne, and National Tube in McKeesport, Clairton and Donora Works. From Pittsburgh to Donora, a thirty-seven mile stretch, US Steel operated eight major steel plants. The overall attitude of the people was that everyone was busy earning a living in these manufacturing cities, no matter what the cost.

Thanksgiving brought turmoil and confusion for Agatha, who was more in a quandary than ever before in the kitchen of her new home. Pondering which side of the turkey went into the oven first, and did the breast remain up or down, she erased the whole thing from her mind by sitting down beside her dining room table to finish polishing her last bright pink nail. Looking beautiful at this dinner, however it turned out to be, would prove to be the grace that forgave her for not cooking well.

"Oh that openhanded Joe, why did he want to celebrate the holiday here." She fretted and shuttered to think of all of those dirty little Albreds running around in their nice new house.

"He better get back here and finish this big old bird. Now let's see what else do we need here?" She'd shoved a loaf of bread into the cavity for stuffing – that ought to do. And they didn't need gravy, those beastie little kids can have all the grease on their mashed potatoes.

This was something that Agatha never had to do with a chef like her Mother Lizzie commandeering food preparation around the hotel. Gosh, maybe she should have watched once in a while. No, she loved shopping and dressing up too much, besides she peeled enough potatoes in her day. Today she had donned a fluffy white ruffled organdy apron over a new short dress, just like the one that the new starlet, Betty Grable, wore in one of the latest *Photoplay* magazines. And in fact she had swept her long auburn wavy hair to the top of her head securing it with pretty combs, copying the hairstyle as well.

Agatha sat down, crossing her chubby legs gingerly, scooping up a handful of peanuts while she waited for Joe to return from the store with the boys. They had moved at the end of summer to a cute cottage that Joe had built himself on Brown Avenue, about a half a mile up the hill from Turtle Creek. And though she had dreamed of a mansion much like the one in *Gone*

With The Wind, she thought that this little five-room brick house would suffice in the meantime.

Oh, how she envisioned a life on a plantation, like the beloved colonnaded beautiful southern mansion Tara, with its resounding porticos east and west, high above the rest of the countryside. In fact she had enveloped herself into the long lovely technicolor movie, last summer, three hours and forty-two minutes that sent her into a romantic whirlwind for months, of dreaming about how her life would be if she had been born in the South during this era.

Full billowing skirts floated gracefully around her ankles as she strolled about surveying the crops and gardens, while ordering the workers about. Her very own "Mammy" stood by to perform any whim that might tickle her fancy and authorizing noontime naps whenever she felt a wee bit tired. If anyone wanted to find her they would be escorted on to the expansive beautifully tiled terrace, where she lay languidly across a large silk chaise sipping a mint julep.

Maybe her sister-in-law, Dell, a lot like that "do-gooder" Melanie, would drop by every now and then trying to give her sound advice, while Johnny was very much like the kind and sensible Mr. O'Hara, making major decisions around the grand estate.

The handsome Rhett Butler or Ashley Wilkes was nowhere around for her romantic interest, but this part of the fantasy she could ignore, not wanting a male partner in any form. After this she'd urged Joe to grow a mustache, who responded that he would not fall into her "theatrics", as he now called it.

Agatha felt that she had finally won her independence from any physical encounter, and was relieved that she and Joe now slept in separate bedrooms. She thanked God for this bit of freedom from the pressures of immoral decadence, not caring if he wandered occasionally to some female presence, as long as he kept it a deep secret.

And as for those two little urchin kids they had, well they'd have to stay out of her hair, having their own nanny to deal with on a daily basis, or so she dreamed.

All seven Albreds piled into the 1936 gray Plymouth Johnny had managed to get a good deal on at a local car garage. The trip to Thanksgiving dinner would be their first voyage in it together. The interior had gray felt striped seats and he had thought it a nice clean bargain to behold. Johnny had supported Chrysler products, ever since he'd sold Chrysler Maxwell's at Dell's father Pop's Garage in the twenties.

He would never forget the day that Pop escorted Walter Percy Chrysler into the place in 1928. What an upstanding man, he would be President and Chairman of the Board of Chrysler until the day he died in 1935. But now Johnny was not to wallow in the past long, for his argumentative children started in on each other.

"Ouch, move over there Joel." Terry yelled pushing her brother at the same time, curly ringlets falling down around her face.

"You can't have all the seat to yourself, Sis, the car's only so big." Joel said, trying to reason with his sister. Meanwhile Libby squeezed in on her brother Ben's lap, while Dell situated Kat in her arms, as Johnny began to start the engine.

"This is going to be good, Aunt Agatha cooking a turkey." Ben remarked, as everyone in the back began to giggle. In the meantime Johnny and Dell tried to be quiet, but had to stifle a snicker.

"Alright that's enough Ben." Johnny spoke sternly, straightening his felt hat.

"Your aunt is the daughter of one of the best cooks that ever lived in Eastburg, your grandmother, Lizzie. I wouldn't be a bit surprised if she makes a wonderful dinner." All got quiet in the back of the car, when their father spoke, but Dell had to smile to herself knowing that Agatha wouldn't know a kettle from a saucepan if someone handed them to her.

"Hey Muggs, where de hecks m' white shoit, did ya iron it or not?" Phil stood throwing things out of his dresser drawers, his temper starting to flare, as he searched for the right clothes to wear to his sister's house for the holiday.

"That woman." He muttered to himself angrily, his dark hair messily hanging over his forehead. Most of his aggression

121

stemmed from having to go to Agatha's house and bad cooking, bah, he thought.

"What the hell good is she? She don't even woik, she sits aroun' here all day doin' nuttin' at all." He mumbled to himself. Just then his meek little wife, Mugsy, came running up the steps looking harried and downtrodden, her sad eyes cast to the floor like a poor forlorn little animal who'd been kicked one too many times.

"You callin' me Breddie?" She spoke meekly, as not to get her volatile husband more upset than he had already demonstrated.

"No, I'm callin' Franklin D., whodaya think de other person aroun' here is, huh? Though I hate to admit it's a goof like you." He shouted. And with these words he gave Margaret a swift shove, which forced her to bounce onto the bed clumsily.

"I told my daddy about you hitting me, and he's going to come out here. You better stop it Mister." Margaret said defensively, covering her thin body with both arms. And though she wasn't hurt this time, she cowered with the imminent fear of permanent crippling from her husband's wrath. During the peaceful times of the day when Breddie worked, she wondered what happened to the happiness they had in the beginning of their relationship, or was it something she had imagined.

Deep down inside she had been relieved to get away from the ranch with this smooth talkin' guy who stole her heart away with a single smile. Maybe Breddie was just her ticket away from her brutal farmer father, who only knew the hard cow punchin' plains of Montana, with never a kind word for anyone, including her and her poor mother. In her desperation Margaret thought about leaving. But where on earth would she go? Who wanted the likes of her?

"Yeah, yer ole man, what're ya talkin' about, he's de one who started beatin' ya when you was growin'up. No one wants ya babe, you're too darn dumb." He stood with hands on hips over her while she sobbed into the white chenille bedspread. Then he added more fuel to the fire.

"Ya can't even have a baby right." Margaret had had three miscarriages, one occurred after Phil had pushed her down the stairs. Now, after he knew her feelings were hurt badly, he inhaled hard on his cigarette, blowing smoke hard into Mugsy's face like he'd seen Dan Duryea do in the movie *"Scarlet Street."* She deserved disrespect, especially since he just couldn't love the lowdown dame anymore.

Actually, he wanted someone like Bette Davis, who would clout him back and take her punishment standin' up like a real lady, not hunched over like poor ole Muggs. A real knock out kind a broad, who'd swear at him sometime, den dey'd make up 'tween de sheets like civilized people. Phil paused for a moment, reflecting on the gutsiest woman he ever met. It had ta be his Mom, Lizzie. Nope, she wouldn't take any guff from any man. He wished he'd a treated her a little better. Then a tear narrowly escaped from his eye.

"Where's Margaret, Phil?" These were the first words out of Dell's mouth when they met up at Agatha and Joe's. He might a knowd it. But he was ready with a dandy excuse.

"Aw, I don' know Dell." He stared at his sister-in-law, who knew not to trust those dark lying eyes, as she further questioned him, already suspicious of his behavior to his wife.

"She's had dis headeek fer a while, just can't shake it." He answered, not meeting her eyes, but looking as immaculate as the village priest in a white shirt and black suit, Dell observed. *Yeah, he's the headache*, Dell thought, deciding to take his latest problem to Johnny. He would have to talk to his brother, even though he'd wanted to stay out of their marital affairs. Dell felt that someone had to intercede for that poor girl so far away from home, who was being mistreated. She wondered what Margaret's relationship was with her family.

"Hey, Unca Phil." Suddenly a football whizzed past them aimed at Phil, catching it on the fly, and was suddenly pulled into the the game in progress as Ben, Charlie and Joel, jumped around across the yard throwing their arms up in the air for a return pass. Concentrating on throwing a long one out to Ben and away from Dell's inquiring eyes, Phil was relieved and thankful for his nephew's interruption. In the meantime, Tommy ran backward for his toss, as Joel blocked and tackled him. The two wrestled to the ground and soon Charley and Joey's black and white pooch, Ruffo, was on them licking their faces all over, while they rolled around the grass laughing.

Dinner was as Dell suspected, half cooked, raw, or over cooked. The huge eighteen-pound turkey turned out with leathery skin and chunks of stringy meat sticking up all around the carcass. Thin pan grease loosened it a little on their plates, but the mashed potatoes were gray and lumpy, while the Brussels sprouts remained hard little rocks. Thank Heaven the canned vegetables and cranberry sauce were as perfect as Agatha appeared, smiling pleasantly serving a runny pumpkin pie holding an odd salty tasting unidentifiable crust.

Johnny, began the meal with a gentle grace, praying for Tommy who was missing from the throng for the first time this Thanksgiving.

"Dear Lord please bless our son, Tom, who is on shore protecting our country." Then as he took notice of the condition of the turkey, Johnny was sorry that he hadn't prayed for the cook.

Joe was enchanted by the first dinner in their new home with his wife, the perfect hostess and praised Agatha from the highest heights.

"And she did this all by herself." He said admiringly, beckoning toward Agatha, who bashfully lowered her head, tendrils of auburn hair falling down over her face, while she giggled heartily. Dell sat amazed that she was oblivious to the dreadful tasting food, and began to feel sorry for her ignorant sister-in-law for the first time in her life.

Phil was upset with Joe, knowing he had wine someplace, but hadn't shared it with the rest, or unless he was a stupid ass, he wouldn't have put up with his wife serving a mess like this.

"Yep – she's de only one who could pull dis off. Dat dame Betty Crocker can get some tips from dis dinner. It's a sight fer soa eyes and bad bellies." He said disdainfully. The boys began to snigger, but then looked up to see their Dad's piercing brown eyes taking them in, and sat back quietly smiling at their uncle.

Chewing endlessly on the tasteless grub, Johnny couldn't believe that his sister actually presented this food as edible. His mother must be throwing up dirt from her grave. But then, he thought it was probably the best that Agatha could manage, and once again he blamed it on the brain damage she'd contracted from scarlet fever when she was a kid. He knew that Dell had called her and offered help, but she had refused, wanting to do the entire meal herself. Johnny understood that his wife had learned so much more from Lizzie than her own daughter had.

Ruffo sat under the table quietly benefiting during the meal, gobbling ubiquitous pieces of turkey meat from the kids, who had also wedged bits and pieces under the rims of their plates. Dell had a napkin full of meat which she could not chew, then transferred the full napkin to her purse. Ben, who had stuffed a couple of his pockets with rock hard Brussels sprouts, filled up on dinner rolls, and piped up enthusiastically.

"Hey, let's go out and throw some more passes after we drink our pie." He then held the saucer up to his mouth crudely. His words and actions brought camaraderie from around the table, as everyone laughed heartily, even Johnny, abandoning courteousy to the wind.

Two weeks later on an ordinary winter Sunday as the Albred's rode home from six o'clock Mass, war was being declared on America. Johnny picked up a special edition of the *Pittsburgh Sun Telegraph* to read the alarming news of the bombing of United States bases on Pearl Harbor in Hawaii. Dell was frantic with worry about their son stationed somewhere in the Atlantic, never having let them know the exact location in his letters.

"Do you think that Tom will get shipped over to Japan, John?" She said. Her voice quivered with fear that he might be in the middle of the action. Johnny laid his hand on her arm as he was driving, trying to summon up strength to say the right things at this desperate time. He glanced into his wife's bright hazel eyes.

"Dell, this war has been going on for two years all around Europe, now we're all in it. And mark my words it's going to affect every one of us, not just our sons." Dell caught the plural of sons, which raised a new scare in her stomach. Is this what we raised our boys for? To leave home and fight for their country in some foreign city? She thought, and could not imagine having three sons leaving home for this reason. It broke her heart. She looked over at Johnny noticing that he had lost a lot of hair, and was nearly bald since Tommy had left home. She also started to get gray hairs at almost forty years old. Just then her thoughts turned toward Tommy as a tiny boy at the hotel.

"Johnny, I'll never forget when he used to sing for the boarders. He knew all the words to My Bwue Heben. Remember they used to put pennies in his hat. I never liked seeing him out there on display, but Lizzie and Zach loved to encourage him. And eventually I had to join in with the rest. Oh dear, there were good and bad times back then." She sighed.

Ben, Joel, Terry and Libby smiled in the back seat hearing another anecdote about their oldest brother again, as Terry cried out in a sad voice.

"We might never see our brother again, they'll capture him and torture him."

"Nah, he'll come home." Ben spoke consolingly. "Besides he's far away from Pearl Harbor, you know your geography, don't you Sis? Pearl Harbor's in the Pacific, and Tom's in the Atlantic Ocean." The other's all looked over at their brother who was confident in expressing himself, leaving no room for doubt by any of his siblings.

And though his mother always badgered him about where his homework was, and why he never brought home a book from school, Ben would always have an answer, speaking in his quiet demeanor.

"I did it in study hall, like we're supposed to Mom, it's what the Brothers want us to do." Ben liked St. Thomas' High School and seemed to have a bright future ahead, though it was most likely he'd be going into the Army, the way things were going.

Johnny's words rang true all around neighborhoods of the nation, as the United States began preparing for the long time conflict. The campaign being so close to home took most Americans by surprise, and mobilization came with many sacrifices. Auto production stopped immediately, as the last car in Pontiac, Michigan, came off the assembly line. A gray sedan with black victory trim, which meant no more shinny chrome, an embellishment that Americans revered in their automobiles.

Factory's re-fitted their machinery to construct tanks, planes, small boats, and gun mounts, as Pittsburgh was turned into a giant war machine with companies like U.S.Steel and

126

Westinghouse overloaded with orders for overseas equipment. Shipyards expanded with great speed, as did the aviation industry, which was the first to hire women to fill the drafted men's positions, proving that female workers did the delicate and tedious aircraft work better. A much lower absenteeism rate gave them a permanent place and higher salary than other jobs at 70.5 cents an hour.

Men like Johnny and Phil were personally affected when they were limited to two packs of cigarettes a day. Whiskey in particular became scarce, and beer becoming a watery pleasure, which Phil claimed he wouldn't touch with a ten-foot pole, as distilleries switched to one hundred percent manufacture of explosives. Dell was secretly happy about all of this abstinence, even though she knew it was temporary.

Mr. and Mrs. Farkash across the street struggled with the new government system of rationing foods in their little neighborhood grocery store. War Rationing Book #1 came out in March of 1942 with 190 million copies printed. Pushing up the withered sleeves of her old gray knit sweater, the poor elderly woman complained about the inconvenience.

"Oh, Mrs. Albred, I can't figure this out, please be patient with me, oh those crazy government agents. The Mister and I looked over the list, oh, I have to get my other glasses," she said nervously. Dell sympathized with the elderly woman having to go through the difficult aspects of war while consulting her list of directions. Storeowners and all Americans had to make proper adjustments to buying goods in wartime.

The official book of twenty-eight consecutively numbered stamps started out with sugar, and then came shoes and coffee, which Americans tended to hoard the most. Meat and butter were the highest in points, lowest being canned milk. Red and blue stamps in war ration book four were worth ten points each, with red and blue tokens used to make change for red and blue stamps only when purchases were made, while brown and green stamp point values never changed.

Allotment stamps limited food and gasoline as well. An "A" card for cars limited them to a mere three gallon of gas a week. The government control was difficult, but people everywhere repeated, "there's a war on, and our boys and girls are over there fighting for our freedom".

Soon military uniforms appeared on the streets, in stores, movie theatres, church and many other public places. Dell hung a Navy banner showing a single white star on a dark background in their living room window symbolizing their son and brother taking part in warfare. Every day a new neighbor's son was called up by the draft, with a new law soon going into effect stipulating that additional males between 45 and 64 years old who had not before been required to sign up must do so immediately at their local recruitment center.

During one of the many evenings of shrill air raids when all of Eastburg and surrounding areas were required to darken their windows from any offending light, the Albreds' phone rang in the corner of the living room table. Joel ran to answer it.

"Mom, the operator says she has a long distance call for you." Twelve-year-old Joel began to feel bad that he was part of what might be a harbinger of bad news. Dell's heart nearly stopped as she snatched the receiver, with thoughts of Tommy being wounded or missing in action as she had just heard had happened to the Sokolowski boy. She waited with trepidation while the operator connected her to the party calling.

"Hello Dell." Spoke her sister, Mary pensively.

"Oh, hi Mary, you scared me." Her voice calmed.

"You know I'm on pins and needles here waiting for news about Tommy. Well we did get a letter the other day, but it was delayed a couple of weeks, so we still don't know what base he's stationed at. Of course I thought you were him."

"I know Dell, but this is good news for a change. I'm pregnant; we're going to have a baby. The doctor said I have to take special care, but everything should be fine." Mary sounded so happy, Dell joined in with her jubilation, wishing her the best, and offering to come out and help her when the baby was born. She missed her sister who now had a beautiful home in the suburbs of Cleveland. They had always been close, but visited just a couple times a year now. She still seemed so far away, though it was only two hours by train.

After hanging up the phone, Dell thought of what she could hand down from her kids to the new baby. Many baby things were not being made these days with a war on, and toys were one of them, since those same companies were now making small parts for large equipment to be shipped overseas. Homemade wood scooters, wagons, dolls and pull-toys began to appear in yards.

The kids were all busy in the war effort now; Joel collected cans, scrap iron and waste paper with his friend Kovick. They would pull their wagons around the streets, with a dumping off place where a huge truck would pick up the barrels and boxes full of the precious cargo to be melted down into machinery. Terry and Ben started a Victory Garden in the backyard. Libby helped plant the seeds along with her brother and sister. Every one of their friends were now involved in helping with the war effort in Eastburg.

In the evening Libby would run to turn on the Philco for the family's entertainment. They were lucky to have their console radio, since they were no longer being made, since all of their spare parts and tubes were being used for war materials as well.

The favorite mystery program this Friday night was "The Fat Man". "He's stepping on the scales..." Spoke the deep resonant voice of Raymond Burr.

Libby and Joel loved to sit right up close to the sound system, listening and capturing every reverberation registering into their imaginations, picturing characters by descriptions, dialogue between voices, and deciphering the foils they encountered during the story line. Sometime their eyes lit up in horror, as their mind filled with fear projected from individual images. Six-year-old Libby was particularly impressionable to these urges.

"I'm afraid to go to the bathroom, now." She said during the KDKA station break.

"Yeah, the boogie man's gonna get ya." Joel put in.

"Joel don't scare your sister." Dell reprimanded, concerned that Libby shouldn't be listening to scary stories. Usually this one wasn't, but it was hard to monitor radio programs.

Terry, who was learning how to crochet by her mother's side, was concentrating on her knots; therefore she did not join in. For this Libby was grateful, because her sister might have said something unpleasant. In the end Joel had to stand in the hallway until his little sister finished.

This program would be followed by the broadcasted series of The Adventures of Mr. and Mrs. North. Nicki and Nora set out to solve every misdeed, proving once again that crime did not pay. Everyone would guess who the suspect might be.

On Sunday, the funny papers were spread all over the living room floor, as Terry and Joel read their favorite cartoon characters, who had all joined up with the military forces battling conflicts in their comic strips. Joe Palooka was in the army, Tillie The Toiler, Terry and the Pirates, and Smilin' Jack Smith were suited up in military outfits, as were many others.

One of Dell's worst nightmares was to come true during the next few weeks, as a new homeowner bought the home they were renting. Adding to the consternation, Johnny harbored resentment toward Mr. Fischer, their new landlord, knowing things about this man that upset his principles.

"I've got bad feelings about these Fischers buying the house, Dell I know that bastard and he cheats on his wife with some blond that works near me. Let's go out and look at that house in the country that Goss told me about at work last week on Saturday evening." Johnny was working most nights, double and triple time during these war days, which enabled them to save quickly for a good down payment.

The next Saturday evening, Dell, Terry and Libby went to see *"How Green Was My Valley"* at the Frederick Theatre. When they came in the door they could hear a commotion in the hallway. It was Johnny hurling insults down the inside staircase, which the family never used. He had begun drinking after supper, which caused him to loose his usual self-control.

"Yeah, come'on up here, ya damn asshole, I'll break your bloody neck." His face turned fiery red with fury, as his husky body grew taut with fomenting rage and resentment for a man without any morals. Then to think he had the audacity to move in under the same roof instead of renting it out to someone else repelled Johnny even more. Dell could hear Fischer, who seemed to be standing by his inside door.

"The sooner you gypsies get the hell out, the better." Was his last response, making Johnny even madder as he started

130

down the stairs. Ben and Joel, who had already grown to their father's five foot nine height, stepped forward to hold him back from something he would regret. Dell, who knew he'd had one too many which gave him the courage to act out like this, pleaded with him in her soft appealing voice.

"John, don't do this, you'll be very sorry tomorrow if you hurt that man. Let's just find a place to move to soon." Johnny looked at his wife and knew she was right.

8. Churchill

The younger Albred's would grow up knowing their way around expansive fields and pastures bordering the new family home. The old brown insul bricked farmhouse built in 1885, sat at a vertex next to the steep grade of Churchill Road, altitudinous over all the landscape within miles around. Once a well-trodden horse path, the route was an artery leading to business route twenty-two which ran east and west to and from the main city of Pittsburgh.

The tall and asymmetrical structure in appearance due to two front rooms, additions added on last, elevated the dimensions from the original backside of the house. Nonetheless, the five spacious rooms stood poised and ready to accommodate the exuberant Albred family upon their retreat ten miles northeast from the city of Eastburg. This would be an enormous change for Johnny and Dell, whose families had come from Hungary and Czechoslovakia to settle among the ethnic neighborhood of Bessemer Terrace, and Eastburg, the town where Lizzie and Zach started their successful hotel at the turn of the century. Their growing up years and courtship had begun in this valley where they still had many friends.

Their relatives stood by in astonishment.

"Ooh, sa far from everything, way out here in the country." Agatha and Phil Albred, Johnny's sister and brother moaned. Their faces all scrunched up in disbelief. No friends. No stores around.

"And you're goin' t' sell your car t' put cash down on dis? How are ya goin' t' git around." Phil croaked out in a gruff voice. His rugged lifestyle of gambling, drinking and vice had taken its toll on him through the years, to say nothing of the miserable marriage that ended in disaster well before Johnny tried to moderate. Poor Margaret had packed her bags and taken a train back to the life she had in Montana for another better or for worse.

Johnny and Dell were elated with their six thousand dollar discovery in Wilkins Township, School Taxes set at twenty-three dollars yearly. They had saved long and searched hard to find a house to raise their family away from the smoke fumes of the vile city.

Moving day to the quiet countryside became an adventure for all the young Albreds, who took turns taking care of their two year old sister, Kat, who was just beginning to get into trouble. Exploring the big house that would be all theirs, meant climbing all the way to a bare attic, having no floor, only cross beams, which they would straddle to examine each corner for interesting objects left behind by former tenants. Hearing Dell's loud distressful wail down in the kitchen had them tumbling down the steps to her rescue.

"Ooh no, take the children out in the backyard, Terry, we're going to tear these all out. Joel and Ben stay here and give us some help here. We've got to rip these out". Dell could turn into a civil engineer at the drop of a helmet - when action was called for - and this was one of those occasions.

"What is it mom?" They begged to know, hating the look of their mother feeling so disgruntled about something they knew nothing about.

"Just go out with your sister. Terry please take them out in the yard, now, and keep them out there." Since it wasn't often that their mother reacted this way, shouting out like this, they were startled into obeying immediately.

"What is it Terry?" Libby asked her again. Terry seemed to know what these situations were about well in advance. Her older sister had been Libby's worldly guide to knowing why people, even their mother, behaved in the way they sometime did.

"They found roaches deep in the cracks of the cupboards." Terry said.

"They're a sign of a very bad housekeeper, mom doesn't want that on her record, and she doesn't want word getting out that we even had one. Understood?" Libby heeded her ten year old sister, who knew the ropes about what people were feeling, especially their mother, one of the cleanest people she knew in the whole world.

Libby learned later that day, that roaches were indeed found in the beautiful oak cabinets that lined all the walls of the kitchen. The prior homeowners had been slipshod with their living habits and Dell, having worked under the antiseptic hand of Lizzie Albred, knew how to clean expertly from bottom up rapidly, knowing some of these household pests personally. Mostly she'd despised the dreaded bedbugs which would show up every now and then on an untidy border coming from some strange land straight into their hotel rooms.

A long and wide sloping backyard stretched over an acre in the back of the house, featuring cherry and apple trees and an extensive vegetable garden, of which Dell was titleholder. A locust tree lined border ran alongside deserted Spellman's Lane, providing the only barrier running between the Albred's yard and the rugged and stony pasture of the Swiss Farm Dairy. This landlocked area permitted the free and easy cows to graze and gaze lazily while they went about chewing their cud.

When summer came Libby and Terry would discover the smooth verdant mounds of the Edgewood Country Club, beyond the cow pasture where they could run barefoot all summer, never having to wear a pair of shoes, except to church on Sunday. On hot summer nights the greenkeeper's sprinkling system provided showers to splash through in bare feet, a recreation that did not exceed wintertime sledding down the steepest pinnacle on the golf course called green eleven.

When school friends challenged any kid's sledding and tobogganing skills with a night on green eleven, they had to be ready with speed and accuracy and a steering run set fast and furious downhill. It could be a treacherous ride full of rough terrain around a huge cement sewer at the bottom, a hazard to be avoided at all costs. Accordingly, the adept "sledders" were always singled out as quick and praiseworthy, and looked up to by the more cautious others who stood by and warily watching for fear of imminent danger.

The history of this homestead originated before the turn of the century as a local provisions store, as older neighbors told of buying basic necessities there. In as much as proof of this, two large display picture windows looked directly out onto Churchill cemetery across the street, where many of the inhabitants of the area now lay buried.

In time, Libby would learn the name, shape, and location of tombstones as so many individuals, almost the way a child learns the alphabet or a mental map of the street they live on. Names of family groupings like Advise, Belle and Jonah, pink granite monument markers with engraved grapes above their connected names stood prominent above the rest. The Brown family had a large monument in one corner, a dark dulled grey stone, black and neglected with age.

She and her friend Joanie, whom she'd just met in second grade at Gray School nearby, were the only ones who seemed to visit the abandoned Brown family after death. There was also a tiny tombstone for a baby girl, Cynthia Ann Brown, who had lived just one month. Libby and Joanie would wonder how the infant had died, but her friend seemed to have had some experience with life and death.

"She probably choked to death, my baby cousin Mary had the same thing happen to her and we were so sad about it." Her eight-year-old friend said matter of factly. Joanie was one year older than Libby, her dark, wavy, thick hair shone next to Libby's straight blond pigtails as pepper next to salt. They would sing together from the *Hit Parade* magazine, reaching high clear notes, and developing duets in ranges only their young emergent vocal chords would allow. Many of these were war inspired songs, being played and sung for our troops fighting all over the world.

These heartfelt tunes of loneliness and sentimentality struck every American deep in the core of their being, since the person fighting on another shore was a son, sister, daughter, brother, father or all three. Tunes like; "The White Cliffs Of Dover", "Say A Prayer For The Boys Over There," " Don't Sit Under The Apple Tree With Anyone Else But Me" or "You'd Be So Nice To Come Home To." People sometime sobbed openly out on the street for a loved one killed or missing in the war.

The horrors of warfare were deep in progress when broadcaster Gabriel Heater, made today's announcements in a deeply concerned voice, attracting his listeners to the radio.

"Ah there's good news tonight." Johnny listened hopefully this November 12, 1942, as he relayed a major victory for the United States Navy over the Japanese at the battle of Guadalcanal on the Solomon Islands in the South Pacific. He agreed with Heater that this was good news, since many disasters had fallen to Americans and its allies thus far. Knowing that Tommy was off the coast of Normandy, the rosary was recited daily for his safety.

They'd gotten some nice letters recently that he was safe and couldn't wait to see the new home on Churchill Road. But Johnny had only to read between the lines to detect his son's realm of fear about being right up in the front lines of this terrible war. Within the news context Heater commented on the allegiance of the American railroad, which had been weakened by the depression less than ten years earlier, and now carried the whole burden of the war effort, transporting cars, trucks, rubber and gas, making the tracks the only alternative for distribution. The high percentage of 97% of the troops and 90% of military materials were also moved by rail.

The Chicago Bears dominated football along with players Sid Luckman and Harry Clark. Tommy Harmon, All-American halfback at the University of Michigan led a charmed career in the Air Force. Sports figures were admired for sacrificing their career for the armed forces.

An automobile ad followed the sports, which caused Johnny to wonder who was buying them, when they couldn't drive them without gasoline. Maybe the manufacturers had a huge inventory in Detroit. And then again, the ration took place in only seventeen states. He wondered what the other thirty-one were doing with all their gasoline.

He missed his old '36 Plymouth, but they needed the rest of the money for the house payment and he could only get three gallons of gas a week due to his "A" sticker for a government named "non-essential" vehicle. And heck there was a regular bus service to carry him to and from Eastburg to work at 6:30 a.m. and home at 4:30 p.m., since it was the transportation for Westinghouse employees. Johnny liked the hard working Belledaino Family, who came from nearby North Braddock running a pretty reliable busing business.

Utilizing this transportation worked well unless they took the round about route at 2:20 or 10:00 in the evening, then a half hour trip became an hour, since this route would take them ten miles out into Crescent Hills and through another township,

Penn's Hills, mostly remote farms. Fare was a reasonable twenty cents or three tokens for a quarter. The kids could walk two or three miles to wherever they were going. Libby and Terry just walked over the hill to Gray School; they could even come home for lunch.

Johnny worried incessantly about Joel getting in with bad companions and some how going astray, probably because he was a mild mannered boy. Now attending Wilkins Junior High, further up Churchill Road. He didn't believe his son had much ambition academic wise, though he was a smart boy, if he'd only apply himself. Nonetheless Johnny figured he'd be a craftsman like a carpenter or plumber or even a landscaper of some kind. What really made him mad was the way Dell would defend their son. He had to give her a look a couple of times to stay quiet.

Joel was such a good kid, though skinny and wiry in stature, helping Dell around the yard, and God knew there was a lot to do around there. One of the most recent tasks was to take all of the garbage and cans out of that heap at the bottom of the driveway. The former tenants had dumped everything relentlessly over by a fence, presenting a health risk. Dell had now found out that garbage collection was available, and soon boxes and barrels of unknown decaying materials stood by ready to be hauled away by heavy trucks. Joel buried the rest deep in the ground and started a compost behind the proposed chicken coop he would build.

The unsightly area would become a veritable flourishing rock garden populated with blooms of every variety. Bright hues of spring yellow and purple irises encircled the bed of orange summer tiger lilies and tall blue and pink delphiniums gracing the center of the rocky bed. Sweet Williams and late season golden chrysanthemums glowed in the bright autumn sun. In the midst of this flowering choir, Dell placed an ornate and lovely statue of the Blessed Mother.

My inspiration, she thought, saying her daily prayer to the Virgin Mary. *O Mary conceived without sin, pray for us who have recourse to thee. Please keep our Tommy and all of our children safe over there, wherever they are. And please let this darn war be over soon.* She would cry, interceding to the Blessed Mother. Tommy had been home a couple of times, but seemed very edgy and nervous which was understandable having been in the line of duty. Saying he'd seen men die beside him, but did not talk about it, but raging nightmares told the real story.

Dell was pleased with her accomplishments in improving the landscape of their home; of course a lot of the plants came from Heartland Greenhouses next door. The workers there would throw many nice plants over the hillside, and right into their backyard. Dell would take her pick basket and inspect the rejected sprouts and older discarded plants, dragging them over to the yard for tender nurturing. She discovered she had a way with these "foundlings"; she was pleased when tiny buds appeared, multiplying in the spring.

The old house itself needed multitudinal repairs, like a new roof and shingles over the old insul brick layer. The big country kitchen needed to be tiled around the sides, since the fifty year old walls were uneven and needed support. It could also use new windows and a new cabinet sink, though she didn't know where the money would come from. The unsightly old fixture stood with a skirt in front of the pipes. The two bedrooms upstairs for the girls and boys would have to be painted after the old unsightly wallpaper was removed.

Eventually they would get to everything, but right now she trusted Mother Nature the most, cultivating the fertile soil, which had always been farmland belonging to the Martin's in the eighteen hundreds. A noted early family of the Churchill area, their daughter, Mrs. Leax, lived right next door. A beautiful rose garden of every variety bloomed in her front yard. Dell loved the roses; wanting to grow a special garden of her own someday.

The Martin's land had been part of the Swiss Farm Dairy. The landsite looked very much like the mountainous highlands of Switzerland, therefore Dell could understand how the familiarity with the land encouraged the Koniz and Fribourg families to settle here around 1928, bringing over friends and relatives to help with the milking, bottling and other farm work.

The Koniz family lived right on the downgrade of steep Churchill Road, while the Fribourgs lived on a dirt road, leading down into a lower area at the bottom of the rise, past the barn and the bottling building to their large old country Swiss style home. Mrs. Fribourg could be seen carefully nurturing her beautiful many colored dahlias and bright blue delphiniums robustly growing in her garden in front of the house. A long white braid crowned her head, framing her friendly cheery face, always ready to greet visitors to the dairy at any time of day. She would smile and talk with the Albred children if any of them appeared unannounced for an emergency quart of milk, even though they had regularly scheduled delivery every day.

"Ah so, it's the Albred guhl, vich von are youh?" She would inquire in her melodious broken Swiss tone. Mr. Fribourg was just as pleasant, chatting openly with them, his dark eager eyes shone down above his thick dark mustache moving happily, as he laughed with his wife. They had a grown son named Hans, who towered over the children wearing high big black rubber boots, on his way to the bottle washing station. He would talk loud and rough on his way to work. They would try to avoid him, even though he was only teasing them in his brassy voice

"Ah so, und vere ist da Lilly one's going?" Then he would challenge them, as he stood in their path. This gesture would force his mother and father to laugh uproariously.

Mr. and Mrs. Koniz were a quiet family, raising a family of four sons and a daughter, who were friends of the older Albred's. If perchance any member of their family stopped at their lovely home on Churchill Road at Christmas time, Mrs. Koniz would greet them kindly. A fragile sickly woman, she would graciously wrap delicate cookies and Swiss chocolates into a package for them to bring home.

Johnny, the official administrator of the "domain", searched through farm journals and catalogues for products to cultivate the soil, and this year their new serious vocation was to raise chickens. Already purchasing a few peeps, now living in a small pen, he ordered supplies from a local lumber store to build them a coop as soon as possible.

Dell fell into the role of production engineer, carrying out plans to begin to live off the land, assigning everyone tasks to do in the big yard. Ben and Joel each had a large section of lawn to plant and groom throughout the summer. They were appropriately named: Ben's lawn and Joel's lawn. Competition lay between the brothers as to who had cultivated the greenest stretch of newly seeded grass. The entire lower part of the property bordered by tall robust locust trees, boasted their first garden; yards of tomatoes plants, corn rows, cabbage, lettuce, onions, peppers, and green beans growing in the fertile earth. Dell and Joel headed up the rest of the Albreds, being put to work to pick an abundance of harvest at the end of that first summer.

Next year Dell planned to have a much bigger spot just for tomatoes, since they grew so rapidly in the sun there. A friend of Johnny's from the Westinghouse, Howard Enders, owning one of the only motorized plows in the area, would once again dig up the half an acre garden area for them. Examining the fruits of her work that sat on the basement shelves neatly canned and ready to heat for winter meals, Dell thought about once again experimenting with the pungent assortment of piccalilli, planning to grow all the ingredients for the mixture of cauliflower, pickles, and onions again next year.

Dell looked out of the tiny basement window above the washtubs that Monday while putting her last load of colored clothes through the ringer. It was a fair November day, Should she hang out the wash on the large length of clotheslines encircling the upper lawn above Ben's lawn? She decided no, that she would just pin them up in the dry basement, since the days were now growing too short.

As the ubiquitous clumps of laundry slid into the rinsing tub, Dell spied Libby and Ben in the backyard. Ben always seemed to have some kind of a plan up his sleeve, not at all impetuous like his older brother. He had worked at Kennywood Park as a lifeguard that summer right after graduation, but now the U.S. Government already made his future plans for him.

Dell would never forget the day he strolled in the door with a pile of the mail, leafing through the cards and letters and resting on a single one. He started to laugh, as if it was a postcard from his buddy.

"Ha, here it is, I've been waiting for you to write to me. A nice letter starting with Greetings." Ben chuckled, but Dell knew it was the government claiming yet another son of hers to fight for their country. Reading the look on her face Ben responded, taking it all in stride, glad that the suspense of entering the service had finally been broken. It had just been a matter of time, since many of his friends had already left home.

"Don't worry, Mom, I don't think the war has much longer to go, and who knows maybe I'll get a desk job." But Dell was heartsick that another member of the family would be gone.

"Hey, there's no one left to even pal around with here anymore, it's getting lonely."

Ben had filled out handsomely, growing quite tall during this last year, graduating from St. Thomas High School in May. Her sister Mary, Paul and their new baby, Sylvia had come. Little Sylvia was a sweet dark haired child who seemed to play nicely with Katrina, a year older and now already walking. Terry and Joel watched Sylvia and Katrina while they went to North Braddock for the ceremony in Paul's Packard.

"Benedict John Albred, with honors." Pronounced the principal, as Ben strolled across the school stage to receive his diploma. Johnny and Dell sat with pride, their eyes misting over. This was a solemn moment. Their son shook hands with the priest, smiling to himself on his way back to his seat.

Later on the way home, Mary had remarked, wondering why her sister wasn't as savvy as she about worldly happenings, and what was going on with some of the kid's lives.

"Dell, did you know that Ben would be valedictorian of his class?" Ben had always been one of Mary's favorites, sometime spending summers at their home near Cleveland, and it was obvious that she was interested that his future would be bright. Dell meekly shook her head no, staring at her sister, who's hair had always been almost white, but now appeared to be snow white, while Dell's remained dark brown lined with grey streaks.

"Ben has always been a quiet boy, keeping mostly to himself. Do you know he rarely brought a book home, Mary? It must have all come easy to him; he's like his father that way." Johnny stared out the window thinking there was no money for college, it didn't matter how smart his son turned out to be. He glanced down the street where the hotel had stood for forty years before it burned to the ground that election day. There had been plenty of cash back then – they had been rollin' in dough – but then Lizzie had also been in charge. God knew she spent a lot of money on his education, but with one goal in mind, that he would become a priest. Any other vocation was unacceptable for Lizzie.

Libby was a happy go lucky child, who could rise out of her doldrums in eager anticipation of doing something interesting each day of the year. Her blond pigtails bounced as she raced around the yard loving all of the seasons. And though allergies seem to consume her with incessant sneezing in the fall, and eczema in the winter, she seemed to be a peaceful child.

For the most part Libby seemed to avoid the turmoil of family personality clashes boiling over, usually at the breakfast or lunch table, and seemingly when the omnipresence of their father was absent from the meal. Terry was beginning puberty, and Dell sensed that her moods had shifted to angry and sadness as young womanhood loomed on the horizon. But then, Joel was also growing into a man, and Dell did not know how to help ease this passage for her son, hoping that Johnny would talk to him patiently about growing into manhood.

Consequently, when Terry and Joel argued, she would end up being hurt, running upstairs to her sanctuary in the huge bedroom she shared with her sisters. Dell would sometime go up after her and talk about what life held for a woman, and how she could approach the rough times ahead. Terry was a different person than Dell at age eleven. For one thing, she had a stronger disposition and was already physically developed for her young age, and a stubbornness which sometime made her hard to talk to as well.

Nevertheless, Dell would sit down next to her on the bed, putting her arm around her daughter, who faced a different world than she knew in the twenties. Dell felt the sadness and discomfort of her children, and tried to get them to talk it out.

"Honey, what is really the matter, it's not the way Joel spreads peanut butter on his toast. He's not to blame for everything." She said compassionately. Terry lay on the bed, her head in the pillow, curly dark hair tangled in her tears.

"Mom, none of the boys like me, they'll never like me. I look too funny with my scars. If only I could be normal." She continued to sob through the words. Dell looked at her with a pained expression. She didn't feel that Terry's nose looked too bad, but knew that she would probably have at least one more plastic surgery on her scars. Dell looked into her beautiful eyes.

"Well then they're not worth it. Don't worry when that special boy comes along, you'll know it. You have a pretty smile and a good personality and you look nice all the time. That will be enough to attract the man of your dreams. And he will be worth it." She hugged her daughter lovingly, wishing it could be different too, but knew that God had blessed her in every other way.

Later, Terry was once again set free from all troubles sitting behind the sewing machine, a bird flying out of entrapment. She would seam up a new pillowcase or repair some of the family's pile of worn clothes that Dell had given her to mend. Her dream was to someday buy one of the new electric sewing machines that would soon be available, maybe even become a seamstress when she was older.

Libby never understood her sister's moody ways, and tried to avoid her wrath. Terry could be generous and giving when she wanted to be, but most of the time she would stay out of her older sister's way by returning to the never ending task of weeding the garden, or cleaning and lining the canning shelves with pretty paper for her mom's new seasonal addition of goods. Washing the bathroom fixtures was required almost daily. Afterward Libby would go to help Ben or Joel with their outside jobs, which were much more interesting than housework.

Swinging under two cherry trees beside the cellar door was her favorite summertime pleasure. Pulling up a strong rope thrown roughly over a branch with a piece of wood for a seat, Libby was in heaven. It wasn't very comfortable, but she was able to go a little way up into the air, holding on tight with both hands.

Today, Ben had carried up flat stones from the land below to lay in a walk along his lawn, and after finishing he smiled at his accomplishment and looking in his sister's direction with enthusiasm. Libby could tell by his interest in her new concoction, that they might do something exciting together. He just stared concentratedly for a few minutes, then like clockwork he said the magic words.

"C'mon, Lib, we're going to make you a good swing. Where do you want it to hang?" He exclaimed in his best big brother voice, his dark eyes shining with adventure. She ran as fast as she could ahead of him in great anticipation, to the different corners of the yard, trying to make a quick decision.

"Over here, no, over there." She said, running enthusiastically back and forth in bare feet, knowing that this day she would have his full attention. Spare time was something that Ben didn't have, since he had worked all summer and would soon be going away to the service just like Tommy who had just reenlisted for five more years.

"No, over here." She ran to the bottom lot of their property, which ran along Spellman's Lane down to a little old house where an elderly couple lived. Maimie and Pap Spellman. There was no water or heat in their little white dilapidated cottage. Just a rain barrel where Maimie washed her long white hair. They lit candles to ward off the darkness at night. During the winter cold, Pappy brought in a scuttle of coal to burn inside their huge iron stove, which they also cooked on.

An outside toilet took care of their other needs, but Dell and Johnny were concerned about the elderly couple's health, becoming their patron family, a place where they could come for water and then usually Joel would take food and holiday meals down to them.

Maimie seemed to favor Joel the most, because he worked closest to their house while working in the garden, it was then that Maimie would sing in her yard entertaining him while he worked.

"Put on your big white bonnet with the blue ribbons on it while you hitch old Dobbin to the sleigh...." Then she would laugh, and Joel would laugh with her. This would make her happy.

"I know the ideal place for your new swing." Pronounced Ben.

"Where? Where? Libby shouted back at her brother, happy inside that he'd made the final decision. Since it was all his idea.

"Down here under the plum trees. It will be shady and private and your friends can come up the lane to visit you here."

144

At that he set to work fashioning a long branch to fit across several small trees and a proper board seat with a new rope through the holes. It was the most beautiful swing she had ever seen. But most of all she couldn't believe what a good carpenter her brother was. She wondered how he knew how to do these things so well.

Once or twice he visited what would be her "camp" under the plum trees to make sure the swing was operating perfectly, but soon he would leave their home to fight in the world war. Libby would be forever grateful for that day, and thought of him far away as she swung mightily into the air singing all the sad sentimental war songs from the radio.

The cemetery across the road would soon be full of snow, but during the past summer evenings at dusk on hot days, she and her new friend Joanie would stroll cautiously through the cement-pillared entrance into the graveyard. After a while they would reach the end of the gravel road to a section where an aluminum pillar marked a grave. A corroded metal Paraclete sat at the pinnacle, its wings outspread ready to fly into the sky. Walking down the red-slagged silver maple tree lined road toward the veteran's monument, they would dare each other to go over and touch the relic.

"Go ahead Lib, you're the fastest runner between us. Give a good knock on the side. Let's see what happens." Joanie would say daringly. Libby, seldom passing up a dare or a challenge, would steal up to the iodized marker, its name of Schmidt nearly worn away with time and weather. Two sharp thuds brought a "tink" back from inside, prompting a shrill of fear inside Libby, who sprang back beside Joan, the two of them running fast fearing for their lives, breathlessly gasping with laughter toward the iron entrance gates.

Dell would often repeat to houseguests, elaborating on the standing family joke.

"Those people across the street never cause trouble. They're the best neighbors anyone can have" Dell would jest, all the while thinking about what was really scary about living out in the country during their first six months as country greenhorns, when the night loomed as dark as ink penetrating your mind with fear of an unknown creature lurking nearby and the stark quiet became overwhelming.

The absolute and complete silence at night, contrasted with the cacophony of living right next to the trolley tracks where streetcars came and went all night long clacking steel wheels loudly through the dense darkness. With passersby shouting out conversations with lunch buckets in tow on their way to and from different work shifts at the Westinghouse plant. There was always someone they knew, a close neighbor or even Mrs. Farkash in the store across the street, who would hear a cry for help and come swiftly over to help. But now, to add to her nighttime fear, Johnny was also working double shifts since the beginning of the war and was hardly ever home with the family in the hours of darkness.

One winter evening Dell heard a loud sound, as if a wolf were howling, outside close to the house. Frightened out of her wits, she went upstairs and woke Ben, who came lumbering downstairs in his pajama bottoms and no shirt, though it was winter. She was relieved that he hadn't left for induction into the armed forces yet.

"It's coming from the back of the house." She whispered. He immediately turned around, running back up the steps two at a time, for his twenty-two rifle, which he kept for shooting rats that would occasionally run in and out of their back wall when they lived in the city. Now, Slithering slowly down the steps again, he held his gun out high and circled round the house. Wakened by the commotion, Joel, Terry and Libby followed by tiny Kat, all moved down the steps in unison stumbling over their nighties and pajamas huddling together by the door. Eyes wide open, they crouched apprehensively at the back door waiting, filled with fear of the unknown creature somewhere out in the black abysses of the cold dark night.

"Hoo, hoo, hoo." they heard, pinning their ears to the outside door. Ben soon came running back with the news of a huge owl flapping his wings at the top of the tallest locust tree in the yard.

"It must be after some field mice." He said. Claiming the looks of admiration from the younger members of the family, slinging his gun behind his back.

"But it's as big as Kat here. Boo!" Ben warned with good humor. At this, they all chuckled, as they had never heard an owl or any animal in the city, for all the trolleys, automobiles, sirens, bells and people moving about all through the night right next to their bedrooms.

"Well, I guess it's another thing we'll just have to get used to." Dell said, feeling a little bit sheepish after precipitating an upset in the household.

"Thanks for waking us all up, Mom". Terry remarked sarcastically, before running back to the room closing the door before Libby and Kat could get there, who would have to find their own way back to the bed in the dark room.

In the beginning of December, vicious rumors began circulating around the plant that Phil was part of a ration coupon scheme in Altoona, a new business that racketeers latched onto that was similar to bootleg liquor. Johnny was furious when he overheard two guys talking about this new scheme to cheat the government. Consequently he set out on his lunch hour to track down his brother to find out the truth. He found him at Tiny's number joint across from the plant guardhouse. As usual, he was holding court among the mangiest and shadiest characters in the valley. No wonder he has such a vile reputation. Johnny thought.

"Play dat 495, Johnny, I boxed it. Dis is my ole house number. Dat way ya kin win for 594 too." He spoke with the spirit of the game, seemingly enthralled with his would be winnings. Phil's beady eyes lit up toward his brother, a smile spread across his lower face, nattily dressed in a freshly laundered blue work shirt and neat gray creased pants. Oh brother, Johnny thought to himself, he was the odd man out among the filthy cruds crawling around that place.

Wimpy the owner had dark pants and a shirt on mapped with food and perspiration stains, and could probably walk around on its own volition. The huge decoy candy counter hung out over a dirty wooden floor with cracks as wide as a finger, around which dirt and grime had piled for ages looking very much like rat feces.

Johnny approached his sibling a few feet away with his back to the counter, in a confidential manner with the filthy clerk, taking in the aroma of his brother's provocative aftershave lotion. *He's got to be the fanciest dresser in the company, hmm, I wonder who's doing his shirts these days.* Johnny mused.

"Hey fellah, what's this I hear about your new business venture in Altoona, PA?" Johnny cracked, putting his arm around his sibling.

"Nah I'm goin' straight brother, wisht I'd a piece o' dat action, but no I aint got no business dere. Yer barkin' up de wrong tree. You spendin' too much time in de chicken manure? Ha ha ha." He laughed at his own joke.

"I was tinkin' 'bout da bootleg gas dough, aw, guess Im gettin' too old for dat baloney. Johnny winced at his bad English, wondering if his six years of school counted for anything at all. Wondering if he should believe his distrustful brother, just this once, he fixed his stare on him hopefully, cautiously believing that he just might have grown up a bit.

"I hope so, and wiser." Johnny quipped. Looking him straight in the eye.

"Hey, I'll have to bring Cora by to meet you guys." Phil said with a gleam in his eye. Johnny laughed, now he knew who was doin' his shirts.

The next Tuesday, Johnny listened to the news, before his favorite radio show, Amos and Andy came on the air. Sure enough there was an announcement of a blazing gun battle that had taken place in Altoona, PA, where state troopers captured two tough professional criminals, Charlie Falker and Merle Mercer. They were caught making counterfeit coupons. *Oh thank you God*, he said, when realizing that for once in his life, his brother was telling the truth.

Two days before Christmas, Dell and Johnny had just pulled the warm pedina comforter up close to their chins in their downstairs bedroom. The nighttime temperature had dropped to ten degrees below zero, colder than it had been since the beginning of the winter. Dell was exhausted, but not more than usual, when she spent the entire day working outside. She hardly even combed her hair these days, there was so much to do around there, much less bathe and put on a clean housedress.

Dell had spent this day baking cookies and sweet breads; poppy seed, nut and lekvar rolls, with thick prune butter filling. She'd already baked the usual four loaves of bread for the week

148

yesterday, so that part was finished for the week. Terry worked by her side, cutting delicate shaped Christmas cookies out of rolled dough to decorate with colored icings and candies that looked nice all spread out in the holiday tin.

Later that evening after the kids had gone to bed, she took up her basket of crocheting to finish their mittens and caps to wrap for presents. Coming across a pattern for "fascinator" scarves in the *Sun Telegraph Newspaper* for the girls to wear to school, Dell had meticulously counted the single and double stitches in the newspaper photo that made up a big snowflake design. She then crocheted a border in her own motif of a shell pattern. Over all she was pleased with her handiwork and hoped the girls liked it.

All of a sudden she and Johnny glanced at each other in bed in the dark, both hearing a noise like a car door slamming at the same time, followed by the crunching of running footsteps in the frozen snow and ice covered driveway. Johnny grabbed his old flannel robe, looking out the door, only to be confronted by thick solid frost designs woven thickly into the windowpane. All of a sudden he was startled by a hard thumping on the outside door, he looked over at Dell who prudently guessed at the identity of the intruder.

"Oh, Maybe it's Ben or Tommy coming home on leave for Christmas. Please God." Even though they had not had any word from either, some opportunity might have presented itself to them in the last minute. Holding her heart in wishful awe, Dell ran across in her long flannel nightgown and bare feet to stand behind her husband, anticipating the best.

"Hey look who's here." Johnny shouted with glee, opening the door against a sudden cold waft of freezing wind blowing up, almost blowing the door back off of its hinges. He and his son hugged in the middle of holding the door keeping their balance simultaneously.

"How are ya Dad? Hi Mom, how's my girl?" He spoke tearfully, holding their warm bodies against him tenderly. Then he introduced the new love of his life.

"Mom, Dad, this is Dottie." They both looked at the freckle faced red head next to him and found themselves hugging her as well, trying to discern for themselves what stage their relationship was in, and how it all came about, since he was supposedly on the German warfront.

Only Tommy would know the slim odds for winning the poker game he'd taken part in two weeks before with two other mates and Lieutenant Commander Jeffries. The Commander had gambled carelessly on his last cards after a night of hard drinking, and was sure his spread of three queens and two tens was a winner. Running out of money two hands ago, prompted him to throw out a fast trip back to New York harbor on the next munitions ship to anyone who could beat him. As the fates would have it, Chief Petty Officer Albred showed his cards as a straight flush. Early the next week, Tommy was packed and ready to go, or shame shame on Jeffries, gambling far into the night way past his curfew.

Euphoric relief surrounded them, as Dell said the first thing that came to her mind.

"Where's your sailor suit, Tom?" At this they all laughed, as mother and son walked arm in arm into the bright cheery kitchen. They settled into chairs around the large round table, while Dell filled the huge percolator coffee pot full of water, spooning the pungent grounds into its inside drip cup. Talking all the while, Tommy poured out the story of how they had arrived so precariously this bitter cold night.

" We got here by the skin of our teeth. Mom and Dad." He said excitedly, in typical Tommy manner, his blue eyes twinkled, as several strands of dark shiney hair tumbled down over them, his Adam's apple bobbing up and down with excitement. All the while, Dottie smiled approvingly.

"My buddy, Stan, lent me his car, a '41 Ford convertible. Nice car, but the dumb ass didn't put any antifreeze in it." Terry came bustling into the room with her wide chenille robe gliding behind her, being the first up when she heard her favorite brother's voice.

"Convertible? In this weather?" She went over and hugged and kissed him, staring curiously at his new girlfriend, greeting her coolly.

"Hi, so you're the new girlfriend." She said. Accessing her new adversary keenly. Dottie looked her in the eye pleasantly, having heard all about the family.

"No, I'm more than that." Then she splayed her hand out, proudly displaying the tiny diamond. Now all the Albred's gawked at Dottie, seeing her as a potential new family member, but none of them knew what to say in reply, and Tommy did not seem ready to discuss their engagement.

"No antifreeze in the radiator?" Put in Joel, who shyly waved on his way to the basement door to stoke up the layer of coal that lay waiting to light up for the frigid morning awaiting them.

"No, and my toes are froze." Said Dottie. Answering Tommy's brother, who could turn out to be an ally when she jockeyed for her position in the family.

"Anyway, I forced the engine up this hill. Hell, it wanted to quit in Indiana, and all the way from Great Lakes. He bragged, lighting up a cigarette and offering his father one.

"Tommy, you take too many chances." Said their Dad, who tried not to lecture too much about his son's experience, since he appeared to have learned a lesson, now he thought about his serious quest of marriage.

"Now you won't have to cry when you hear *I'll Be Home For Christmas*, Mom." Libby hurriedly got her remark in before being shut out by another older member speaking. This prompted laughing from all. Little Kat stared at the brother she never remembered, as Tommy went over and picked his little sister up into his long thin arms.

"Hi, little booger," he smiled, kissing and holding her tight. The kids giggled, as Dell reprimanded, putting some of her nut rolls in a plate for the table.

"That's a nice way to talk to your little sister, Tom." Even though she smiled too.

"Hey Mom, where is Ben stationed, I wrote to him at the address you sent to me, but he hasn't written back yet." Johnny came back in inhaling hard on his Lucky Strike.

"He's up in the Aleutian Islands, Tom. I don't think the mail plane goes in and out of there much. "Holy Hell." Tommy yelled. Sorry for his younger brother.

9. Gray School

Libby shuffled her new Buster Brown oxfords loosely through mounds of maple leaves fallen from the trees lining the cemetery banks along the road down to school that afternoon. Tops of lonely tombstones protruded, nature stripping away their camouflage and exposing symbols of another shape of existence. Looking down at the large ripped hem in her new plaid school dress, she longed for her brother's old pants with the old brown cloth military belt that she had knocked about in all summer. Not being much in the frame of mind to do school work this day anyway, she'd been singled out as a daydreamer in yesterday's geography class when her teacher caught her gazing out the window.

Oh if only she was back up at the old fallen apple tree in the cow pasture again. It wouldn't even be tough having five year old Kat dragging along behind her, always having something wrong, like a cut or splinter on her finger. Sometime she would even wet her pants, then she'd have to go all the way home with her again for a change having to run away faster so that she wouldn't have to take her little sister the next time.

Libby would never forget that glorious morning after the terrible thunderstorm when she and her cousin, Joey found the huge apple tree lying on the ground struck down by lightening. They'd tried in great desperation to climb it when it stood tall among the rest, but even with a rope in tow, it was useless. But now, they ran up the large trunk through the branches effortlessly. And the best part was that it was still partly alive with half of its roots still sticking into the ground, so that there were sour green apples on it just for the picking.

Joey had a small penknife that he used to make notches everywhere, pretending that he was a big game hunter. As she watched him from her vantage point in another section of the tree, she kept hearing his pants ripping on small wayward branches, so that by the time they left to go home, his entire inward seam was ripped, creating a dress-like effect as he walked. Libby laughed and laughed doubling over at her cousin, to the point of wetting her own pants. And though her Aunt

152

Aggie was angry with him for ruining his clothes, she still could not stifle her giggles.

They were not allowed to go to the tree for a while, staying on her swing twisting it around and around until they both threw up near the garden. Secretly, they thought it might have been all the green apples they had eaten.

Now why couldn't they have classes outside, she mused, going through the double doors, with those beautiful colors outside. She and her brother, Joel both agreed that fall was their favorite time of year. Many varieties of colors outlined the area, starting with the red of the maple trees, golden weeping willow, pink and orange barberry bushes and the basic dark green of the evergreens always present in the background. Together they collected and catalogued the many hued maple, locust, oak, ginkgo and chestnut leaves in a book to catalogue and look at later.

The opened chestnuts gathered would taste good roasted in the iron skillet with a little oil. Each chestnut had to be punctured with a can opener or knife to let the pressure out of the nut as it was cooking. Terry had to be careful to put a heavy pot on the lid in case the nuts exploded. That was the signal that said they were cooked. One of the iron ones from the old hotel they always heard about would do. They still had lots of things, like huge heavy cups, a porcelain top table, and big kettles and a couple of chairs that remained from the hotel they'd heard so much about. And though they heard that the place burned down sometime after the Depression, somebody must have gone in and retrieved all the kitchenware.

The magic moment when their Dad poured the roasted chestnuts out onto newspapers on the table to absorb the oil, all the Albred's ran to crack the hard shells open to eat their sweet meat with excitement and gusto.

Their Mom never seemed to want to talk about the Albred Hotel days, she would only say things like. *"Oh, we worked so hard from morning until night."* and your Grandma Lizzie was the one who actually taught her how to cook. But then she would grimace and talk about how Aunt Aggie got away without doing any work. And knowing their Aunt now, they could believe it, since when she visited them she just sat and talked and never helping herself in any way, wanting to be served all the time.

Halloween was always present at the top of the hill with the graveyard looming next-door, as skeleton branches of trees lay hauntingly bared in the silver harvest moonlight beaming overhead. Traditionally, she and Terry would go around to their few neighbors' trick or treating, walking long eerie distances between the large fields separating the houses. In the end, the quest for more candy and goodies would win out over their fears of the dark and spooky places, where shadows lurked to snatch them up.

Before Ben went to the Army, the two sisters's had to beware of him lunging out from behind the biggest tombstone, as they cautiously walked past, scaring them out of their wits. They would laugh uproariously, enjoying it all.

This lunchtime, her Mom had cooked tomato soup and a cheese sandwich because Libby had chosen to come home to eat that afternoon. Most of the time she purchased her meal for a dollar a week at school, where she would sit in the school basement cafeteria with her friends who lived at the other end of Churchill Road. Most of their father's were doctors, lawyers and businessmen who had big offices in downtown Pittsburgh and lived in huge mansions there.

Usually they went places together on the weekend, like ice-skating in the winter, girl scouts, and a Polly Pigtails club that was formed by her new friend, Mary Frances Smith, who came from a wealthy family. Mary Frances lived in a palatial estate, with a patio as big as the house, and stone sculptures placed everywhere.

Libby would walk up the road past the Edgewood Country Club for over a mile to get to her friend's house, thinking that Mary Frances was lonely living there with just her mother and father in this huge place that must have had twenty rooms. It was easy for the girls to loose each other when they played, and they would have to yell to find one another again. Sometime on Saturday Libby walked up to her house to play paper dolls or just have tea with her friend. There was an enormous kitchen where servants seemed to be in charge, and though she never saw any there, her mother would refer to them by name when she spoke to Mary Frances.

A number of other children in her class hiked up the hill to Gray from Linhart, a town at the bottom of a steep hill going down past the school. Some of them were from Italian families. Miss Simon would look down at them distastefully after smelling the strong odor of garlic from the spaghetti sauce they'd had for supper the night before. Libby felt sorry for them being singled out, but she wanted to stare at them, knowing they were different, and an interesting, nationality. Dark shiney curly hair stood out in ringlets all over their heads, almost like Terry's beautiful locks.

Their homemade dresses of colorful printed material stood out against all the store bought clothes the rich kids wore, different from any Libby had seen before. But Libby remembered pictures from her parent's photo album of some of their family members who had come over from Hungary and Czechoslovakia and found similarity between the costumes. Their mother had probably made them, as her sister Terry had sewn some of her skirts.

The yellow brick school had two floors of grades; the first through fourth grade was on the first level, and fifth and sixth was on the second floor. On one side of the basement, Mr. Barnridge, the kindly janitor who shoveled coal into the big blasting furnace to keep the place warm. At Christmas he received more gifts than the teachers.

With a shortage of teachers, during the war, her class was made up of fourth and fifth graders. She knew this when over hearing her mother and father talk about the war taking all of our good people, and this probably meant teachers too. She would look at Miss Simon, who was the principal and Miss Cartin, knowing that they were getting old, given that their old crepe dresses had stitches sewn everywhere around the seams. Miss Simon's tight silver curls bobbed when she wrote on the board drawing heavy lines under letters or sentences with yellow chalk. Sometimes she would use a wood and wire gadget that held four pieces of chalk at a time to write lines on the board. When one of the pieces broke or fell out, the boy students would laugh out loud, Libby thought they were rather odd thinking this was funny.

Classes were encouraged to have their parents come to the PTA meetings on Thursdays, and they would all get credit for this by having cookies after class. Libby knew her mother would never be there, because she was too embarrassed to go out in public in her old garden clothes, saying that the wealthy parents at the other side of Churchill would think she looked like a hobo. Instead, she sent Terry to PTA. This did not make a very good impression, because the next day Miss Simon spoke sternly with a strict warning, her brown red eyes blazing down with disdain toward her student.

"Don't ever do that again Libby, PTA is just for parents. Your room will not get credit." The kids all turned around and stared as if she also smelled of garlic. One of the girls even pushed Libby aside at recess, with her snotty nose needing to be blown. Wiping her sweater sleeve against her face, she spit out the mean words at her target.

"Libby, is your mother sick, or don't you have a mother?" She said cruelly. Libby just ignored her, thinking she just wanted to make a few of the girls around giggle. Only Maria and Angelina looked at her regretfully. Libby then went over and took their hands to go off and play in another area behind the school.

"C'mon, let's go down to the big tree in the meadow." This was a favorite gathering spot where they all set up camps in the field grass where they could hide, sometimes getting prickly jaggers from the grass all over their socks and the bottom of their cotton dresses.

The next day Terry told her something that bothered Libby for a long time after.

"All those foreign mothers and fathers were there together at PTA, they all came in together laughing and having a good time lookin' at their kids papers and stuff. They were nice, oh yeah, and the rich kids parents all went to the other side by the windows like they were too good to mix." And she wondered why the two groups stayed separate. What was so wrong with the Linhart students?

This prompted Libby to tell her mother about how bad she felt about her not coming and sending Terry instead. Libby felt sorry for her, but was also upset at her not having one nice dress to wear. She didn't believe that her family didn't have enough money, but thought that her Mom just didn't have time to go to the store and buy a nice dress to come to the PTA.

Then she began to feel guilty for being angry with her poor mother who worked hard so that they could all have a good life. She was a humble and kind person, who Libby thought was very close to the Blessed Virgin Mary on earth, except when she stood by Terry's side during an argument. Her mother would always stay close to their beds while they were sick, patting their heads and bringing mint ginger ale to the bedside, whispering nice things so that they would get well.

When one of them were really ill, Daddy would also come to the bedside, like when she got a diphtheria shot at school and her arm swelled up and she became feverish. Libby heard them both there talking over her as if she'd already died.

Lately Libby and her Mom went grocery shopping early on Saturday mornings on the eight thirty bus. They would go down to Eastburg where they used to live and shop in all the old stores where her Mom knew the shopkeepers since she was a young girl. Then Libby would get a chocolate sprinkle ice cream cone for a dime or an Isaly's Klondike, and most of the time she'd get a coupon for a free one the next time. They would then board the bus to come back home, which had been parked in an alleyway in Eastburg waiting to pick up passengers.

They would have three or four bulging cloth shopping bags, which the bus driver, Joe Winn would help, carry up the steps. Spending almost twenty dollars for groceries for the family for the week was a lot of money. Joe the bus driver would sing little songs and carry conversations with the people on the bus all the way home. Her mother never bought anything for herself, and neither did her father.

The war came to a close after many lives were lost that spring and summer as both conflicts with Germany and Japan ceased. Then the United States sent a B-29, "Enola Gay" to drop warfare's first atomic bomb on Hiroshima, Japan. More people were sacrificed as President Truman announced that 80,000 inhabitants were obliterated there. Then a second bomb was dropped on Nagasaki. This prompted the surrender announced by Japanese Emperor Hirohito. Thus a new fear of Atomic warfare became a never-ending threat to human life on earth everywhere.

Many people grieved for President Roosevelt, who had died from a massive cerebral hemorrhage on April 12, 1945. Franklin Delano Roosevelt was the only President to be elected for four terms, thirteen years in office, and a parental likeness to a whole generation of children who knew him as the father of the country. When it happened, he was having his portrait painted by a Russian born artist, Madame Elizabeth Shoumatoff, when he looked up and said that he had a terrible headache. Lucid until the end, signing papers earlier in the day, he then slumped over.

The end of life came for one of history's dynamic, influential and controversial chief executives at Warm Springs, Georgia where he had gone regularly for rest and relaxation. The American people cried openly in the streets at the loss of their beloved President who had guided them out of the great Depression and through the terrible war years.

While reading yet another article in the Press about the passing of the Commander and Chief of the United States, Johnny among many others realized that one of the wars best kept secrets was the critical status of FDR's health during his last years of office. He felt that he was a man for his times, and there would never be another President like him in their lifetime who was so in touch with the common people.

The wars end brought men and women home to American soil once again. The landscape was filled with mingled joy and heartbreak as transports and aircraft landed at United States bases. Families embracing and uncontrollable weeping at dockside, while widows at naval stations such as Norfolk waited in silence to ask how their husbands had died. Many wives did not wait for spouses, and 502,000 divorces in 1945 occurred. Thirty-one for every one hundred marriages. America maintained her status of the highest divorce rate in the world.

Upon integrating back into social life, civilians experienced positive after effects of the terrible war. One of these included increased physical and social mobility, and more inroads into interracial problems. Military personnel returned to the smallest communities with tales of the world far beyond. Universities were filled with students taking advantage of the G.I. Bill offered by the government for their education, over seven million studied under this measure.

That summer also brought an abundance of tomatoes and Dell was in her glory, as neighbors came from everywhere to help them can over one hundred bottles of ketchup. Every bottle, including old beer bottles found in the dirt cellar were filled to the brim. The nearest neighbor, Mr. Leax set up huge vats in the backyard bubbling over with red liquid. Everyone who did not help stood by and discussed appropriate spices for the brew and how long to keep it simmering. In the basement sat crocks of piccalilli, combinations of pickles, onions, green tomatoes, cauliflower, and other vegetables fermenting in vinegar and spices. This precious concoction was carefully covered with cheesecloth, and added to as the cook allowed.

One hot day as Dell, Joel and the kids were picking more peck baskets of tomatoes, they turned around to see a tall figure emerging from the corner of Joel's lawn beside the crab apple tree where they were warned not to go because poison ivy grew there in abundance. Carrying a big duffle bag and in full army uniform and tall combat boots with his cap lopsided on his head, Ben came walking down in his quiet way to the garden.

"Hey, how about a tomato?" He said. They all laughed and hugged their brother and son, his mother being the first to put her arms around him, tears forming at her eyes as her nose became red with deep feeling for her second son's homecoming. Walking arm in arm with his sister's and brothers, they talked about all the new things happening around Churchill, like all the ketchup they had just made that summer, and how Tommy would be going to Great Lakes Naval Station for a while to finish out his reenlistment. Ben had gotten the word from Alaska that the war was over, but had to wait for transportation to the

U.S. Dell thanked God for sending her two sons back home safely once again.

Suddenly, the four-year war production boom ended and factory gates opened all over the land to unemployment claims spiraling at half a million at a time. Westinghouse Electric's American Federation of Laborer's union leaders called a strike, and Johnny was one of these, worrying about their household income.

"Aw don't worry John." Dell sympathized, understanding his worries.

"We have lots of food coming from our garden now, and thank God the chickens are laying good. The basement shelves are well stocked with lots of canned goods already, especially tomatoes. We'll get through." she spoke with her usual optimism. But her husband had another concern.

"Dell, Ben needs money to start college in September. One hundred and seventy five dollars a semester to be exact." he said, concertedly.

"The G.I.Bill will go through by that time, but we'll have add to his tuition." Johnny brought in forty dollars a week, and it was all going out for food, the mortgage, and he wasn't sure what else, since Dell paid the bills.

"Maybe I can call St. Vincent's and talk to someone in admissions." Dell smiled at him, because if anyone could talk his way through problems, it was her husband. She knew he could handle it. And with that he went to the phone telling the number to the operator, who placed the call to Latrobe, Pennsylvania.

"Give me the President's Office" Johnny spoke assertively, but he was all nerves inside, not having spoken to administration since he dropped out of the seminary in 1927. Oh sure he took the kids to the lake there, showing them around the beautiful grounds of the Benedictine Fathers of St. Vincent in Latrobe. But to actually talk to any of his classmates who would now be parish priests in many of the area's Catholic dioceses, made him feel awkward. All the same, when it came to his children, Johnny would go to any length to help them.

Soon a voice answered in College Administration.

160

"Hello, this is Father Cumiford." Johnny immediately recognized the name and the voice as someone from his past. Now his stomach still fluttering with his morning coffee, began to quiet as he heard his friend from long ago.

"Pete Cumiford? The Irish mafia man?" Johnny joked laughingly.

"Oh you old so and so," spoke President Cumiford, joining in with a chuckle.

"You're now in charge? The guy who couldn't play halfback in '25?" Johnny said

"One and the same," replied the priest honestly.

"The school ran out of good people and I was at the bottom of the barrel, so they finally picked me to run the show here." The former classmates now cackled uproariously.

"I'll tell you why I'm calling my friend. Do you mind if I don't call you Father, since I was there when you threw up in the room after the frat party." The two men had met when they were just fourteen years old, too young to be designated for the priesthood.

Johnny began to state his reasons for calling administration.

"I need a favor, buddy. My son Ben, just back from the army, wants to start the first semester in September, and the Westinghouse is on strike, so we're short here. He'll have the GI Bill helping him out, but is it possible to waive the rest of the payment until later? Father I'd really appreciate it." Cumiford did enjoy his old classmate addressing him with reverence and smiled.

"Oh, I think we can arrange this for you, even though you never said good bye to us and didn't even invite us, your teammates, to your big hotel wedding. Well anyway, you sound happy Johnny. How many children do you have now, and what are their names?"

"They're all named after saints Father, and I thank God for them most of the time. Let's say I'm a better husband and father than I would have been a priest."

"Sometime I have a regret or two." The priest answered back.

"But my life is in God's hands now, and I'm on a mission here."

Johnny thanked him graciously, greatly relieved that his deed was accomplished.

Just then Dell came in and nudged him out of his thinking, with her usually soft way, squeezing his shoulder affectionately. Johnny was in a better mood now, and put his arm around her, thinking that here is the woman I gladly left the seminary for, and I'm not sorry.

"Johnny, let's go to a movie tomorrow. I want to see *Going My Way*. Bing Crosby's in it playing a priest who organizes some neighborhood kids into a church choir. And as you know, he's one of my favorites," she cajoled.

"Barry Fitzgerald is in it too, you like him, don't you?"

"Aw Dell, you know how I hate those show business people, and that damn Hollywood is going to sink into the sea like Sodom and Gomorrah." But then he thought of her feelings.

"But yeah, Crosby's not a bad singer. Where's it playing?" She didn't tell him that Ma and Pa Kettle Down On The Farm, was part of the double feature. They both loved Marjorie Maine and Wallace Berry in these movies about a haphazard husband and wife living on a broken down farm with all of their kids mixing mishap and bedlam with well-mannered everyday principles. This made for a very funny movie and Johnny would love it. Dell thought it might take some of his cares away temporarily.

"We can take the 6:00 bus down to the Rivoli." Dell was glad because they hadn't been out since they saw *The Song Of Bernadette* in 1941. And she could just throw a coat over a clean housedress. It would be a pleasant evening.

Pop Gessner sent an enormous Christmas package that year full of individual gifts for everyone. This was unusual because most of the time he just wrote a check for Dell to buy food for the holiday. In their eagerness, the children opened the intriguing brown parcel from the mailman immediately, with Ben leading the way. He never could stand the suspense of a wrapped package. Then Libby, Terry and Kat opened their presents of scotch plaid wool outfits of pleated skirts, vests, with

162

white blouses in the same trim in material. The boys opened presents of beautiful argyle sweaters and socks. Dell and Johnny were happy with any contribution for a Christmas ham, this in view of the fact that he had finally gone back to work after a few months of their union strike.

The week before Christmas, Libby, Terry and Joel met their Dad after school to do Christmas shopping at the five and ten cent store in Eastburg. This was the first year that Libby was included in the expedition and she was enormously excited. Snow had fallen all day, and the streets were slushy with melted dirty snow. The steel streetcar tracks were especially slippery as they crossed the street from the bus stop to go into the warmth of the bustling activity of the five and Ten Cent Store.

The swinging red doors with silver handles opened into an area where their Dad was sitting in one of the many lined up wooden chairs in the front of the store. Once inside, strong smells of fresh roasted salted peanuts wafted into cherry red noses, as the nostalgic melody of It's *Beginning To Look A lot Like Christmas,* filled the air along with cash register rings and chirps of canaries singing from their cages in back. Thin wooden floor boards creaked with people rushing back and forth seeking the gifts of their choice for loved ones, carrying mud and slush to every part of the interior.

"Hi Dad." They all resounded together, with which Johnny handed each a brand new dollar bill. Libby held the money out. A whole dollar to buy presents for the family.

"Now if you need more, come and see me. I'll sit here and wait for you." Johnny smiled with a twinkle in his eye, with his cheery red cheeks and wearing his old work coat and his gray felt hat in his lap, he could have been St. Nick himself.

Libby watched Terry disappear beside a counter of women's bedroom slippers, knowing just where she would begin to buy. Joel sped down an aisle filled with toys of every type, also having something particular in mind. Not knowing her way around the place as well, except for when she and her Mom went shopping on Saturday mornings, Libby sauntered over to the stationary and books. Noticing the entire series of Nancy Drew mysteries, she wished it were possible to get those instead of presents just for an instant. *The Secret Of The Missing Cave* was one she would pick out first to read.

Passing by open counters full of underwear and perfume, Libby thought maybe she could buy her mother some Evening In Paris with a beautiful blue silk tassel hanging down from the dark blue bottle. Her dad would love a red work hankey and Joel might like a wallet having an inter sanctum hiding place for his secrets. Tommy would be home for Christmas too, she had no idea what to buy her oldest brother, or what he would like, since she had not seen him for a long while, but her Mom had said the boys always needed socks.

"Can I help you, please?" A friendly salesgirl looked out at her, smiling.

"Yes, I want to buy my brother a tee shirt." Libby said shyly.

"Ahh, I don't know the size, but he's about as big as that guy over there, though."

"Well then you want a medium. The prices are either thirty nine or fifty nine cents."

Another decision, after three purchases her dollar was now running low; Libby thought she would go for the thirty-nine cent one.

"You only have thirty five cents here." The lady said kindly.

Libby was embarrassed at this and ran back to her dad, who had been watching her from a far. Johnny winked at the salesgirl coming over to hand her another quarter dollar to take care of the sale.

Everyone got the 6:45 bus home together with many secrets stored up inside their many packages. Guessing what each other's present would be discussed daily until Christmas Eve, and as always, Ben wanted his immediately without holiday wrappings.

Gray had an annual Christmas Pageant, which began with the singing of Christmas solos. Libby was sad when the music teacher Miss Garrick did not pick her after earnestly trying out. And after repeating this to her mother, she was embarrassed when Miss Simon announced in class the next day, that her mother had called the school to tell them that Libby had a beautiful voice and sang beautifully on the swing all summer. The rest of the class laughed as the teacher said this out loud, asking Libby to stand up in front of the class to sing a song.

Libby walked up in front of the room poised herself graciously and faced her audience, bellowing out a popular tune made famous by Perry Como.

"A you're adorable, B you're so beautiful, C you're a cutie full of charm, D you're a darling, and E you're exciting, and F you're a feather in my arms..." She sang with gusto and enthusiasm, so that the class cheered, and Miss Simon had a big smile on her face. This gave Libby a good feeling about the way her Mother had caused the situation to come about, especially since she had not wanted to come to the school for PTA previously.

This would be the beginning of many local singing appearances in Libby's life, people would love to hear her sing and music would take high priority in her life. She sang a lovely Christmas song at the pageant that year and at school Cantatas throughout the coming years.

She despised her image in the mirror dressed up in widow's weeds, especially since black was never her color. Scarlet O'Hara might have pulled it off to entice Rhett Butler when she worked at the Charity Ball in *Gone with the Wind*. But Agatha looked old, drawn and decrepit, though she was still in her thirties. And besides, her mourning period was over, Joseph had been dead for nearly a year from a heart attack. It was over, kaput; they had tolerated each other for ten years. And never again would she have anything intimate to do with the male gender, they were vile creatures who existed on earth for only one purpose.

However, propriety was propriety – and she would prove to the neighborhood that she was as refined as the rest of them. Besides, she wanted pity and lots of it from anyone willing to listen. Therefore she would continue to take advantage of widowhood.

The short black rayon dress kept inching up over her belly now, what skimpy material, not even enough to cover a woman's derriere. Ever since the war shortage on cloth all the civilians had to suffer, especially the well dressed such as she. Everything that was worthwhile had been rationed; thank God it was now over. Refusing to wear the military style short-skirted dresses, at least two inches above the knee, with epaulets and enormous shoulder pads, Agatha instead chose an older style that no longer fit her ample body. Giving her dress yet another yank and a newly purchased girdle a tug she yelled for the boys to get ready.

"Hey you two quit fightin' in there, and get ready – we're gonna catch that eleven o'clock bus up to Aunt Dell's". She couldn't wait to have some of Dell's good nut roll and kielbasa, not to mention the huge ham usually sitting in the middle of the kitchen table all day long. Carefully placing the fitted dark velvet hat strategically over auburn hair now peppered with a few strands of gray, she smiled at her reflection once again.

Agatha grieved at having to cover the huge pompadour she'd created in the front, with her chapeaux, but she pulled the black net down over her pretty face, staging her mourning performance. She couldn't wait to have some fun with the Albred family, since everything in her life had become monotonous all of a sudden. Darn that Joseph, forcing her to become a sad and lonely pathetic woman in the world. Whatever would she do now?

"I yust go nuts at Christmas, when each kid hangs up his sock. It's a time for kids to flip their lids, while their papa goes in hack," sang a Swedish Spike Jones, as the Albreds slowly showed up in the living room to have a holiday laugh with their uncle. Soon Dell wandered into the room wiping her hands on a new apron Terry had sewn for the holidays, which she had put on in haste to grind up the horseradish. This would be the garnish for the ham that would sit temptingly on the cabinet sink, since no one could touch it due to the observance of the Catholic meat abstinence during Christmas Eve. The delicious looking ham served as penance as well, for the drooling Albred children.

Uncle Phil had tip toed into the front door and put the new record on the victrola, with his overcoat still over his arm. Everyone laughed as Spike Jones' band played another one of

166

his zany classics on the new Philco phonograph, a gift for the children from their mother and father.

"I taught youse would like dis." He spoke sprightly, as he joined in the laughter with his nieces and nephews. Johnny just shook his head in disbelief at his younger brother, always up to something.

"Hey Dell, Johnny, I'm gonna bring Clarise by for Christmas, okey dokey?" He yelled on his way out the door, leaving the record to play on for the kids to listen.

"Sure Phil, bring her to dinner." Dell said following him to the door, secretly hoping he wouldn't ruin another life, but just maybe it would be a match made in heaven, who knew, she thought.

Pilgrimages to church began with midnight mass in late evening, as Dell and Terry, wore their new Christmas hats for the long walk down and back up Churchill Road in the early hour of the morning. Tommy, who would spend his last unmarried holiday at home, and Ben would go with Libby to the six o'clock in the morning service. Joel and his father would be home from the later mass in time for lunch. Little Kat had one of her winter colds and lay wrapped up in bedclothes on the couch beside the lighted tree most of the time.

Libby felt proud walking with her two big brothers to and from church, but could hardly contain her excitement as Father Shields screamed out the mass and sermon. She dreamed of getting back to her wonderful Christmas gifts. No longer believing in Santa Claus, she knew her mom and dad had bought the Irish storybook doll dressed in beautiful white and green satin, just for displaying with her other storybook doll collection, and then she had brand new roller skates. Learning to skate well would be fun, though she would have to practice in the basement until the weather got better. Then she would go onto the cemetery road or over to Gray school to practice.

Somehow in her heart, she knew these moments would never come again in life. Tommy would be going away permanently to live in Illinois, where his new wife to be lived, and some day they would have to share Ben with another strange woman too. But for now, their family was close, loving and sheltering.

EQUILIBRIUM

PART THREE

"The human heart dares not stay away too long from that which hurts it most. There is a return journey to anguish that few of us are released from making"

Lillian Smith
American writer-social critic
(1897 – 1966)

10. The Big Snow

"Were you praying for snow again?" Ben said, looking inquiringly disgruntled at Libby, chugging down his third cup of coffee in a nervous state, as his mother chuckled wiping the oil clothe over the breakfast table cleaning up butter, jam, picking up empty used dishes.

"I always pray for it, why?" She looked up into his clear brown eyes defiantly.

"Because I have to get back to Latrobe for school, that's why. I hate this white stuff, it makes it hard to travel around, just getting down this hill is enough trouble."

Libby didn't know what he was talking about; she loved the fluffy white covering of pure snow. It was always fun and picked up the pace of the long cold winter days. They could sled ride right down through the backyard and up to green eleven, or build snowmen, and sometime school was even canceled.

And while it was true that she prayed for things that she thought were important, a plea for a television set for their family and a job for Joel were also included in the list of current meditation requests; Libby had found a close association with the Lord and His Blessed Mother, very comforting in the life of a fourteen year old, trying to establish ground in her life.

The nun in Catechism class at Saint Coleman school always talked about the power of prayer and encouraged all of the religion class students to visit the Blessed Sacrament on the altar in church especially when they had troubles, as someone to talk to, like a special friend always there to help. Putting this into practice, it never occurred to Libby to complain about personal problems to a stranger who didn't know the secrets of her heart.

However, to institute Sister Mary Seraphina's idea of a family who prays together stays together became a difficult thing to accomplish. Libby would gather her sisters and brothers together before seven o'clock every night after supper into the kitchen before the local Pittsburgh priest came on the radio station to recite the rosary. Then they as his radio audience would answer the proper responses. This worked well for a while, but Joel, and Ben when he was home, would try to rebel by ignoring her and going about doing other things, like reading the paper or working outside.

Libby would not relent; she coaxed her siblings in for the devotion, and might even enlist her Dad to get them to kneel down with their beads in hand. After a while the pattern took hold, except when out of the way activities were planned, she was persistent in keeping her vigil, since she found that her life always went along smoothly whenever she sought divine help.

Strong northwesterly winds unceasingly whistled and blew with breathless force at the top of their hill, layering deep blankets of snow over the entire region. Five to six foot drifts crested around their backyard alone. The storms continued, falling hard from Thanksgiving until almost Christmas. Snowfall came down in record proportions, marking the beginning of the 1950's decade, as the Albreds and many others became walled into their dwellings, with only a path tunneling out to the garbage can, the driveway and mailbox. The news reported the Union Railroad had hired men specifically to clean their tracks. Officials, buying up every shovel in the area, had the rails cleared of heavy snow and reported the trains were moving again.

Churchill Road was not navigable by car. Nevertheless, the Albred's would wake up in the morning up to the sounds of skidding, sliding and loud screaming of car wheels, as some brave workers tried to gain access to busy route 22 to traveling to Pittsburgh. Some of the fearless drivers accelerated their gas pedal relentlessly until they reached the top of the road, eventually leveling out onto another course of drifted blizzardy wind gusting across the uncovered road which ran parallel with the golf course.

Even Mr. Oldheart, who traveled up and down in his little Willey's Knight spreading ashes that had been previously piled along the road, abandoned his useless Township upkeep duties. The poor man decided to hunker down with the rest of the residents as a sensible gesture and when the Albred's could no longer hear his rear engine car stopping on the grade at each little pile, they knew the weather had turned impossible.

Dell worried when there was no word from Terry, who had gone to baby-sit in another town close to Eastburg near where they once lived. There had been no word from her all morning, and with all transportation down, she and Johnny wondered about her return and how she would ever get home. All of a sudden the telephone rang, with everyone running for it as usual.

"I'm not home." Joel exclaimed as usual, having an intense dislike of talking into the instrument. Johnny would always give his son a look of disgust for shunning his social responsibility.

"Hi Mom". Terry spoke defensively, ready to encounter her latest feat.

"I'm walking home, I don't want to stay around here any longer, or else these people are going to have me watch and play with the kids all day after I watched them last night, I want a rest." She whispered to her mother as if someone was close by listening at the other end. Dell cringed thinking about her daughter's long walk from Ardmore Boulevard to Churchill Road, a distance of over ten miles.

"You don't even have boots, honey. Can't they loan you a pair there?" Dell made an attempt to make the situation better, with little knowledge of what actually was going on where Terry had been delayed.

"No, I just want to get out" She seemed desperate to leave.

"Well alright, Joel will meet you half way with dry clothes." She said, looking up to see Johnny listening in on the worrisome situation. After Dell hung up, he called the township police and ambulance to see if they could provide an emergency vehicle to help get Terry, but the two cars were out on other calls.

In the meantime, Joel began the long trek down hill over the blustery snow covered road to meet his sister somewhere along the way. His thick glasses kept fogging up under his dark wool tassel cap and he stopped to clean them now and then. Nonetheless, he trudged on not wanting to disappoint his mom and dad, and did care about Terry, even though they argued most of the time now that they were older and he found himself more vulnerable to criticism.

Joel hoped that a job would come his way soon; in the meantime he worked out with weights, a part-time interest now after high school.

"You've got to get in shape kid." Ben had reprimanded him about his skinny frame. And though he worked hard around the house, he guessed his muscles were all in the wrong place. Consequently, they had both retreated to the cellar to lift the barbells his brother had bought. But now he could hardly believe his eyes when he saw his sister at the bottom of the road.

"How did you get here already?" he said looking at his poor forlorn sister, whose wet dark ringlets completely circled her face, while her thin leather shoes and light coat were soaked through. Thinking appearances are deceiving, knowing that under that poor image was a tough girl, Joel admired Terry for the strong personality she revealed and was happy and relieved that her disposition was a cheerful one.

"Were you already walking when you phoned us?" he said. She smiled courageously at her brother, sipping the chicken soup carried in a brown paper bag still quite warm in the canning jar, that her mom had sent. He was surprised at the speed with which she had traveled. It was a bit of a miracle, he thought, but Terry laughed.

"Ha, I got a ride from some Eastburg policeman, said he could only drive me to Turtle Creek. He knew Mom and Daddy from the old hotel days". Arriving home, Dell wrapped her daughter in blankets and put her to bed with a hot toddy to stave off pneumonia. Afterward she and Johnny breathed a sigh of relief that Terry was home, and laughed at the news of the troublesome Kovic boy who was now an Eastburg policeman.

The next morning found Ben, Joel and Johnny shoveling some of the heavy snow off the roof as a preventative safety measure. Seeing how all of them worked so well together, Dell was thinking of having them get together on another home fixing project. Johnny was on strike once again with the company; Ben was busy biding his time home from school, mostly playing his new Peggy Lee records over and over again. *The Old Master Painter,* a tune that had her dueting with Mel Torme, and the new Nat King Cole hit, *"Nature Boy"*, which had hit pop charts all over the Pittsburgh area.

In his last year of college, Ben was completing studies in psychology; he had majored in for three years. Eventually seeking a career in psychological testing in schools, he might enter the student guidance field, which was wide open for entry. He knew a good career path lay ahead, though one still had to obtain a masters or PhD in this young science, still in its early stages since 1930.

Dell set out bringing her team of workers to the cellar, grimacing at a clothesline filled with wet gloves, scarves, and snow pants drying in her nice clean basement. Trying to ignore these, she turned her volunteer team's attention to the heavy rolls of bright yellow tile sitting in the corner by the dark brown glue cans. It would be a messy job but with all of them working together, they could cement it up in the kitchen in no time flat, or so she thought.

Then the fiasco of labor division of who would put cement on and where and how to install the cut rolls brought confusion and anger among Johnny, Ben and Joel, and in the end of course Johnny made the decision about who would do what, with both sons exchanging weary eye contact.

All day long Libby, Terry and sometime Kat would head out to green eleven to sled ride, where Libby might meet her friend Randi McCabe. Randi, named after her father Randolph, was an outgoing tall girl with dark straight hair and bangs over her forehead. Randi had brought Libby on the bus to her house on Homer Drive.

One of the first things Libby noticed and liked about her new friend was her ability to recognize all of her friends and neighbors, calling them all by name, and actually starting little conversations with them. Libby wished that she could be that friendly and mean it as well, though she wasn't nearly as outgoing as Randi.

They had struck up a relationship around their love for music; Randi played the piano and Libby sang some of the popular tunes of the day, *Lavender Blue Dilly Dilly* and *Somewhere Over The Rainbow*, as Randi's mom Mrs. McCabe stood with her arms folded in the doorway enjoying the twosome making melodic harmony together. Exhibiting inherent confidence, Randi was older than her sister Lea and unlike, Libby, did not have five other siblings around to disapprove of her conduct. The two would call each other frequently on the phone, talking about school projects.

172

One of these was the circle skirt they were making in home economics at Wilkins Junior High. Randi and Libby had spent last Saturday afternoon in nearby Turtle Creek shopping in old O'Neil's yard goods store, filled with creaky wooden floors and just one of the area store owners that had seen the moving destructive waters of Turtle Creek floods in winter and spring.

Finding just the right colorful brown rodeo figures print, the two friends were pleased with the unique design that matched the full-skirted pattern. They then chose zippers and brown thread before heading over to Isaly's for a whitehouse ice cream cone. Another friend named Dee Dee also bought a huge fresh dill pickle from a nearby barrel.

Sewing the seams together was not difficult for Libby, but she lost patience with hemming the full garment, and Randi was wearing her pretty skirt months before Libby's got seamed. And though she begged Terry to please finish it, her sister said it was a home economics project, which she had to do herself. Eventually, Libby wore the lopsided crookedly hemmed skirt with a white sport blouse and brown silk scarf tied around her neck. Thick white cuffed socks hung over brown Saddle oxfords.

Since school was canceled until further notice, Joel took Kat along on the sled down to the nearest store for food after taking orders from some of the older neighbors. The smaller neighborhood kids who now lived on Garden Drive waved as they passed while sledding down the steep grade past their houses.

The new homes farther down Churchill Road, and up into another mountainous grade, were built immediately after the war to provide housing for returning veterans. The colonial style brick two story houses were priced at an exorbitant amount of money, from ten to fourteen thousand dollars depending on the number of bedrooms, and many of the returning military readily obtained GI mortgage loans to purchase them.

The young families who bought them also made baby-sitting jobs available for Terry and then Libby and her new friend from Garden Drive, Frances. Frances was a shy backward girl whose nasty mother usually frightened her friends away, and Libby was no exception. She was the youngest girl of seven brothers who all seemed to be favored by their parents, only Frances was ignored.

Terry with her outgoing personality was liked and trusted instantly by many of the new mothers. However, Libby who did not have the built-in confidence her sister possessed, had to eventually prove that she was capable to stay with their children for an hour or two, mostly on the recommendation of her sister who already knew the older women on a first name basis. Terry would graduate from High School in June and enter nurses training in the fall, when there was enough tuition money put aside. Libby was happy to take over her baby-sitting clientele.

Libby's savings grew while earning fifty cents an hour, and five dollars for all day Saturday at some homes. Now she could finally buy some new clothes for school. She was glad not to have to wear Terry's hand-me-downs any longer. Nevertheless Kat, though more petite than her sisters, now wore third handed clothes after Terry had altered them to her size.

Because of all the AF of L Union strikes, Johnny and Dell were getting behind in their bills; consequently Johnny took a part-time weekend job selling cars at a new Ford garage on Ardmore Boulevard near Eastburg. He still made a professional appearance in his blue vested sharkskin suit, and his sales ability was up to par with eager automobile buyers. This was reminiscent of the twenties for him when he sold Chryslers for Pop, Dell's father. Pop still drove Chryslers to this day, even though he was past sixty years old.

This new faster routine induced Johnny to smoke even more than his four packs of cigarettes a day. Refusing to start using the new filter tips just new on the market, which were said to be better for your lungs, he continued to light up from early morning until late in the evening. Stopping for a drink in neighborhood bars, mostly with some of the local politicians, since he had now just acquired the post of part-time Building Inspector and Health Officer for the township, became a regular practice. This routine worried Dell who hated his new schedule, and the excesses it brought, and invariably they would end up arguing that evening with her crying and pleading once again in her mild manner.

174

"John, I know you want to take these jobs, but why do you have to stop at the Rodi Road tavern along the way. You're such a good man when you don't drink. You're out there celebrating, and I'm here cooking and cleaning and taking care of the house and kids. The only place I ever go is to church on Sunday. Why don't you and I ever go anywhere together? " She would then break into tears, her nose turning bright red as she wiped it, with Libby or Kat consoling their mother as their father sat out on the back porch with Greg, their new dog, sulking.

This last comment would fan the flames of Johnny's guilt even more, since he felt he was helping the family in the best way he knew. After six months in his part-time job, he came home with something new for the family.

"C'mon out kids, there's a surprise out here." He shouted into the big country kitchen, which now looked bright and shiney with new yellow tile installed around the walls. Everyone ran outside thrilled at the sight of a new light green 1949 Ford sitting in the driveway.

"I got a good deal." Johnny smiled and winked at Dell, who just rolled her eyes knowing full well this new car would add to their present debt, which they could do without.

"Look at these sleek and smooth sides and new rear quarter windows that actually open." Johnny proceeded to demonstrate by opening doors and windows and other moveable parts of the automobile. His flamboyant sales pitch related that this model had integration of body and fenders setting a standard for automotive design. Sales of this model were highest for Ford since 1929 worldwide, he exclaimed before the captive family audience.

Terry, who had just taken drivers education last year at Turtle Creek High School, and had acquired a license, entertained thoughts toward taking out the family car as soon as she could bargain with her father, which would have to be soon and before she went into nurses training.

History would later say that most Americans were becoming satisfied with their lives during this era, as essentials such as electricity, telephones, refrigerators, good roads, and antibiotics made life more comfortable. In addition, strong unions and government and economic policies supported the middle class.

President Harry Truman gave approval of the hydrogen bomb to be produced after receiving word that the Russians had tested atomic weapons. The bomb was first tested by the United States on May 1951. After detonation, people came in to see the after effects. The government and scientists kept the bomb a military secret to prevent any other country from copying it.

Conservatism and change came swiftly for the nation. In the Pledge of Allegiance, the phrase "under God" was added. Women and men were dressing moderately in conventional heels, dresses and flannel suits. Channel, Bill Blass, Dior and Givenchy were some of the designers during this period. Blue jeans were starting to be seen more out in public, worn mostly by young people. A new flannel suit for women "straight from Paris" sold for $19.95.

The culture that produced good people, however, had changed rapidly during the last twenty years as technology, communications, and the economy made it tougher for people to live up to the higher social values achieved by previous generations. The advent of television exposed millions of Americans to world situations which they had never before seen in everyday life, as the black and white moving pictures in their home influenced their thoughts, understanding, likes and dislikes, manner of speech and even dressing adding up to their store of additional knowledge.

Few people could imagine that in a decade or so television would become a peremptory force in American culture, defining the news, reshaping politics, reorienting family life and remaking the cultural expectations of several generations of Americans. No one predicted that in a few decades 98 percent of all households would own a television set, exceeding the level of telephone ownership by five percent, and by a far larger margin in the homes of the poor.

Those members of an average household would watch the screen glowing constantly day and night some six hours a day. Few people foresaw that television, more than any other force, would provide the unifying images that would define the national experience and consciousness. American writers and creators spoke out against this severe bottleneck to creative expression, which struck out free expression in the minds of growing children.

Taking pleasure in television entertainment, the family gathered around their Air King console style for weekly programs with the rest of the nation. Terry enjoyed Hopalong Cassidy, Gene Autry, Roy Rogers and the Cisco Kid. Everyone watched along seeking the adventure the Wild West stories told. In the meantime, when Libby and Kat came home from school, Dell could be seen glancing at Kate Smith's afternoon homemaking show as she prepared dinner.

The new medium competed with other activities in everyday life. Shopping at the new serve yourself checkout Kroger Super Market in Penn's Hills on Friday nights, Johnny and Dell would hurry home to turn on "I Remember Mama". The weekly series featured an immigrant Swedish family integrating into society in New York City while maintaining the traditional beliefs of their native country. Johnny in turn, would quiet the household down on Tuesday evening to view Bishop Fulton J. Sheen's lecture of the week.

Every family had enchanted moments rooted in everyday life. The joys and sorrows of family are as mixed together as salt and pepper can be. It can be a complicated mix of intense emotional people. Arguments about politics, religion and how they make diverse decisions about love and work can come to the forefront in day-to-day discussions. No group can make their members feel happy and sad in an instant than the interior of these personal encounters.

The pugnacious Albred family would prove these principles time and time again as their strong personalities struggled to emerge and blend together to define the family unit. The fear of being a likeness of Aunt Agatha, in her selfish indulgent ways, hung over all of the Albred girls, as Dell sometimes revived stories of her sister-in-law avoiding work in the hotel kitchen, and usually ended with the threatening words, *you don't want to be like Aunt Agatha, do you?*

The strong legacy of Lizzie and her infamous authority held over everyone at the successful hotel, would haunt the household, as Dell watched her daughter Terry take on the characteristics of her strong paternal grandmother's domination over her sisters and brothers and sometimes even herself.

Libby and Katrina shared one double bed in the big bedroom with their sister having the other one all to herself. Immediately after World War II hard wood furniture became available again, and Johnny and Dell set out for Turtle Creek and Fallers Furniture to buy a new shipment that had just come in. The maple wood dressers and bed set looked nice with criss cross white organdy curtains hanging across the large picture window facing the cemetery in front, and the smaller back one, which looked out onto the long back yard.

Two old pieces from Dell's past sat in the back corners; a dark oak cedar chest with oak spindles around the top sides, and a large dressing table with a white onyx hand mirror and silver brushes and a comb sat in the middle, a plush stool in front.

Sometime when tempers were flaring and they came in contact with each other in this upstairs area away from their parents' jurisdiction, the two older siblings would thrash out their anger with one another, creating a battleground more often than not.

"Were you wearing my skirt again?" Terry yelled at Libby, her face angry with vengeance and hatred.

"Yes, I wore it, I had no clothes to wear the other day." Libby would defy her sister by looking her in the eye as no one else in the family would do and telling the truth, knowing her impudence would come back to hurt her.

"You little snot, you look like a slop in my skirt, it doesn't fit you, what are you trying to prove. That does it, I'm getting that steel cupboard I saw in Faller's to put my stuff in so it will be safe from the likes of you when I start training at Shadyside." Terry shouted angrily.

The huge floor model steel cupboard was delivered the next day. And that weekend Terry took the bus to Shadyside to begin training to be a nurse.

The curious cabinet had locks on every door, and no one knew where the keys were, especially Libby and Kat, who sat up in bed evenings while Terry was away, wondering what precious possessions their sister had that required secrecy of this kind.

The intrigue of this locked Goliath flamed the curiosity of the two younger sisters, especially Kat, who suggested one day after school that they break into it.

"I'll get a table knife, we can pry it open." Kat said. Libby laughed at her little sister, who showed more spunk than she gave her credit for in the past, since she still watched the antics of Buffalo Bob and Howdy Doody every night. Just then Libby felt bad for not taking Kat on walks with her and Frances. But Frances just wanted to talk about boys and didn't want Kat to hear, for fear she would tell their mother.

"You know we're gonna pay." Libby said regretfully, trying to warn her little sister of the dangers involved, but then she had an interest to satisfy as well and decided to join in on the break-in with some old keys she thought might fit, but none surrendered the tough Yale lock.

"I know, but it might be worth it. But at least we'll know what's in there. After all we share half the room, Lib." Kat said. Little dark haired Kat, always a fragile girl, had her own form of retaliation. Libby thought.

"Okay, I'll pry the bottom of the door open, and you reach your little hand in there and feel around, maybe you can pull something out." Then they both started giggling mischievously, as Kat squeezed her little hand through the wide crack.

"I think there's silk scarves, a book of some kind, and a glass bottle, oh it feels like perfume...oh oh, I think it spilled." She warned, pulling her dripping beautiful smelling fingers out of the opening.

"We're dead girls, we better stay clear when she comes home from school this weekend." Libby said, trying to think of a counter plan but none would absolve them from the terrible deed.

"Do not tell Mom, Kat, she won't defend us, especially now since Terry is away and she misses her a little. Pretend it didn't happen. But then, maybe Terry misses us too, and then maybe she'll laugh at our little search." Kat looked admiringly at Libby, like she just might know something about human nature. But that night Libby turned to St Theresa The Little Flower, whose statue sat on Terry's highboy dresser, that her sister would not be too tough with them.

That Friday evening, when Terry came home for the weekend, she ran straight up to her room to change into blue jeans. Hmm, it smells nice in here, she thought. It smells like my Faberge I got for Christmas from the people I baby-sat for.

"Hey Libby." Terry came down into the kitchen, and grabbed the bottles of peanut butter and jelly out of the cupboard to make a sandwich. Since her voice sounded calm, Libby came into the kitchen to face her older sister inquiringly. Kat backed into the corner of the big room sitting sheepishly on the covered radiator.

"How did you get into my cupboard without a key?" she spoke authoritatively, her clear blue eyes searing through Libby. *Here it comes. Oh, God, help me.* Libby prayed, then tried to side track her older sister.

"So how's nurses training? Did you save anyone from dying yet?" But it was a futile attempt, since Terry concentrated on the forthcoming answer.

"I didn't, I tipped the corners so I could dust underneath, and whatever you had in there must have spilled." *Sorry for my lie, St. Theresa, but its going to prevent a lot of blood shed here.* Then a miracle happened. Terry smiled, apparently finding another fresh way to incriminate her younger sister, especially since when she opened the refrigerator that there was no milk left. And now Joel became her target, who was ready for his sister.

"I'm going down to the dairy." he replied, instantly ready for her onslaughts.

"Make it chocolate," she said.

Terry smiled, coming back to Libby's reply.

"Oh are you really cleaning up there these days with me gone? I am the only one who keeps that room clean." Terry elaborated, but seemed to be sidetracked, which brought relief to Libby who winked at her nervous little sister in the corner.

Terry could sometime be a force to be reckoned with, and only Johnny could suggest to his daughter in no uncertain terms that she restrain herself. This procedure would take more than just a look her way. He knew that in their efforts to protect their daughter from cruel outside community harm during her school

180

years, the entire family had overcompensated, and now it would be difficult to get back some of the self-confidence of some family members.

Dell was pleased that the kind and mellow nature of her dear departed father-in-law Zach was evident in the good nature of Joel, as he demonstrated toward his younger sisters Libby and Kat. Libby had inherited her grandmother Theresa Gessner's fine singing voice. Dell and Johnny knew that their daughter could not go forward into a profession with this talent because she had not adopted a musical instrument for training.

She would need a piano which they could not afford to buy due to many other family priorities. They both hoped she would eventually meet a nice young man and marry, but as she prepared to enter high school, Libby went into college preparatory subjects hoping to enter as music major. Her friend Randi and Frances and a many others were planning to be nurses or teachers. None of these careers appealed to Libby, who wanted to further her classical singing into an operatic career.

Teachers encouraged her to sing regularly at events in school, giving her the needed confidence to know that she could compete as a professional. Now training at a prominent music studio in the fashionable Shady side area, she would meet Terry after class, while she was in nurses training at Shadyside Hospital. The two sisters were given a chance to meet on neutral ground away from home subsequently establishing a little better relationship.

The climate for certain types of career success for Libby and her classmates would prove to be a difficult road in the late 1950's, as most young women flocked to college, predominantly into education and nursing and traditional female disciplines, so they would not compete with men. College administrators decided that coeds needed a curriculum that would serve society's demands that girls grow up to become happy homemakers.

The professions were for men, and most universities employed quotas to reserve their seats. At the University of Texas, for example, 95 percent of those accepted to law and medical school were male, and of the one hundred students in each new dental class only two could be female. The reason being cited was, "girls aren't strong enough to pull teeth."

One woman, who graduated with a journalism degree from Columbia, was offered a job at one paper in the cafeteria, not the newsroom, and another company refused to hire her because a female reporter had been raped in their parking lot. All women started at a lower salary than men, and in hard times they were the first to be fired.

Joel Albred got notice to pack up and leave his loving family home to join the Korean War. This would be the first war in history in which troops of a world organization acted as police to fight an aggressor nation. The war began on June 25, 1950, when troops of Communist-ruled North Korea attacked South Korea in an effort to unify the country by force. The United Nations charter, signed by the major nations of the world in 1945, had outlawed all such aggression.

Consequently, the United Nations asked member countries to aid South Korea. President Truman ordered US air and naval forces to help defend South Korea, and then U.S. ground troops came to the aid of South Korea. General Douglas MacArthur commanded the UN forces in the Far East.

"Aw he won' have ta go, his eyes 'er too bad." Phil said when he stopped by one Sunday soon after Joel had received his draft notice. Wearing the new Bermuda shorts with high knee socks Phil thought he looked cool, but Joel had to chuckle at his Uncle's new look. Most people did not believe that men should show their knobby knees in public.

The family, but especially Dell, wanted very much to believe Phil's declaration about Joel, even though he fell short of all of their trust with his hair-brained schemes, especially his latest cheesy potato chips snacks recipe he was perfecting in the basement of his home.

In some respects Uncle Phil had newfound admiration among the family with his marriage to Twila Tower, whose father owned Blue Tower restaurants, a popular hamburger place in the area. Twila would give each of them free passes for hamburgers when she came to visit. She was the first woman they had seen with bleached blond hair, and they saw her as a Marilyn Monroe look alike.

"I passed my eye exam, Mom, I'm shipping out in two weeks." Joel told his mother in somewhat of daze as she stared at him in disbelief; leaning on her hoe in the middle of the garden that warm summer day planting additional lettuce plots in the garden.

"What did they say about you having to wear glasses all the time?" She said.

"Ha, they said they'd give me a pair of safety glasses to wear." Dell's heart fell, as she thought about sending another son to war, especially in this decade of what had almost seemed like peaceful times at last. And where was this Korea the newsmen talked about?

Oh God have mercy on us. She prayed, looking up to the Heavens after he had walked up to the house to change clothes and come back to work in the garden beside her.

The day before Joel would leave for Seattle, Kat sat on the basement steps watching her brother do bench presses with weights. She couldn't imagine what life would be like around there without her brother around. She was always by his side in the yard as he worked; riding in the wheelbarrow on top of leaves or soil he hauled from different parts of the yard.

"It'll be good for him. He's too backward – for God's sake he never leaves the yard or goes anywhere or meets anyone." Ben said to his parents. Later he laughed with Joel about his new combat glasses, trying to make light of his brother's apprehension about leaving home. Ben now taught school and coached in a northwestern Pennsylvania high school near Clarion, meeting a shy girl who worked in one of the stores there.

"Not at all his type." said Aunt Mary after meeting Marjorie, a slim blue-eyed dishwater blond. Mary's hair had turned pure white over the years, and her trim figure had filled out a bit too much in some places.

"Well, for one thing, he's an educated man, who will go up the ladder fast in education, and she seems to be scared of her own shadow. I don't know, did she finish high school." She said sardonically.

But Dell had found Ben's fiancé to be sweet, if a little timid, and not at all as outgoing as Tommy's wife. It would take many years before the Albred's would get to know Dot Albred, their new sister-in-law, since the couple lived far away.

Soon they would learn that Charley would also go to war, as Aunt Agatha tearfully told her brother Johnny over the phone. She now had a man in her life, though the family did not know who had captured the heart of Agatha.

General Dwight D. Eisenhower was elected president, though the nation mistrusted his military status, saying that he would not make a good commander in chief with his tough war record. He would be the first Republican in the White House for the first time in twenty-four years, with Richard Nixon as vice-president.

The conflict in Korea would go on until a truce was signed on July 27, 1953, but there would be over a million casualties and almost 500,000 prisoners of war. Joel Albred came home a changed man with a heavy heart over loosing his buddies to bloody warfare.

Senator John F. Kennedy married Jacqueline Bouvier and Queen Elizabeth II was crowned in England. Joseph Stalin died and Khrushchev became the Soviet party boss.

In science, the double helix structure of DNA molecule was discovered in research laboratories.

Television still dominated American family life with *Father Knows Best* reining as one of the most watched television shows, exemplifying the perfect family in the now called "suburbs". Jim Anderson was wise, warm, and understanding; his wife Margaret was a perfect mother and thoughtful homemaker.

This complacent mood prevailed throughout the country, with only a minority of citizens concerned about the true sociological picture of America. There were problems in the nation, and in the late 1950's three issues would gradually appear: life in the atomic age, the role of women, and the status of blacks, who were being ignored by white legislators.

Another father, Johnny worried, to the point of loosing sleep at night, about his two daughters going out into the mainstream. His concerns were mostly centered on the boys and men they would meet.

Terry had turned into a lovely well-developed woman, and one who could attract the kind of low-grade man that he scorned in his life, a worthless guy who only had one thing on this mind. He expressed his concern to his older daughter, who had graduated from nurses training and was now making a decent salary at Magee Women's Hospital in Oakland. His bushy eyebrows moved together in a troubled look over clear brown knowing eyes as they spoke.

"Why don't you trust me dad?" She spoke up to him, stating her position profoundly.

"I'm not going to let any man touch me, don't worry."

"I trust you, Terry, God knows most of the time you can take care of yourself. But there are some reckless guys out there, and you won't get away until they have you in their clutches."

His last thought motivated him to anxiously enter into the same circles as a 24 year old, frequenting the same after hour's place she went to drink and dance after working the graveyard shift at the hospital. Why she wanted to be a nurse and work in a hospital with sick people baffled him, since she spent most of her life there having almost continuous plastic surgery since she was born with, but nevertheless it was the profession work she had chosen.

Johnny strolled into the classy Shadyside Bar near the Cathedral of Learning at the University of Pittsburgh and Carnegie Institute of Technology nonchalantly, chatting informally with the bartender about the weather being unseasonable and the bad parking situation. And soon he spotted his daughter walking in with a friend of hers, Kathleen, he recognized immediately.

His daughter's brown wavy hair shone under the colorful strategically centered strobe lights of the café, which irritated him, especially when he saw the formfitting red and white print dress she had designed and sewn looking seductively attractive. *Damn it, why couldn't she wear her nurse's uniform here. That way those leeches wouldn't look at her so longingly.* He seethed.

Terry couldn't believe it when she saw her father sitting by the bar having a beer and staring at them coming into the lobby. She walked right over to him smiling. *He would talk to her tomorrow about how much red lipstick she was wearing*

"Checkin' up on me, huh, Dad?" She said laughingly.

"Did you find anything yet?"

"Oh, I just wanted to see the place." He lied.

"Hello Kathleen." He said, as if they met there every evening after work.

"How's your father feeling?" He changed the subject immediately, asking about her father's recent gallbladder operation. Both girls smiled at each other understandingly.

A musical group began to play back in a corner, and both girls said goodbye. Soon Johnny left as well, feeling very much out of place as couples began to dance. Terry would not be asked to dance that evening and would forever hold her father responsible for spoiling her fun.

11. Doing What Is Expected

No, she would not sell the house for back taxes, where would they go? It was a horrible world when poor widow women were always bad off, and to think it wasn't their fault; it was their husbands for dying in the first place. They were the ones who were supposed to take care of their wives, even though they were six feet under. Joseph had promised her father that she would never want for anything, and now look what she was facing.

What's more, it gave her chilblains to think she might have to work. Lots of women were working outside the home now, but what kind of a job could she get? The only place she ever worked was in the hotel, and that was drudgery, the kind suited more for Dell who was very good at housework of any kind. She could plough into anything around the house and make it beautiful, cooking, cleaning, gardening, you name it. Too bad she couldn't do the same for her scraggily appearance. Johnny had to be blind in one eye.

Unlike her sister-in-law, Agatha had done just the opposite in her house, with roaches running around in the cupboard, thick grease on the stove burners, and ancient food in the refrigerator starting to smell, this made her think, how could one tell when food was rotting? None of the drains worked well, and the bathroom sinks and tub had the perennial rust line running down from the spigots. The red smelly Lifeboy soap was mushy and slimy in the washbowl, turning the whole area into a colorful messy swirl.

Dust was a daily companion, as much as she tried to wipe it every couple of months. She wasn't sure where to store the dirty clothes; the ringer washer had broken down a year ago and had not been fixed. Now they would just wash something out when a change of clothing was needed. Sometimes the shirt got pressed, sometimes not. It was all just too much for Agatha to keep up with all day.

Another terrible thought suddenly occurred to her, the daily grind would be very unsuitable for her delicate bunions, just waiting to be tampered with to cause soreness, not to mention the strong lye soap she might have to use on her lovely hands. No, she would never ever do that again. Not with God as her witness would she deliberately step into the misery of hotel or restaurant work again.

Turning the television on to *The Ed Sullivan Show* this Sunday evening, Agatha lay back against her grimy gray frieze sofa to nibble hot roasted peanuts. She loved to devour the hot roasted red Spanish kind she bought at the five and ten cent store. The grease stained bag sat on the table, while she daintily pinched them one by one with thumb and forefinger laying the tiny morsels onto her tongue. Licking her salty oily fingers clean, she wished with all her heart that she had had an extra quarter, just enough money to buy the latest Photoplay magazine displayed in the Pullen's Drug Store on her trip downstreet to Turtle Creek that afternoon.

A big glamorous picture of Marilyn Monroe in diamonds and white fur flashed across the cover, since the movie, "How To Marry A Millionaire" was now showing everywhere. Betty Grable and Lauren Bacall were also in the picture, which she might go to see. But it was shocking the way the stars today were wearing next to nothing. In her day, the more clothes they put on the more glamorous they looked. What was the world coming to with all this naked flesh around?

"Eeeek." She screamed as a little furry critter of some nature, ran past her naked toes next to the couch. Immediately shuffling her feet back into her satin mules she cried out.

"Joey, I told you not to leave those chipmunks up here, keep them in the cellar." God knew what else was running around down there. Rats, squirrels, foxes and all kinds of vermin. It was too much for her to think about right now.

Oh well it didn't matter, as long as he kept them down there. Now shoo, shoo." She took a newspaper, heralding the little brown-stripped creature to the basement door, just in time for Joey, who loved outdoor animals indoors, to throw it a peanut.

"Aw mom, look how cute they are. " And he steered it toward a whole family of chipmunks peeping out from behind the tool bench.

"Don't let them come up here Joey. You're nuts, you oughta go up and live with your cousin, Katrina, she's got cats, dogs, a bunny and even though the Albreds don't have a bunch of chickens anymore, she's still got "Henny Penny" living in the old chicken coup. That kid must not have any friends, just animals."

"Don't worry about that Ma, look over there, and see the trap door by the window? They can come and go as they please." But his mother had already lost interest. He'd kept quiet about all the damage they had done chewing the insulation in the basement wall, though it wouldn't matter to her at all, since she didn't understand about such things. If it wasn't something fancy to wear or featured in a movie magazine, she wasn't interested at all.

Sixteen-year-old Joey and his older brother Charley, who'd just returned from an army stint in Korea, had learned a long time ago that their mother wasn't completely hooked up when it came to learning about the important things in life. In fact, they felt that the tables were turned and they were more the parents while she remained childlike in their home.

Joey didn't think that she was mental, just slow and completely comfortable in her own world of make believe dress up and picture shows and television. Sometimes he'd be angry because he didn't have a normal mother, like Aunt Dell, but this was the deal they were dealt and they had to make the best of it. Charley had moved into his own place after he returned from Korea, because he ran out of patience with her, he guessed.

No, Johnny didn't have to know, it was none of his business. Her brother would just give her that "why are you so stupid" look again. There would have to be another way to raise the money to keep the wolves away from the door. Now this month, all those silly bills were due again, especially the last four years taxes. The last notice said one hundred dollars was due in their office by the next month. The sheriff who had come to the door mentioned the word foreclosure, which had scared her to death. At least she had gotten their monthly check from the Orphan's Court, Johnny had set up the appointment to go to Pittsburgh and sign for it, Dell had gone with her.

Glancing down at her stubby worn fingernails sent Agatha into an immediate depression of the worst kind. Once beautifully laquered with the reddest paint she could find in the dime store, she would splay them out at every given opportunity in public, holding her purse, showing her lovely hands at every turn. Well, they didn't matter; she could wear her white gloves everywhere now. Reaching over to dust the mirror over the oak buffet, she peered into it as her hand wiped the filth from it with an old tee shirt.

Just a hint of auburn streaks lay between the gray hairs she'd acquired thanks to her husband dying on purpose. But now she remembered a cupboard full of hats for every season and purpose. Running to the closet, she stretched up to pull a number of decorative round hatboxes down from every fine woman's store in Braddock.

Gently fitting a large white straw picture hat in the center of her head, the problem was solved, as she was posed, exuding with glamour and sophistication once again.

Spring was imminent, at least the snow was melting as she looked out of the dirty side window, truly this was a sign which foretold the wearing of suits, of which she had many, for Easter Sunday would arrive in a couple of weeks. Taking a dark navy Chanel fitted outfit from a padded coat hanger, Agatha remembered back to the days when her mother would give her two hundred dollars to go shopping on Saturdays. She would return with handbags and boxes filled with complete outfits, dresses, suits, shoes and accessories. What fun she had trying them on over and over again.

Standing in front of her reflection in the bureau mirror, she knew a tight girdle would make a whale of a difference in appearance, and heck, the pain would be worth it. Then looking into one of the hatboxes she glimpsed a corner of green under a string of pearls. Most likely a dollar, she grabbed for it. No, it was an old one hundred dollar bill, but how could she not have spent it. A wave of euphoria came over Agatha, filled with hope sitting on the corner of the bed; everything would be okay for them.

A visit to her cousin Millie in New York City would be just the ticket to cheer her up. "Joey, come up here." Agatha hollered.

The sun shone brilliantly, filling the big Albred kitchen with potent springtime rays, as Dell and Mary busied themselves with the task at hand. Mary had come to stay the week before the wedding. And even though the reception would be catered, the two sisters baked and cooked just for all of their houseguests who would arrive before the end of the week.

Mouth-watering smells wafted up onto the second floor where Joel applied the last brushstrokes to painting bedroom doors. Smells mixed to almost nauseating heights, but as he bent his head towards the stairway, his nostrils could discern the good cooking from the paint fumes. Promising himself that he would definitely stop at the kitchen afterward as a reward, he continued to ready the place for all of the pending wedding guests.

Large roasters full of pirohi's, delicate butter dumplings filled with prunes and mashed potatoes, sat on one side of the new electric stove that Dell had purchased with her inheritance money from Pop's estate. She was thrilled to cook on the beautiful new Westinghouse range sparkling in the bright room. And though she missed her father, who passed away from lung cancer, she secretly thanked him every day for her good fortune.

Mary carried over additional pots of hot stuffed cabbage to store on the counter, sliding over the large pot of creamy chicken paprikas' with sour cream and homemade noodles. In the chair next to the window beside a warm radiator sat a big open canister, which both women had access to from either side of the table. Mutually reaching into the bin for generous handfuls of flour, they threw a portion across the ancient breadboard on which her mother Theresa had made delicious perohi every holiday. Preparing the area, they began to gently knead the mounds of lemon smelling dough for nut and poppy seed rolls.

"Mary how much yeast did you mix into your recipe?" Dell was concerned that ingredients were getting mixed up in the process, since this was a task she always tackled alone. Smiling at her sister, she was pleased inside that she would stay and help and help her with the preparations for the family dinner before Terry's wedding.

"No, no, I'm making the kolache Dell, remember we agreed?" Mary was her same assertive self, an attribute that Dell always admired.

Then they both laughed at their forgetfulness.

"Gee, I'm glad Terry found a nice man. She's had her share of sadness in life." Mary said compassionately. Dell nodded back across the table.

"Can you imagine Mary, she spent all that time in hospitals when she was just a baby and now this is where she works, and she met a nice boy there. William had that terrible accident and ended up in the Emergency Room at Magee Hospital, with pieces of glass stuck in his arm and leg after falling from the scaffold up there working on that construction crew in Oakland."

"Well, I hope he's a tough guy. Terry might give it to 'em if things don't go her way. You know how stubborn she can be." Mary said, laughingly, but knew she could only go so far criticizing Dell's kids, even though she loved them like her own, especially Terry who had come a long way from her early years.

"William's a quiet guy, but he worships the ground Terry walks on." Dell bragged.

"Dell, whatever happened at Ben's wedding? Her sister inquired. "They had no music or photographs. That sure wasn't well organized."

"I dunno Mary, her parents are very odd people. They had an arranged marriage in Europe. Her mother, Mrs. Spivak is afraid of her husband. I think he pushes her around."

" I can't believe Ben would get into this kind of family." Mary replied.

"Mary, I try to stay out of my kids affairs – John and I just listen. Dell said.

Just then Kat and Sylvia came running down through the kitchen. The two sisters looked at them admiringly, both glad that the youngest family members got along so well. At twelve, they still liked playing with paper dolls. Mary was pleased that she and Dell had daughters close to the same age, and hoped they would remain as close as she and Dell were.

"Mom, we're going down to feed Henny and Bugs." Kat said, violet eyes smiling at her cousin, as they ran out the back door. Sylvia giggled, with shiney brown curls bouncing as she ran behind her cousin. Frolicking in the warmth of the season, they ran outdoors, this time without the drudge of a heavy winter coat. Hulda Honawickle, Kat's gray-stripped cat, named after the olde time movie star segment of Howdy Doody, ran at her heels hoping to play with her mistress this morning.

"Hello Hulda." Katrina said sweetly, bending down to pet the affectionate young cat.

"Aw, she's so skinny. Doesn't she eat at all, Dell? " Mary said, after they had let the screen door slam haphazardly behind them.

"Well, she's healthy, Mary, what else can I do? I give her eggnog and rich foods to build her up. I was a bean pole too, remember?" Dell said, on the fringes of annoyance.

In the meantime a cry of distress came from upstairs, having them bursting into guffaws and chuckles once again.

"Ouch you're sticking pins into me." Libby shouted.

"Well stay still, I have to get this seam straight." Terry said sternly. Libby frowned meanly, knitting her eyebrows, resembling her father who expressed deep disappointment in this manner. She did realize that this would be the very last painful duty she might have to undergo within the walls of this bedroom. Hallelujah. A quiet excitement and relief momentarily subdued her anger.

Next week her sister would be gone gone gone from living full time in this house. Not just that, Libby would be queen of this big bedroom. Oh well there would always be Kat around, but she could manage her younger sister.

"Now, move over this way." Terry yanked her by the waist.

"If this looks horrible, you'll be the one to blame, girl." She threatened once again.

Terry had designed the wedding dress personally from beginning to end. Yards and yards of satin and laces were cut, shaped and seamed creatively into a fairy princess original. The new "A-line fashion" lines flowed onto a cathedral train, with tiny hooks carefully sewn inside the hem for detachment for dancing later. These would lift the long skirt to clear the way for Terry's feet and legs to move swiftly to polka rhythms at the reception in the hall, which would take place later that evening at a nearby clubhouse.

It was a hot summer day when the queenly vision in white, a delicate sequined tiara atop the brunette curls gathered around her crown, set out to marry the love of her life. The fine tulle veil studded with seed pearls fell down the front of her countenance, as Terry strolled slowly down the aisle with her father. It was a moment in inertia for Johnny, clad in a new light colored sharkskin suit walking slowly beside his eldest daughter.

"God bless you both". He whispered, handing her over to William, who looked as white as the white bib inside his rented tux." Dell's eyes teared up watching and waiting in the pew to witness the prouncement of wedding vows with the man Terry would spend the rest of her life with, William Soronson of McKeesport.

Tommy, Dottie, Ben and Marjorie sat together; Katrina and Sylvia sat with Aunt Mary and Uncle Paul, as Libby and Joel took part in the wedding. Agatha, bedecked in elbow length white gloves, reaching up every now and then to straighten her big straw picture hat, enjoyed every minute of the summer event of the year. Phil and Twila did not show up at church, but they'd heard that he had traveled to Buffalo where a new potato chip factory was being built.

Historically, America still embraced the traditional role of husband as the head and wife as the homemaker in the home. A survey found that household chores of cleaning and washing, only ten percent of husbands helped their happy homemakers. She embellished the home and then created another recipe for dinner. In 1955 the two nonfiction best sellers were "Better Homes & Gardens Decorating Book and Betty Crocker's Cookbook.

Smith College reported in 1961 that their institution was old-fashioned, but they felt that a woman's place was in the home. Marriage is a career, and it is inappropriate for them to compete with men, so "Why don't we stop competing with them

194

and instead cooperate?" Mr. Right was security and would be a good father and provider. College became the "world's best marriage mart".

As a consequence, teens were "going steady" at record rates during the fifties, and women married younger than at any time in the century and the divorce rate plummeted. Marriage equaled success. Divorce equaled failure. No unmarried person could be happy and no female wanted to remain single and become an old maid.

The most spectacular success was having babies, especially since women possess a natural maternal instinct, as opposed to the fathers who do not have an inherent paternal nature. The birth rate soared to four million births annually; the baby boom, hence the theme "Cheaper By The Dozen". And now a new film, "Father Of The Bride" starring, Elizabeth Taylor was a popular box office release, further romanticizing the sacred union of Matrimony.

It was Saturday morning in August, and Libby slowly walked down to the bottom of the field with a cup of coffee to sit and think at the old picnic table, now abandoned after a summer filled with memories. A robin flew into the nearest tall locust tree carrying a large worm to a nest there. The garden was green and lush with tomatoes just ready for picking, and huge green peppers hanging low, waited for their benefactor to pluck them from the stem. She would not take liberties with the harvest. No, it would have to be the head gardener, her mother, since once before she'd brought a few tomatoes up to the house only to be told that they were not quite ripe enough.

The plot was only half as big as it used to be, with only five of them still living at home. Everything seemed to change when Tommy and Ben were married. When they visited their new wives had to be included in everything, it wasn't any fun anymore, her brothers were changed somehow, and they couldn't just go off without asking their partners. Time and situations had separated Libby from the closeness she once felt here as a child. For instance, she had never seen the new rose garden and decorative birdbath her mom had planted in front of the garden. Where had she been? Maybe it happened while she was involved in high school activities while a senior at Turtle Creek High School.

Looking down to the other part of the yard where the plum trees once held the swing that Ben had built, she wondered when they had disappeared, then remembered her mom saying they had contracted some form of disease and had to be chopped down. Now a huge forsythia bush proudly flourished in the same spot, where she and her cousin Joey had eaten so many green onions from the garden and apples from the cow pasture tree hide out, having thrown them up behind the trees. They were so sick from winding the swing rope around tighter and tighter and spinning 'round and 'round that their stomachs couldn't take it. Libby had to chuckle to herself.

She'd graduated from high school hoping to enter Duquesne University's School of Music in the fall, but now this would not take place. Daddy had said there was no money available for school. Auditioning and finally qualifying for a scholarship there had not provided enough funds for her to proceed into the freshman class, without being supplemented by other money from home or somewhere.

Libby had performed to the best of her ability, sounding the notes and words sharp and clear for the judges there, singing an aria from the opera La Gioconda, based on Victor Hugo's play Angelo, *tyran de Padoue*. This was the blind mother, La Cieca's part, and so called, "The Blind Girl's Song". Her clear contralto voice sounded up into the rafters, bringing attention from the crew, as Libby's vibrato resounded out over the theatre lights.

Afterward, someone had said that maybe a sponsor could finance the rest of Libby's music studies, but there was no one available to assist with the venture. And she already knew that her mother and father would not approve of her going forth and associating with "show business" people, as her dad called them. Consequently, she was beginning to loose confidence that her aspirations could ever come true.

By late September, Libby had taken a job at a small corporation on Parkway East, the main highway to Pittsburgh, called Union Switch and Signal Corporation in the town of

Swissvale. And oh how she missed this open yard, running free as a bird without any worries. Working now as an advertising typist, she spent eight hours a day behind an IBM catalogue print machine with a team of people working on a government contract compiling an Air Force Manual.

She missed her high school chums, and the fun of being together every day. Those days now seemed faraway. After school they'd congregate at the local drugstore for cokes and chips, the boys going over to Pinky's Poolroom.

Quite often Libby and her friend Helena, a pal from senior year would make visits to the Blessed Sacrament at St. Coleman's Church after school. The solitude of the old Gothic church held consolation as they prayed for a bright future after high school. The cold dark building had seen better days, before the floods from the nearby stream of Turtle Creek.

The tile floors and wall paint were peeling, giving it a decaying look; nevertheless, for them it gave solace in their anxieties at a time of change. They had both been baptized and made their first communion and confirmation there, feeling inspired after a brief visit.

One day as they were blessing themselves with holy water from the huge marble fount, a sister of Mercy approached them, who had seen them come and go a few times.

"Hello girls, do you feel that you would like to enter into the religious life?" She looked deep into their eyes with a kind-searching look, and handed them each a pamphlet on religious vocations. As they walked around the corner of the church, giggles drew forth.

"Get thee to the nunnery." Helena exclaimed. Discussing this further they thought about the material things they'd have to give up, even though they loved their faith.

"We would have to give up shopping." Libby said.

"And boys." Helena responded. They then laughed nervously. The next time they saw Sister Mary Aquinas, they were honest with their intentions for the future.

Now though, Libby seemed to be suddenly thrust into an entirely different adult world, far away from the frivolous fancies of youth. Dressing up in nylon stockings and high heels, she tried to fit in with all of the grownups at work now. The salvation and familiarity of stopping in for a visit to nearby St. Anslem's church became part of her lunchtime. Libby felt particularly glad about saving money for college; this was not hard to do, since she was grossing five hundred dollars a month, almost as much as the secretaries at U.S.Steel Corporation, and she didn't have to go all the way to downtown Pittsburgh to earn this salary.

As Johnny and Dell were viewing television one October Friday evening, a news flash came on announcing the Space Age had officially begun as the Soviet Union launched Sputnik, the first man-made satellite, into orbit. Russia had preceded America into the space race.

Later that evening, as they were preparing to go to bed, panic gripped Dell, when she finally convinced Johnny to let her look at the inflammation and irritation of his foot and toes. Worrying sick about his refusal to go to the doctor, she had wearily watched him hobble up the bus steps to work each day agonizing with pain for more than two weeks. His last desperate measure of cutting open the toes of his shoes to let air pass through, prompted her to take action.

Hearing him rustling the paper around the bandage to dress his sores that evening before bed, Dell pushed opened the bathroom door. She stood in horror, gasping at the putrid and decaying condition of his toes. At first she couldn't believe it, staring at the dark sickly yellow, almost black wound from which a stench of worse than moldy cheese emanated. Fright and panic struck in the pit of her stomach, while Johnny tried to rationalize nervously. Dell hardly recognized the man stooping down tending to himself in front of the bathtub.

"Its numbness, Dell, I think my toes have died, could this be gangrene?"

His voice quivered, confessing his darkest fear to his wife. Dell's heart swelled up with compassion for her poor wounded husband, too choked up to say anything in response. This was something far beyond her comprehension, having never seen anything of this nature before.

"C'mon John we're going to the doctor as soon as possible." Dell demanded, not caring if he objected or not. She would drag him to Dr. Newhouse, who might not be the best one to see in his old age, but he could certainly diagnose something like this and recommend another man to go to for further treatment.

Then Dell's terror turned into anger, as she lashed out at her husband.

"Honestly John, you're supposed to be a smart man, how could you let this happen?" Her once strong and swift husband, through all their adversities as a couple, had taken a wrong turn, trying to defy nature and failing miserably.

"Who would support this family Dell?" He spoke sadly, down trodden.

"You might have been helped John, you're only in your fifties for Pete sake."

While lying in bed tormented by worry that night, Dell clasped and fingered the sorrowful mysteries on her worn pearl rosaries that Tommy had sent her one Mother's Day from when he was stationed in Germany. She reflected on their life together.

They had been married for almost thirty years and she had deferred to him on almost everything in her life. After all, he was the man in the family. Now she was learning too late that men could make stupid mistakes, especially concerning their health. Johnny was a coward about going to doctors, and in this way he took after Lizzie who never went to a doctor under any circumstances. Their life together would never be the same after this; her strong and willful husband was seriously damaged. From that day forward, Dell took control, never trusting her husband to make the right decision again for their lives.

The next day a specialist hospitalized Johnny immediately at Magee Hospital in Oakland. Dell secretly wished that Terry was still there as a nurse. Terry had the kind of confidence that Dell needed now. Her daughter knew how to take charge in these situations, since she rose naturally into the role of responsibility. But Terry had moved to the state of Ohio after her marriage and worked at a hospital there now.

Dell called Tommy and Ben and their wives to tell them about their father's prognosis. They were in complete consternation as to how this could have happened. The rest of the family gathered around to pray novenas for their father's return to some kind of normalcy, never imagining the worst situation that could come out of this circumstance. Libby put her arm around fourteen year old Kat, who was troubled with concern for her father.

One day later, Johnny faced the awful prospect of having a leg amputated. Then he would face the inevitability of surgery to explore for the clogged artery that would improve the rest of his circulation. The Albred family was further devastated, as their father lay suffering with a grim diagnosis for the recovery of his leg and foot.

However, as he lay in the hospital bed in prayer, a surprise visitor lifted his spirits. Libby's friend Randi, now a student nurse at Presbyterian Hospital in another part of Oakland, stopped by to see him.

"Hello, Mr. Albred, how are you doing?" Looking up to see who had come, he felt as if it was an angel stopping by to lead him into the pearly gates. Instead he smiled up at the young woman who he'd seen as a young girl visiting in their home. Her poise and confidence were striking, especially when her bedside manner came across.

"Hello Randi, I'd forgotten that you were going into training. Guess I let this go a little too long." He confessed, embarrassedly.

"Don't worry." She spoke with compassion.

"These cases sometimes deteriorate fast. It will turn out okay. You may have to watch your diet and get prosthesis, but you can live a normal life again. I see people going through this all the time." After this she walked over to see him often, cheering him up when she came into his room. But two weeks later he came home to face another trial.

Rich was a malcontent. He loved fast cars, pretty girls and tried hard to emulate James Dean. With clear blue eyes that saw right through a person, and wavy blond hair brushed back in a DA hairstyle, Rich was a rebel without a cause living in an era that seemed to have no future available for a guy like him who was tired of the same old narrow choices life had to offer. He was among the growing number of disillusioned young males brooding a setback to get it out of their systems.

Sure there was a lot of injustice in the world, but the people in government who could do something about it, turned their heads the other way. The double standard ruled, with a President who was out on the golf course most of the time, a smoke ring of malaise seemed to encircle the youth of American cities.

Spotting Libby across the room, he strolled over and began to talk "cool".

"Hey baby, whadaya say we have a pop later on our morning break?" Libby smiled disconcertedly, wondering how this guy could work in a professional office with this kind of laissez-faire attitude. It was just inappropriate in a business office. Besides, she felt nervous about being called "baby". She had never dated men older than her, and he was worldlier. Did he want to take her out, was that it?

She couldn't understand what he wanted.

"I beg your pardon? Do you have a question about the last page I typed for you? Did I put the proper spaces in the nomenclature chart"? Whew, he thought exasperated, checking out her crinoline and black suede flats; this chick is out of it. What boat did she get off? A Natalie Wood she wasn't.

Libby knew he was one of the technical writers working on the manual, but thought he was more serious natured and she stared incredulously at him. Then Rich realized, that maybe he should try a better approach with their new young typist and smiled into a big dimpled grin.

"Hey, I have two coupons for a free movie ticket. Wanna go see "Pete Kelley's Blues" at the Stanley Theatre." Libby looked at him sharply, hazel eyes blazing.

"You're a working man, maybe we can go on a proper date." Later she would ask herself how she gathered up the gumption to speak up to practically a stranger this way. But there was something about him that titillated her senses and excited her inside like no one else she'd ever known before. He wore a white corduroy shirt with an insignia on the side pocket, claiming it was his family's crest. Libby believed him and his expressive ways. In a way Rich was refreshing with the terrible gloom that had descended over her house now. They soon started to see each other out of the office, and one afternoon he even accompanied her on a noon visit to St. Anslem's. As they knelt and started to pray, Rich broke out into stifled snickers, which brought them both into giggles as two small children.

"Don't get serious about him, he's not a very nice person." Her friend Mary Lou told her one day. Libby thought this was just plain gossip.

"Why?" She inquired

"I don't know, he just has a reputation for treating people malicious." Libby dismissed this information, and decided to pray for him. Rich was fun and they were just dating, but by Christmas day they were engaged to marry.

EQUILIBRIUM

PART FOUR

"Give us strength to encounter what is to come, that we may be brave in peril, constant in tribulation, temperate in wrath and in all changes of fortune and, down even to the gate of death, loyal and loving to one another."

Robert Louis Stevenson

12. What You Make It

Idealism rang royally at the threshold of the sixties, and John F. Kennedy became the standard bearer of that overall national feeling. In speeches leading up to his first year in office, JFK confronted the complacent 1950's, resounding, "The torch has been passed to a new generation of Americans." He promised to move America forward with vigor, ushering in an era of rising expectations with a group of youthful advisers known as the best and the brightest culled from corporations and universities, across the homeland

Student unrest around the nation was corralled into the Peace Corp and tasks in campus organizations like the Student Peace Union, grew from 150 to 4,000 three years later. The Young People's Socialist League tripled to 800 by 1962. Ruled by the self-satisfied standards of the 1950's, these organizations were radical because they no longer were afraid to state their views at a small demonstration; and by the late 1960's they became debating societies.

This new pulsating political mood inspired the nation as people everywhere set out to change their corner of the world. In the Township of Wilkins, the home of almost ten thousand citizens, County of Allegheny, Johnny Aloyisius Albred worked valiantly, both physically and mentally rising to the guidelines required for the elected office of Tax Collector.

When the year before, having lost both legs to the surgeon's knife, he emerged from his hospital bed a sad and forlorn man feeling doomed to a useless life as a recluse, Johnny shared bedfellows with the true meaning of hopelessness and despair. How would he spend the rest of his pitiful life? He had to find a reason to go on living.

"C'mon John, watch this television show with me or look at this cardinal in the yard," Dell would yell from the next room, once again encouraging him to get interested in existence, though it would be half-hearted. The doctor's said he was healthy in every way, and with the proper diet he could live twenty more years. But more than this, he had the unlimited love of a strong and positive woman in his corner. He called her his angel, Dell.

Then out of the blue, an opportunity presented itself. A brand new township building had been erected just across the hill from the top of Churchill Road, which seemed to be beckoning to Johnny in some way. And as if on queue, one day in November, George Barton, the municipal secretary visited him during breakfast.

Dell had prepared his usual dietetic breakfast of oatmeal, rye toast and grapefruit with lots of hot coffee, when they heard a knock on the outside storm door. Looking out through the kitchen into the hallway, Dell ran to the door and opened it when she spotted the friendly intruder, motioning him into the kitchen. George had been one of Johnny's first visitors his first week home from the hospital. She liked him and also knew his wife from the Confraternity of the Holy Rosary meetings at Church.

"How are you George?" Dell said, wiping her hands on her apron, as she led him into the sunlit kitchen, fragrant with strong coffee. Johnny wheeled his chair around, smiling at his guest. Even now he was getting used to commanding his new vehicle and glad for the month of rehabilitation at Harmarville learning to be navigable once again. Becoming skilled at getting in and out, and down from the chair in times of emergency had been part of the course there. Ultimately he even took their authorized drivers test, eventually hoping to get the gas and break in his own car mechanically moved beside the gearshift so that he and Dell might travel. Though Johnny did not feel the impetus to conquer this next step yet.

"Hi John. How are you feeling today?" The personable man said.

"Oh, I'm getting by George m'boy. It's a long hard process. I've been going over those building permits and health inspection reports you dropped by the other day." Holding the position of Building Permit and Health Inspection Officer for over fifteen years, Johnny was thinking of turning it over to a younger man who could get around easier to slap fines on all the illegal garbage dumpers a lot easier than he could in his present state.

Then George zeroed in on him with the message he had actually traveled to their side of the hill to deliver.

"Ya know John, the position Al Bakley vacated when he passed away last winter is open and ready for a replacement, and the board is looking for a democratic candidate. I'm actually representing them today, to ask you to consider running for office in the May primaries." Then he sat back and sipped black coffee from the huge mug that Dell had given him, letting his statement settle with John, who seemed to want to avoid the topic of politics for the time being.

"Oh boy, Al was a hard line politician, the old tough kind. Remember the big picture he had of FDR in his office, and how he would tell anyone who didn't like the New Deal that pulled us outa the Depression, to get the hell out of his office. Nope, they don't make 'em like that any more." Johnny said laughingly, with George joining in.

"You're right. He was one of a kind." George responded. Then a somber look came over Johnny, thinking back to himself as half a man, though deep down inside he was excited at the statement George had just made. The prospect of working in politics and making a living at it as well had moved his senses. His thick knit brows covering the upper half of his face crowned clear brown eyes, now focusing level on George.

"What would the people think of a double amputee handling their precious money, George, do you think they'd have trust in someone like me?" Johnny remarked humbly, but his friend was ready with all the support his colleague needed.

"Hey, you have a good education fella, you're smart and people like you, what else do you want?" Johnny and Dell both laughed, a little embarrassed at his straight forwardness.

"I'll tell you what. We'll see you at the next township meeting – you can tell us then." He said, sure of himself, and the new candidate. George had been in local politics a long time and he could spot a good civil servant when he saw one. Johnny would make a good tax collector; he just didn't know it yet.

Johnny and Dell reflected on the issue of him running for office, finally making a firm decision that this would be a good long range plan for them to support themselves. Consequently they would undertake an honest effort to get him nominated.

Joel, who was a strong well-built young man in his twenties, assisted his father through the physical encumbrance of guiding his wheelchair into the township meeting to confront all the tough local politicians. This difficult maneuvering alone became a humbling experience for a man who never felt restricted physically or socially in his life.

Johnny was elated to gain quick support and endorsement from some of the many different opinionated heavy weight officials who ran their local government, in addition to a few from their jurisdiction of Allegheny County. This initial meeting set the wheels in motion as George had stated, for a nominee to go forward as a prime candidate, and actually put Johnny's name on the ballot. Now he realized that he had more important goals to think about, his first being a dedicated obligation to these people who believed in his ability to fulfill the objectives set for this position.

Dell began to feel good about Johnny's decision to run and was excited about the opportunity to go forward to meet the challenges ahead of them, and as Johnny said, they had nothing to loose. As the days wore on, she saw her husband in a new light. He became less morose and searched the *Pittsburgh Press* for news every week, feeling very much in tune with the political scene and the new President, John Kennedy now in office. Watching him now, she began to feel good about herself as well, knowing that she was falling in love all over again with the man she had married, but now for different and more concrete reasons than thirty-five years ago.

She admired and loved him for his courage and his new lease on life and knew inside he would be victorious in May and November. A steady stream of visitors called to encourage him to "keep up the good work", "stay strong and try not to falter". His brother Phil was a regular caller, who though he had past run-ins with the law, gave his brother advice on how to handle his oncoming public life.

"Keep yer nose clean, an' don' take any crap offa dem guys. Im sure dey all got records anyways." Dressed in the latest ivy league striped shirt and vest with his graying hair cut short and parted on the side in a distinguished manner, Phil

206

could pass on sight for a Harvard professor, until he opened his mouth. Johnny and Dell would laugh about this later.

When May brought the national and local primaries, almost every member of the Albred family except Tommy and Terry, both living out of state, were stationed outside every school, fire station and church hall of the township voting districts. Now the fruits of the hard work of their campaign for the last six months would be paying off as every neighbor and friend cast their vote.

Libby and Ben stood in the chilly spring weather at Eastmont School greeting the public on their way to the polls. Ben and his wife Marjorie lived closer since he had taken a teaching job in nearby Plum Boro and was now working on his masters at Duquesne University. Libby had come up to help immediately after work that evening from her job at the Westinghouse Airbrake in Wilmerding, to volunteer for her dad.

Reaching out her hand with her dad's card to the next prospective voter with his picture and slogan in dark printed letters, "For a Good Today and a Great Tomorrow Vote for John A. Albred," and smiled receptively.

"John A. Albred would appreciate your endorsement for tax collector, he's a double amputee." Libby said kindly.

"Can he add two and two?" The man responded sarcastically, looking her square in the eye. Libby was slightly taken aback but now knew these kinds of opponents were out there.

"Yes, as a matter of fact he has a college education from St.Vincent and St. Bonaventure College." She responded quickly, a little shaken with resentment. And momentarily it turned into a personal issue and not a public one. In a few seconds, it donned on her that her dad could be the horrible object of public scrutiny and she was hurt by this contrary outside opinion.

As the man smugly passed by, Libby looked across the way at Ben, standing there as solid as a monument in his cool London Fog raincoat. As stoic an image as ever, his eyes were smiling and he winked, as if to say, *we know all of this, but the public has to be convinced as well. And don't let it bother you*

Lib, this is John Q. Public, and Daddy has chosen this road to go down in his life, so we have to deal with it.

"Aw don't worry about that guy, he's goofy, always causing trouble." Joel said belligerently. He had descended upon the scene bringing more cards to hand out and some hot coffee to warm them against the evening chill. Ben laughed at his brother, sipping from his steamy Styrofoam cup, but wondered too about the thoughts of the average cynic.

"How do you know?" His psychologically educated side spoke. Knowing this would not be enough to satisfy the curiosity that met his brother's estimations of a weirdo, Joel continued explaining what he knew about the political die hards in the party system.

"Hey I go to all the meetings now with Daddy too, ya know? There's a bunch of them that don't want Daddy in there, they say he's tryin' to run on the sympathy vote. It makes me sick, these local politics can be just as cutthroat as the national level." He said with angry determination. The two siblings nodded their heads in acknowledgement, staring at their brother who now had a place of prominence in the family, taking on the emotional setbacks now, as well as the work he had always done around the house.

Ben and Libby understood that Joel had been witness to conversations they knew nothing about, beside playing a key role in the new episode of their father's life sharing the sad and depressing days with him while they were absorbed in problems of their own. At least one that Libby knew about was the fact that neither of her two older brothers had any children, and Marjorie and Dottie were unhappy about the situation.

Libby was happy to be spending time with her brothers, even under these circumstances. She missed them so much these days. It was as if she had moved onto a desert island somewhere, married life was so different and demanding than her old life growing up at home. *Was this the way everyone felt the first year of marriage?* She thought. There seemed to be so much happiness and bliss in the movies and watching some of her friends. What was missing?

A year ago at just barely nineteen, she and her mother had walked down to the Justice of The Peace close to their house so that her mother could sign her application for a marriage license, as she was under age to be married in the state of Pennsylvania. Walking down Churchill Road that day, she felt as if she was sleep walking and going through the motions in making this monumental decision which she was not prepared to go through with. Though it was true that she had watched the example of her mother and father's relationship everyday and it seemed to be a good way of life with two people loving each other and spending their lives together.

Tommy had walked her down the aisle at St. Coleman's, due to the fact that her father just had his first surgery to remove one of his legs. He looked deathly ill making his way into the church on crutches, and she felt terrible watching him struggle while she was trying to feel festive in her beautiful white taffeta gown and lovely veil. But at that time her mother had insisted that they go ahead with the plans for the wedding, honestly believing that Johnny would be on the mend by the time of the actual event.

Consequently, Rich and his parents were moving with breakneck speed, as he had always done, to carry out arrangements. Libby had found out half way through their relationship that her fiancé was hyperactive to the point of being extremely unkind to people, just to accomplish his objectives, never stopping to consider the consequences to the people who were being pushed aside.

Libby had been confused. Her heart was breaking for her father's pain and anguish, and her love for Rich merged with this feeling, filling her with a guilt beyond compare, while they went ahead with the untimely wedding. Her dad did not attend the quiet dinner after church, and their families and the people invited tried to keep a celebratory mood for the benefit of the bride and groom, but Libby could hear them mentioning her father's health at every turn.

The next week while working at her desk in the Personnel Office of The Westinghouse Air Brake Company in the town of Wilmerding, closer to where she and Rich now lived, she pondered on all the events leading up to that moment. Stopping in for noontime visits to St Leocadia's, a Polish church nearby to say a Novena so that the Holy Spirit would stay with her father in his desperate situation, Libby realized that she had deep regrets and wished that everything hadn't happened as fast just to stay on their wedding schedule.

The old WABCO Plant stretched out for miles through the Turtle Creek and Wilmerding Valley, dated back to 1868, when the first successful test on passenger train air brakes was manufactured two years earlier. She liked the little town of Wilmerding, named by William Negley, the landowner, after his wife Joanna Wilmerding Bruce Negley. In another part of the city lay a huge castle like structure, where George Westinghouse had owned and worked during his lifetime, sitting high on a hill looking down into the valley.

Nineteen hundred workers, mostly immigrants moving into the area at the turn of the century, lived in the surrounding lands in company manufactured homes. Employees completed one hundred sets of airbrakes a day in their plant location, beginning in the core room in hot furnaces, these were molded and sent on to be completed in many other sections of the shops.

Libby and Rich lived northeast from there in Eastport on the third floor upstairs of his parent's house, Mr. and Mrs. Robert Honford. She and Rich were comfortable there, and Mrs. Honford tried very hard to bring her into the family, insisting that she call her "Mom", which Libby found very hard to do, since she felt that she already had a mom whom she missed terribly. Mrs. Honford would buy her gifts and trinkets everytime she went shopping to try to make her feel comfortable, knowing this was a difficult time for a young bride making adjustments with her husband, who had very little to change.

It was obvious to Libby that Rich was tense living in his married state in his mother and father's house, a stately three story home standing very close to others on a busy city street. Rich had changed over night from the laughing and devil may care guy that she used to see at work and on dates, into a serious husband and a man beset with rules, especially for her, dictating how she should act and dress, and critical of everything she wore. He insisted that she wear black clothing with extreme costume jewelry, making her look ages older than her twenty years.

If perchance she wore what she wanted to wear that day, he would look at her in disgust saying, "I can't believe you put that dress on; you look awful in that thing." Libby would be hurt at his remarks, starting to question her own judgment. Not a natural beauty, she worked hard to be attractive, brushing her long auburn hair every night, and pulling it up in a ponytail by day. She wore very little makeup, only lipstick. A friendly and kind girl, Libby just didn't know who she was now – it was as though Rich was running her entire life now.

It seemed to Libby that nothing she would say or do pleased him, and after a while she stopped trying. Needless to say, the lovemaking part of their union was nonexistent, and though it was a month before their marriage was actually consummated, both avoided the subject. Libby had never been counseled in sex education, having been told at a very young age that good girls did not allow boys to touch their bodies in any way – not even if they felt as if there was love, and of course parental worries projected over the fear of pregnancy was always a factor.

Hoping this would not be the objective in their relationship – except to have children, Libby knew nothing about her own sexuality, and even less regarding her husbands wants and needs, even though she had always been told to try to be available for his erotic demands and needs. All that aside, when Libby tried to hug Rich platonically it seemed to mean to him that sex was eminent, when she was only looking for simple reassurance. This discouraged her from attempting simple day to day affections.

After a few months into the marriage, Libby's inherent eczema, which had only appeared in tiny patches on her body in past years, started to break out all over her skin in multiple proportions, covering her arms and other extremities eventually enveloping her body like a giant wave signaling distress within. Rich tried to understand, but had little patience with his bride suffering with this horrible skin disease, never realizing that he unleashed a whole new variety of anxieties into the realm of her suffering.

Nights were sleepless and torturous with bedclothes sticking to open sores that had already become a source of daily torment with her clothes rubbing against the eruptions. And in less than a month her skin had become an inflamed and infected organism. When Libby finally found a reputable dermatologist, through the WABCO plant doctor, he immediately placed Libby in the care of Mercy Hospital in Pittsburgh.

Upon entering the hospital Libby was connected to intravenous bottles to clear her body of the infected substance that had permeated her nervous system. After a few days of the liquid miracle dripping slowly into her vein, all traces of the medically diagnosed neurodermatitis had vanished and she was released to go home.

President Kennedy held the first presidential news conference carried live on radio and television, with everyone tuning in to get a candid shot of how the commander and chief was running office. All of a sudden, everyone was interested in government policy, even teenagers watched their young president invite impromptu questions.

And in England The Liverpool Four, also known as the Beatles, infiltrated the United States, as their original tunes were played all over radios here.

The Food and Drug Administration approved a pill as safe for birth control use, and Alan Shepherd became the first person in space.

American boys and girls were sent off to yet another distant country. A faraway place that no civilian had ever heard of before, Vietnam. The Viet Cong had become so successful fighting there, that the U.S was forced to choose between allowing the collapse of the South Vietnamese government and supplying larger military forces. Consequently, by February 1962, 4,000 U.S. military advisers had arrived to aid the North Vietnamese.

The next day, Sunday, just after Libby had been released from the hospital, she drove back up to her old homestead on Churchill in Rich's pride and joy, a '57 Chevrolet Impala he'd owned since before they were married, to visit her mom and dad. Recently acquiring her license, she could now go and visit them all the time, or so she thought.

Pulling into the driveway this early spring day, Libby smelled the sweet scent of lilacs in full bloom, summoning up nostalgic memories of the senior prom. She remembered herself and Randi getting their hair set in an elaborate style to go with their new strapless gowns and dyed- to-match shoes and evening bags, hoping their escort would bring a corsage to go with the outfit. Joel had just finished mowing the lawn and a fresh fragrance permeated the newly cutgrass, conjuring up a longing for her swiftly passing youthful days. Now they were gone forever. She was overcome with a sad empty filling.

Walking up the cement walk along the back of the house, she thought the new construction project undertaken by Randi's father's firm, turning the back corner of the house into a new modern office for her Dad's Tax Office looked great. It was a peculiar feeling coming back home, having missed all the planning stages that went into projects now, and she felt more homesick than ever going into the back door and seeing her sister there.

"Hi Lib, how are ya doing?" Kat yelled up from the kitchen floor while playing with their new miniature dachshund, Hermie, whose tiny tail wagged profusely as Libby bent to scratch and pet the new little addition to the family. Kat had turned into a beautiful young woman over night, and now as a teenager in high school, she was a stunner. Clear violet eyes shone smilingly behind her Dark thick wavy hair, now disheveled from her recreation with Hermie. But even in an old shirt and jeans Kat looked beautiful.

"Did you see the May altar?" Kat said. This was a project they always did lovingly together every spring, and Libby was glad that her sister was carrying on the tradition of decorating an altar to honor the Blessed Virgin Mary in her designated month. She and Kat had always set up a lovely edifice in blue and white crepe paper with streamers down the front and lots of flowers in season, violets, lilacs, and the sweet smelling lily of the valley. Everyone in the family would make their pilgrimage to venerate the Mother of Jesus in their own special spiritual way.

Dell and Johnny looked up from deep concentration sitting at the long desk against the wall, where they were counting the days left for the tax discount date to be announced to the senior citizens who would benefit from the break. As a kind gesture, Johnny would make a personal call to all of the elderly who might forget the chance to save money on their high property taxes this way.

"Oh hi there kiddo, oh your skin looks nice now." Dell said approvingly. Johnny smiled, as his wife came over and hugged and kissed her daughter, knowing that she had just gone through her ordeal at Mercy hospital. Her mother might have had a hunch about the difficulties Libby was having adjusting to marriage as well. Libby didn't know since she never complained to her mother whom she always thought had enough problems of her own without Libby adding to them.

The room was cozy and new compared with the rest of the older part of the house and Dell had hung plants and cute curtains on the large picture window looking out into the yard with birdfeeders and now, apple blossoms. Her mother had on a pink checkered housedress, that Libby had never seen before, and had just gotten her short white hair permed. She thought her mother and father both looked better than ever now that her father was adapting to his handicapped lifestyle.

Libby tried not to look down at his stumps now practically uncovered by his Bermuda shorts, he was still her dear dad and on this warm day, she noticed beads of perspiration on his brow. Remembering back to a time when she was a little girl, she commented.

"Dad, do you recall when you used to come home from work and sit in the big chair in the living room reading the newspaper, and I used to run to wipe the sweat your face with tissues," Libby said laughingly.

"Yes honey, I used to love that, it always so nice of you." Johnny said. "I always felt like it was healthy to perspire, when my body stopped reacting that way I knew something was wrong." He added. Then she knew he had something important to say to her, starting out his first sentence to be taken seriously, with her Christian name.

"Elizabeth, I'm worried about you these days." He began, lighting up the ubiquitous cigarette, smoke curling slowly up between them, though Johnny waved it away. Libby knew she had a talk coming, and wondered how far he would delve into her new married life since she knew it was against her parents' principles to mention any of their children's married lives – especially taking sides of any kind. Accordingly, none of them had ever come home with any of their marital problems.

Libby could hear Dell and Kat making lunch in the kitchen with their clatter of dishes and utensils, and now she wished with all her heart to trade places with Kat who giggled lightheartedly at something, sounding carefree and full of fun. Her father continued on his course, repositioning his lower body with his strong newly developed arms, to make himself more comfortable in his wheelchair.

"I haven't really had a chance to talk to you, because of all that has happened with my operations, and I feel awful that I was never able to walk you down the aisle on your wedding day as a father should" He said apologetically. Looking into his cheerless eyes, Libby hadn't realized just how important this had been to her father until now. She felt so sorry, she thought her heart would break for all that had happened and how the course of events had him missing out on this crucial occasion in his life.

"Oh Dad, I know but you've made the best of a distressful situation, look how nice it is for you now." She said. Looking around at the comfortable surroundings. Libby had always had an easy time talking to her father and was glad to have this moment for a little heart to heart conversation on his terms.

"One thing I want you to do for yourself, and that's to be the person that God made, a unique individual. Don't let anyone make you into something you aren't. Believe wholeheartedly in yourself, because it's the quality of your life to other people that allows you to love and feel loved. Don't forget it." Johnny spoke solemnly. She listened intently to what her father was saying, and thought about how his statement applied to her side of the partnership in the marriage, and knew she had lost herself.

Libby knew that none of her family knew anyone the likes of Rich Honford, and how he could be vicious and ridicule them all when they were alone, and how she would cry out in desperation against him.

"Your parents are stupid." He would sound out in a jealous rage. She even dreaded coming home that day for fear he would start in on ridiculing the people she loved. This hurt her deeply, and she wished for his miserable mood to pass quickly.

As they all sat down at the table for lunch, the hissing pressure of a bus door reverberated out in front of the house through the open kitchen window, bringing on anticipation of a visitor coming into the back door.

"I wonder who that can be? I'll bet it's your sister, John." Dell ventured a guess. And no sooner said than done, Agatha appeared laughing at her own unexpected cleverness, appearing in the doorway. Dell jumped up to get a dish and silverware to set another place for her sister-in-law.

"Well look who the cat dragged in today." Johnny announced, smirking at his sister, who sat down grinning at her brother obstinately.

Libby couldn't believe how stylish she looked in late life, with big golden hoop earrings dangling down around her forever pretty face. Her complexion was still completely flawless as her high cheekbones magnified her beauty. Graying, but still auburn short hair was combed and teased on top of her head. Agatha was a bit rounder in the middle, but even now had a striking figure showing through a roomy green sack style dress.

Now in her forties, she suffered from years of wearing tight ornate shoes, setting a precedent for foot trouble. As a result she now wore sensible shoes that had to be cut open to let her bunions breathe, which was the single unsightly and grotesque feature about her aunt. Agatha smirked slyly at Libby, leaving her niece to believe she was about to say something ambivalent about her wedding or married life.

"Oh hello Libby, are you still married to that gigolo? I know he just married you for what he could get outta you." She said cynically, while Johnny and Dell looked disdainfully at each other across the table at lunch in shocking disgust at her comment.

"What do you mean?" Libby answered.

"Aggie, you don't know what you're talking about." Dell put in sharply, always the female lion protecting her young, and knowing the terse antics of her sister-in-law. Then Agatha laughed wickedly, somewhat mischievously playing down her comment. And they all tried to ignore her as changing the topic, as she was known to do right in mid-sentence, before the subject was closed.

"I dreamed I was at the opera, and you were on stage singing La Traviata." She said grandly. Her aunt hit another sore spot with Libby, who had abandoned her opera career completely, wondering if she would ever sing again, but she smiled at the image her aunt portrayed, and thoughtfully gave her praise for knowing the popular opera.

"Oh I looked unbelievably stunning in a powder blue gown trimmed in sparkling sequins, wearing diamond studded opera glasses." Agatha gestured daintily as if putting them on and haughtily watching a far away lighted theatrical stage, daydreaming and obviously enamored with herself in her imaginary world, she'd disappeared from their midst for a few seconds.

After a nice lunch of Dell's luscious fried chicken and creamy potato salad, Libby hugged and kissed them all in the driveway before getting back into her car, except Aunt Agatha who preferred to stay in the kitchen to finish the rest of the scrumptious meal. Her mom put her arm around her daughter in consolation.

"Now, honey don't pay attention to Aunt Agatha, you know how she never thinks about what she says, her i's have never been dotted. We have to try to understand the poor soul."

"Yeah, I know mom." Libby said.

"Besides she's been maintaining her little apartment upstairs of Mrs. Dugan's house, and we're grateful for that. I know that Charley and Joe come to see her often. Now, honey please take care of yourself and try not to scratch your arms. Don't bother your skin, or it might get infected again or you might even end up in the hospital again. It looks so nice." Dell said compassionately.

Libby wanted badly to cry out, *Mom, please let me come home again, this married life isn't all that its cracked up to be.* But she resisted, and somehow knew her mother would urge her daughter to give the union the best effort she could.

"I'll try not to, mom, but it itches so bad, its hard not to touch it." Little did they know. Libby thought. It was like a million nerve endings driving her crazy under her skin, it was miserable, especially at night but not as bad as a month ago.

Now taking Librium twice a day, as prescribed by Doctor Schultz, the dermatologist, to calm her nerves, she noticed dark circles under her eyes when she looked closely in the mirror. When she ran out of the contents of little plastic bottle, she would panic until she was able to stop at the pharmacy to get it again on payday. The cost was ten dollars for a small amount. Rich didn't know that she was continuing to have it refilled; it was good thing Libby was working, so that she could purchase it without discussing the matter with him.

Arriving home, she found her temperamental husband in a good mood, sitting at his desk working on the design for the new home to be built some day, and excited at the prospect of his drawing coming to life. Rich's bright blue eyes lit up with joyfulness as she came up the last tiring short pair of steps leading into their cozy little apartment.

His parent's house was an edifice of many sets of steps. The century old enormous wooden house had four floors and had been built into the side of a huge hill, featuring at the turn of the century, a long sweeping lawn in front. As commercial progress moved into the Eastport area, highway zoning officials dictated that most of the luxuriant frontage be excavated away to make room for a super main road running south into the busy manufacturing city of McKeesport, a city of over three thousand people, which grew from 2500 to 20,751 in the years from 1870 to 1890 and was noted to be the fastest growing community in the nation.

This relegated the home within the confines of a cement fortress in the front area shielding the house from the heavily traveled thorofare. The façade of their family estate was never the same afterward. Nevertheless, Mr. Honford took good care of the structure, painting it white every spring and tending to thick shrubbery crowding the outside steps up to the big front porch.

"Come here, honey." Rich said, motioning her over for a kiss. Putting his arm around her waist, they both stared down at the make shift drafting table he had set up in the back attic room.

"I think we're going to build this baby in the spring." He said.

"Oh Rich, that's great. Where will the lot be? Maybe up near my folks somewhere."

And then she wished she hadn't said this, but he kept his composure, and answered carefully and deliberately.

"Yes, maybe, but then I'll have to find an affordable lot somewhere." He said slowly. Libby was pleased, at least for the moment, and wondered if she even had a choice in the matter. *Would this be his place? Where would she come in?*

"It's about time you got back here, the work is piling up." Her boss Jack McDuff growled her way on Monday morning. Somehow Libby knew that Jack's action and appearance did not speak for the gentle man inside, who was capable of having the keenest understanding for his immediate employees. She knew in fact, that he felt sympathy for her stint with the terrible case of acute dermatitis, and looked truly sorry about the affliction, shaking his pure white haired head to the side and wiping his mouth with a soiled hankey.

A man who'd been born and bred in the small city of Wilmerding, where Airbrake contracts from around the world meant the difference between being employed and not paying the rent, he'd learned at an early age to sweat it out with the townies wary of prosperous and impoverished times. The official news of the "hires and fires" started at his desk before matriculating into the larger sections of the Personnel Department. Libby would then follow up the process by immediately removing the blue record cards out of the file to match each pink slip.

Conversely, his superiors were interested in just how far his bad habits had manifested themselves into his work ethics, since Jack was a bonafide weekend alcoholic, sometime imbibing his way through the dry labor week. Nonetheless he was quite knowledgeable about his job, and could probably perform his tasks backward. Every detail of the omnipresent tray of IBM cards which ultimately were sent to data processing; plus every employees history, and possibly their ancestors, no one, not even Howard Paxton, the Personnel Manager, could get the goods on Jack. But all the same, the witch-hunt was on by his immediate superiors.

The next week, Libby, who was quite oblivious to the inclinations and routine of her boss who had always treated her fairly, was called upstairs into Mr. Paxton's office. *Well, what could this mean?* She thought. *Maybe a transfer to another department, a demotion or worse still, a dismissal.* But Paxton seemed in a searching frame of mind, as he kept eye contact with her as she entered the secluded office.

"Sit down Libby" He said. Paxton was a balding stocky man, always neatly dressed in the same serge suite, a bit of a boring conservative man, but who always seemed to like her work as an employee.

"We have a problem here in this department. We have had word that Jack McDuff has been drinking on the job and might have a stash somewhere." Libby was shocked and wondered how this could be happening right under her eyes, moreover, in a place of business where people came to do a job everyday. She knew what drunkenness was, growing up in the Eastburgh and Turtle Creek Valley. Beer gardens were every other establishment, and all one had to do was walk down the street to view a man in a stupor, but she refused to believe that it was here beside her.

"So what I'm asking you to do, is to please look out for this happening, and report it instantly to me." Paxton ended the conversation.

In her confusion and embarrassment for Jack, Libby wanted to disappear immediately, but reluctantly agreed to be vigilant for them. Having trouble looking at Jack when she walked into their shared office, she went straight to work separating transfer slips, which alerted departments of a change in their personnel. Nevertheless she felt Jack's red rimmed blue eyes following her inquiringly.

Spring turned into summer, and the Vietnam War escalated and became a major issue in the Cold War giving rise to communist countries, particularly China, considering the war an important test of "national liberation". American soldiers were being brought back in body bags.

President Kennedy announced an air and naval blockade of Cuba, following the discovery of Soviet missile bases on the island, inciting that this crisis threatened world peace and intensified the Cold War.

Rachel Carson published "Silent Spring", and Betty Friedan's "The Feminine Mystique" was printed, pronouncing the beginning of the women's rights movement.

Citizens grieved for the loss of the President John F. Kennedy, who was assassinated by Lee Harvey Oswald in Texas on November 22nd at 1:30 p.m. For the next three days the country was absorbed in the story of their lifetime. Not since the death of Franklin Roosevelt had Americans been so focused on a single event.

"Women must learn the self-love, the self-idealizing, the self-mythologizing, that has made it possible for men to think of themselves as persons. The first step is to acknowledge that one is a woman and to begin discovering what that may mean".

Laura Chester and Sharon Barbara.."Rising Tides" 1973

13 Seventy Degree Angle

The women's movement was born in November of 1872, with the hard work of feminist leader Susan B. Anthony and fifteen other women in Rochester, New York. The second revolt came in 1971, a few years after the publication of Betty Friedan's "Feminine Mystique" in 1963. The controversial book raised the consciousness of women everywhere, and the sisterhood grew in numbers.

No matter what their station in life, women were encouraged to do the best they could to achieve a higher level of success. In the early 1800's, there were many duties but few rights; a married woman had no right to property, even if it was her own by inheritance. If she worked, her wages belonged to her husband. If she left home, even if she was forced because of intolerable circumstances, she forfeited everything, including her children. A dying man could even give or will his children away from his widow.

With the antislavery movement in the mid-1800, came individuals dedicated to improving the lives of women. They tirelessly circulated petitions, sent feminists on lecture tours, and lobbied congressmen to change the repressive laws. But preachers compared the fervent group with prostitutes; angry mobs pelted them with everything from prayer books to rotten eggs because of their "unladylike" behavior.

Most feminists assumed the battle was won when women's suffrage brought about the nineteenth amendment by giving women the vote, but by the 1970's women still had not fully realized other suffragist goals: equal pay for equal work, equal employment opportunities and education, equal political representation together with representation under the law, not to mention child-care centers for working women.

Constituting thirty seven percent of the work place, women were paid less money than men, and the wage gap between men and women was actually wider than it was in 1955, with women earning on the average of only three dollars for every five earned by men. Women college graduates earned less than male high school dropouts, and men earned almost twice as much as women when their educational backgrounds were equal.

Consequently, *The Feminine Mystique* found "trapped" suburban housewives, awakened and reawakened latent feminists across the country and the rebirth of feminism began. Psychoanalysts and social scientists tried to explain this problem overtaking the country in terms of Sigmund Freud: Anatomy is destiny, and American women had not learned to adjust to their sexual role.

But Friedan felt that theorists ignored the fact that women have minds, pronouncing that a woman, no matter how gifted or intelligent, finds her greatest glory and fulfillment by giving up all interest in the affairs of the world and devotes her life solely to husband and children. And also pointed out that women were literally and figuratively ensnared in the image of themselves as mindless, beautiful creatures with no personal identity and no real role at all.

The National Women's Political Caucus was formed as a bipartisan coalition of democratic and republic women to involve more women in politics on a full time basis. NWPC included authors Betty Friedan, Gloria Steinen, congresswomen Bella Abzug and Shirley Chisolm, former republican national committeewoman Elly Peterson and actress Shirley MacLaine.

By demanding the enforcement of existing laws, the feminists began making significant gains for women, a major goal being a constitutional guarantee of equal rights for women. The proposed amendment simply reads:

"Equality of rights under the law shall not be denied or abridged by the United States or by any state on account of sex".

A 1972 Harris Poll showed that only thirty six percent of all women were opposed to the women's rights organizations, as compared to forty two percent in 1971. And forty two percent of all men favored the feminist programs.

223

Sitting in a humanities class at Allegheny County's Community College in Monroeville, Libby, now a mother of two, led the discussion for support of the new movement sweeping the country. When Mr. Riley, the instructor asked just how effective this enormous social transition would ultimately prove to be for women's rights, she stirred in her seat eager to answer him.

Attractive and confident at thirty, and one of the older students of the class, Libby stood up ready with an informal oration. Taking on a fragile outward shell of confidence, Libby wore the fashion mode of the day; dressed in wide bell bottomed jeans and high platform shoes, her long silky straight auburn hair hung past shoulder length.

"Of course the campaign will be successful, this is a great chance for all women who have been secondary to men to jump on the band wagon and make big strides toward competing with them for the same good jobs and better pay." She spoke from her heart, though her stomache was in knots, not knowing inside just where her life fell in step with all of this hoopla.

As soon as Libby sat down, a Viet Nam vet, an ex-marine jumped up defensively.

"You girls have it so good, us guys do everything for ya, and yet you wanta be like us, you're crazy." He said laughingly with the class, of which half were women.

She didn't care if she was labeled a "women's libber", she felt good about her position to do a small part in her little corner of the suburbs, and joined the local chapter of The National Organization of Women (NOW). Sanctioned by the sisterhood, she knew there was a better place out there and that it was just a matter of time before she could strike out on her own, but had no plan as to when or where she could go as a single mother with two small daughters. Some of the choices were not good places for her precious girls who were dearer to her heart than anything else in the world, including the tenuous ego she was cautiously developing.

Working a few part time jobs in secretarial positions to earn enough money for the next college semester, she believed as many of the prominent women leaders, that education was the key to freedom. The musical calling that she had so passionately sought at one time had dispersed as so many dreams into thin air, now superseded by the practical position of speech therapist, recommended by a college counselor, which Libby could coordinate with the grade school schedule of Beatrice and Sonja. Knowing the position required a masters degree, dimmed her hopes of an early start into the profession, hence she had to continue to be tolerant of her way of life with Rich.

Despite the fact that she and Rich had spent the last ten years building a home and marriage, Libby still questioned the quality of their relationship every day, knowing that other couples had a quality of life together that they did not have. Certainly maturation played a role on her part, for as recently as the past summer she had been slowly realizing that most men as partners did not have all the answers and could not be drawn upon to bring the required security and stabilization needed in a relationship, as she had unreservedly believed in her life.

What kind of a false security had she grown up with while observing her father and brothers handle emotional predicaments and problem solving? They always seemed to have the situation in hand, and without a doubt her mother always deferred to them in any domestic crisis. And indeed Libby always felt intrinsically safe with male decision making in their home, and saw this as a way of living. But now she questioned those fundamental principles, seeing no one but herself as trustworthy. It was a brand new feeling, nonetheless, unsteady.

The intricately designed two story brick colonial style home that Rick had built in the suburbs near yet another country club in the Penn's Hills area, had been a heartfelt effort on his part to give his family the best he could offer on his terms. The tree-lined, well groomed street, where a throw away carton from a carryout store stood out like a rhinoceros parked on the lush carpet of green, dared anyone to blight its shimmering blades waving in the breeze. Libby was secretly opposed from the beginning to the impeccable lawns, fearing that chemicals had to play a role in picture perfect neighborhood, especially with the new environmental restrictions recently outlawing DDT for commercial use.

Contrary to the faultless outward appearance of the surroundings, the individuals living there made up for the artificiality. The couple across the street, Ruby and Arthur MacDonald, "call me Mac", were as happy a family as any suburban outlet in America could produce. Libby enjoyed talking with Ruby, who seemed to have the basic parental skills down, and she soon became Libby's mentor helping with the concerns and consternations of motherhood.

The MacDonald's were retired army officers, who had left the military to raise their eight children, collect their pensions and enjoy life by working part-time jobs and hobbies. One of Ruby's most admired celebrities was the unyielding Captain Von Trapp, the ruthless disciplinarian in the new movie, "The Sound Of Music". Nonetheless, the family was a perfect example of regimentation-gone awry. For when Ruby blew her tiny shrill whistle, only two or three of their offspring would appear – the rest would amble over eating a cookie or would stand behind their mother disrespectfully making gestures with their thumbs in their ears, splaying their fingers and mocking outwardly.

Yet Libby had to admire her neighbor, because every day at three o'clock she was tooting away in their backyard carrying the ritual through, and between this afternoon ceremony and the church bells at Beulah Church high on the hill, one could set their time pieces at home. All the same, Ruth and Arthur continued to wear khaki, and the children were obligated to do the same, even down to the youngest two year old wearing diaper and bib in the same material. They appeared as one khaki wave standing and sitting down together in the church pew on Sunday.

Inhabiting the house next to them was a ruddy Scotsman, who loved to play the bagpipes from morning until late in the evening. On a hot summer night with all the windows open, as Dunny MacFeerson pumped the air through the pipes, squeals and sounds of all ranges blew down the street forcing the residents to block their ears. Libby loved the sounds of the people, though Rich thought them all to be unbalanced.

As the years went by, his edifice, filled with all the right custom made furniture, grew to be a cold and empty structure lacking in the warmth of a close family loving and supporting each other. The atmosphere was far removed from the family circle that Libby had grown up in Churchill Road. A pretentiousness grew out of the perfect image portrayed by the people living there, which turned into bitter resentment as they drifted further apart.

Some weeks they did not see each other at all, since Rich worked until ten o'clock in the evening, and Libby was going to classes almost fulltime or studying for an exam. She was also in to the grade school world of the children, taking the role of girl scout leader, seeing teachers and attending PTA meetings, which Rich had managed to avoid so that he could devote his life to being a studio designer. As a result of their not having spent any time together, weekends found them alienated and not having anything to say to each other.

The astonishing births of Beatrice and Sonja were the only bond that held them together over the years, and for Libby, the loving support of Johnny and Dell, whom Libby visited along her travels to nursery schools and kindergarten almost everyday. Her mother and father adored both girls, and often stopped by to take them along on short trips to Ohio to see their Aunt Terry and new cousins Martin and Gerald.

Beatrice had been born first, an event which flabbergasted Libby onto a temporary higher plane of living altogether. In their baby's first couple of months, she and Rick would turn off the television and pull up a chair and fix their eyes on the adorable subject they were able to produce with God's help. What masters of divinity they had become in the genetic connection of this tiny bald headed specimen, who slept around the clock enabling Libby to learn how to become acquainted with the other fantastic world of motherhood.

Libby couldn't wait to show her little darling to her old group in the office staff at WABCO, especially Jack, who was getting ready to retire in the years to come.

"Where'd she get her blond hair?" He remarked in his rugged sarcastic way. Libby laughed and noticed that he was even more miserable than ever, which made him an angry "sober" person suffering without his daily intake of alcohol. This pleased her, that the old man was now walking the line, and secretly she was happy to have not reported the miniature whiskey bottle she'd found one day while filing a "new hire" employment card. Swiftly closing the metal file drawer shut, Libby had told herself that Jack was worth it, as they both had their devils with which to deal. Her only regret was that he had not allowed himself to become a consummate professional because of his drinking habit.

For the time being, Libby's skin had cleared up beautifully. The obstetrician had said it was the hormonal adjustment after the birth of the baby. Certainly she had suffered during the nine months she carried Beatrice, taking oatmeal baths and lathering with cortisone throughout. Being so caught up in motherhood, she prayed that her good luck would continue, as they readied their possessions to move into their new home just a few miles away from the Albreds family home.

Kat's beautiful wedding had taken place in 1969, while Libby was pregnant with their second daughter. Sonja had been conceived that summer during spectacular Fourth of July fireworks at the nearby Country Club, and Libby secretly wished for another daughter. And since we all come into being in the arms of God, this deity was a patriotic spirit.

The nation had been crippled with despair upon loosing two great leaders when Robert Kennedy was assassinated in California while campaigning for president. And later, civil rights leader Martin Luther King Jr., had also been murdered Memphis, Tennessee.

Neil Armstrong became the first American to walk on the moon, and Marlon Brando starred in The Godfather, making it a top grossing film. On television every evening came reports of Viet Nam war protests by the burning of draft cards and flags from universities; tens of thousands marching in Washington, DC.

"Aw they're all a bunch of spoiled brats out there. What do those kids know about real responsibility? We all got drafted, we all have to serve our time." Rich shouted scornfully at the angry crowds, on the TV screen. There was no understanding there. He spoke as if he had seen action, when in fact he worked with engineers in a comfortable office between wars.

The nurses in the maternity ward of Mercy Hospital in Pittsburgh called Sonja "buttercup", as she stared up at them

228

with bright hazel eyes. Never sleeping, always active, Sonja joined the human race with enthusiasm. Rich eagerly held his new daughter when she was brought into the room, and they felt blessed with the miracle of birth visiting them once again.

It was spring, and the wonderment of new growth filled their home with Beatrice joining in on the joy of having a new sister to perform every childhood maneuver her four-year-old mind could originate to entertain the tiny baby.

Libby was furious when she found out she would have to get permission from the pastor to sing at Kat's wedding, since women soloists were still not permitted to "perform" in the Catholic Church. Paying no heed to the patriarchal consensual clause, and refusing to believe that God would not allow her to follow through with her singing, Libby sang two religious songs. As her sister walked down the aisle, melodious strains of "The Our Father" and later in the ceremony the solemn and beautiful "Ave Maria" encircled the hollow concaves of the century old church where God was so prominent for their family.

A vision in white silk organza and lace walking down the aisle of St. Coleman's, Kat took her father's hand near the gate of the sacristy, where he had been stationed in his wheelchair. He then placed her hand in Timothy Houlihan's with his blessing, with family and friends as witness. Libby was personally pleased that her father had a new chance to give another daughter away properly.

All of the neighbors and most of Johnny's political constituents from Wilkins Township came to Kat and Tim's wedding reception at the new Bel Air Country Club, which had been built in an area where they'd played as kids called Oat's field. Firmly established in office now, after the last election he was delighted to hear from Joel after working at one of polls, a supporter had said that a vote against John Albred was like voting against motherhood and apple pie.

A great celebration followed, with dancing and socializing and all of the neighbors taking part like the Albred's had never seen them do before. Members of the Swiss Farm Dairy family showed up in their Sunday finery and wearing their cheery healthy faces to congregate with the Albreds whom they had known as small children especially Katrina.

Now all of the Albred's were married, including Joel and his ideal mate, Glendora. Glendora was a lovely homespun young woman who liked to bake her own bread and sew from morning until night. She was his ideal mate, and just right for the laid-back likes of Joel, who loved to stay at home and mosey around. And though he worked days at WABCO, he was already counting the years until retirement, when he could devote his time to gardening.

Kat and her husband Tim moved the day after the wedding to Michigan where he took a position in sales at Westinghouse there. Dell and Johnny were saddened by this, though they knew there seemed to be a trend in families migrating to find better jobs. Ben announced that he and Marjorie would also be relocating to Long Island, New York. Ben had finally landed his ideal career in counseling at Locust Valley High School. They would live in Bayville. Johnny just shook his head in wonderment at how the members of the family were moving in such great numbers that he would never see them again, since they were so far away.

It was Sunday evening; Johnny and Dell were about to watch their favorite, Little Joe on Bonanza, when the black phone on the desk rang long and sharply giving them a start, almost ominously. Johnny wheeled his chair quickly and purposefully toward his desk. Dell watched Johnny's face trying to get an inkling as to which member of the family was calling, but Johnny's face turn out to be grim and then deeply saddened, as he questioned the caller.

"When did it happen?" He responded sorrowfully, and then regretful words came.

"Where will he be laid out?" Johnny stared into space, still shocked by the news. Then he hung up and cried openly into a soiled handkerchief he'd pulled out of a shirt pocket, having difficulty through his sobbing to tell Dell that his brother Phil had succumbed to a cerebral hemorrhage. They both held each other in shocked grief.

"I can't believe he's dead, even before me. He was always so healthy and vibrant planning his next place of business. You know what he was doing when he had his attack?"

"No, where was he, John?" Dell said compassionately. The thought crossed her mind that he might be out doing one of his dirty deeds again.

"He was down in the basement working on his definitive potato chip." Then they both had to laugh, knowing his brother's devotion to a perfect chip and finding a worthwhile business venture.

Philip Ambrose Albred waxed sterling, lying in the immaculate white satin of the casket with his Eastern Indian inspired Nehru jacket. His still mostly black sleek hair in his late sixties was neatly coiffured in an ivy league cut. Always the epitome of stylishness, he could have stood as a manikin in Hugh's and Hatcher's men's clothing shop in Turtle Creek. Agatha stood nearby clasping a white lace hankey and dabbing at her red eyes from time to time, doing her best to mourn the brother she never had a good word for while he was living.

"She looks sensational in black." Terry whispered into Libby's ear in the deep calm of the luxurious funeral parlor, as their heels sunk into thick dark floral carpeting and plush satin draperies hung from the front windows. Then the two sisters fought back giggles in a place that forbade jocularity. Terry, now a mother of two young sons, continued to work as a career nurse and was happily married to William, and no one knew otherwise. But Libby could attest to the fact that her sister would make the marriage work or die putting forth a strong effort.

"What I wonder is, who is that woman over there?" Terry said with her usual inquisitiveness, as they both stared at a solitary well-dressed blonde wearing an attractive dark business suit and black satin pill box hat with its large webbed veil pulled down over her face. She appeared to be a lot younger than their uncle. Behind her sat two men who looked as if they had just stepped out of the new Godfather movie, with dark stripped suits and white ties.

"Probably some of Uncle Phil's gangster cronies." Her sister said.

Tommy sat with his wife Dottie, reflecting on the uncle who made them all laugh showing up with all kinds of new records, and who never complained on the outside about any of the foibles in his life. And who'd lend you a five or ten without questioning where it would be spent.

Dell knelt by the coffin staring down into Phil's still youthful face, feeling somewhat guilty for the numerous times she could have been more understanding to her n'er do well brother in law who seemed to be hell bent on living his life beside the devil. He was always looking for trouble, and it usually found him first.

On the other side of the room, Ben was wondering just whom he could talk to about acquiring all or some of Uncle Phil's fine wardrobe to take with him for the next school year. At his new position at Locust Valley High School in New York State. He and Marjorie had been out the weekend before looking for a home directly on the ocean. It was an opportunity of a lifetime, and one that would fulfill all of his educational ambitions.

Joel sat with his dad, and reminisced about the funny side of Uncle Phil, who narrowly escaped jail.

"Yep, your grandmother kept him out of jail many times. Especially when he was caught with the Bathtub Moonshine Ring up in Bessemer Terrace, when he was only eighteen. You'd think he would have learned then, but he only went on to bigger and better scams in the Burgh."

Johnny reminisced, brushing back a tear.

"But you know, I'll bet he wouldn't have done it any other way growing up in the hotel the way he did with a mother who didn't have the time of day for him."

Many friends and relatives followed them home from the cemetery after the service the next day to consume a huge plate of sandwiches and mugs of hot coffee from a huge urn.

It was Tommy, the most socially gregarious of the family who brought the mysterious attractive woman into the family circle sitting around the table.

"Mom, Dad, do you remember a friend of Phil's named Belle?" Then he stood by smiling at the blond woman who smiled beguilingly. Dell was the first to recognize the girl who had dated Phil in his young years, often being part of his renegade crowd making easy money.

"Yeah, I used ta love the chump." She used the old street language to identify herself.

"There was no bigger dare devil than that man we just laid to rest. I can't believe he lasted this long. He knew where I was; he just called me in Texas. My married name is Mrs. Jackson Wise, my husband's company is buying Phil's potato processing machine." Johnny and Dell and the rest of the family were rendered speechless at her astounding news.

The last ground troops of the Viet Nam war came home. And one of the greatest scandals in American history began evolving in 1972, starting with the break-in at the Democratic National Headquarters in the Watergate Hotel. The scandal would end with the resignation of President Nixon. An investigation would prove to the American people that conversations in the White House from the sixty-four tapes led to his direct involvement. The House Judiciary Committee approved three articles of impeachment. The public stayed glued to their television sets to watch Richard M. Nixon announce on August 8, 1974, that he would resign the next day.

The popular Beatles from England continued to create expressive music, perking up the ears of every music lover in America with their latest album, Abbey Road. Everyone loved their original music, with poignant tunes like *"Something"*, *"Here Comes The Sun"*, deep down heart rendering songs that everybody young and old began to hum along with.

In their early career they catered more to a younger set with the ilk of *"She loves you"*, *"Please Please Me"* and *"Help"*. They were fast moving numbers that many adults ignored, but as their music matured with songs like "Yesterday" and *"Let It Be"*, the older generation could not ignore their artistic work any longer.

They truly were one of the strongest musical forces of the twentieth century capturing the spirit of the time, turning rock and roll into dominant pop harmonious form. In terms of social resonance, no other contemporary artists or group achieved anything like Paul, John, George and Ringo. *"Let It Be"* became the album announcing personal tension that broke up the band, an eventual parting for a group who could no longer stand to work together.

Sunday afternoons in fall and winter found Rich, Libby, Beatrice and Sonja and all Pittsburghers glued to their television sets in heavy concentration on the antics of the men in black and gold working hard to make their way down the grid iron. Their beloved football team, the Pittsburgh Steelers had won two super bowls and were destined to become NFL world champs again at the end of this season.

"Go, go, go Franco." Libby and Sonja screamed with sportsman like zeal, scattering the two cats into another room, but feeling remorse on the other hand for upsetting their lovely Russian blue, Mia and her little adopted feline son, black and white vested, Mr. Rudyard Kipling, familiarly known as "Kippy", nesting in a big easy chair in the corner of the comfortable family room. These two had been inseparable ever since one of Beatrice's schoolmates told her about a tiny kitten found in a garbage can at the other side of their neighborhood, sending the kindhearted Bea in hot pursuit of the little tormented animal. Sonja's Christmas present, the gentle and loving Mia accepted him graciously, greeting him with a thorough washing of her expert tongue, cultivating a companion for life.

In the third quarter the action was stepped up as the team scrambled toward the sixty-yard line with skillful running tackle, Franco Harris, enthusiastically pushing his weight through the strategic play, which would ultimately finish with a sterling victory for an immaculate reception of a pass thrown by Terry Bradshaw to receiver Lynn Swan. Everyone learned the dynamics of the game at an early age in this area, and to end the play-offs in triumph was a dream come true as another great season landed them in football heaven.

Owner Art Rooney grew to know the team personally, and along with Coach Chuck Noll, once they put a team together, the Steeler management stayed with them for years working with the rookies, hoping in due course to make magic. The Pittsburgh Pirates baseball team had won the pennant a few years ago thrilling the people with the *"We Are Family"* theme, and now the city was on fire with wild and ardent fans from all over taking every win or loss to heart.

"Dad, we're on our way to another super bowl, aren't you excited?" Libby said with her usual exuberance, as she stopped by the house to pick up her mother to go Christmas shopping that morning. Grabbing a mug of coffee as usual, she sat opposite her father to discuss the latest team win, but felt dismay upon looking into his eyes, which were not crystal clear brown as always. Feeling a quick jab to her stomach, Libby worried that he was seriously ill, or that something else was wrong.

As Libby and her mother drove through the town of Monroeville toward the mall, she inquired about her father's health and immediately sensed her mother's worry, though she hadn't said anything.

"Mom, daddy's eyes are yellowish tinted, is he okay? Has he been getting enough sleep?" She ventured. Her mother was surprised that it was this obvious to her daughter, and responded quickly voicing her concern.

"Yes, there's something wrong but he will not go to the doctor. I believe he is suffering with something abdominal. He seems to grab his side a lot during the night, and I can see him wince and cry out in pain at times. He also prays out loud with great fervor and intercession, I know he's terrified. I've suggested he see Dr. Williams, but as you know, your father is stubborn." Dell said, sadly defeated.

"Well we've got to make him go. I'll call Dr. Williams and have him come to the house to examine him." Libby asserted, not wanting to give in to her father's stubborn affront. Returning with all their purchases, mostly toys for Bea and Sonja, which she would hide before they came in from school that day, Libby ran in to see her father one more time before she left for home. She bent over her father's wheelchair, putting her arms around him and hugging him longer than usual. He felt frail to the touch; all of the brawn that he had acquired when he was first rehabilitated over ten years ago seemed to have vanished.

"Dad, I think you should go to the doctor for a check up. I can take you right away." He became immediately defensive, probably since Dell had told him the same thing earlier, Libby thought.

` "No, why? I'm fine, there's nothing wrong." But Libby was her father's child and could be just as obstinate.

"I know they make house calls, because when Rich caught the chicken pox from Sonja, Dr. Williams came first thing in the morning." Libby left Churchill Road with much trepidation that day, and called the doctor as soon as she got in her door. But he declined, saying he could not treat a patient who was so adamantly against being examined.

Rich was proud of himself. He had a brand new bright blue and gold-stripped sweater, parka and an entire ski ensemble to match. His bindings were the best, Pyrenees, imported from Europe. Paralleling down the highest slope of Seven Springs Ski Resort looking regal was one of his delights in life. Now if only Libby would try to go along with him and not screw around like she usually did, in view of the fact that he'd also bought her a pair of Head skis and had them initialed. Rich thought she might be won over, especially since this was one of the latest things to do for "true" ownership, the salesman had said.

They were finally going to have a ski weekend for two whole days with the kids at the Albred's house. And though it was March, there was plenty of snow on the slopes and some of the new man made powder as well. A picturesque winter couple to behold, everyone will be staring at them, he thought, and there may even be time for some romance on the day's agenda.

But as usual Libby was being her odd natured self in the car on the hour-long trip. He should have known they could barely be in the same room with each other much less travel in a confining car. It was tense to say the least; there were walls of discord between them. She had her lips pursed in that resentful way, and then the dam broke.

"I can't believe you charged all this stuff on that one credit card, the one I'm trying to pay off." She said angrily, with her arms crossed.

"Its okay, I'm going to personally send a check in at the end of the month. Why is it always about money? Why can't you just enjoy yourself?"

"Yeah, I know, but you never do, and I'm left trying to get rid of all the darn interest."

This was a new Libby sitting next to him and was probably taking this opposite side to torment him all the way there, when usually she would soften and laugh, but she had become hardened with age just like an old piece of cheese. Where was that lovely feminine nature she had at one time? Whoever planned this trip made a big mistake, he thought. He spouted out at her.

"You're just like a tough old truck driver girl, and now that you're about to graduate from college you're more stupid than when you started. You don't even know how to balance a lousy checkbook and you have a degree in business management." He added belligerently. Now the battle raged even more as he drove higher into the Laurel Mountains of central Pennsylvania, as Libby dug deeper into her "angry archives" against him.

"Well you're the money man who's always writing checks and charging up everything in all the stores in Pittsburgh on your lunch hour, like all that redwood furniture you bought last summer for the patio which was over six hundred dollars. Don't you know by now, Rich, that no amount of material goods are ever going to make you happy? You have to find it within yourself. And isn't it interesting how we have nothing in common but our finances?" She lashed out at him.

"Oh boy, now you're starting to sound like your dad, okay Johnny. Like he knows what end is up, he won't even go to a damn doctor when he's sick. What kind of a weirdo is that?" He seethed. The last remark brought silence about, since he knew he'd struck a chord with his wife who was dreadfully worried about her father's health.

Early Saturday morning started with a warm spring sun beginning to melt the snow, as they skied out of breakfast in the lodge.

"I don't feel like going up to the top yet, it's a little early." Libby said, still holding back kindness from yesterday's argument. Her only comfort lay in the fact that the girls were not around to witness another terrible encounter taking place between them. They would urge her *please be quiet mommy, don't say anything back to make daddy more angry.* Her heart would bleed each time they witnessed parents who went at each other like two blood hounds gouging each other's flesh until they had beaten away all love and human decency.

Rich grabbed the rope tow hard, looking back at Libby with narrowed angry eyes, feeling deeply the wider chasm they'd created together yesterday on the road. Watching him disappear over the mountain, Libby started slowly traversing over to a gentle slope near a grove of pine trees, where Rich suddenly appeared expertly making his way down the grade in his usual good form, doing parallel stem Christies in enviable motion. Downhill skiing all his life, even on the toughest mountains in Europe, he was progressively better every year, whereas she was an intermediate who was into smoothly traversing back and forth, but she enjoyed the quick movement, the crisp wind gusting sharply into her face.

Now in late afternoon, the warm spring sun had melted much of the bottom stopping area into deep slush. Libby made her last run down the mountain, edging more and more around the wet choppy ice to maintain balance. Then a swift fast turn threw her down into an awkward fall. After twisting her left ski around, she stood up and felt no pain as she brushed the dirty wet snow from her ski pants. Then she felt her left leg crack. Rich skied marvelously into a fast stop beside her, with a disgusted look on his face.

Johnny knew he was dying. Some kind of cancer, he thought. Looking in the large hall mirror he now noticed his skin was yellowing with the same jaundice as his eyes. But no, dammit, he wasn't going to let some doctor prod and puncture what was left of his once vibrant body. It would be too humiliating. He lit up a cigarette, and looked out the picture window above his desk at a cardinal couple flitting around the bird feeder in the crab apple tree. Next month it would be filled with bright pink blossoms.

He reached down to his lower side, kneading the sharp soreness, which felt like it was spreading into a larger area. Tommy had called from Highland Park earlier where he had just built a home north of Chicago. Starting his own construction company at the end of the sixties, he was now doing well with a good team of subcontractors. Johnny was proud of him.

"Hey buddy, how are you doin'? I hear you're under the weather. That's a helluva note." His oldest son spoke in his usual candid tough guy tone, and Johnny wondered how much of it he learned from his Uncle Phil.

"Aw, no. I feel chipper. A little indigestion that's all." At this comment Dell raised her eyebrows and pursed her face in disbelief on the way through the storm door to sweep the porch.

"In fact your mother and I are going to Kennywood Park later to go through the Old Mill and Noah's Ark." At this Tommy laughed, though he believed the old park might just be opening for the season. Their family had had many fine times in this old amusement Park in West Mifflin.

That night before bed, Johnny took out the Teilhard de Chardin book on love and suffering. The words of the Christian neurophysiologist were reassuring to him in his state.

It is in accord with the nature of living things that man is mortal, as it is in harmony with his nature to suffer. The biologist is ideally equipped to see the happy end-result of protective suffering and death which renew generations radically, thanks to sexuality, more radically than can simple unicellular division which, barring accidents, produces no corpses. That grief and death are in the real nature of mankind is the principal crows of our nature. Medico-fictional dreams of conquering death or grief will not alter it.

Reading by his small bedside lamp, Johnny found a phrase which Jesus Christ himself affirmed as the greatest of all the commandments to live by, that faithfulness to human nature, the brain of man being what it is, demands incessant effort directed to humanization. Only humanization is directed to the aid of others, for man is a social species that finds psychological equilibrium only in the balanced love of others. "You shall love your neighbor as yourself," is the psychobiological law of cerebral equilibrium.

14. Undiscovered Country

Dell was grief-stricken and angry at the same time, a combination of feelings left her with deep remorse against the man she had spent the last forty-five years knowing intimately. In death he had betrayed their loving and trustful relationship. Because of his physical limitations as a double amputee, Johnny became increasingly eccentric. This forced him to garner all of the security within his realm for personal protection. But did he know that someday it would boomerang and Dell would be left perplexed as to why he did it. Her thoughts tormented her that morning before Libby would come to take her to the supermarket.

"Maybe he thought I was going to go off with another man somewhere," Dell told her daughter, mournfully, who was looking solemnly around her dad's old office at the new sitting room her mother had furnished, with a crocheting basket in the corner and a flowered chair alongside, and no sign of its former occupant. The huge void, as if someone had taken a chunk out of the back of their house with a bulldozer, hit Libby each time she came in the door, still expecting to see the glimmer of her father's smiling brown eyes. But that was two months ago. Time marches on, and certainly her mother was progressing forward.

"He even took a few thousand dollars and put it into an unknown bank, at least one I never heard of, and today I found out the car is in his name only." She expressed with incredulity. Libby pitied her mother, but knew her dad to be paranoid, though she didn't think it would extend this far, to the one who had taken such good care of all his needs. And hadn't Libby even lately walked into the house to witness Dell administering a strong mustard plaster to her father's sore back. Even up until the end she had admired their obvious devotion to one another.

Dell wiped away a tear, blowing her nose, which Libby knew would instantly turn vividly red. Even as a child Libby had watched this barometer in the middle of her mother's face, to see if she had been saddened by worry or heartbreak. Her dad had the power to make her mom laugh and cry in a heartbeat. *Was he still doing this?* She asked.

"He must have had no respect for me at all, honestly Lib it breaks my heart."

"Oh mom, you know how daddy was, he loved to pull people's strings. Don't forget, he watched everyone come and go at will for the last twelve years, and for a handicapped person that had to cause some mental anguish. Somehow he's getting the last word with you here on earth." Libby was a firm believer that the line was thin between life and death, and in her illusion she could see her father still hovering near the earth smiling at his own clever mischievousness.

"We traveled to Canada, and all the way to Florida in our little car. He did get around." Libby looked at her sweet mother who still glowed with naiveté. She truly was an angel on earth, and Libby felt it more than ever, but also knew her father's sardonic sense of humor. He enjoyed teasing her mom mercilessly, winking at his daughter or any of her siblings, when she got angry at his prank.

Libby remembered the day they had pulled up in front of her house with the new shiney red compact car. Her parents were both somehow embarrassed driving this loud colored ostentatious automobile around. But nothing held Johnny and Dell back, as the special controls on his car served him well.

In an instant mood change, Dell spoke in a new confident voice that relieved Libby.

"Honey, I'm not going to let that car sit in the garage." She said forcefully.

"You kids shouldn't have to drive me all over town, I'm going to learn to drive. Joel or Rich can teach me." Her determined proclamation came with such verisimilitude, that Libby had to laugh out loud. And though her mom looked incredibly vibrant at sixty-five, she wondered if perhaps she had found some small form of unforeseen freedom with the passing of her husband whom she'd had to wait on most of their married life. Then Dell brought up a sore subject to Libby.

"How are you and Rich getting along these days?" It was obvious, especially during the funeral that things were more and more outwardly tense between them, since he had never forgiven her for the "clumsy" fall at the ski resort, where she'd broken her left leg in two places. Compassion was another one of his nonexistent virtues, especially when it came to his dear wife.

Rich was wretched all during the laying out of her father. Even as they were getting ready to go to the funeral home, when Libby had to hobble up and down stairs on crutches, he scolded her about her inconsiderate family.

"Tommy and Tim are running the whole show. No one ever asked your advice on anything. Why? Because you're a nonentity in your family." He spilled the words out scornfully. She attributed his words to jealousy and hatred for her brother and Kat's husband, who had gone to grade school with the funeral director.

Tears drenched Libby's pillow each night as she sobbed herself to sleep, tears for her dear dad, whom she'd grown closer to late in his life, and for the mistake of the roughshod marriage she was deeply entrenched in. Her fractured leg was symbolic of her broken, shattered life. She was living through the frustration of not being able to get out of a marriage gone rotten. Rich was even responsible for her fall at Seven Springs; if he'd had her ski bindings checked at the beginning of the season, they would have released when she fell.

"Mom, he has short intervals of being the nicest guy in the world." Libby started to feel a tinge of guilt about talking openly about her husband.

"He is so devoted to the house and takes pride in everything he does around there, and makes us laugh with some of his antics. Then while we're eating dinner he lashes out at all of us by being extremely critical of Beatrice, who's just being a teenager the way she dresses in army fatigues and behaves around the house. She's such a good girl, but he's undermining her confidence as well, by calling her friends names. This hurts her deeply and she ends up crying. Sonja sasses him back, aware of her sister's humiliation.

"It's a vicious circle. We will have to separate for our own welfare and the sake of our daughters, who I fear will pay a price someday." Libby felt bad, but relieved for confessing their ruined domestic environment to her mom who already felt down and out, but then as her mom responded she was a little taken aback.

"Okay, but can you and the girls make it on your own without Rich?" There it was again coming straight from her mother's mouth. Oh boy, that men are the strongest individuals in the world attitude again, she thought. Superman, Tarzan, the President of the United States, they could do no wrong. But then what else did she expect from a woman whose generation was raised to worship their men, putting themselves last on the agenda.

"Of course mom, I'm graduating and then I'm going to get a great job remember?" She tried not to be smug, and smiled watching her mother grinning back with contrived enthusiasm, her faith wavering. No one Dell knew had ever accomplished such a feat, it seemed.

Libby had also resented the fact that Dell had called Rich and Joel when Johnny was rushed to the hospital fighting for his life at the end, but then what could she have done in her father's last moments. The medical report said cancer of the pancreas; Rich said when he returned home in tears of anguish. It was then that she truly believed that Rich really did love and respect her father, since she had never seen her husband grieve so passionately.

The Albred family had given their father a final tribute worth talking about for years to come that evening after his burial. Since his political constituents, neighbors and friends had come to lunch after the funeral at a nearby community center, later that evening they gathered in the Albred's huge kitchen where an abundance of food had been brought by their nearby life long neighbors.

This big cheery room with pink flowered geraniums at every window adorned with yellow checkered café curtains, and familiar objects from their childhood was always the heart of their home, a place now missing its key member. An emptiness filled them all, as when Libby first saw her father's office after returning from the funeral home the first time, seeing her dad's precious Schaeffer pens and pad placed neatly on his maple desk. A solitary grief had overtaken her at the stone cold absence of Daddy.

Libby propped her broken leg up on a chair alongside the large maple table, opened the big family songbook, and strummed her guitar to an old familiar song, her dad's favorite, "You Are My Sunshine," He had played it on his mouth organ often. Then Ben, now a well built handsome man somewhat balding at forty, came over to her side leafing through the pages to songs of their dad's era, the roaring twenties and Depression ridden thirties.

Johnny had been raised in the manufacturing town of Eastburg, he had tended bar at the Albred Hotel, rubbing elbows with some of the roughest characters around, especially his brother Phil's gangster bootlegger pals, and even the cops had been questionable in that city.

Later at the turn of the century, his mother Lizzie had catered to the new immigrant clientele workers needed at the new George Westinghouse plant across the street. Bed and board at her spotless thirty-room hotel assured them of a new home, far away from across the ocean in Europe, where most of their families had stayed behind.

Tommy, Ben and Joel, the only children who had lived at the hotel, reminisced about their grandmother's sternness, for the rest of the family present.

"She was diminutive, but boy she wielded power and no one talked back to her, a force to be reckoned with in her high white apron and tight babushka wrapped around her hair. I don't think she ever smiled. We were all afraid of her when she walked in." Ben added. Tommy laughed, shaking his head in agreement. Dark full haired slight built, even though he worked in the tough occupation of construction, Tommy loved being home bantering with the rest of the family.

"You boys were probably doing something bad, like peeing behind the shed in back of the hotel. You certainly were not angels." Terry said, pouring a cup of coffee from the percolator on the stove. She would always have the reputation of having another opinion in the family. Aunt Mary laughed loudly at her niece. Dell, who worked hard living at the hotel in her early marriage years, knew only the day-to-day humiliation of drudgery.

"She couldn't be pleasant, there was too much work to do, and we were up at four o'clock in the morning just baking bread. Your grandmother was up way before that shopping and planning and preparing meals for the borders. Right Agatha?" She looked over at her sister-in-law, who usually was never around to do the hard work, but Dell wanted to razz her a little.

Their aunt sat in a nearby chair nibbling some cake, and giggling, but followed the conversation that took her back in time, when money was easier to come by, and when she was the belle of Eastburg growing up with many luxuries in the bountiful twenties of the hotel.

Everyone was at attention listening to Dell talking about the old days, standing in front of the kitchen sink unwrapping a huge bowl of potato salad from the people who ran the greenhouse next door. She spoke from the heart of the hotel years under her mother-in-law's tough rule. Except this time it was different, daddy wasn't there to give his input, which might or might not agree with Dell's observations and they felt the emptiness among them.

Then Libby played the chords to "Its Only A Shanty in Old Shanty Town." a rollicking 1932 paen to poverty song, written when shanties were built throughout the depth of the Depression. Johnny would have appreciated this symbolic song of that period. Dell remembered for both of them, singing robustly, and laughing with the music. Everyone was brought up to   carry a tune in the Albred house.

Ben looked over Libby's shoulder as she turned the pages, when "Tea For Two", their mom and dad's theme song turned up. Her big brother patted her shoulder gently.

"Oh let's not play that one," He whispered. "It will be too sad for mom." Everyone in the room hushed, as they peeped over her shoulder acknowledging the moment. Libby could visualize her mom in past days, looking up at her dad when it played on the radio all throughout their life together. It would always generate into a tender affectionate moment together no matter what else was happening around them.

During the period of this 1924 song, her dad would have been twenty-four and her mom just eighteen, the height of their courting years when Johnny was selling Maxwell's at her father Pop's Chrysler Garage.

Joey and Charley, who had brought his two young sons and daughter up, sat beside Aunt Agatha, the last remaining member of the immediate Albred family. Agatha and Dell through their mutual family association would become better friends in their older remaining years.

All the younger cousins, and children of the six Albred's joined the full chorus singing out robustly through the happy flag-waving "I'm A Yankee Doodle Dandy". Then Kat, still the baby of the family among her older siblings, marched around the room with a tiny American flag that had been stuck into a plant from Johnny's office. Now a dark haired beauty with striking violet eyes, who would always be the doted on as the "baby of the family," lived with her husband in Michigan.

Everyone laughed at her exuberance, remembering how their dad had loved playing John Phillips Sousa's marches on the radio, waking them up on Saturday mornings with the loud pulsating rhythms preventing them from oversleeping in too late.

Libby couldn't help but feel, but for the fact that her father was no longer present, the eating and drinking would not have gone on indefinitely as it did that day, which went on late into the night. Johnny the disciplinarian would have wheeled in at some point expressing that it was time to suspend the festivities. However, the bereaved family all felt better afterward. Nonetheless, Dell watched Ben's wife Marjorie imbibing more than others, a habit which would begin to control her life, eventually leading to alcoholism. Another exhibition, which would not have taken place had Johnny been around, as in later years, Marjorie would threaten family members, especially Dell, with outbursts related to alcoholism.

Red, white and blue was showing everywhere these days, and though the 1976 Bicentennial party of the United States wouldn't be until next year, patriotism permeated the air as the nation prepared for America's big birthday party. Two hundred and eighteen million Americans would celebrate on July 4, 1976. The event was in concert with John Adams, patriot, and second president of the United States, who proclaimed a major commemoration at the time of the signing of the constitution, with salutes, ringing bells, exploding fireworks, blaring bands and thousands of parades commencing in tune.

Australian author Colleen McCullough was a best seller with "The Thorn Birds," and Guillermo Vilas, Bjorn Borg, Jimmy Connors and Chris Everet were the most successful tennis players in 1977.

California State University, situated along the Monongahela River in the town of California, Pennsylvania, was the site for Libby's graduation with honors. She would be the first woman in her family to graduate from college. Commuting two hours twice a week southwest over the Pennsylvania turnpike to this neat little country college, Libby had found it easy to learn in a small class environment as opposed to the large course groups she'd heard about at the University of Pittsburgh or Carnegie Mellon. Her confidence soared, after receiving a Bachelor of Arts Degree, and she found out during her job search that it was still unique at the end of the seventies for women to qualify for positions in business management.

Her resume looked especially attractive after she'd acquired experience working part-time in many corporate offices in Pittsburgh, where she'd gained experience on every office machine, with the exception of the new computers swiftly coming of age in companies.

The last "temp" job she'd completed had been at an IBM Corporation on the north side Pittsburgh paying ten dollars an hour, where Libby had filled in for a woman on vacation. IBM "Mag card" typewriters was a concept easily within her grasp to learn. Nevertheless she strongly hoped it would not be necessary to enter a professional position through a secretarial entry job, especially since her last two interviews had offered attractive administration positions. Sadly for her they were both in Texas for Pittsburgh Plate Glass. *Now if I were a man, I'd have all the freedom to hop on a plane and go for those jobs.* She thought.

But being a mother of two teen-agers in school, she could not pursue a career relentlessly, just leaving them to "fend" with their father, though she knew some women who were throwing that caution to the wind nowadays, just to get their careers started. No, she could never leave them without a full time mother, not until at least they were ready for college.

At the end of the seventies, however, a recession of great magnitude loomed over the Pittsburgh area, an economic upset stirred by the fact that the steel industry began to go through a serious business slump, reducing shipments of steel in 1980 to 83.9 million tons, down from 100.3 million in 1979. The federal government's "trigger price" mechanism for restraining imports had come to an ineffectual end, and U.S. Steel pressed ahead with major court suits aimed at forcing the government to take action against foreign producers that dumped steel in the United States.

Historically, even by 1970, the U.S. share of world production was down to 20.1 percent. What was thought of as the traditional American steel industry – big integrated companies – had already lost its competitive edge over foreign producers and domestic minimills. Production share continued to fall over the years having a declining consequence over the entire region. Libby could still visualize the diminishing returns graphs on the board that Professor Jefferson had drawn in micro Economics class, determining business growth with U.S.Steel and the auto industry. These two barometers determined a sick or healthy economy that she could now understand personally as a workingwoman.

Al Galora, the son-in-law of the Leax's next door, had just finished plowing an early winter snow that had fallen overnight, and Dell stepped out to clear the rest of the loose piles around the garage door so that she could drive to 9:30 mass that Sunday. Now chauffeuring a few women who lived down the street, who wanted to go to church but had no transportation, she was proud of her new driving achievement. And even though it had taken her four times to pass her test, she had gained complete independence as a result of her perseverance.

The roads looked wet this morning; therefore she wouldn't worry about travel down the steep hill and back again. Turning around to go into the house to have another cup of coffee, Dell breathed deeply, filling her lungs with a long gust of fresh air and gazed down over the back yard. A beautiful scene was displayed in the long yard as white clouds of snow and glistening icicles clung to tree branches, featuring Mother Nature at her finest.

The thought of their children sledding down their hill and filling the air with merriment brought tears to her eyes. Oh how she and Johnny would laugh at their antics as they frolicked over deeply drifted blankets of snowfall. *Oh where have all the years gone?* She asked herself. Now leading an almost solitary existence, she yearned for her bustling family coming and going for over forty years. A strange blanket of loneliness encircled her like a dark groping monster. Dell knew that no one could fill the chilling emptiness she now suffered, however, the strong faith that had guided her throughout life was always present and the Blessed Mother stayed vigilant.

She missed her helpmate, Johnny, who had been in her life all this time. Often she found herself talking to him as if he were still there in his wheelchair. Last night she had dreamed about him, at least she felt his presence, but instead Philip stepped out in garish clothes. When she asked him if Johnny was next to him, he spoke out.

"Oh, no, he said." Johnny is in another place entirely," we're separated." She'd sat up in bed afterward, mostly upset because she had not seen her husband. Dell had told this dream to Libby the next time they saw each other, trying to interpret what it might mean.

"Maybe my time to die is coming, Lib." She told her daughter in her meek and mild manner. "I want to die in my sleep quietly, that would be a nice way to go wouldn't it?" Then they had hugged each other spontaneously, almost as a departing gesture.

Last summer she'd had the smallest garden ever, since the only ones around to pick lettuce, tomatoes and onions had been Joel and Libby and their families. And now that Libby had started to work full time, Dell didn't see her much, mostly because she worked on the weekends. What kind of a company would have people work on Saturday and Sunday? Sunday had always been the Lords day with them, a prescribed day of rest.

Maybe I'll sell this place and get a new senior apartment down in Turtle Creek. Dell thought. She didn't want to be around there the next time Ben brought his wife Marjorie from New York. Last Christmas she had lashed out at her mother-in-law in a brash intoxicated manner. Dell had asked her to please not drink too much over the holiday, when an unleashing of all of her evil spewed forth in vile language.

Dell had been struck speechless at her daughter-in-law's despicable mouth. Marjorie had pointed a wicked forefinger in a drunken stupor at her mother-in-law, her stringy gray streaked hair falling down around her face and bright green eyes looking horribly into Dell's, shocking and terrifying her with filthy bold innuendoes.

"You, you're so **perfect, the perfect mother**. You adore your precious son so much, would you like to sleep with him?" Dell burst into tears of revulsion, not knowing what stance to take against her daughter-in-law, who then grabbed a knife from the table to lash out at Kat who'd try to defend her mother. In all her years she'd never encountered a wildly inebriated woman such as this, who'd dared to insult her in her own home. Even through all of the years of witnessing drunken behavior at the hotel, she hadn't been the object of such ludicrous and debased conduct, and from a family member no less.

Kat and Tim, the other houseguests for the holidays, stared in disbelief, and ultimately Ben had had to subdue his wife. They were all left to wonder if his counseling would work with his emotionally unstable wife, who had not yet been diagnosed as a bona fide alcoholic.

Dell worried incessantly afterward about her son's life being threatened living with this mad woman, who was now angry with every member of the family, who were trying to be cordial to her for Ben's sake. When Marjorie had left Churchill Road after Christmas, Dell and Kat had found bottles hidden around the house in various places, confirming the fact that her alcoholism had become more of a problem.

This year, as providence would have it, two days before Christmas, Dell was hastily packing her suitcase to take a trip to Chicago. It would be strange leaving home for the holidays, but Tommy and Dottie needed her desperately to go there. Tommy was seriously ill.

"Mom, he's going to have chemotherapy starting next week. It would be nice if you could come out. It may be his last Christmas, the Doctor thinks it may be cancer of the bone." The conversation had left Dell in tears and clutching her rosary all day praying to almighty God for her oldest son's health. He had always been strong willed, going off to the Navy at such a young age, driving his poor body ragged, *oh my poor boy.* She cried into the solitary black night.

The New Year would bring in the decade with technological developments being founded right in their own backyard at The Robotics Carnegie Mellon University, established to conduct basic and applied research in robotics technologies relevant to industrial and societal tasks. And Acquired Immunodeficiency Syndrome, or AIDS would be identified in Los Angeles, with more than six to eight million people dying from the disease. In the far Middle East, followers of Ayatollah Ruhollah Khomeini seized power in Iran.

Libby loved her new job working for Dravo Corporation in downtown Pittsburgh in one of the tallest skyscrapers. As proposal coordinator in the Engineering Sales Department she worked with kind and professional people who encouraged her to do her best work. After a few months, Jim Higgins, the Sales Manager, whom she had gotten on well with immediately, sent her for a week of computer training.

The intricate process of preparing large sales reports and forecasts from all over the world required computerized comparative data, and Libby undertook the daily and weekly output. It was actually fun being cooped up in an office after spending most of her life being out of doors. But as chance would have it, the depressed economy of the region was bringing most companies to their knees financially, and Dravo Engineering was no exception. Consequently, after six months in her dream job she was laid off, and notified that she was one of the first to go because of her low seniority. Though it would just be a matter of a few years when the company would declare bankruptcy, and by then Libby would be securely installed in another job.

15. Uncharted Waters

Confrontations of the worst kind continued in Libby and Rich Honford's residence. With Libby working almost every day of the week, her emotions were threadbare and their short time together filled with tension. Except for her closeness with Sonja, Libby's heart had left their war torn home. Beatrice was now a junior at Clarion State University, and Sonja was getting ready to enter Penn's Hill Senior High School.

"When are you leaving here anyway?" Rich had shouted malevolently last night. Of course he'd come back drunk again to thrust his "Friday night seizure", as Beatrice called it, upon the household. He would be all wound up talking and shouting, mostly at her, his adrenalin flow never stopped especially when under the influence.

"I think you should be the one to leave, you're causing all the trouble with your drinking and coming home so late in the morning. Or should I say so early." Libby said.

"Oh yeah, this is my house, I work sixteen hours a day to pay for it." He said. Libby had heard this last phrase many times over the last twenty-one years, and was exasperated from defending her position, with her dander up again at his hateful selfish words.

"Maybe I will be the one to leave." She said willfully, thinking that now that she was in the job market, there were ways to free herself, which she hadn't told her husband about yet.

"Ha, you'll never make it out there, it's a cold cruel world girl, you just can't compete. I see these really sharp women at work and you can't cut it. "

She knew he had never recognized her as an equal partner in their marriage in all their years together. He thought of all their "possessions" as his. The original material man, thinking the sun rose and set on tangible objects. He never could deal with live human hearts since they would take too much magnanimity, a condition he somehow never did comprehend.

Each day now brought fresh fatigue of mind and body stressed from yet another emotional plunder. Only one thing had changed over the years; she no longer sobbed senselessly, since over time she had become embittered with an impenetrable shield of armor, no longer hurt by his slanderous words, simply because she no longer cared about him. Libby's love for Rich had died during the first ten years of their relationship.

It was Memorial Day, the end of May 1980, and an unusual holiday since there was no picnic supper planned at her mother's that afternoon, probably because of all the sadness and deaths in the family. Tommy had died last year from cancer of the pelvis; they had all grieved for their oldest brother, who had everything to live for at forty-two years of age. Dell particularly, had not reconciled his death and had taken it to heart with great pain. First Johnny and then their oldest son were gone from the world of the living, leaving a deep hollow in the Albred family.

"Ring, ring, ring." The shrill wall phone rang abruptly, blasting resonantly off the sides of Libby's kitchen and dining room walls, crashing into the solemn angry silence.

"Hello", Libby answered, anchoring the long yellow-coiled wire around the kitchen chair, while buttering a slice of toast with the other hand. She thought it was probably Kat, who was visiting at her mom's. They loved to chat about little happenings in their lives, and it would be a nice diversion to talk to her this day. They had grown much closer in the last five years, their age difference dwindling over time. Instead, a man's voice on the other end of the line hesitated. She could hear him take a short breath before he spoke.

"This is Trooper Jack Harris, can, can I speak to your husband please?"

"Yes." She answered disconnectedly, wondering why a trooper would be calling Rich. Perhaps he was in trouble with the law for driving under the influence. Or maybe it was some woman's husband, who had found them in bed together. Though she doubted the latter, Rich had been doing a lot of peculiar things these days, like staying out until two a.m. in the morning, which he'd had too much pride to do in past years. However, carousing around with women was never one of his shortcomings.

"It's for you." She shouted across to the family room, where she suspected he was once again bowing over the file box containing their alphabetized monthly bills. It was a joint venture and one of the only things they had in common these days. Libby hesitated; listening suspiciously as Rich walked over and lifted the receiver from the table. A split second into the conversation, she caught the expression on his face, which told her that the voice was strange to him as well.

He frowned first at her, and then out the back window into the tall fir tree in the backyard, his brain deciphering and registering remorse with the relayed information. He hung up slowly, staring at the receiver while gathering his words. Libby knew his familiar distressful look well; the news couldn't be good. Then he spoke softly, which was out of character as well, since they'd just had another major battle.

"Libby, there's been an accident on the Parkway West. Your mother and Tim have both been killed. Kat is in critical condition at Sewickley Valley Hospital. They were taking Tim back to the airport to catch his plane back to Grand Rapids ". Libby looked away, outraged at the Trooper for not giving her this information directly. Venting her anger at someone, anyone, wanting to kill the message bearer, she thought, *why were men always protecting women*? Why was it Rich, who didn't exactly have a good stronghold on things, who had to break the devastating news to her?

Rich, Libby, and Sonja walked in a daze to their car in the driveway. *Could this be a mistaken identity, someone's cruel and inhuman joke?* She thought. *Or maybe it's God punishing us for fighting like cats and dogs lately.* Just yesterday her mom had brought over a large pot of stuffed cabbage for them, only to be greeted coldly by Rich. But she had ignored his stiffness, as usual, as she offered the meal welcomed by at least Libby, who was glad to have dinner brought over and not have to cook that evening after her rigorous work routine, which she was reluctantly adjusting to.

"Here, this is for you, sometime I get hungry for these dishes, but they can only be made in large portions, there's too much for me to eat alone." Her humble mother had said. Libby wanted to invite her to eat with them, but also wanted to spare her from the ongoing wrath of their household, but she knew her mother was more than aware that their environment was no longer family conducive.

Entering the antiseptic wing of Emergency Patient Care, their heads were bent low; Libby willed her heavy feet to carry her forward into the door. And deep in her heart, she still wished for the mistake to reveal itself along the way – that everything was not as bad as the trooper had described to Rich. Maybe her mother would even be here to greet them, telling them she was fine and that everything would be all right. She certainly knew how to combat bad news, especially when things seemed grimmest. Hadn't she practically resurrected her dad's terrible handicap into something that jumpstarted his entry into politics?

As they walked closer into the visiting room, Libby heard Kat's violent screams echoing through the otherwise quiet waiting room. She rushed through the "No Admittance" room incoherently, trying to interpret what kind of medical care could elicit this outburst from her sister. Bright lights and a team of hospital experts in green scrubs stood around covering Kat from view. Libby broke through one in the circle, who seemed to be joined together pulling and yanking her sister's broken body into a form of traction, which would ultimately lead to the straightening of her fractured pelvis.

The scene played out like a life versus death struggle in an old episode of The Twilight Zone. A little later, Joel and Glenny told them in the visiting room that Kat had been next to the driver's seat, when they had been hit head on by a truck. The truck driver had had a heart attack coming down the hill beside White Swan Park on Parkway West, his truck gaining momentum, and crashing into the small compact car with great force. By some grace of God Kat had come out of it alive but gravely injured. When she heard Libby's voice come through, her head and shoulders turned, alarming her caregivers.

"Libby, Mom and Tim, they're dead." She cried out agonizingly, her usual bright violet eyes now clouded with bloody pain from the depths of her soul in unbelieving despair, hoping with all heart that her older sister would say that everything was alright, and that their mother and her husband were recuperating as well in another room of the hospital. Then as if Kat thought that Libby really didn't understand that they were killed or hoped it hadn't happened, she cried out again.

"They've been killed Libby, oh God help me." Libby wished with all her heart that she could say, no, it really didn't happen, wake up Kat, its all a bad dream, I'll take you home soon.

"Kat I know." Libby said, grabbing her arm firmly. "But you are meant to survive, Mom and Dad want you to go on living. " It would have been easy to sob uncontrollably along with her sister, but instead her strength increased forcing her to stay her ground and not break down, because by some divine miracle Kat had been spared. She has to recover from this horrendous accident; it was the one precious ingot of life they had been granted in this huge fiasco.

Libby focused on her little sister, bringing to mind what their dad had always told them. *I want you kids to love and take care of each other.* And now more than ever, Kat would need all of them helping her mentally and physically in the years to come.

And without thinking about the loss of her dear mother, who would never be there again for her, Libby realized that Ben, Joel, Terry, Kat and herself were now the future of the Albred family, with both their mother and father and Tommy gone. The swift arm of fate had swiped Dell away forever. God had made a decision to remove Dell from all of her pain and suffering of this earth and place her spirit next to him.

Adela Elona Gessner Albred, and Timothy Oliver Nelson were laid out in two different rooms in the funeral home. Their mother looked beautiful lying in the red silk suit that she had worn to Kat and Tim's wedding. Libby had seen her wear it for many happy occasions, and though she looked beautiful in death as well as life, Libby noted the cosmetic contrast from a few days before when she and Joel had morosely gone to the Allegheny County Morgue to identify their mother's body.

Her bluish white hair that had just been permed last week had been washed with the rest of her body, bearing no marks from the dreadful accident. A serene glow shone out of her face, which comforted Libby in her fear of seeing her mother in this state. Her presence had always lit up the room like a candelabrum, but now that Libby thought about it, the glow was within all the time, not just at death. She had truly been an angel of God – and now Libby knew that she was in a safe heavenly place to celebrate her next life with Johnny. They were a rare selfless loving couple who always thought of themselves last.

When the double funeral was over, the mourners all went home after a short breakfast at the local community center. Libby and Rich sat exhausted in the comfortable family room, each having been brought to their knees by the harsh awareness that life is, as the Bible says, "A vapor, that appeareth for a little time, and then vanisheth away". Then Libby was motivated by her voice of reason, which broke into the relaxed setting.

"Rich, I think you and I should separate." She said, in a moment of complete emotional exhaustion. She was motivated by a force stronger than herself, and couldn't believe it was her voice speaking. Could it have been some form of divine intervention acting on behalf of her well-being? Worried about the reaction she'd receive, Libby looked straight ahead out the windows at the bright emerald golf greens of the local country club on the horizon not knowing what to expect. The fact that Rich looked up shaking his head slowly in acknowledgement surprised her.

"Alright, but you'll have to give me time to find an apartment. I'll move as soon as I can." He said, further surprising her with his willingness to move, making her slightly suspicious. Libby stared at his impeccably tailored suit, black wavy hair, and stunning good looks. He will most certainly marry again, she thought, some woman will fall head over heels for him. Especially when everything is going his way, until he turns his evil side up, she pondered.

A separation would give them a chance to clear the air; she needed a rest from their pugnacious way of life. But then he mentioned one of his future goals.

"I thought we'd look for a bigger house Lib, have a change of scene." He said.

She just shook her head negatively at his comment, thinking *it doesn't matter if we live in a mansion or an attic, It's still us, with our out of kilter relationship.*

In just a couple of weeks he had found a roommate in Shadyside, where he could easily commute to work in Pittsburgh. The day that he moved out proved to be extremely sad. Libby knew it might prove to be complicated, especially since most of their home furnishings had been his special selections, with an artistic flair displayed in every corner of the rooms; from tiny ornate master paintings to majestic brocade chair and wallpaper coverings.

Beatrice was home from school that weekend and both sisters' were deeply affected by their father's departure. Their hearts went out to him as he carried twenty years of possessions out the door and into a rented van. Libby had worked at her office almost the entire day mentally rationalizing, *let him take what he wants; none of those "things" bring peace of mind or happiness in any form.* But as she walked up the steps from the garage into the kitchen, an empty sadness greeted her, as she viewed most of his artifacts gone and bare spots remaining here and there with an overall oppression pervading the almost empty house.

Beatrice, with her long thick auburn hair hanging down over her shoulders as she sat low on the couch, spoke remorsefully.

"Mommy, it was a bad scene seeing daddy loading all of his floor plants onto the truck. especially since he babied all of them. He looked so downtrodden." She moaned into a tissue.

Libby shook her head miserably, feeling deep guilt. First the girls had lost their grandmother and uncle, and now their family was being dissolved. Things were changing too rapidly for them. Sonja, sensing her mother's feelings, put her arm around her for consolation.

"All I can say is that you two made each other miserable day after day, and this will be a wonderful relief for all of us." Her wise teenager said. Then they hugged and held each other for a couple of moments, knowing that ultimately it would be for the best. At least Libby knew it would.

Libby had always felt that she should be the one to move, since Rich had put so much of himself into designing and building their home both inside and out, single handedly attaching a redwood deck in the back, landscaping the small yard, repairing downspouts, building the family room and painting the trim on the red brick home; he was always in motion doing something else around there.

She started out paying all the bills herself, hence not wanting support from Rich of any kind, except to pay college expenses for their daughters. Not having Rich's share of the money was the minor part of their separation, since she was consumed with guilt. And she realized that he would need money to essentially start his life over. At first it was lonely without his presence, especially at night, but then she began to relax and revel in her independence. Most of all, a sense of peace and calm came over the house.

Perhaps the biggest adjustment, without the anxieties that accompanied their relationship, Libby's skin completely cleared up and she felt beautiful again. Her auburn hair now had traces of gray shining through which she had never hidden, since as Bea had always told her, "Mom, be proud of your gray, you look terrific for almost forty." Therefore, Libby took her daughter's sage advice, and decided to be herself, as her dad had always advised her. A promising sign would appear when Sonja stayed on the honor roll for the rest of her high school years.

Nonetheless, the decision to separate from Rich would haunt Libby every day with questions of *could she have hung in there for their daughters' sake? Or would counseling have actually helped them in the last stages of no respect for each other?* She always came up with negative answers to these. She had to keep remembering the misery they'd caused each other.

Certainly she had been to blame as well as he at the point of no return, but there was a double connection here. Libby hated him for the way he treated her poor mother, who was no long around, indirectly blaming him, which she knew was wrong, since it was an accident. Oh how many *times had she reached for the phone to call her mother or I have to tell mom about that when* I see her, but there would never be a next time, since she was no longer there to respond.

After a few weeks Kat came home to Churchill Road from the hospital with a fractured pelvis and broken toes, Bea and Sonja spent the rest of the summer helping her to slowly recuperate onto crutches. Joel and Glenny were always there as well, with their two teenage sons, cutting the long lawn and taking care of the house. Bobbie and Philip, named after their Uncle Phil, were fair haired and tanned from a sunny outdoor summer and loved the land, as did their father before them.

Terry and William came on weekends from Ohio to spend with their sister, while Ben and his troublesome wife; Marjorie would call to see how Kat was convalescing. But all in all, the Albred's would avoid meeting up with their alcoholic sister-in-law, who insisted on harassing them with phone calls from New York, especially to Libby and Kat. There was now a wedge between them and their brother. If they wanted to talk to him – they had to call the Guidance office of the school in New York where he worked.

One evening when Libby came over to pick up Bea and Sonja, after work at their family home, Libby had wondered into their mother and father's bedroom gazing around the empty shell looking for signs of Dell. This peach colored room had been filled with life at one time. The place where they came as kids when they were sick – where just the thought of lying down on their soft mattress brought relief from any illness. Their parents had the healing power to just lay a comforting hand on them and magically make them feel better.

Her mom's dresser looked as if she had gone out for a brief period and would be back momentarily, with her brushes and combs in place next to a perfume atomizer filled with Lily of the Valley cologne all set on an ornate mirror tray. Blue crystal rosary beads were piled up in the corner. Libby stared dismally at her reflection as she saw Kat hobble up behind her.

"Oh Lib, our beautiful mother is gone forever." She cried out mournfully. Libby could only stare; her forlorn look frozen in a time capsule with the space of vivid memories. She held her sister tight, wondering if she would ever recover from the dreadful accident she had survived physically but not mentally.

Libby hated her new job at Domaini-Manfred. It was exactly what she did not want to fall into, but times were bad and she now needed money to keep the household and her life going properly. Coordinating correspondence between suppliers and sub suppliers for engineering contracts was not difficult, but working with Mr. Puppendorf was unbearable. The one blessing each day at a miserable task, was a co-worker named Felicitas, a dark thick-haired immigrant Italian girl with a tough hard-core disposition who was ready to defend Libby at every turn.

And even though Libby was the lowest paid of their engineering group, Paulo Puppendorf would hold her solely responsible for all communications lost between companies.

"Elizabet". He would holler from his office, as if she was part of the job militia, then he would call her into his office and demean her in any way he could in his high style German.

"We cannot have mistakes on this Continuous Caster steel project, you must be professional in every way." He would drum this edict into her on a daily basis, then he would ramble on about the numerous tasks she should accomplish that day. Puppendorf had been part of the Luftwafe in the Second World War, priding himself in dictator style office politics.

He was charming in a prison warden kind of way. At least during their initial interview he had actually come across as polite and debonair, whereas she had probably appeared desperate since she needed a job NOW, and he must have sensed her urgency. Oh God, after a day with this demanding man, it would have been so easy to call Rich and consent to reconcile, but her new friend Felicitas stressed her declaration.

"Don't you dare call him, after what you told me about him." Libby heeded her command, simply because she knew she'd gone around the corner into a new way of peaceful independent living, to return to her former life which seemed farther and farther away now.

Felicitas dominated the office with her European savvy, intimidating the newly transported Italian and German engineers with her multi-lingual German and Italian language skills. Sometimes she shouted at them in their native tongue. "Scusa mi! Pietro" or wrote memos with Achtung! at the top of the margin. Someone had put her in charge of the office, and Libby couldn't wait to meet them.

Libby had a hard time seeing the big picture of this company's existence in the United States, but could rationalize its actions. The foreign steel companies had come into the area at the beginning of the 1980's to sell their technology in Pittsburgh, since most of the area steel companies became obsolete because no modernization had ever been done to make them competitive with the rest of the world. And although there were many problems with labor and management, this was just one of the obvious problems. There were times when driving past J&L Steel on Parkway East, when one of her German co-workers would casually remark.

"Look at that awful looking place, nothing should ever be that neglected, never modernized, just laying there like a piece of junk." This would make her feel very embarrassed, and even sad for the families living all around, now unemployed. She would then argue that European countries had rebuilt brand new companies after the World War, installing state of the art steelmaking devices; this is why you have the edge on the world market.

Libby soon found out that the company was moving into a new office across from the Pittsburgh airport; her daily route to work would be on the same road that the dreaded accident scene took place. The trip from home would take one hour each way every day. Maybe this was the time to leave the job, but to go where making the kind of money she required.

Television these days was highlighted by two events, "Shogun" and the shooting of J.R.Ewing on "Dallas". The prime time soap opera "Dallas" became one of the most talked about series of the year, especially after the evil oil tycoon J.R.Ewing, played by Larry Hagman was shot during the final episode of the 1979-1980 season. And Musician John Lennon, who helped found the Beatles had been shot to death on a New York City street. He'd just resumed his career with a new album, "Double Fantasy," after five years in retirement

Ronald Reagan was elected President after serving two terms as governor of California. In the 1980 election, he defeated President Jimmy Carter, the Democratic candidate. The nation faced serious problems both in foreign affairs and in the economy

Mother Teresa, an Albanian-born nun, won the 1979 Nobel Peace Prize for more than thirty years' work with the poor and ailing of Calcutta, India. In tennis, John McEnroe, a 20-year-old left-hander from Douglaston, NY defeated Vitas Gerulaitis of

Kings Point, NY in the US open final on September 9th at Flushing Meadows, NY.

In the spring of 1982, Kat slowly started out on her own once again, taking short-term assignments at temporary jobs in East Liberty, and finally settling on a clerical job at Pittsburgh Theological Seminary. This religious organization lent itself to her nurturing need for consolation, after most of the staff there began to find out about her role in the horrible accident. Some members there who had actually read about the calamity, recalling it being published in the newspapers last memorial day.

Libby saw her sister often, since they only lived a few miles away from each other, and especially on the weekends, when they were away from their perspective places of employment. But they spoke on the telephone almost daily, and when Kat was having setbacks Libby would talk her out of her mood.

"Lib, I was also meant to be killed – I don't know why I was spared." She would sob into the phone. But Libby would constantly reassure her sister of her need in the world.

"Mom is feeling good right now about your achievement to get back on your feet, Kat, please take that into consideration, and keep going, you have a family now." Kat had acquired two new dogs, Conor and Sadie, along with ten-year-old Augie, and had adopted two more cat's in addition to her older ones, Whisper and big, white Warlock. The pure, black kitten, Woodie, found in the woods behind Carnegie Mellon University and Winnie, a darling little Persian kitten. Her house full of animals kept Kat busy while she was convalescing with their care, feeding and constant walking.

Bea and Sonja, went along with their aunt to Animal Friends Pet Adoption Agency to choose them, which resulted in them begging Libby to bring into their home two new felines which they called Geoffrey of Orange and Charlotte, both tabbies of opposite nature. Now Mia and Kippy became a family of four. Bea, who had graduated from college, was now helping Libby prepare Sonja for her first year at Edinborough College near Erie, PA. Bea would spend the summer working at Hornes Department Store at the Monroeville Mall, while contemplating graduate school. The girls visited their father often at his home in the Shadyside area.

The van sub-culture which Libby had now joined for transportation to Domaini-Manfred's new Airport Office Park location, proved to be an interesting event in itself, with six male employees from American Bridge, a subsidiary of US Steel Corporation. The vanpool carried on interesting conversations during the hour to and from work each day, ranging from politics to personal hygiene. Corkey, the driver would sometime get into traffic, which would increase the laborious commute, but then the chatter would rage with what was the best route to take.

The crew consisted of Jimmy, a fiery red haired accountant; Peter, a short stocky balding middle-aged engineer; Jack, handsome and knowledgeable, who would sometime brief them on the history of bridges while crossing the Ohio River; and fast talking Ricky, who never took no for an answer. There were two who rarely gave an opinion on any topic. Libby found herself somewhat confiding in the group about her work situation at the foreign office across the way.

One cold dark winter day, just when she thought her career was on the skids for good, Dr. Fretzen, a tall dark robust German, the head of their office division in Pittsburgh, called her into his office to ask if she wanted to head up the new computer department they were trying to organize. Libby was thrilled and the next week was sent to Chicago to train for Wang Office Computer Management.

A separate office was set up for the VS Wang, a 32 Mega Byte unit mainframe, which stored all the contracts and clerical documents from two office floors of the company, and maintained them on three generations of discs. Puppendorf called her away from her new interest by giving her mountains of correspondence, running defense against the computer management job she was trying to develop, since he wanted Libby to do only do his work.

But Libby persisted with her own agenda, by holding classes for the new computer operators, instructing them on how to take care of the system of their workstation, and trouble shooting to bring them back into any of their lost documents.

The latter occurred often in all of the new computers, since saving and storing documents instantly was not yet improved.

Essentially, she thought job security was hers for the taking, but having very little social time, except when Felicitas would coax her to go out for a drink after work into Pittsburgh to Froggies nightspot. This was where she met up with a friend she had known at Dravo. He began to call her at her job, and eventually they started up an uncomfortable affair. Inconvenient for Libby, since Mark was still committed to his marriage, and she was getting ready to divorce Rich.

When the continuous caster plant was completed, she was called in to Dr. Fretzen's office.

"Libby, as you know the job is finished, we will now place you in a new position, as assistant to Mr. Pizzaria." He spoke in his broken German English. Her heart sank. All the nights she had traveled over forty miles from her home to this office during thunderstorm breakdowns, which would have shut down the mainframe, toggled at her brain. And why couldn't some men see that women have ambition as well, where did their mental obstruction come from?

Heaven help me – her mind screamed. She stood and listened, ears pounding like the downward thrust of a construction worker on a jackhammer.

"You know Dr. Fretzen, how I organized this computer department from scratch. I wrote up the purchase order, buying the work stations, holding training sessions, and trouble shooting with all employees on the system for the last two years." She protested. But these fell on deaf ears.

"On Monday morning you will show Bill Roberts how to do your computer programs." He went on, with his practiced speech, his eyes somewhat sympathic, but his mind telling him to *go ahead with your orders,* since he was taking direction straight from Germany. Libby's objections were disregarded. She stared incredulously at his pile of mail in the corner of his office, and then remembered how he insisted on censoring each piece that came to each employee into the building. This was another sign that warned Libby of her "undeserved loyalty".

The quiet witness to this conversation was her immediate supervisor, Puppendorf, who replied hastily in his highest aristocratic English.

"Don't worry Elizabet, I'll take you to lunch today." She turned to look at him as if he was a snake running up her leg. Her aspirations were dashed, so that she could not talk any more. These last words were the final stroke, and proved that the women in this organization were some kind of pretty tokens, and that she would have to find another job in order to grow in her career.

Essentially, she had set up the department for Bill Roberts to take charge of, not for her own advancement in the company. That evening she vowed to leave. She could not stay with a company that did not reward its employees.

"Do not look back. And do not dream about the future, either. It will neither give you back the past, nor satisfy your other daydreams. Your duty, your reward – your destiny – are here and now."

Dag Hammarskjold, United Nations Secretary-General (1905-1961)

16. Metamorphoses

The winter of 1985 began with various job interviews for Libby throughout Pittsburgh and the surrounding areas. Most of these positions came under the title, administrative assistant, but would actually be office management, covering anything from managing accounts to supervising workers. Libby tried to sort through the job descriptions, trying to qualify for each one during dialogue with the managers in charge, but she was either over-qualified or wanted too high of a salary with her related experience. Her difficult quest would never again lend an opportunity to Libby in the area again.

In the meantime, an opportunity came her way through a group of co-workers that she could not turn her back on, though she was reluctant at the outset. A trip to Badgastein, Austria. The beautiful resort nestled in the Alps and located south of Salzburg was at one time the health spa of the Hapsburg royal family empire.

Felicitas and her German friend Helga spearheaded the group, which would be affordable for everyone, especially since the exchange rate of the dollar into schillings would be advantageous to American tourists in Austria at this time. The prospective travelers met at a tavern in Shadyside to talk about the coming trip, and Felicitas insisted that Libby go as well.

"Alright I'll meet with everyone, but there is no way I can go on this trip, I can't afford it first off." She argued with a reserve that deep inside said, she wished there was a way to finance such a venture.

"Alright, alright, I know, but come along anyway, you'll meet some nice people there." The attractive young woman spoke with her usual abruptness, and sometimes Libby wondered how she could befriend such a rough character, but she knew that inside she had a good heart.

Also Felicitas was never put off my rejection of any kind, and Libby admired her friend for having this virtue. Libby liked all of the people immediately, and wondered if this could be a good omen. The next day at work she expressed her desire to go with them.

"Borrow the money from the company." Felicitas said, assertively.

"They have emergency funds for employees, and well, this is a bit of a crisis, after all, you need a little R&R away from the crazy company." Felicitas said. The wheels began to work inside Libby's head; God knew she had acquired difficulties. With the bad winter they were having her fuel bills were escalating. But maybe she could ask for more. She needed only six hundred dollars, which included her airfare and hotel for one week. Dr. Fretzen, whom she had disdained in the worst possible way, now seemed to want to fulfill her wishes monetarily, which surprised Libby. Felicitas was elated when she told her.

Libby knew it would just be a matter of months before she left there. No one knew how earnestly she was trying to find another more fulfilling position. The more she thought about the week in Austria, the more Libby came to the decision, *why not take advantage of the travel plan laid in her path?*

"Drive down to Pittsburgh tomorrow for a passport, I'll cover for you girl." Felicitas' blue eyes lit up at the prospect of going skiing in Europe and having a good time together in the little town with the native Bavarians. Libby couldn't believe it was happening, her first trip to Europe, was it actually going to happen?

On the flight over, they found out that the ski resorts in central Europe were experiencing a weird reversed weather pattern, called a foehn, a warm dry wind blowing down the side of the mountains. It was a phenomenon they would have to deal with when they arrived.

"Don't worry we'll go shopping. I'm going to Munich by train." Shopping in the Alps? Libby could hardly comprehend this, since her conceptions were of great mounds of snow, with St. Bernard dogs with a jar of brandy tied around their necks, like Rowdy at the Swiss Farm Dairy where she grew up.

As they arrived at their hotel, it was indeed temperate, and in the tiny town of Badgastein, classy stores abounded for them to charge their goods as high as they wished on lovely hand stitched wool sweaters, purses or even dark green loden coats and jackets. Libby knew her charge card would suffer for all of this shopping, but it was a "one time only" and she knew the rate of exchange for the dollar was now high.

Almost every night the happy throng met for dinner or drinks together, laughing at the day's events. Many still went skiing on the limited amount of snow on the Alps, with a few having accidents of one kind or another. Libby met a handsome man from one of the government controlled steel companies, who described the Ring Strasse in the center of Vienna in detail. Hans helped her make up her mind about which city she would travel to when Felicitas and Helga went to Munich.

The Railroad station, die eisenbahn left for all destinations throughout the rest of Europe, stood at the top of the hill. Felicitas, Helga and Libby walked up the next day to buy their tickets in the middle of the week. Libby was excited at the thought of traveling in Europe, seeing places she had only read about in the past.

Traveling alone along steep craggy mountain cliffs, over rivers and beside beautiful lakes during the course of four hours, she wondered at the ancient countryside. What historical figures had traveled over these borders? What wars had been fought there? And how many different civilizations had roamed there, barely existing on the yield of the land. She thought of the panoramic span above Julie Andrews in "The Sound Of Music", and how the kind Austrians had influenced millions with their patriotic stand against the Nazis.

Hans Segelschiff had described Vienna well to Libby, and she left the Bahnhof in good spirits. Taking a swift notion to take a cab, since her time was limited, she asked the cab driver in her shaky German, to take her into the middle of town.

"Stattfinden, bitte, Ich reise." And most certainly he knew she was coming for a quick look at the city. Smiling, he answered her in the soft Bavarian blend of Deutsche.

"Americaner? Stephan Platz?" He said, driving ahead steadfast. *Okay, she thought. Since she hadn't seen any part of city this would do for now and probably forever.* As she stepped out of the cab and viewed the formality of the city, she was glad she'd brought her good camel wool coat along. Libby had never seen so many attractive people in her life; it almost seemed a prerequisite for walking down the street. She marveled at St. Stephan's, a beautiful gothic church with 450 ft. spires rising high above the old distinguished city.

Walking into an attractive Viennese restaurant and ordering schnitzen, reminded her of her mother, who had made the breaded meat often for dinner. In fact Libby felt very much at home here in Vienna. She made light conversation with her waitress, hoping she sounded as sophisticated as she felt right now.

"Danke, das essen ist gut." She complimented and left a nice tip afterward, and then ran for a taxi to catch her train back, regretting not having enough time to visit any other city sites within the Ringstrasse, which Hans had described so eloquently. Finding the right train that evening proved to be a dilemma for Libby, since none were marked appropriately "Badgastein".

She was finally directed to take one of the last trains out of Vienna headed for that part of Austria, but two hours into the trip she began to get nervous and contacted one of the conductors.

"Entschuldigen, Ich gehe Badgastein, bitte" And somehow the kind man brought the message to the chief conductor, who stopped the train at her destination. Libby was flooded with relief when she found out the train was headed for Bulgaria, which she did not choose to see that night. The rest of the touring party laughed when she told them the next day at breakfast.

Arriving back in the United States on a cold snowy day, Bea and her friend Bridget picked her up at the airport. The marvelous adventure was over, but her comprehension that the world was much much bigger than Pittsburgh, Pennsylvania, remained in her heart forever. Two days later she began to send resumes out to far distant places, like Austria, just to see what kind of feedback she would get. Not getting any worthwhile response, just a thank you for inquiring, seemed to be customary all over the world. The same results occurred with all the

270

interviews she had gone to in her hometown as well. Libby did not qualify for some senior positions, because of all the unemployment; there were at least fifty people there before her, and with much better qualifications.

One spring Sunday morning when she was reading the Press after church, she noted in the want ads that representatives were coming from Boston to interview people to hire away from the business depressed Pittsburgh area. Boston needed professional people with computer experience and consultations would be conducted at the downtown Pittsburgh Hilton.

"I think I'll go down and see what they're all about." Libby told her sister Kat, who seemed to be still happily employed at the seminary. But then Kat had sounded sad on the phone.

"Oh, no, don't tell me you're going to move away?"

"No, not yet. But remember that last interview on the north side that ended with my not having enough anatomy experience?" Libby said. The company manufactured perfect anatomical dummies for demonstrating CPR to students and needed an all around sales-office manager type. With so many people out of work, it was an employers personnel market out there. She was frustrated with the situation, and there were no choices.

"There probably isn't anything there for me, but I've not progressed in my job search. And I've got to leave this company that does not appreciate the efforts I've put forth. You know Kat, I've got to advance to another level and get more money in the interim." Kat understood. She was in a dead end job herself.

Libby's interview at the hotel ended on a positive note, with the principle agency practically begging her to come to Boston, promising many interviews with prospective employers. Good companies. In fact they had so many businesses calling them, that the two men doing the employment search, named Dave and Ryan, claimed they could fill one whole day up from morning until night with scheduled appointments at her convenience. Airfare and expenses would be no problem.

"Boston is in the midst of a climbing business trend, we've almost recovered from the textile industry slump. Biotechnology was born at MIT, and there is massive industrial growth. Professionals like you are needed to run all the new businesses, which have been spawned from this new technology." At forty years old, Libby had met many shysters. She looked these men straight in the eye to see if they were lying to her, and instincts said that there must be something to what they were saying. It seemed logical, mainly because of all the scientific schools located there, and she knew that technological evolution existed, having read about this taking place in Boston, Massachusetts.

It was 1985, a new era was beginning to bloom in laboratory systems, through computers, and knowledge in this area led to good positions for those who had been introduced to the high tech industry during their careers. Another rationale was that Ryan had just relocated to Boston from Oakmont, a city in nice residential area along the Allegheny River. Libby knew Oakmont to be a town with people of integrity; old families lived there. He began with his selling points of New England.

"You'll love the city, the ocean, the Cape, you never have enough time to do it all." He said excitedly. She saw it as far-fetched from her personal point of view. She was not ready to leave Pittsburgh, where friends and family, what was left of them, lived and supported her, and yet, thinking of this, she was not truly sure that her family knew how her ambitious goals were not being fulfilled. There was a fire inside Libby that was burning to get out soon.

Worldwide events showed Mikhail Gorbachev becoming the last Soviet premier, presiding over the breakup of the Soviet Union, with President Ronald Reagan becoming an assertive president who proved to be able to handle international affairs with adversaries like Russia during the Cold War. The Doobey Brothers had won four Grammy awards at the National Academy of Recording Arts and Sciences ceremony in Los Angeles.

"Good evening ladies and gentlemen, we want to welcome you to Boston's Logan Airport. Have a nice stay and thank you for traveling with us this evening." The stewardess stood above the brilliantly lighted runway announcing the entrance into the city, as Libby gazed out through lights sparkling off the ocean.

"Have you ever flown into Logan? The runway appears to be in the middle of the harbor." Kat had told her on the phone the day before she left. Now she opened her eyes wide, searching for sights of the largest city in New England and the birthplace of Liberty. At the end of May, a spring rain splashed against the tiny window next to her seat, as tall buildings emerged far out of Boston Harbor.

Libby's history book knowledge of this area began at a young age when one of her teachers at Gray School had impressed upon the fifth grade, that all of America's clothing and shoes were made here. She remembered Miss Martin's comment most everytime she put her shoes on. *Now where did that famous Boston Tea Party take place?* She thought. There really is a kind of mystique about this area that visitors cherish.

She'd told herself over and over that this would be in many ways an exploratory trip, finding out just what was here as far as employment opportunities. What if she did suddenly become a tourist in the middle of it all, and happened to see some part of this historic landmark as well?

The DC-9 came to a stop with the clamor of unclicking seatbelts filling the air, as passengers scrambled out to reach for their belongings in the overhead bins. She had only one overnight bag containing a silk crepe matching skirt and top, a dark printed outfit that would be appropriate for two scheduled interviews tomorrow. She hoped it wasn't too crushed in the small piece of luggage, rolled up neatly in a Turkish towel to keep all of the pleats in the skirt in place. She had bought it to wear at her mother and Tim's funeral, which seemed just like yesterday.

"Will you try to reach my bag in the top compartment above youah head?" A voice behind her inquired, as she moved into the aisle along with the rest of the passengers.

"Sure I will." Libby replied, yanking the heavy black cloth duffel bag forward and down with a thud onto an empty seat. It really was beyond her strength, but the young man had asked so politely, she wanted to respond with an honest effort. Besides, the accomplishment of having come this far on her journey, made her feel exhilarated.

"Is this your home?" She asked.

"Yeah, I live in Somaville, that's about a half houah out of the city. It's one of the last stops on the Red Line." Having no idea what a Red Line was, Libby queried him again, wanting to get a feel for the type of people who lived in this city.

"Do you know where Wakefield is? I'm supposed to be staying there tonight for an interview in Boston in the morning."

"Youah staying in Wakefield? That's way up nawth." He said dropping r's like they infected the English language with an unknown virus.

"Why don't you stay in the city?"

"Hmm, that's a good question," she replied a little upset. "I guess my travel agent needs a map."

"Well good luck." The first person she'd met in Boston ended their conversation.

"Yeah, thanks. You too."

The procession of travelers ended at the airport terminal, where loved ones, business associates and limo drivers claimed their human cargo. Following all the correct signs to rental cars, buses, taxi's, and baggage pickup, she looked quizzically for someone to instruct her on just how to get to Wakefield.

"Just wait out theah. A shuttle'll come along soon fah the Village Inn at Wakefield." The man at the car rental desk barked out. He did not smile or make an attempt at any eye contact; a common courtesy Libby had been familiar with all her life in Pennsylvania. But again, reminding herself that she needed to be helped, not to make a friend, Libby felt the loneliest feeling she'd ever experienced, telling her that she was far away from home.

Standing out in the darkening late afternoon, a slight chill overcame Libby. Coming from a close knit community in western Pennsylvania, a large family and friends who had sheltered her from any outside danger, she wondered if all of a sudden she was exposing herself to some unforeseen negative element.

"I don't know why that travel agent booked this room out here. I can't believe I'm staying so far away, at least ten miles north of Boston" She said, feeling frustrated with her hometown business people, who were actually the company's travel agents. Her sister, Kat listened to her complaint at the other side of the phone.

"And the worst thing about it is that my credit card would not go through. The manager said he would call the bank. Oh well, I'll just chalk it up to another experience. I'll let you know how this all turns out. It's scary. "

"I hope it doesn't turn out." Kat said. She was really hoping against Libby getting a job where she'd have to relocate out of Pittsburgh.

Later, lying in the strange motel room and unable to sleep, Libby questioned her mission on coming to interview in another state, and there was an argument going on inside her. One was the ultimate fear of unseen, unexplored places, which could be holding some danger. It was an elaborate way to self-destruct, but she had worked like a West Virginia coal miner for five years, unrecognized, hammering away at two jobs.

Waking up and showering bright and early the next morning, Libby dressed, assumed a professional stance, and set out for her two interviews. The first one was right in the heart of Boston at 9:00 a.m., another reason for arising early with new resolve to go into the city early to look around before the interview.

"The Manager cleared your credit card with the bank." The check out clerk responded.

"Oh thank you very much." She said, assuming that there would never have been a problem. The truth was that she was getting behind on her bills, and this particular charge card had been one of them.

"Wheah do you want to be driven to Miss?" The limo driver spoke matter of factly, his eyes straight ahead.

"Take me to Quincy Market." Libby declared, not knowing why, but thinking it might be a good place to see at 6:45 in the morning, deciding to start her sightseeing adventure as early as she could, since who knows where she might be the rest of the day. Obtaining a good map at the hotel lobby, she was able to pinpoint her walk down through Downtown Crossing, Washington Street, and onto Kneeland Street, where the first interview was scheduled. It seemed like it would be easy enough, just walking pleasantly through looking at everything on her way.

"Heah you ah deah." Announced the driver, as he pulled up alongside what appeared to be the commercial district with two old huge square brick buildings standing side by side.

The pavement was wet from the washing of all of the incoming produce in Quincy Market, as workers unpacked large ice-filled cases of haddock, flounder, oysters, lobsters and other varieties of seafood. Other outside stalls boasted large quantities of fresh green produce. Men in long white aprons stacked large dripping heads of lettuce in even rows, alternating these with cauliflower, broccoli, and other budding vegetables, projecting a beautiful array of fresh lusciousness.

Big rosy apples from Maine and Washington State lined the fruit stands, with an abundance of strawberries arranged in baskets. She had never seen such a delectable assortment, and thought that perhaps they had been grown on all the farms in other regions of Massachusetts and New England. Strolling through as a solitary figure this early morning, Libby heard a pleasant voice.

"Good mawning." The high-aproned green grocer shouted, so as not to miss his first customer of the day. His red cheeks glistened as if two bright shiny apples had suddenly flown against his face. Smiling back at him, she walked on past peddlers carts, which surrounded the stalls of fresh foods. They were covered with handmade merchandise. Leather goods featuring handbags, belts, gloves and jewelry decorated one cart – while another exhibited scarves of every design and color. Since these were not officially on display at this early hour, she sauntered by noticing Faneuil Hall just adjacent.

Straddling the uneven quaint red brick yard with her high heel, she stepped closer to read the small billboard outside Faneuil Hall which announced the time of the next reenactment of a debate to take place that day. At one o'clock that afternoon, the colonists would argue their protests against British Rule. The merchant Peter Faneuil erected the building in the 1740's for just this kind of banter to take place.

The red streak of the Freedom Trail stretched out before her, as she read on the side of the building the route it would take: The Granary Burying Ground – with graves of John Hancock, Samuel Adams and Paul Revere, The Old South

Meeting House, Old State House, Paul Revere's House and Old North Church. Well, not today she thought, looking for the Park Street sign at the end of the next corner.

The employment agency office where Dave and Ryan worked welcomed her as a celebrity within their midst.

"How are you doing so far?" Dave asked. "The people you'll meet today are consummate professionals and will not waste your time unless they have a positive position and salary. So don't worry, Libby. You look nice." Libby liked Dave, who represented Boston in a warm friendly sort of way. Ryan also showed up to say hello, as Dave walked Libby to the window to point out the direction where she would walk to Biotech Ventures.

Libby thought the best part of all of this was the fact that she did not have her usual job interview jitters. Libby would not allow herself to dwell on the real seriousness of accepting a position and everything that had to take place with selling the house and moving, plus leaving Kat and the girls in Pennsylvania.

This chilly spring day, which seemed to be warning up a bit, she strolled jauntily through what was called Downtown Crossing past the world famous Filene's Department store and basement, trying to picture herself working and living there. Stepping into a small chapel on a side street, and making the customary three wishes, she knelt down to pray in the dimly lit church. *Oh Dear Lord, is this town where my future lies*?" If he wanted her to live in this beautiful city, she would make an effort to move here. Libby sat back in the pew trying to hear and find a sign of what was expected of her by the supreme powers that guided her life.

She was in a state of euphoria, as if she had a bright future. Libby followed the directions to Kneeland Street that Dave had given on the telephone at her job in Pittsburgh, to the first interview. The plan was to call him afterward with the results, and then he would give her instructions for the next appointment out in a town called Waltham. This position seemed more adaptable to her present skills. Kurzweil Computer was making high tech products for the hearing impaired.

This industry interested Libby, though she really wanted to work in the city of Boston. If she did in fact come here, she started to think that quite possibly her continuing love affair with the city would have to replace all of the loneliness brought on by living alone for the first time in her life. A fraction of this was shattered when she took a left turn out of Downtown Crossing, during what appeared to be the end of Washington Street, and noticed a block of down trodden businesses, topless bars, strip joints with billboards of scantily clad women outside and pawn shops with bars on the windows. Libby would later find out that this stretch of the city was called "The Combat Zone". Realizing that every city had its undesirable side, she walked through as if late for a meeting.

Finally what appeared to be a unique art deco, nineteen twenty or thirties building, greeted her around the next corner. Ornate brass relief leaf and stem ornaments shone across the outside doors, and Libby thought it might have been a theatre or public building in some era. She pushed the revolving door into a stark well-worn and neglected lobby.

Libby was greeted with a flurry of activity, as she took the elevator up to the tenth floor area. There were people walking everywhere, it was as if they had just unloaded the moving van at the back of the building. One person still in motion looked her way.

"Hi, are you here for an interview?" She got the feeling that they were hiring many employees, and didn't know which position she was intended for exactly. Finally a young man came from the back of the unorganized office. He was the only one with a formal suit on, but even that was dressed down, with a plaid shirt and a nondescript tie that was out of place. He seemed very academic, probably had a PhD from either Harvard or MIT, she thought, finding out later that it was Harvard.

"Hello Mrs. Honford, or is it Libby?" He looked into her eyes and shook her hand.

"Libby, thank you." She immediately liked his demeanor.

"I'm Jim Sherman. Andre Duveaux is out of town today. He is the President and the man you'll be working for at Biotech Ventures, Inc. we've just moved in here, but then, I'm sure you can tell." Laughing at the end of every other sentence, she wasn't sure if he really had a great sense of humor or was just nervous during the interview. After all he was in the process of choosing an assistant for his boss.

She smiled and spoke of all the experience that she had acquired in an office, including a current computer background and what it was like working for an international company, where many of the employees did not speak English.

"We had to orient some of the engineers to the culture here. It's been quite an experience." Jim seemed to like this "multinational flair", and she wondered how many international employees worked there. He didn't seem to completely know what the position entailed or was reluctant to say it was a "secretarial position."

It was a short interview, ending with Jim saying they'd get in touch with the agency for another interview when Andre got back, after which Libby went to the white tiled restroom. The tiles were broken out in some places, giving an unclean appearance, which gave her an ambivalent feeling about working there, since the office she now worked in had bright shiny new lavatories. This reminded her of some of the vintage office buildings in Pittsburgh. Very old and unkempt, and there was always the veritable bucket with a mop in the corner waiting to be put into use.

Oh well, I'm finished here, its very unlikely that I'll be back again. She said to herself. But the challenge of getting this position still lay there curiously unrevealed. Libby knew she came across confident, almost cavalier, like she could do most anything in an office, which she probably could. But was this what this company wanted in this post? They've probably got plenty of people to choose from right here in Boston. Many technology grads, who wanted to get into the front door.

Jim, whom she found out was the CFO of the new company, had spoken about the promising future of the company, and that there would be stock options with the job. Getting in the front door of a brand new company sounded exciting.

"Hmm, I wonder what this Andre is like? She mused, thinking he definitely was French.

"Take a cab to Waltham, and give the driver this address." Dave said later, handing her a couple of twenties. After they had met first thing that morning, they planned to meet again after her first interview at the local bank downstairs of his office where he took the cash right out of his own ATM account. This was the first transaction that Libby thought was a little unprofessional. Dave hadn't gotten the results of first the interview yet.

The cab stopped in front of a beautiful red brick office building, far out in the suburbs for the second interview. This discouraged her since she liked being able to walk everywhere in Boston. Besides working there would be a veritable lifetime of historical touring.

Mr. Samuelson believed heartily in their software program at Kurzweil Systems, to help the hearing impaired, and showed her around the workshops extensively. They seemed to be truly dedicated people, and their work had become life itself. Libby tried to like the position, but could not fake the right words. The trip back and forth cost forty dollars, which told her a little bit about the high cost of living in New England. This would be the downside, and then she knew that living way out there would be against her better judgment.

Landing at the Airport in Pittsburgh, brought reality back into Libby's life. Her old comfortable life style, with the same old problems lurking out from everywhere, as opposed to a brand new city and fresh challenges abounding. Libby would pray hard that night to make the right decision. Going back into her old job the next day felt kindly familiar and comfortable, even though the same old humiliating problems faced her. What kind of an impression had she made at the Boston interviews? Was she meant to relocate, was that where her future lay?

17. Equilibrium

A week later early in the morning, after she had walked to the desk with her cup of coffee, the call came, forcing her to make a decision that would affect the rest of her life. Relocating into another city, lock, stock and barrel, sent a wave of anxiety deep into the pit of her stomache.

"Libby, Andre Duveaux, The President of Biotech Ventures was very impressed with you, and wants to make you an offer." Dave said, probably excited at the chunk of money they would make from this prosperous business enterprise.

Well what did Libby expect, after she'd made the second trip to meet Andre on People's Express, all in one day, which was jet-setting in her world. In a way she couldn't understand it, in view of the fact that her approach had been so cavalier. She'd walked about his messy office with an overconfident flair, advising Andre outright what she would do to organize his huge office. Then she heard herself responding.

"What is the offer?" Libby said. Then overwhelmed with the spontaneity of the moment, she heard herself say, "*I'll take it.*" Had she completely lost her "commies", her Dad's word for common sense, altogether? Then her brain fast-forwarded thinking that one of the high powered Boston executives needed her talents, her confidence soared into colorful fireworks bursting and zooming up through the white stained ceiling tiles of the office.

Felicitas was surprised and happy for her co-worker, announcing her next vacation plans right there and then.

"Oh, guess who's coming for a nice vacation, I've always wanted to see Boston and Cape Cod." She danced around with the good news. Puppendorf had gone on to another engineering assignment, and Dr. Fretzen naively wondered what had motivated his employee to make such a radical move as to take a position in far away Boston, and a woman at that.

The vanpool men seemed jealous of her forthcoming move, all except Jack, who wanted to make a professional change himself. Libby had hoped to stay in touch with the nice engineer, who had actually given her some votes of confidence from time to time, when she had needed it most during the two hour long daily commute.

Libby was proud of her two independent daughters, who had made many of their own decisions along the way. Bea had announced last month her plans to attend Cleveland University on a tutoring grant for a masters in English, while Sonja completed her junior year at Edinborough State University. She would finish the year with a flourish as an art major by now taking part in a huge exhibit in the town of Edinborough. Rich and his new partner, who were now living together, had made a special effort to see her talent displayed there at a gallery.

Leaving the only permanent home Beatrice and Sonja knew, made Libby apprehensive, and she hoped and prayed fervently that they could adjust to the new changes ahead. Years of memories and friends they'd made would remain in the suburbs of Penn's Hills, Pennsylvania where they had grown up and gone to school maturing into young adulthood. In fact it was ruthless and heartless of Libby to accelerate her own professional life.

Essentially she was asking both daughters to return the devotion she'd given to them for more than twenty years. Was it fair? But if not now, when would the timing be appropriate? Libby had graduated from college at a later age and was now forty years of age, almost past her prime. Was this risk worth taking?

When Libby picked Sonja up at school that Memorial Day weekend for her summer vacation, she announced the oncoming plan to move to Boston. Sonja seemed excited and ready for a change, showing exuberant enthusiasm.

"Oh, I love Boston, there are probably lots of jobs there, I can work all summer and save money for my last year of school." She said.

Libby felt temporarily relieved, that her daughter was excited and eager to leave for the east coast. The plan was to stay Friday night in the Brookline area, then find the designated realtor in a city south of Boston, called Milton, as in the literal sense, the English writer of the epics," Paradise Lost" and Paradise Regained".

They would seek out this town because the realtor selling their home in Penn's Hills initiated transference relative to another agency in the state where Libby and Sonja would settle, an enterprising Real Estate contract made between state agencies. Libby and Rich parted amicably with a divorce pending five years after their initial separation. With their home now on the market, Rich kindly helped Libby and Sonja pack their car with a few essentials to take with them until the actual sale of the house.

Libby vowed that it would be her last entanglement with the complicated Machiavellian ways of men and marriage in general and had pledged to work among the bright and knowledgeable scientific community until she retired in twenty years. Her religious faith had remained intact, except for the twinge of guilt, which gnawed at her now and then. The church would say that she would be in sin as a divorced woman. And only God knew how horribly Libby had suffered through twenty years of marriage, she thought, convincing herself that she and Rich had actually done each a big favor by parting and not hurting one another anymore.

Driving into the city of Brookline and checking into a hotel, proved relatively easy, but big city fears would set in late that night, as Libby tucked her large wad of money deep under clothes in the huge suitcase. Later, lying in bed, she clutched her mother's blue crystal beads entreating divine intervention. Whew, this is going to be one giant hurdle to get over, especially with Sonja asking a series of "what if's" like, "What if this doesn't work out mom?" and What if we have to go back home after all?"

"Well, the house is still there with all the furniture in it, it hasn't been sold yet." Coming up with answers, she tried to convince her daughter, who was after all, yearning to have some permanence in her life. It wasn't her fault that she had an over ambitiously motivated mother.

Setting out to find Milton proved to be an introduction to the southern shore of Boston, as they circled and recircled routes 95 and 128, looking for DeWalt Realty. One man's direction was to take Route 128 to Randolph/Milton exit; another's was to take 95, and they were not sure where one ended and the other began. The two Honford ladies were in a quandary about keeping their ten o'clock appointment with Miss Susan Darlton. Eventually they followed directions to Adams Street leaving East Milton. This route took them past enormous "old money" mansions and lovely landscapes, and then all of a sudden Sonja hollered out in relief.

"Oh my gosh, mom, there it is, finally, the Realty we're looking for."

"Thank you God for looking down on us." Libby said in a whisper.

The DeWalt Real Estate turned out to be a beautifully reconditioned Victorian mansion, where Miss Darlton, and many others honed their craft of finding attractive homes to suit their client's discriminating taste.

Stepping sprightly out of a side office, Susan Darlton turned out to be an extraordinarily astute agent, dressed smartly in a red sport coat and trimmed skirt ensemble and looking as if she had the perfect life style altogether. Hearing their story, she was immediately sympathetic to their predicament, setting to work finding an appropriate apartment or house to rent. Susan queried Libby regarding her living preferences.

"One bedroom or two, furnished or non, and what prices are we looking at here?"

Libby hadn't thought about what kind of living accommodations she would need, since the new job offer had taken precedence. And since she'd always owned a house, first, last and security had never been something to consider. Consequently, her brief education on rented dwellings on the south shore would happen all in one morning. Every now and then Sonja would stare at her mother, bringing back that insecure queasy feeling again.

"Mom, we need a place for the cats, remember?" She said. Susan, hearing this statement, spoke up responsively.

"Oh, that might be a problem here, they may not want animals, but then you could pay a security deposit."

"Sure." Libby answered resentfully. *Hmm, of course that damn Rich wouldn't take them, they would be too untidy for him to handle in his perfect house.*

In less than fifteen minutes, Susan had come up with three rentals: a huge house for nine hundred a month, a cape style home completely furnished for eight hundred and an entire first floor of a house for five seventy-five. Since the lowest price appealed to Libby, Susan called the young couple that wanted to rent, to meet their prospective client. Nonetheless, they could not come until the next day to meet Libby and Sonja. The Pantone couple owned what was called a two-family home, where Libby would live downstairs.

"Can you come back tomorrow morning to talk with them and bring your earnest money along?" Susan spoke matter of factly to her two new clients, who probably looked like they needed to be pointed in the right direction. Sonja looked sharply at her mother, saying in a whisper.

"Oh no, mom, we have to find this place **again**." Both women laughed, and Libby tried to reassure her daughter.

"Don't worry, honey, we'll look for signs along the way, we'll write it down, and we'll leave an hour ahead of time. Now let's go get a nice lunch somewhere." She said, trying to keep the enthusiasm in her voice. They left the Lower Mills, where at one time they found out later; the wonderful aroma of Baker's Chocolate factory once permeated the area with a mouthwatering aroma, tantalizing the taste buds of all the area residents living there.

The next day found Libby and Sonja confronting their new young landlords, Deena and Patrick Pantone, who had no idea they were "Angels in disguise", to Libby's way of thinking.

Deena, a svelte strawberry blond, came forth from her sitting position smiling widely upon their introduction, instantly settling some of the jangled nerves inside Libby's stomache. While dark haired Patrick sat back a little more reserved, Libby began to think that it was Deena's decision to say yeah or nay to the hopeful renters.

"Hi, its nice to know you. Wow, you're relocating?" She said in a friendly manner, seeming like she would want to do the same. *Good, Libby thought. We can use friends like these now. And are these two really old enough to own a big home like this?*

"Yes, we're interested in renting your apartment. Tell us about it. And we have cats, sorry." This will either make or break our prospects she thought.

"Oh we have a cat too. I love cats." Deena said. *Oh, and I love this young woman*, Libby screamed inside. Then off they all went to see their new possible dwelling. The white and blue painted building featured an extra large front door with a tiny vestibule inside leading to another door to living quarters. Nice hardwood floors everywhere, won Libby over, and four huge rooms, would provide more space than she could ever realize for her first apartment. They would move in the next day, which only meant walking in with their suitcases, a table, lamp, and a television set. But that evening Susan brought by a small table on which to eat and a couple of chairs. They had blankets for sleeping and Deena brought an old mattress in from the garage, to use as they saw fit for the next week or until their furniture came.

Libby and Andre got along famously from the first, coordinating Biotech Ventures. The day-to-day business of scheduling his appointments with other biotech and drug companies went smoothly for her, especially since she had no harassment as with her past employer. Her new boss seemed to put himself in her hands as far as getting to the right places at the right times, and since he too was new to the city, as were many of the scientists, they all helped each other find their way around Boston. The laboratories were staffed with transfers from many other countries and states whose studies had prompted them to come to that city.

Deena and Pat proved to be more than landlords, in their quest to help the nomads find their way around Milton, giving directions for the local food shopping centers, pharmacies, doctors, dentists and the south shore mall. Libby recognized the rarity of these two individuals instantly, as her beacon in the new environment she had sought for a better position in life in general.

Riding the T proved to be an interesting experience, and Libby thought she was most fortunate to have this public transportation close at hand, though she did have to drive a couple of miles to the commuter parking lot. Most participants, who had been riding the T for years, had an established "this is what I expect" look, unlike Libby who did not take the commuting convenience for granted. Pittsburgh never had a train such as this one. And except when there was trouble on the tracks, she could time herself to the minute getting into the office each day.

The little town of Milton, Massachusetts, estimated population around three thousand, presented itself as a lovely New England town. White church steeples peeked over lush green parks and massive well cared for estates. Milton Academy stood behind many successful military and business leaders, while Aquinas and Curry College also turned out fine students. Turner's Pond, in the center of town gave respite from busy Brook and Adams Road running perpendicular. The little Mug and Muffin restaurant was a favorite breakfast place, and one had only to get on to the nearby Interstate 95 to shop at the famous Southshore Mall.

Attending church on Sunday at St. Agatha's reminded Libby of her own Aunt Aggie, who was now good pals with Kat, still living in the Albred family home. But weekly calls to Kat told Libby that things were not well with her sister's relationship with the rest of the Albreds. The sympathy that had been forthcoming after the accident had turned sour, and family members wanted the house sold without any more delay. Prompted by her wicked sister-in-law Marjorie, who had the most to gain and the least to loose in the matter, with Terry and Ben both following suit to remove Kat from the house, and eager to collect their share of the estate settlement.

"Libby, I got two more letters from attorney's today in the mail, even more threatening than the last ones. Terry has an attorney now in Ohio, besides the one from New York. They want me to get out of the house now. What am I going to do? They're making my life miserable." Kat cried sorrowfully on the phone, as she had so many times before, complaining about the pressure her sister and brother had brought against her.

Libby was angry with her miserable sister-in-law who had nothing to do but harass family members into torturing poor Kat, who had no one but Libby, and Joel for defense. Libby thought that his "neutral status" had inadvertently pulled him and Glenny into the fray.

"Damn them all, they're all wimps, not knowing how to speak up to Marjorie. What a devil incarnate she is. Daddy was right about her from the beginning, causing this rift in the family." Libby was torn up inside about how desperate and helpless her family members had become. Not one older sibling had ever tried to help Kat try to find a rented place of her own. *Maybe Kat should come up here and live with me?* She thought.

In a few weeks what was left of the furniture in the house in Penn's Hills arrived at her new address on Warren Avenue in Massachusetts. There were beds to sleep in, and a couch to lounge on. Luxury was once again theirs to behold. Libby and Sonja even went out one Sunday to purchase a lovely coffee table to enhance the nice living room. Civility was restored to their new living conditions.

Bea and Kat drove up to New England the next weekend in a rental car with pet companions, Mia, Kippy, Charlotte and Geoffrey, who scampered around the apartment seeking their favorite window to peer out onto the busy street. The two pairs of sisters toured Boston, hiking the Freedom Trail, the Boston commons and The Public Gardens, and lunching at a distinguished Back Bay restaurant. Kat then flew back home leaving Bea to stay on in Milton, until her classes began again.

As the end of the summer approached, Libby and Bea drove Sonja to the airport to return to Edinborough State University to resume her studies; her father would drive her onward from Pittsburgh. Bea would not leave until later in September for Cleveland State University. And while Libby worked, Beatrice bought a bright new shiney bicycle to tour the picturesque town, taking pictures along her trail.

"Mom this is such a great place to live, I hate to go back to school next week." She said. Once more Libby was reassured that she **had** done the right thing, and was beginning to feel at home there.

Autumn brought beautiful sun-lit days with picturesque colorful scenes even more vivid than the summer before, as Libby found herself enjoying walks to the quaint library nearby on Saturdays to research the historical town. But in just a matter of time, her peaceful revelry and escape from reality were interrupted by a frantic call from Kat.

"Libby we have a buyer for the house. They're all going to get their damn money." Her sister said. Libby was surprised at the speed with which the house sold, but then Kat went on with future plans that included both of them.

"Do you think you can find a place that we can share with three dogs and our combined cat community of eight? I know it's a tall order, but maybe there is a house for us." Somehow Libby knew her sister would follow her up to New England. It seemed as if Kat was always just a few steps behind. Hanging up the phone, Libby sat down and put her head between her knees.

"God help me." She said. *Where in heaven's name would she find such a place?* Meditating deeply for help on this new dilemma, Libby realized this favor from God and the Blessed Mother would take powerful Divine intervention. Perhaps even a pilgrimage to Lourdes.

Then she gave thanks that the new job was working out so well. In fact her challenges there were few; only yesterday, she and two of the nicer new employees, MBA's emanating from prominent MIT, Walter and John, had walked into town to purchase software for the computer in their particular office environment. Libby enjoyed being one of the pioneer's in the new company, which was growing fast, as the scientists continued to do more extensive clinical trials with new pharmaceuticals.

The first home the Albred sisters would share was found in Scituate, beside a tiny pond and a stones throw away from the Atlantic Ocean. Libby thought of it as "Paradise Regained", as she stared out onto the unbridgeable horizon of the rolling seaside. Photographs could never capture the breathtaking essence of spindrift filtering through the weather beaten dark shingled house on a bright autumn afternoon, nor the dank wet nights that had them hunkering down into their warm beds.

This had not been an easy accomplishment for Libby, who had made call after call from the Patriot Ledger Newspaper rentals with no availabilities forthcoming for the two pet owners. Finally, after a few weeks, she reached a woman who gave her a glimmer of hope.

"We have some animals, too, that's alright, we just want to get the current tenants out in a hurry. There's something going on in that house and I don't like it at all." She said in a husky knowledgeable voice. Libby couldn't believe her ears.

"My sister and I will probably move in at the end of the month." Libby said hopefully.

"Okay, you can pick up the lease at my daughter in law's across the street." *Oh this was too good to be true. Thank you, God.* She planned to ride down Route 3 that evening after work to see the house she had just rented sight unseen.

Leaving the Pantone's proved to be heartrending, but Libby knew she would never forget this nice couple, who had been the port in the storm for their unsteady vessel that Memorial Day weekend. And now they announced they were getting ready to have a baby.

"I'm so happy for you both". Libby said excitedly, knowing she would miss them.

"Your new place sounds great, though, Libby. I think you'll be happy down there right on the ocean. My goodness, everyone wants to have a place like that." Deena said.

"However, I have no idea how to commute to Boston from there." Libby said.

"Well the Boston Harbor Commuter Boat leaves from Hingham Harbor there. Why don't you call them for the times." Pat said. Once again they had helped Libby find her way around.

"Oh thank you, that will probably be the answer. Good luck, and we'll be in touch." Libby would say goodbye to her solitary lifestyle in Milton forever, to move twenty miles farther south along the coast.

Now driving into the commuter parking lot, she could see two luxurious long sleek Commuter Boats docked at Hingham wharf. Libby rolled down the car window to get a closer look at the pure blue sky covering the Atlantic Ocean framing this breath taking golden October morning. She and Kat had decided that commuting to work by boat would be both time-efficient and interesting. And it was the closest mode of transportation to work from Scituate, half an hour's drive down shore.

Parking her car in the spacious boat marina beside many enormous yacht's and summer cruisers of every variety and style just recently put into dry-dock, Libby walked cautiously down the gangplank to go aboard. The comfortable cabin interior confirmed her decision; this would be a relaxed mode for everyday travel.

Conspicuously holding onto the handrails toward a seat, an apprehension revealed under-developed sealegs. The newest passenger sat down quickly, preparing for the vessel to rock while they embarked for the trip across Boston Harbor to Long Wharf. The soft plush seat appeared to be a restaurant booth arrangement complete with table in the middle. Maybe they actually served breakfast she thought, breathing a sigh of relief for having made it to this point in her journey.

Observing the other commuters boarding, Libby was gradually reassured by their confident air and sure footing. They had a uniformed demeanor of "proper Bostonians", wearing Burberry raincoats and armed with large briefcases and Wallstreet Journals. Most bought coffee at the galley bar, and balanced their morning mainstay while walking toward their regular seat.

Libby sat inconspicuously among the others and opened her textbook on Public Relation Practices, a course she had just begun at Boston College, to further her career at Bio-Ventures, when a tall rugged-looking man hastily arrived. He threw down a large piece of worn wardrobe luggage that revealed many frequent flyer miles, almost on her feet.

He certainly must think he's important. Libby thought. But then most of the men out here at Hingham probably are a spoiled breed of people, having celestial wives, perfect children, two well-trained dogs and of course the mandatory station wagon waiting for them every night for transport to their perfect little cottages by the sea. An air of trepidation, cultivated over the last five years, still manifested itself in her disposition, and separated her from these ostensibly untroubled passengers.

"How about keeping an eye on this for me, I'm going to get some coffee." Ordered the man with the deteriorating luggage, while making his way to the beverage bar. Libby looked the other way, incredulous at his abrupt assignment to her, a stranger, who was just getting her orientation to this new system of travel. *What arrogance.* She thought. *Oh well it goes with the territory.*

"Looks like they're digging for that new sewer pipe out there in front of your house, Hank. When do you think that thing's going to be finished?" Said an apparent friend of Hank's, who now juggled a cup of steamy coffee, sitting back down beside her in the booth, a little too close for her comfort.

"Oh I don't know, Pete, you know how slow the Town is with construction projects." Listening with continued indifference to the two neighbors small talk, she gazed out the window at the trees showing their brilliant colors on the other side of the channel, as the boat took off at great speed. The sun glistened on the water, reflecting the decorated Harbor Islands with bright spectrums of red, purple, yellow, and orange leaves of every variety. This resplendence is for everyone she thought, with heartfelt gladness, not exclusive to Hingham Harbor.

Libby's mind traveled back in time and space to fall scenes from her old dining room window in Pennsylvania. Mostly maple trees grew there. The kids used to have such fun jumping into raked piles of leaves, screaming uproariously. It really wasn't until Bea and Sonja were teenagers that the love in her marriage had been squeezed out like a well-used lemon waiting for disposal.

All at once a high-flown motorboat raced directly in front of their craft, which rocked turbulently in its wake. Instantly she grabbed her books and handbag, hugging them and the side rail vehemently, as laughter at their predicament dispersed from all corners.

"Whew, look at that, I think its one of Tom Clark's new Flyte-Crafts." One of the men said, standing up to examine the speed and direction of the showy boat.

In the meantime, Libby searched the faces of the passengers, wondering why they weren't advised to wear life jackets when they boarded. But all were having a good time, that being the last thing on their minds this morning. After all, she was the odd woman out; they did this everyday of the week, and had probably gone through many ocean side experiences together while traveling.

Gliding neatly alongside Long Wharf, the crew jumped instantly onto the dock and quickly tied the mooring lines onto the hooks at the edge of the pier. Then passengers rose to disembark with Libby taking her cue as well. Stepping out onto the gangplank, Libby made an effort to fall into step with the crowd as they proceeded up the deck. At the end she was not sure of the direction where the quaint red brick sidewalk led, and cautiously made a left turn toward her company's part of town.

Beginning her long six-block trek southward down to her office, she turned to hear a voice coming up along her right side.

"Sorry for distracting you on the boat like that, I know you were trying to study." Hank shouted over at her, stretching his long legs, attempting to close the gap between them.

"That's okay, I'm used to people not being friendly in the city." Instantly sorry for her negativity, Libby looked up into his friendly face, and he seemed sincere, as if he wanted to make up for all the rest who had failed to give her a proper welcome. His soft, undemanding voice sounded pleasing as they made small talk while waiting to cross another street.

"Hank Simmons." He said shaking her hand. "Can I call you when I get back from business in Houston next week?" She finally smiled back. *Oh brother have I heard this one before.* Although the Houston excuse was different. Reaching into the front pocket of her purse, she handed him her new company name card. It looked as though he was trying to do the same, fumbling through his coat pockets with no success of having found his.

When they reached the street where his Engineering Company resided, they departed. Libby thought he might be a nice friend to talk to once in a while on the boat, and the guy did deserve credit for trying to assuage her aloofness and cheering her up as well, whether he knew it or not.

A week later, Libby watched the black steel gated doors close in the black and gold art deco elevator of this interesting building where Biotech Ventures was located. She had learned that a popular New England architect had designed it in the 1920's. The doors opened to the tenth floor, as she tried to recall the name of the man she had just met, it wouldn't come to mind.

"Good morning Libby. How are you this morning?" Andre said energetically, as she entered the office. Andre was a dapper Frenchman, as brilliant as he was handsome. He wore the best quality tailor made suits well on his slight frame and moved with a debonair flair of confidence. He and his wife Maria had invited Libby and Bea over for dinner on their terrace late this summer after Sonja had gone back to school. The Duveau's lived in a lovely French chateau style home in the fashionable section of Roxbury.

"I'm enjoying my new commuting experience, Andre, having coffee and reading the paper on the way to work is a nice way to start the day." Libby said, smiling at her boss, knowing he would appreciate hearing about it. He smiled wide, showing perfect gleaming teeth.

"I'm pleased that you have adjusted so well, that is better than tiresome driving or riding the T. Besides you'll work so much faster after your restful boat ride." He laughed. *Ha, typical boss after all.* Libby thought. *Little does he know that this job is child's play?* Since her usual ease at transactions with people had taken over, Libby was just doing what came naturally at work. Soon she would be planning an exquisite Christmas party at none other than the historic "Hampshire House" on Beacon Street. What fun, and Jim their CFO had told her the budget was carte blanche. She would be meeting with the Restaurant Party Planner tomorrow.

"Libby, the phone's for you." Her assistant Rita called from her desk across the office. She had been at the fax machine getting ready to send a press release to Reuter's. They had worked on the piece all morning so that it read properly to their client companies, who would get notification of the announcement of their new products released and approved by the FDA.

Libby came over and pushed the telephone console button down, raising the receiver to her ear.

"Hello, Libby speaking, can I help you?" She spoke softly into the phone.

"Hi, this is Hank Simmons, calling you like I said I would." Libby listened to his innocent straight-laced voice. There was a distant sound to it; different than any of the men she'd met in the past. Kind of an uncool, unpretentious tone that she didn't quite know how to interpret. She'd always prided herself on her skills on personality demeanor, usually being able to second guess what a person's motive might be from the beginning, but this guy had her baffled.

And secretly, Libby liked the feeling that Hank could not be fit into any stereotype she'd ever come in contact with.

"Would you like to go to lunch somewhere today? There's a good German or Chinese restaurant right across the street from where you work." He said. Hank seemed kind, and what the heck, a free lunch, especially now when she was trying to keep track of her money.

"Alright, I love sauerbrauten. Where shall we meet?" She said.

"I'll see you downstairs in your building. That's interesting, she mused. I gave him my name card, but had he done some other investigative work besides?

"How was your trip to Houston?" She said, coming up to him in the lobby later, wondering how a friendship with this new man would blend into her new life. Libby did have a history of being overly friendly and much too trustful with everyone. Now as she began to make new friends in a new location, she vowed to stay a little more removed from close personal involvement.

She would take time getting to know people, not overwhelming them with her gregarious personality. And maybe give them a chance to tell their story from beginning to end – really find out about their lives. God knows the world needed good listeners as well as intelligent conversationalists.

Consequently, Hank talked continuously, as she wrangled with her sauerkraut, enjoying every forkful. Following his every word, she noticed there was something about his appearance that spoke of neglect and despondency, when they took off their coats in the old style German restaurant. And looking around at the creaky old uneven wooden floors and mahogany bar that seemed from another era, probably the thirties, Libby established, nothing had changed here either except the personnel and customers, who seemed to keep getting younger as she grew older.

"We just couldn't talk to one another. And then our oldest son went off to college, it was lonely without him around." Hank went on with the story of his broken marriage, as if he was just looking for someone who would understand. Maybe someone who had been there before. *Well, his judgment is right.* She thought. *I have.* But Libby would not dole out any advice. She was proud of herself this time. She listened intently, glad that she was removed from personal feelings this time around. And she would stay detached from any personal feelings.

Libby managed not to say a word about her own experiences, just maintained eye contact throughout, knowing for certain there was a bee's nest here – which just might yank her in. Hank seemed like a nice man, and this time another trait came through. The guy was extremely vulnerable, and someone out there had taken clear advantage of those sensitivities. But wasn't that the cruel emotional upheaval that happened in most relationships? People had to use people to some extent, depending who was on the up or downside. And if the love was gone, there was nothing to keep them together.

"Would you like another cup of tea?" The long white-aproned waiter inquired.

"Okay." She said finishing the dish of apple strudel. This probably was one of the infrequent lunches, when she actually ate and let someone else do the talking.

"So, are you getting divorced or are you trying to get counseling at all?" She said. *There, that was objective enough.* The thing was that she'd heard these kinds of stories before, and usually the guy was leading up to telling her he didn't want a commitment, but can't we at least go to bed together? Somehow she knew this would never go in that direction, but who knows, he might have another technique here in Boston that she never heard of before.

"I wanted to go to counseling at first. But now I want out. I have an attorney. I am definitely getting a divorce and the sooner, the better." Hank spoke resolutely, and there was something in his tone of voice that made her believe him. The sadness he projected, made her want to reach out and hug him, or at least pat him on the back and say with a voice of experience, *Don't worry it will be alright, I've been there and it does get better. Ride the waves till the water gets smooth.* But she said nothing.

When they reached the revolving door in front of her building, she reached out to shake his hand, and he grabbed on clutching it securely.

"Thank you for lunch. We'll have to do it again sometime, next time it'll be on me." She said, smiling into his blue eyes, not expecting him to come into the lobby with her again. It was almost as if she had thrown him a lifeline of some kind without intention.

"I'll call you." He said, lingering longer than she thought he should, his eyes hanging onto hers. Libby walked to the elevator thinking about their encounter. *What the heck was that?* She asked herself. *Oh no, she would not let this happen to her.* Hank would be a nice friend who she could listen to at this crucial turning point of his life.

He seemed to be a very quiet introspective man, with a demeanor she had never encountered before. Every man she had known had been up front and outgoing in nature. Libby would probably have to bring all her sensitivities to the forefront to tune into where this guy was coming from. Now she questioned herself. Did she really want to go to those extremes for someone she had just met last week on the boat?

Her phone was ringing as she walked back to her desk.

"Oh, hi Ben, how are you?" She answered the voice of her brother calling from the school counseling office of Locust Valley High School. Their relationship was strained due to the antics of his alcoholic wife, who still denied her sickness. She had set out with her bitter jealousy to divide their family and had succeeded, especially now that they had obtained their share of their parent's estate, after the house on Churchill had sold last month.

Libby was upset that Ben had let Marjorie continue to badger them with her bad behavior. He had a master's degree in counseling and could not find help for his own wife. He had even checked in with ALANON and had learned to cope with Marjorie's malady.

"We're thinking of coming up to Boston to see you and Kat." He spoke as if all was hunky dory with the four of them.

"Ah, I'll speak to Kat about it." She lied. Knowing that neither she nor Kat wanted to risk loosing their peaceful world by coming face to face with Marjorie, but they both missed their older brother.

"I'll tell you what, we'll see you both for lunch in one of the downtown restaurants on the wharf, okay? I'll call you back next week." Ben said. Yes, they would love to see him, too bad Marjorie would probably come along. And in many ways, Ben had enabled Marjorie to treat Kat and Libby horrible, by not forcing her to seek professional counseling. But what was the real problem there?

Meeting at the ocean side restaurant, "Tides", Kat and Libby walked in to see Ben and Marjorie already seated and having drinks and sharing a cigarette at a corner table. Their brother wore a colorful sport shirt, showing off his good taste in clothes, but his complexion had a slight pallor, which Libby observed instantly. Marjorie sat close to him, repeatedly sipping her bloody Mary, anticipating the encounter with her sisters in law, who were outraged inside at the drinking and smoking they witnessed, which would be the demise of both of them.

Libby's heart ached for her brother, who once had the courage to blaze his own trail through life. A rugged individual, Ben had been bred with sound healthy values as an Albred, but instead chose to poison his body with cigarettes and alcohol. Subsequently his confident voice emanated affection, reassuring them that he did still care about their welfare.

"How is everything going with you two here?" He said. Brushing his gray moustache in a downward motion with his fingers. It seemed he wanted to convey something to his little sisters here and now, sending it forth through bloodlines that Libby seemed to grasp, with words he could not express.

"We're fine, it's a new challenge for us again." They answered together mechanically, not taking their eyes from his clouded hazel ones, which told them that he was proud of them, and that they should stick together like family always had in past years.

After eating lunch and peppering it with small talk, the two sister' arose to go back to work.

"I have to run, I don't want to be late." Libby said.

"Yeah, I just really started this job at the bank." Kat added.

"I'll hail a cab. Then we can talk on the way." Ben said. Then some of their old good-humored brother's mood emerged, the one they knew from the backyard on Churchill Road, who'd always have a plan to create something different, like a brick barbeque pit where they could roast hot dogs and marshmallows outside.

"I'll never be a fogey. You know, in fact, I still like to tango." Ben had always made them laugh with his outrageous dancing, and just the thought kept them smiling, until the taxi stopped at Libby's job. They kissed goodbye. Both sisters thought the meeting helped amend the relationship, and felt glad at heart.

Hank called the next day, saying he would save a seat for her on the boat that night.

"Sure, I'll see you then." But that evening she saw him standing, when he probably had a chance to get a single seat way before she came aboard.

"Sorry, the seats were all taken by the time I got here." He said in his boyish way. She thought Hank was a handsome and appealing man, and with the bluest most honest eyes she'd ever seen.

"Don't worry, I wasn't expecting a seat." She said. *Darn it,* she thought. *I have to tone my feelings down a little. He's really just trying to be nice.* But as she was walking to the parking lot later, she noticed him getting into a station wagon with a tall dark haired wife sitting in the driver's seat and the inevitable German shepherd in the back. *Well, there it is.* She said to herself. *Another husband out there cheating – and what a story he cooked up for me, boy was I vulnerable.*

From that time on, she avoided Hank's calls, thinking the worst. But a week later on Friday, he called again to say he was coming down on Saturday to fix the outdoor light the saltwater from the ocean kept spraying and burning out. Libby had mentioned this sometime in their conversations and he'd amazingly remembered.

"Alright." Libby said reluctantly. A handyman would be good. Somehow she felt like she had to clear the air about the woman in the car that night.

"Oh, was that your wife who picked you up at the boat the other night?" She was ready for the answer, thinking its okay; he's a kind Samaritan and a good friend.

"Oh, that was Theodore, one of my sons, he gave me a ride to my house while my car was being worked on.

When Saturday morning came, a little red headed boy with freckles, named Jay, ran into the house searching exuberantly for one of the cats to play with.

"Where are they?" he yelled. Kat and Libby laughed, because the smart cats had found secure hiding places from all of life threatening events like this one, by now. It was this day that Libby found out that Hank lived in nearby Hull where his children visited him often. Slowly, she began to trust this tall quiet gentleman, whom Libby was beginning to believe was indeed a unique individual.

Libby's telephone rang while she was at her desk working hard with an office team putting together a Biotech Venture prospectus for introduction to potential investors. It was a call from her brother Joel.

"Libby, Ben died this morning of a massive heart attack at school". She was not prepared for this announcement, and when she met Kat on the commuter boat, the two sisters' held each other. Her sister handed her an arm full of flowers

"Here, these are for you, because you're alive and here today and I love you." Kat said. Holding each other's hands on the way home, Libby vowed to call Marjorie that night.

"Okay, you can come to the church, but you won't stay here at the house." Her sister in law said. It seemed to Libby that Marjorie was now blaming them for her brother's sudden death. *Poor sick woman.* She muttered. Marjorie knew nothing about the internal workings of families, and how they grew and learned to love each other through the years. Libby was glad that they had had that final meeting with their brother, who knew how they were on the outside looking in, with Marjorie at the gates.

They traveled to Ben's funeral through New London, Connecticut, in Libby's new car, ferrying over to Port Jefferson. Kat, Sonja and Libby and Bea sat estranged from Joel, Glenny, Terry and William, who had gathered around Marjorie as she mourned. The family that was once so close had become split

300

right down the middle because the devil incarnate had been unleashed. Marjorie would die soon after in a drunk driving accident.

Fall turned into spring, and Libby was invited to Hanks cottage for dinner with two of his sons attending. Jay could not make it, but Allen the oldest and Theodore the middle son were very cordial and she was reminded of her own three brothers when they were young. Later that evening when Hank told her he was being transferred to Texas, Libby mentally crossed him out of her little black book. But when he left town, she was aware of a big fat empty hole in the pit of her stomache.

Epilogue

Libby knew from the first that providence had played a major role in bringing them together; they were so exceptionally well suited for each other. Catholicism had played a part in both of their lives, putting them in an awkward place to remarry after divorce, and yet the attraction to each other was strong. Writing long letters, calling periodically during the week only made them more lonesome. Of course Hank came home every other week to see his sons, and she visited *the lone star state* at every chance available.

A tenderness that Libby never knew existed lay between them, as making love took on new dimensions. There was a thrill of excitement in his nearness that was brand new to Libby, who uncovered feelings that were long under wraps, or never cultivated at all in her lifetime. Never in a hundred years did she ever believe that falling in love with someone would be an issue to deal with while establishing her ideal career in this great city.

Love and romance suddenly appeared in both of their lives, and demanded immediate attention. When the sound realization of how rudely they were both mistreating this fragile, beautiful state they were wrapped up in, she called Hank that evening.

"Honey, I think I'm going to come down to be there with you. I can get an apartment, and our company has a client there in Arlington where I can interview."

"Alright that sounds like a great idea, Libby. I'm coming home at the end of the week, we'll make plans at that time." Libby knew she loved Hank, but did not know yet if he was worth quitting her dream job for. She went over for a visit to St. James Church in Chinatown the next day for a visit. *Please let me be doing the right thing here. You've thrown this good man in my path. Are we meant to spend our lives together?* Then she sat back in the pew to hear her answer.

The next weekend when Hank came home as scheduled, they had dinner together that evening, and after their last cup of coffee when Libby turned around to leave, she spied a tiny black box sitting on the table. In it was a beautiful two-carat solitary diamond ring, which she immediately put on her shaking finger, sealing their precious love forever.

"I love you Libby." Hank said. A man who rarely revealed his true feelings. He'd fallen in love for the first time in his life. Libby looked into the deep sincerity of his blue eyes, knowing that when Hank made a proclamation it was carved in stone, and she was ecstatic.

Hank believed whole heartedly in concrete principles, in the field of engineering, where constructing firm foundations were a way of life.

He had been born into a strong New England family, where his mother and father had guided their four children toward a life which included searching for independent goals to benefit society. Rose and Thomas Simmons had raised their children with a strong sense of purpose and integrity, and a sound background of family devotion.

Hank had felt dubious after meeting Libby, recognizing that he had to reconstruct part of his solid background to support their new loving relationship. He also knew that Allen, Theodore, and Jay would survive as strong young men. Consequently, he set about mentally designing a scheme of building a new set of values for their life together, while enforcing their love for each other. This excellent format came swiftly through in his engineering profile.

After obtaining an annulment in the church, invalidating both previous marriages, Libby and Hank were married aboard the Boston Harbor Commuter Boat with a Catholic priest and all five children standing up for them. It was a beautiful fall day, with the golden sun sparkling off the water and on to the happiest couple alive, and the new family.

"And this is our life, exempt from public haunt,
Finds tongues in trees, books in the running brooks,
Sermons in stones, and good in everything"

Shakespeare, As you like it, II, i, 15

BIBLIOGRAPHY

Is My Baby All Right, by Virginia Asgar, M.D. and Joan Beck
   1972,Trident Press,
   Division of Simon Schuster Publishing Co.

This Fabulous Century,
   1969 by the Editors of Time-Life Books, Inc.

Gangsters and Hoodlums by Raymond Lee and B.C. VanHecke,
   1971, South Brunswick, NY: A.S. Barnes & Co., Inc.

The Unpossessed by Tess Slessingers, The Unpossessed Women
in the 1930's,
   Simon & Schuster Publishing Co.

And The Wolf Finally Came by John P. Hoerr, 1988, The
Decline of the American Steel Industry,
   University of Pittsburgh Press

Photo by Tom Bender

Elizabeth Lydia Bodner was born and raised in Pennsylvania. Upon graduating from California State University of Pennsylvania she moved to New England where she met her husband, an engineer. As they moved around the country with her husband's business she wrote her first book, "Uncompromising: Family Style," which looked at the late 1800's and early 1900's through the eyes of immigrants passing through her grandmother's hotel. In her new novel "Equilibrium" we see how the values acquired in those early years enabled a family to not only cope with the tumultuous last two-thirds of the 20th century but also maintain the family stability and strength.